TURNING JAPANESE

DATE DUE		
AUG 2 0 2009		MAY 0 2 2009
JUN 2 4 2009		MAY 2 9 2009
		SEP 2 4 2009
		JAN 0 3 2011

ALSO BY CATHY YARDLEY

Novels

Surf Girl School
Couch World
L.A. Woman

PO-P

Romances

Ravish
Crave
Baby, It's Cold Outside
One Night Standards
Jack & Jilted
Working It
The Driven Snowe
The Cinderella Solution

Nonfiction

Will Write for Shoes

CATHY YARDLEY

TURNING JAPANESE

THOMAS DUNNE BOOKS
ST. MARTIN'S GRIFFIN
NEW YORK

This is a work of fiction. All of the characters, organizations, and events portrayed in this novel are either products of the author's imagination or are used fictitiously.

THOMAS DUNNE BOOKS.
An imprint of St. Martin's Press.

TURNING JAPANESE. Copyright © 2009 by Cathy Yardley. All rights reserved. Printed in the United States of America. For information, address St. Martin's Press, 175 Fifth Avenue, New York, N.Y. 10010.

www.thomasdunnebooks.com
www.stmartins.com

Book design by Jonathan Bennett

Library of Congress Cataloging-in-Publication Data

Yardley, Cathy.
    Turning Japanese / Cathy Yardley.—1st ed.
        p.   cm.
    ISBN-13: 978-0-312-37880-6
    ISBN-10: 0-312-37880-7
    1. Japanese Americans—Fiction.   2. Comic books, strips, etc.—Fiction.
3. Cartoonists—Fiction.   4. Americans—Japan—Tokyo—Fiction.   I. Title.
    PS3625.A735T87   2009
    813'.6—dc22

                                                        2008036273

First Edition: April 2009

10 9 8 7 6 5 4 3 2 1

For Tanner

ACKNOWLEDGMENTS

I'D LIKE TO THANK THE VERY HELPFUL PEOPLE AT OHZORA Publishing in Japan, as well as Belinda Hobbs at Harlequin Japan, for letting me tour their facilities and answering all my questions.

TURNING JAPANESE

CHAPTER 1

"HOT ENOUGH FOR YOU?"

I had been minding my own business as I waited at the crosswalk, but this made me look over. The person—sort of—who asked the question was easily six foot two. His bald head was an ominous medley of red and black, with small horns scattered about. His eyes were blazing yellow. He had to weigh in at three hundred plus pounds, and his robes were thick, some rough weave, in a solid black. He was sweating profusely.

"Sure is," I finally said, before getting jostled by a group of hobbits, with pointy ears and curly hair, who were apparently complaining about their hotel room. The big guy was still staring at me expectantly, and I found myself adding, "But back home in New York, it's hot *and* humid. Like they say, at least this is a dry heat."

"Oh? You're from New York?" His yellow eyes lit up, and I immediately regretted giving him the opening. He had successfully initiated a conversation. I should've known better. "The city? I love the city! I was there for a different convention, a few years ago . . ."

"No. Groverton." I watched him stare at me blankly, then I laughed. "It's a tiny town, upstate."

"So you're just in San Diego for the Comic-Con?"

"Um, yup," I said.

"I'm Chad Pennington," he said. "I'm local. Oh, and I'm also Darth Maul."

"I'm Lisa Falloya," I answered politely, before gesturing to my non-costume clothes. "And . . . I'm not anything else."

Just then the crosswalk sign lit up and I started moving, carried by the wave of the convention-goers. I darted ahead, because the friendly guy who'd started the conversation was a Star Wars guy, and I knew from experience that most Star Wars guys could talk for hours. I just wanted to get to the convention and find my friends Stacy and Perry and maybe convince them to go home a day early.

It wasn't that the convention was too weird, even though I was surrounded by people dressed as everything from comic-book and video-game characters to monsters and, in one funny incident, a human Three Musketeers bar. Actually, I liked the atmosphere. I even liked the people. Darth Maul, my crosswalk buddy, was probably a very nice guy, if possibly overtalkative.

It wasn't the city. As far as cities went, San Diego was really as lovely as everyone said. It was eighty-nine degrees, and locals were acting like it was the apocalypse. If this were Groverton, people would be commenting on how unseasonably balmy the day was. The sky was an impossible blue, and the air was bone dry. It was as close to heaven as you could come, after Groverton's sweltering heat.

And it wasn't that I missed my boyfriend, Ethan . . . although I did, terribly, because I always did when I was traveling. Of course, it wasn't like I traveled extensively, either. In fact, my annual trek (no pun intended, for those Star Trek fans I felt sure were crawling around) to the Comic Book Convention every August was the only traveling I did. Which was why I was now feeling the aftereffects.

"There you are!"

I finally saw Stacy and Perry, my two best friends, walking toward me. Stacy was a short, somewhat stocky redhead with a matronly disposition. Thirty-four years old, she looked like a cross between a fairy godmother and a linebacker. Perry, on the other hand, was very tall, almost six-five, with corn silk blond hair. He was whipcord thin and lanky. Even at twenty-eight, he looked like he was maybe nineteen. Fortunately, neither of them were wearing costumes, although Perry was wearing a Green Lantern icon T-shirt.

"You missed *so much*," Stacy said, sounding out of breath.

"It's only ten thirty," I pointed out.

"Yeah, but they were showing movies this morning. I got to see *Steamboy*," Stacy gushed.

"You've seen that like thirty times," Perry pointed out. "I met a few cool artists and got my *Camelot 3000* copy signed. Finally."

"Cool." We were all friends in geek, as Stacy used to say. It was nice to have best friends like this, the same since junior high. Apparently, it was really rare. "I was tired, though."

"Staying out too late, huh?" Perry said.

"Yeah. You guys both know I don't get out much at home," I said, with a sheepish grin. "Ethan usually stays in and studies, and since I started seeing him, I only go out for our anime club." I decided to lay the groundwork for my next request. "Besides, you know I don't really get along with traveling . . ."

"It's a nice change for me," Stacy said, her voice positively perky despite only getting a few hours of sleep. "Between Roger needing to get up early to go to work and Thomas only being two and a half . . . that whole first year, I was getting no sleep. I wasn't even getting a shower every other day, much less going out!"

"Well, at least you're back at the Con," I said. "You've had a great visit, and I'm sure you miss Roger and Thomas anyway . . ."

Stacy sighed as the three of us joined the crowd crushing into the convention center. "Yeah, but I don't know how long I'll be able to keep coming here. Roger's been talking about having another kid. Maybe trying for a girl, this time. So this could be my last Comic Convention for a while." She sounded strained, as if perkiness was warring with the grimness of that announcement.

"Yeah, but Thomas was totally worth it," I reminded her. He was my godson, after all, and he was an amazing kid. I was starting to feel a bit bad at what I was about to ask. "The thing is . . ."

Perry rolled his eyes. "No, Lisa, you can't go home early."

I blinked at him. "How'd you know?"

Even Stacy shook her head. "Because you do this every year. You're fine the first day or two, but by day three you're dragging, and by the fourth day you're begging to catch an earlier flight."

"And you'd realize that every year we tell you *no,*" Perry added. "Besides, if you leave now, you'll miss the announcement!"

I quavered internally. That was a big part of why I was so gung-ho on leaving early, I had to admit.

This year I'd actually entered one of my hand-drawn comics in a competition. The company was a big Japanese publisher, one that I'd been reading for years, and when I saw that they were asking for entries from the United States, I'd allowed myself a glimmer of hope.

Of course, I'd probably have left it a glimmer if it hadn't been for my meddling friends. Once Stacy and Perry found out, I'd had to fight them as they browbeat me for another month to enter one of my amateur comics in the thing. So I'd closed my eyes, held the proverbial gun to my head, and pulled the trigger by mailing that sucker in.

Today, I'd find out if I made it.

"I have almost no chance," I said, both to argue my case for leaving early and to try and quell my own hopes. Why get worked up? I probably had a better chance of winning the lottery. "You guys both know that. I mean, how many people here probably entered?"

"It's a great story, and your drawings were cute," Stacy argued. "Come on! It'll be another half-hour. We need to get to that pavilion."

"I should get something to eat," I said, trying to postpone the inevitable.

The thing was, I'd had the dream for the past few months. This probably sounds totally pathetic, but once I heard the winner announced, and if it wasn't me, well, I would lose that delicious feeling of possibility.

Of course, the counterargument would be, *but what if I won.*

It was a traitorous internal voice, the same one that had prompted me to start drawing the comic in the first place. As usual, I tried to ignore it. Nothing broke your heart like that little voice, I swear to God.

"I'll meet you guys at the Sansoro Publisher booth," I said, and they nodded, although Perry made a menacing gesture—*you'd better be there,* he seemed to say.

I headed for the hideously overpriced concession stand, intent on grabbing a hamburger, fries, and a Coke. The breakfast of conventioneers, I thought with a grin. But before I could get on line, my cell phone vibrated in my pocket. I glanced at it, then smiled.

"Hi, Ethan," I answered, ducking into a corridor and covering my other ear with my hand. "It's so good to hear from you. I miss you!"

"How are things at Nerd Central?" he asked, then laughed. "Been picked up by any more Star Trek guys?"

"Star Wars," I corrected. "And Darth Maul tried to get me into a conversation at the crosswalk, but I escaped."

He chuckled again. "How's it going? Homesick yet?"

We'd been going together for three years now, and he knew me probably better than anybody. "Terribly homesick," I admitted without shame. If you couldn't be puny and miserable with your boyfriend, then he wasn't much of a boyfriend, right? "But it's just another day and a half."

"That's my girl," Ethan said. "It's good for you to get out."

He was always saying stuff like that. The only non-Con travel I'd done was with him: a vacation to Florida, a trip to Toronto, even a trip to meet his parents near San Francisco. Being with him did ease the traveling malaise, just like being with Stacy and Perry helped. Usually because they wouldn't let me wallow in it, I thought. "So how are things going for you? Working hard?"

"I'm just getting stuff closed out and ready for when the semester starts up again in September," Ethan said.

"I thought you could coast this year, relatively speaking," I said, finally getting on line behind a couple dressed as Superman and what I had to assume was Lois Lane, circa 1940. "I mean, it's your last year."

"Yeah, but I'm going to try to get a different job, maybe in the city, remember?"

Of course I remembered. I'd known about The Plan, as he called it, since the day I met him. I think he'd somehow worked it into his pickup line. We'd introduced ourselves, said what we did. He'd said, "I'm Ethan Lonnel, and I'm getting my MBA before getting a job in the city. Probably a director of operations."

I'd been impressed, since I just said I worked at the Philson semiconductor plant in Groverton. Everybody I knew, practically, worked at The Plant, as they called it—it being so huge and overpowering that it needed no further clarification. I had a job, and that was as far as it went. He, on the other hand, had A Plan. Or rather, The Plan.

"That's awfully together of you," I'd said, impressed. "You sound like you like what you do."

"I love what I do," he'd answered, and his grin had been amazing.

"I like a man who loves what he does," I'd found myself saying, even though I suddenly realized I had rarely met anyone, man or woman, who fit that description. We'd been together ever since.

"So I need to ace this year, especially the outside projects," he said. "I'm going to be busier this year than ever."

I sighed silently. I barely saw Ethan these days as it was. I knew better than to complain, though. Not that he'd reprimand me or anything. It would just make him feel guilty, which would make *me* feel bad since I knew how important The Plan was to him. It was better to just avoid discussing anything but details.

"Don't worry. After June, it'll all get better," he promised, and I knew that, too. "But, yeah, until June it's going to be rough. I won't get to see you that much."

I made a little noise of acceptance, a sort of *yuh-huh,* even as I felt loneliness curl around the edges of my consciousness. "Well, it's just a year," I said, with forced perkiness.

"Then, everything we promised," he said, and I warmed at the tone of his voice. "Hell, you probably won't be a single girl for very much longer. You should take advantage of it. Go out and raise hell with your friends. See the world. Stuff like that."

"Oh, you know me," I said, motioning to what food I wanted and paying the cashier for it. "World-traveling hell-raiser."

"I just feel bad, having to leave you alone all the time," Ethan said.

"No problem." I grabbed my tray of food and juggled the phone. "You're worth it."

"That's definitely my girl," he said. "Listen, I gotta go . . . need to buy books and stuff. I'll call you tonight."

"Love you," I said, reluctant to lose contact.

"Love you, too." He hung up.

As I made my way to the Sansoro booth, I tucked the phone into my pocket, and then found Stacy and Perry. There was a good-sized crowd, all of whom were undoubtedly anime and manga buffs—that is, all fans of the Japanese cartoons and comics that we, meaning me and all my friends, were wild about. They were talking in low, excited murmurs. There was a delegation of people from the publisher up on the stand, and the podium was empty but spotlighted—obviously waiting for the grand announcement.

"Did I miss anything?" I asked, before taking a bite of burger. I grimaced at Perry when he stole a fry.

"Not a thing. But any minute now," Stacy said, unable to keep still in her seat.

I plowed through my food, as if eating would somehow force my jittery stomach to focus on something other than the impending announcement. I finished, and they still hadn't said anything, so I got up to throw out my trash, making my way over people's feet, since Stacy and Perry had grabbed seats in the middle of the room. I was at the trash can when a man stepped up to the podium.

"We at Sansoro were very pleased at the number of entries that came in for our very first American manga contest," he said. He was Japanese, but his accent was very slight. "The entries themselves were very impressive, and we had a very difficult time picking out only one final winner. The judging process went as follows . . ."

The pleasantries went on for a while, and I was seriously considering just hovering along the edges of the crowd, and then bailing before Stacy and Perry could see me. Just for a little while, just to get my bearings. *Don't get your hopes up, don't get your hopes up,* I muttered to myself, pressing my hands against my stomach.

The burger was probably a bad choice.

I would find out in a second. Then, after the letdown (which I'd felt so many other times, in other contests), I'd just hang out and watch a movie or check out the other booths; then I'd get to pack and go home, back to the routine. Not that thrilling, admittedly, but . . .

"And the winner is . . . *sertgh burglethetir!*"

I stared. The microphone had burbled, or something. That had made no sense.

The crowd was applauding, and I had the vague impression that Stacy and Perry were screaming. Yes, screaming.

The Japanese man at the podium scanned the crowd. "Is she here today? We were told she'd registered."

I stared at Stacy and Perry, who were gesturing to me wildly. What the hell had just happened? Did I have an aneurysm and miss it, or something?

The man cleared his throat. "I repeat . . . the winner of the grand prize of a one-year internship at Sansoro Publishing is . . . *Lisa Falloya!*"

A MONTH later, the shock still hadn't worn off.

"Well, *of course* you're going," Stacy said, taking a long drink from her milk shake. "Tell me you're going!"

"I have another week to make up my mind," I said defensively.

I had all but passed out, hearing I'd won the contest. Now we were back in Groverton, sitting at MegaBurger after an anime club meeting, having our usual shakes and burgers. And from the moment that I had discovered I'd won, I'd had a barrage of commentary from Stacy and Perry.

"Why the hell wouldn't you go?" Perry asked, before taking a huge bite of burger and devouring it in nanoseconds. For a skinny guy, he could really pack it away. "It's *Japan,* for chrissake! Only the coolest place on earth! Do you know what I'd give to live over there for a year? To get somebody else to *pay* for me to live there for a year?"

"So you go," I said, only half joking.

"Oh, don't start with that," Stacy snapped. "You've got an opportunity to see how a manga publisher works. We've only been reading the stuff for forever, and you get to actually spend a year doing something other than order semiconductor parts! You've got to be insane to not see how phenomenal that is!" She dipped a fry into the pool of ketchup she had smeared on her plate. "I'm with Perry. I would *kill* to do what you're going to do!"

"And you could come back, and tell everybody you were a *manga-ka*!" Perry said, as if that settled the argument completely.

"I wouldn't make it to *manga-ka*," I said, using the term that meant manga artist. "I keep reminding you, I'm American. They don't make Americans *manga-ka*."

"A Westerner is the head of Sony now," Perry countered. "They're changing."

"Not according to my mother," I argued back, uncomfortable with the pressure. "And seeing as she *is* Japanese, she ought to know."

Perry rolled his eyes, and Stacy *tsked* the comment away with a wave of her hand, almost knocking her metal cup with extra milkshake over. "Your mom hasn't lived in Japan for what, forty years? Japan's changing. I've read about it. Besides, you won the contest, didn't you? You got the internship! Why would they do that if they didn't want you to be a *manga-ka* for a year?"

I kept quiet. I loved my friends, but they'd lived in Groverton all their lives—same as I had, come to think of it. But the difference was, they weren't Japanese, or half-Japanese, or even Asian.

I knew there was a difference. But there was no way I could explain it to them without sounding racist. And even if I could manage to sound rational, they still wouldn't believe me. It was an American thing, I knew—people changed, it didn't matter where you came from, as long as you worked hard and had the talent, you could go where you wanted to go.

"Besides, it's not just that," Perry said. "You're just, you know, being a punk." He grinned at that.

"I do hate traveling," I said, refusing to rise to the bait.

"But it's *Japan*." Stacy's tone sounded almost rapturous. "You can see that fish market, and all the kids in Harajuku, and the commuters . . . and those massive screens and . . ." She gestured, as if words failed to capture just how unbelievable the whole thing would be. "And you'd be getting paid!"

"Not all that much," I said, trying to put a damper on the whole thing. I was jazzed that I'd won the internship, but in my mind, I had done what I had set out to do. Sure, I wasn't crazy, a part of me would love to go, but it just seemed like a huge hassle. "It's a small stipend. I mean, it's an *internship*. And it's expensive to live in Tokyo. Way more expensive than here, anyway." Just number fifteen on my list of *why it's a bad idea to go to Tokyo*.

"You've got savings," Stacy said stubbornly.

"Besides, it doesn't have to be expensive," Perry said. "Remember Yukari?"

"Uh, no," I said. "Should I?"

He rolled his eyes at me. "She's my pen pal from Tokyo."

Stacy and I shared a grin. Perry had Asian pen pals all across the world, it seemed. He made his preference for Asian women no secret. I'd occasionally wondered if that was why he initially befriended me, even though we'd never been anything close to romantic. "Don't tell me you're getting one of your hoochie mamas to hook me up with an apartment," I said.

"She's not a hoochie mama." Perry finished his burger in one enormous, fierce bite. He always took umbrage about this sort of thing. "She's a nice girl. Twenty-one, out of university but still living at home with her parents and her kid brother. I'm sure they would be up for taking in a boarder. You could stay with them, and it'd be a lot cheaper than renting an apartment or even a gaijin house."

I have to admit, I did look into housing. Gaijin housing was housing specifically meant for Westerners or foreigners. They were usually tiny, with a shared bathroom, and they were still not necessarily cheap. Or, if they were cheap, they were probably in ghettos. Not what I really was looking forward to.

"How do you know they'd be interested?"

Perry smirked. "Already asked her."

"Jesus, Perry." It was one thing to be helpful; this was bordering on blackmail.

"Listen, if we left it up to you, you'd come up with excuse after excuse until the deadline had passed," Stacy said, defending Perry. "I looked up airfares. I looked up what it would take for you to get your passport. I looked up what it would take to get a work visa."

"They'd take care of that," I said automatically, then blushed as I realized that they were looking at me with some smugness.

"So you *do* want to go!" Stacy almost crowed it.

"So I've read the paperwork, big deal." I felt embarrassed, so I nibbled a couple of fries. "I didn't just ignore this. I've done some research. And it's not like I said I don't want to go."

"Could've fooled me," Perry muttered.

"It's just . . . okay. Yes. I'm scared, okay?" I crossed my arms, leaving half of my burger uneaten. "It's a big, huge change, and I'm scared silly."

Now Perry and Stacy eased off. "At least you're being honest about it," Stacy said, and she reached over to pat me on the hand. "But honey, it's time. This is such a huge opportunity. What are you scared of?"

"I won't know anybody. My Japanese is so totally rusty . . . I can get by with speaking it, for the most part, but the written is terrible." I sighed. I could recite the list from memory. I'd only been going over it every day for the past month. "I get lost at the drop of a hat. I get horrible jet lag. I don't know what they'd expect of me. I get homesick when I leave for just *five days*."

They listened, quietly, supportive.

"I don't know. Maybe some people are just cut out for small-town living," I expanded. "I love Groverton. I still have my best friends from high school. It's just . . . *nice* here. Comfortable." I sighed heavily and took a sip of my shake—chocolate peanut butter. What were the odds I'd find a chocolate peanut butter shake in Tokyo? "It'd be great, from a certain standpoint, but after a year it'd be all over. So why go in the first place? I'm happy here."

Stacy and Perry looked at each other. "Want to take this one," Perry asked Stacy, "or should I?"

"Go for it," Stacy replied.

Perry turned to me, his eyes filled with compassion and understanding.

"Lisa, honey," he said, "that is the biggest bunch of bullshit I have ever heard in my life."

I sat up straight, as if I'd been goosed. *"I beg your pardon."*

"You're scared, you admitted it," he said. "And fear's the only thing that's kept you in Groverton all these years. Yeah, we're cool and all, but we're not the reason you stayed. And it's not because it's so nice. I mean, it's not like you love your job."

"I . . ." I fell quiet. He was right. I was a desk jockey at The Plant—the same place where Stacy worked. Half the time I was stressed out, and the other half I was trying desperately to kill time while looking busy. "Well, that was blunt."

"And you don't like your apartment."

"It's not so bad," I said, thinking of my little studio apartment. Sure, it still had that college graduate still-in-boxes, Ikea chic thing going, but hell . . .

"Face it. Your life isn't a Frank Capra movie," Perry said, in his best Jack Nicholson tough-love voice. "It's just less work than going out and doing what you want to do."

"So why are you two still in Groverton if I'm such a bum?" I didn't mean it to come out that harshly, but damn it, I felt under attack here.

Perry's smile was sad. "I didn't say that we were better than you," he said. "I know that part of me just desperately wants to live vicariously through you. You're the one who won, after all."

"And I've got Roger and my son," Stacy said. "I'm not going anywhere."

They looked at me, like I was the Great White Hope or something. I felt like a slug.

"There is one other thing," I said, although it was a feeble hope. "Ethan. I don't want to leave Ethan."

Stacy shook her head. "Does Ethan want you here?"

I felt my eyes widen. "Of course he wants me here!"

"Did he tell you not to go?"

I thought Ethan was my ace in the hole, the one factor that was inarguable. "No," I admitted. "But then, I didn't really ask him, either."

"So there you go," Perry said. "Let Ethan be the final factor. If he doesn't mind you going, then you don't have any more excuses except your own fear."

I sat and stared at my so-called helpful friends, who stared back. I was very aware of the clatter of the other diners, the smell of the burgers and fries from the kitchen, the sticky-smooth feel of the booth's red vinyl seat on my back.

"I'm staying at Ethan's tonight," I finally said. "I'll talk to him."

"That's all we're asking," Perry said.

"You guys are insanely pushy," I added, a grumbling footnote.

"Yeah, but that's part of why you're friends with us," Stacy said. "You didn't want to go to the Con with us, either, remember? And now you go every year."

"It's all about that first leap," Perry agreed.

"Well, thank God I have you two to push me off the cliff," I said, and they toasted each other with milkshake. Unable to stay pissy in the face of such joviality, I joined in.

Still, I felt foreboding at what I'd agreed to. What would Ethan say? He loved me, he wanted to be with me, I knew that. But he also wanted me to live a bigger life than I was living. He was the one with The Plan, after all.

And honestly, what did I *want* him to say?

"HONEY," ETHAN said, "I think you should go."

I let out a slow, frustrated breath and plopped down on Ethan's stylish leather couch with a thud.

For once, why couldn't you be a possessive, overbearing boyfriend?

But I knew I didn't mean it. I'd actually had one of those, thanks very much, right before Ethan. I'd gotten enough from that relationship to realize I didn't need another. But still, the fact that he was so agreeable, so practically ready to pack my bag for me, rankled.

"You realize, of course, this means I'm going away for a whole year, starting in January." My voice was a dull monotone, just this side of sulking.

"I know. I'll miss you," he said, and that was a balm of sorts. "But it's such a great opportunity."

"If one more person says it's a great opportunity," I said, "I may scream."

Ethan ran a hand through his hair, causing the sandy brown curls to stick almost straight up. He looked terribly sexy that way, I thought. And I'd be thousands of miles away from him for a whole year, making do with a photo.

I was spending the night at his place, and I could see his dining room table was strewn with papers and binders and folders—all school stuff. He'd been studying when I'd gotten there, and now it was eleven. At least it was Friday. Still, he looked frazzled.

"I thought this was what you loved. The comic book stuff," Ethan clarified, and instead of sounding warm, he sounded annoyed, and rightfully so, I thought with some guilt. Here he was, trying to be Mr. Supportive, and I was just being a pouty little whiner. "If you don't want to go, don't go. But if you ask me if I mind, then the answer is no."

I nodded, biting my lip.

"And if you're trying to use me as an excuse for you not to go . . ." He sat down on the couch next to me, frowning. "Then knock it off. Because that's not going to work."

"You're right," I said. "I'm sorry. I'm just freaked out by the whole thing. It's a big move."

He smiled, more gently this time, and I managed to feel like even more of a crumb. What the hell was my problem? "I moved from Walnut Creek, California, to Groverton, New York," he pointed out. "Three thousand miles. I know the feeling. And, yeah, it was a big change, but I got through it just fine. I met you, didn't I?"

I smiled when he winked at me. "But it's different. You're . . ." I moved my hands in an amorphous gesture, trying to put into words what I felt was impossible to define. "Different," I finally said, somewhat lamely.

"Not as different as you'd think—" he started, but I interrupted him.

"You've always got a plan, and you stick to it. You know where you want to go, and absolutely nothing's going to stop you." It was sort of comforting, actually. "I'm not like that. I'm more of a go-with-the-flow girl."

"I know. That's part of why we work so well together," he said, and he kissed my cheek. Now I knew I'd miss him, dreadfully, painfully. "But, sweetie, you can't just float through life."

"Sure you can," I said, only half-joking. "I've been doing it for twenty-eight years."

"What I mean is, you can't just be my sidekick. You need to have a life of your own. Don't you want to have some adventures before we get married?"

There it was again—that little thrill, and that little tension, at the thought of it. Married to Ethan. It was something I'd dreamed about, but it was also probably the most permanent thing that would ever happen to me in my whole life. "What, you're saying I should sow some wild oats and pick up some pretty Japanese guys?" I laughed, to show I was kidding. The thought of cheating on Ethan, on *anybody,* was pretty unthinkable.

He was laughing before I was, I noticed. He knew it, too—the thought was pretty ludicrous. I was as monogamous as they came. "No, you know that. But you could tell our kids about your trip to Japan. How their mommy went all the way across the world to draw cartoons."

He made it sound like a big vacation or some kind of summer camp. I frowned, although I wasn't sure why.

"It'd be over before you know it," he coaxed. "You'd be so busy, and seeing so much new stuff. The year would just fly by, I'm sure. It's been like that for me, with business school and work and all. I can't believe I've been here for three years already, it's all seemed to be a blink."

I nodded, but in my mind it felt like we'd been together for even more years than that—for practically forever. Maybe because my life was less busy, it seemed to move slower. "Well, I'm sure it wouldn't be that bad," I admitted. "And it'd be new. And different."

"That's the spirit," he encouraged.

"And I've always wanted to see Tokyo," I said, desperately trying to warm up to the idea.

"Exactly!"

"And maybe . . ." I felt weird, voicing the dream aloud, even to the man I was going to marry, "maybe, if they like me, I could get a job. Work on more projects. Maybe they'd actually publish some of my manga in books."

"That could always happen," he said, in exactly the same tone. "Only one way to find out, right?"

I sighed. It was decided. "You really are trying to get rid of me," I teased, my voice uneven.

He sighed in response, surprising me. "Well . . ."

My eyes widened. "Wait a sec. You mean you really want me out of here?"

"Not that way," he amended, irritation back. "But, well, like tonight."

"What about tonight?"

"I've got reading for three classes that I need to catch up on," he said, pointing to the littered table. "I have a meeting on Monday that I need to get numbers ready for. I've got a ton of things to do. Sometimes, it feels like my head'll explode. You know I love having you over, Lisa. I love being with you. But . . ."

"But I'm a distraction," I said, immediately feeling contrite. "Oh, God. I'm sorry."

"It's not a problem," he said, then laughed weakly. "I mean, yeah, it is a problem. But I hate it when I know that you're just at home waiting, and that you'd love to spend time with me. I guess that makes me a selfish asshole."

"Of course it doesn't," I said quickly. "Are you kidding? If anyone's the asshole here, it's me. I mean, I know you're under all this pressure. I'm not making things any easier."

"It's just . . ." He paused, and she could tell he was choosing his words carefully. "You know how you said I was driven? That I always had a plan?"

"Yeah."

"I do have a plan," he said, and his tone was a little fierce. "I'm not ashamed of that. It's how I function. But sometimes I see you, not really caring where you're going. And . . . I wonder."

"You wonder," I said, waiting for clarification.

"This is a terrible time for me to bring it up," he said, and he ran his hand through his hair again, looking less sexy, and more and more like Kramer from Seinfeld. He was really getting agitated. "I mean, I don't want to get into all of this. But I'll have midterms coming up pretty soon, and finals . . . and then I'll set up interviews for better jobs, and still have next semester, and you know work's not taking it easy on me . . ."

I let him continue in that vein, trying to ignore that he was deliberately rushing away from the point that he'd brought up.

I see you not really caring where you're going. And I wonder.

"You're under a lot of stress," I said, summarizing what he was going on about.

"Exactly," he said, and he let out a relieved breath.

"And . . . it might even be easier, say, if I were busy somewhere else."

"I'd feel less guilty," he said. "That makes me a complete shit, but—"

"Knock that off," I said, and saw the look of surprise. I supposed my tone of voice was a little snippy. "You don't have to keep beating yourself up for needing to take time to focus on your career. You worked hard to get here. I really do understand, Ethan."

"Well, good." He paused, stroking my shoulder absently. "So, does that mean you're going?"

I nodded. "Yeah, I guess so." That was too passive. I forced my voice to sound more determined.

"Yes," I repeated. "I am definitely going to Tokyo."

January 5, Thursday

"I CAN DO THIS."

I didn't mean to say that out loud, and certainly not in public, but it was either give myself a pep talk or start hyperventilating. Well, maybe not hyperventilating. I was too tired, frankly. After a six-hour flight from New York, after a twelve-hour flight from Los Angeles, I had only managed to get maybe two hours of sleep total—and that was restless, because the flight attendants had a little coffee klatch in the nearby "kitchen area" while the passengers tried to sleep. Throw in crossing the International Date Line . . . I shook my head. Those two hours of sleep were covering about thirty-six hours of being awake.

I wished desperately for some rest.

All around me, at the Narita Airport outside of Tokyo, there was an orderly swarm of travelers making their way to their cars or to taxis, or trains, or "limo-buses," which were what we in the States call shuttle buses.

I juggled my duffel bag, perching it precariously on the ridiculously large roller bag I'd just retrieved from the carousel. "Ginormous," as my older brother, Tony, called it, I was still getting used to it. It felt awkward. I never traveled this heavily burdened, ever. I normally mocked women who overpacked.

Still, considering that this one roller bag and duffel bag were supposed to cover me for a year's worth of living, I felt as if I'd packed downright spartanly. Even if it didn't look like that to outsiders.

I pulled my carry-sized organizer out of my duffel bag and flipped through the little dividers that said "maps," "Kanai family," and "Sansoro."

Ethan had helped me pull this together. He had an organizer just like it. He said it was how he could function. Lord knows, I needed all the help I could get to function here.

I flipped to "Kanai family" and looked at the instructions I'd carefully printed out from Yukari's e-mail. Then I looked up. Everything here was not only in kanji or katakana, which I had a harder time reading, but also in English, which was a downright blessing. I really was much better at spoken Japanese than written, since they had three different (and somewhat illogical) writing systems that they interspersed at random. I needed to take a train to Shibuya.

The fact that Tokyo had three different and distinct train companies, all independent of one another, didn't help matters, since I could get lost in a phone booth.

I followed the crowd toward a sign that had the word "trains" in it, and for a second I was back at my first day at college in general and Vassar in particular . . . being one in a huge crowd, feeling unsure and unwell and generally unfit. The other people didn't look at me (well, the few people who accidentally got jostled by Godzilla Bag gave me the occasional look) and I merged in as seamlessly as possible, trying my best to follow the people who seemed to know where they were going.

I should've gotten some coffee, I realized, and wondered if it were true—that you could get a can of hot coffee out of a vending machine. I'd have to try that. Hell, I'd try everything.

I'm going to have plenty of time to try everything, I reassured myself.

I apparently went the wrong way, something I figured out after about an hour or so. I had to look at my notes again, the tab that Ethan had marked "Trains"—they were important enough here to merit their own section.

"Is this the train to Tokyo?" I asked the woman at the window, finally.

Nobody looked at me—the woman seemed bored, but at least she was trying to hide it, which was more than I could say about most of the people working at LAX, where I'd made my connection. Or, for that matter, any train station in the States when I'd asked for assistance.

"Yes, miss," the woman said, with a small smile, taking my money and giving me a ticket in return.

"Do I just go over there?"

"Yes," the woman said, the smile never wavering.

Helpful but succinct. I felt bad asking her exactly where I was supposed to go, so I followed the crowd yet again, navigating my bag. I gawked like a tourist, but since I was a tourist, I guessed it couldn't be helped.

A bunch of men and women on the train platform were busily keying away at their cell phones, or ktei, as they were called here in Japan. I knew that getting a ktei was one of my first orders of business after I settled into my new life here, right after getting to my host family and getting some damned sleep.

Almost everyone was in Western-style clothing, not surprisingly:

only one woman wore a traditional kimono, at odds with her Western purse. And several people wore surgical masks, signifying that they had a cold and were way too polite to spread it. Since we'd just left the airport, I also noticed a lot of non-Asians—well, not a lot, but more than just one or two. They were talking in lots of languages: German, Russian, Swedish I think—hard to tell. I noticed that I honed in on the conversations of a few obvious Americans.

"I knew we should've gone with a tour," a woman with a Midwestern accent was commenting to her husband. "Do you even know where we're going?"

"I've taken public trains in Chicago, New York, and San Francisco," her husband answered derisively, but his tone suggested that he wasn't entirely sure. He was also surprisingly loud. I thought that maybe he thought he was speaking softly or that the people around him couldn't understand. "I'm pretty sure I can find my way around here!"

I glanced over at the couple. They were in their late forties, early fifties maybe, but not seasoned travelers from the looks of it. I felt a pang of sympathy. In a weird way, they looked like I felt.

I just prayed that I wouldn't seem like as much of an outsider as these Americans. I knew they couldn't help it. Physically, they stood out, and their English was like a beacon. When they got on the train, I noticed that the Japanese gave the white people a rather wide berth, not sitting too close, despite the crowded conditions of the train.

I'd read about the phenomenon, but seeing it, I still couldn't quite believe it.

Nobody gave me the same treatment, I also noticed. They were squashing up against me instead of steering clear, although I could clearly read the looks on several of their faces as they studied me.

You're not Japanese. I don't know what you are, but you're not one of us.

Unhappily, I scrunched down in my seat. I had a string-thin

woman wearing the highest-heeled boots I'd ever seen on my right, and a young man with a suit and a surgical mask on my left. People were staring at my enormous bag (it was hard not to, it took up as much space as a short, really fat person) and I tried in vain to pull it as close to my body as possible. I could feel the resentment coming from them, but there really wasn't anything I could do about it. I tried for my father's patented Falloya Scowl, something he'd perfected over the years, riding the subways of New York. He claimed nobody ever bothered him.

It worked well enough. But then I got the feeling nobody would actively start anything up with me, anyway. It was Japan, after all. They were right up there with Canadians as being some of the politest people on earth. Using Godzilla Bag as a shield of sorts, I leaned against my luggage, and it in turn supported me.

I was surprisingly comfortable, actually, nestled between my luggage and my squashed companions. It was warm, and clean, and, except for the Americans, relatively quiet. Even the movement of the train was pleasant.

Every stop had a funny little musical interlude. I was practically lethargic when I changed trains at the Tokyo station, hoping against hope that I was on the right line. The Tokyo station was enormous and overwhelming, and I was tripping over my own feet with fatigue. I felt like a small child who had gotten lost in the Mall of America, for God's sake, and I boarded my next train with something like relief, hiding again from the frowning faces of my fellow passengers, who resented my enormous, unwieldy bag. Pretty soon, it was the same thing all over again, and this time, no Americans. Just clean, warm, quiet, with slight rocking motions.

I didn't mean to fall asleep. I really didn't.

I felt as if I'd only closed my eyes for a blink, when I felt a firm hand on my shoulder, shaking me lightly.

I looked up. "What?" I said in English, feeling dazed.

The man who had shaken me was wearing a dapper blue uniform, something like a cross between a cop and a bellhop. So a bell cop, I thought, giggling a little to myself.

God damn, I was tired.

"You need to get off the train," he said, in Japanese. "The train is shutting down."

I glanced at my watch and realized I'd never changed it over. And frankly, I wasn't up to doing the mental calisthenics that would enable me to do the time change from New York to Tokyo. "That can't be right," I said, this time in Japanese—or at least, I hoped I was saying the right thing. "I landed at eight o'clock." I had planned it, with Ethan's careful help. I should have had plenty of time to get to the Kanai house at a decent hour, and the trains didn't shut down until . . .

"It's midnight," Bell Cop said in broken English, realizing that I obviously wasn't from around these parts. "Off train!"

I stood up, unsteady, realizing that I really had to pee. My body protested the fact that it wasn't sleeping, and then gave me a little nudge: I was hungry, too, now that I thought about it. Hell, I was a regular bodily function extravaganza. "Where am I?" I finally asked.

Bell Cop smiled, a little impatiently. "Shinjuku," he said, pointing to the screen. "Off train."

I nodded. "*Arigato gozaimasu,*" I said, bowing slightly, and he responded in kind even as he obviously wanted me the hell off his train. They're nothing if not polite here.

I dragged Godzilla Bag behind me and headed for the street.

Shinjuku was sorta near Shibuya, if I remembered correctly, but nowhere "near" enough. I wasn't going to hoof it over to the Kanai house, that was for certain. For one thing, I don't think they'd be keen on their new paying guest showing up at one in the morning . . . not for the measly rent I was paying them, anyway. And this late, I couldn't even call them to ask directions. For another thing, figuring out a map in daylight when I was well rested was challenging enough. No way could I hard-ass it across Shinjuku in my current condition.

I needed a place to crash, pronto.

I walked out of the train station. Despite the fact that it was midnight, the streets were still buzzing with life. Tokyo was rather like Vegas: there was always a crowd and always something to do. And someone willing to do it.

I needed sleep, my body reminded me. And a restroom, and food, maybe, but definitely sleep. I wandered down the street, roller bag and duffel bag in tow. I was pretty certain the guidebooks Ethan packed for me were buried at the bottom of my duffel. All I could remember off the top of my head about Shinjuku was that it was the electronics section of Tokyo, as in this was where you could buy any gadget under the sun. Tokyo was nothing if not orderly. Of course, that wasn't going to help me get some sleep.

I didn't have the budget for a really sumptuous hotel, I realized in the portion of my brain that managed to stay just a little bit worried, no matter how tired or how drunk I ever got. I thought of it as the Nana Falloya Survival System: if nothing else would save me, guilt might—and since Nana hated "spending extravagance" and made sure I inherited that value, guilt usually kept me from wandering past my financial limits. It was helpful, it kept me out of debt, but in times like this, it was also just this side of annoying.

I scanned the streets, looking for what I could remember meant "hotel" in kanji, katagana, or hiragana. I wound up wandering where the people wandered, using what I liked to call Lemming Logic: if a bunch of people are headed there, it was probably the right direction. It might seem stupid, but it had helped me out in more strange cities than I could remember.

Okay, in like three cities. I'm not a world traveler. Still, right now, I was lucky to remember three of anything.

I noticed several well-dressed young men, wearing herringbone coats and suits, looking out of place in the small, slightly dingy streets. It was as if the entire city was composed of what would be alleys in New York or San Francisco. There were neon or bright LCD plasma displays everywhere, much like *Lost in Translation*—I'd seen the movie enough times to have it burned into my brain.

I saw the young men walking up to other men, striking up a conversation, over and over. Must be selling something, I thought, although at this time of night, in those suits, I couldn't imagine what. I mean, were they after-hour Jehovah Witnesses or something, trying to push pamphlets?

That's when I noticed the signs in front of the buildings.

Oh, crap. I'm in the red-light district.

I was torn between being aghast and laughing outright. Only in Japan would the red-light district be so, well, nonseedy. The pimps wore knockoff Gucci, for pity's sake, and were soliciting business as politely as Salvation Army workers asking for spare change to help the homeless. It was a weird, weird juxtaposition.

Of course, it being the red-light district, I immediately knew what the Taj-Mahal-in-Jersey-type buildings, with the bright green lights and pictures of mermaids or what have you, actually were.

Love Hotels.

I remembered reading about them. They were the equivalent of No-tell Motels over in the States, only very high class, all things considered. And after eleven o'clock at night, in theory, you could get them for the whole night. Not that it was recommended, but the fact was, you *could* rent them, and for not a lot of money.

It took about five minutes for me to steel myself to go up to one of the Love Hotels, looking to see if anyone else on the street was looking at me. Embarrassment warred with desperation. But the fact of the matter was, Love Hotels were built for discretion. I found the "private" entrance, and nobody gave me a second look, assuming no doubt that I was off to meet some lover.

Ethan was going to get a huge kick out of this, I just knew it.

I walked in. There was nothing cheesy or perverse about it. In fact, it was downright decadent: nice wood trim, what looked like marble floors. And on one wall, a lit panel with pictures of different rooms. The rooms that were dark were not available. The ones that were lit up were available, if I remembered correctly.

Tired as I was, I looked in fascination at the elaborate "fantasy" rooms. I squinted, trying to make sense of one of them, then, I swear to God, I giggled like a high school cheerleader. "Good grief," I couldn't help muttering out loud. "I think that's a trapeze."

I wasn't going to pick that room.

I finally settled on what looked like their basic model room, although I was pleased that it had a Jacuzzi tub. I went to the "front desk" and the woman greeted me over the intercom. It was more like a movie ticket-seller's booth, except for one crucial thing: I never saw the woman's face, and the woman never saw mine.

"I'd like a room for the rest of the night," I said in Japanese.

"Of course," the woman said, taking my money, signing me up, and giving me a key. Just like that: no muss, no fuss.

I dragged my bags up to the elevator. I noticed another couple meeting at a small "booth," looking around. They gave me a small, strange glance as they realized I was by myself and laden down with so much luggage. They probably thought my date was inflatable and packed in Godzilla Bag. I started giggling uncontrollably, and they ignored me from then on.

When I got to my room, I thanked God for the Japanese sense of cleanliness. In fact, it was so clean, it was practically shrink-wrapped, and considering what had no doubt transpired in the room . . .

I shook my head quickly. Wasn't even going to go there.

I stripped off my clothes and tumbled into bed. It was my first night, right before my first day in Japan . . . and the first day of the rest of my proverbial life. Or at least, the first day of the rest of my year.

January 6, Friday

Wrestling the Godzilla Bag, I had finally managed to make it to the promised land: my host family's house in the suburbs of Shibuya.

It hadn't been easy. After the Great Train Sleeping Debacle, I decided to opt for a taxi out of Shinjuku and out of my hotel of ill-repute, figuring that was the easiest way to get where I wanted to go. I didn't care if it cost me a hundred dollars, it'd be worth it just to get into something that would drop me off at the right doorstep. Especially with my luggage situation, and the fact that jet lag was making me a borderline narcoleptic. As tired as I was, I still slept fitfully, in two-hour increments, waking up disoriented every time.

It wasn't promising, but I was keeping my chin up. Sort of, anyway.

I'd caught a cab by putting my hand out, the way Perry had taught me, with my palm down—the opposite of every taxi-hail I'd ever done in New York. And a green taxi had dutifully pulled up to the curb, its door opening automatically, like something out of a sci-fi movie. Except the seat was covered with plastic and adorned with a neat white doily. It was *Total Recall* meets my aunt Felicia's house, I thought, giggling. The driver, totally liveried in a full uniform that included neat white gloves, did get out to help me with the bag, at least. Then I handed him the address.

After about ten painful minutes of half-English, half-Japanese conversation, the driver finally got a rough idea of where we were supposed to go, and careened through back alleys and main thoroughfares. I suddenly had a profound new respect for New York cabbies, and fervently wished I were there instead. But when we got to the actual neighborhood itself, that's when things started to get hairy.

"Where is it?" the cabbie asked me.

I wasn't sure if I understood him at first. "I don't know," I said and tried to hand him the address again.

He drove slowly, crawling through suburban spots, before finally dumping me out and leaving me to my own devices. "It's near here," he said, although that left a lot to be desired. I paid him, and then looked around, squashing the feelings of travel fatigue and general despondency at being lost. *You get lost all the time,* I reminded myself. *You'll find where you need to be.*

The problem was, as I'd read in the guidebooks, Japan didn't use anything like the American system of addresses. Instead, you got the city, the section, the neighborhood, and then a very weird numbering system. So, my host family's address said: Tokyo, the city; Shibuya, the area; then the *ku,* or neighborhood, then a number. But you could have a house numbered "18" right next to a house numbered "100." There wasn't any rhyme or reason necessarily associated with it. Apparently, there didn't need to be. Mail was delivered by a neighborhood postman, whose job it was to know where everyone lived.

New mail carriers were basically screwed, apparently. It put a whole new spin on the term "going postal." I also think they have a high suicide rate, not surprisingly.

After wandering around the block aimlessly for half an hour, I finally just sucked it up and started knocking on doors at random. I was probably pissing off neighbors, but I wasn't going to just intuit my way there. Finally, an elderly woman led me to the Kanai house.

It was a smaller place than I was expecting, considering Mr. Kanai was some kind of big corporate muckety-muck, according to Perry. Still, it was clean, and the neighborhood was nice. A middle-aged woman opened the door. She had black hair that hung to her shoulders in a blunt bob, and she wore very little makeup. She was wearing what my nana would call a housecoat, a sort of pink-flowered smock-looking thing, and a pair of red pants. She was wearing house slippers.

"*Kanai-san?*" I asked, hoping against hope.

"*Hai,*" the woman answered, with a polite "can I help you?" smile. Then the smile broadened. "You must be Risa-san!" she said, in Japanese.

I nodded and bowed, my hands crossed in front of me, just as my mom had taught me. Then I turned to the elderly woman, thanking her profusely. The elderly woman did the Japanese version of "aw shucks it wasn't anything," and then, after exchanging pleasantries with Mrs. Kanai, she slowly shuffled back to her own small house. I imagined it was the most excitement the little lady got all week.

"Please, come in," Mrs. Kanai said quickly, her fluttery movements reminding me of a finch. I walked into the small foyer, feeling self-conscious about Godzilla Bag. I prayed it wouldn't trail dirt into the house, which at first look appeared to be spotless to the point of sterility. The carpet was a dove gray, and the walls were a soft eggshell white.

I started to follow Mrs. Kanai into the house, then stopped dead as Mrs. Kanai shot a quick look at my feet. *Oops,* I thought, as I looked at where the tile in the foyer stopped and the carpeting began. I glanced around, and Mrs. Kanai pointed to some thick slippers.

"I got those for you," she said. "Please, try them on."

I hastily took off my shoes, leaving them neatly next to the other outdoor-looking shoes lined up by the wall. Then I put the slippers on. "Thank you," I said. They were thick, lined with fleece or something, and were big but comfortable.

Mrs. Kanai was still frowning slightly, but quickly smoothed it out to a smile when she realized I was picking up on it. "Follow me," she repeated.

I had screwed something up but couldn't figure out what. The jet lag was weighing in heavy, and I just desperately wished I could see my room and lie down.

"This is our house. It isn't much," Mrs. Kanai said, totally self-deprecating, "but you are welcome in it. Yukari, our daughter, tells us that you'll be staying for a year."

"Yes," I said, realizing that my correspondence had been almost entirely with Yukari. "And of course, I'll be paying you every month for lodging and food. I'd also like to make sure I'm paying for my phone calls—"

"It's no problem," Mrs. Kanai said quickly. "It's fine. I'm sure it will all be fine. This is the kitchen."

Okay. So Mrs. Kanai didn't want to talk money. Maybe it was impolite. I didn't know what the Kanais' situation was, that they were taking in a tourist, as it were. Still, at three hundred bucks a month, plus phone calls, it was cheaper than anything else I'd found, and Perry vouched for Yukari. So I'd just pay and then we'd work it out from there.

The kitchen was dollhouse-sized, and there was a hot-tea maker, full up from the looks of it. "I cook all the meals," Mrs. Kanai explained. "And you're welcome to share, of course."

"Thank you," I repeated for the umpteenth time, but Mrs. Kanai was already moving on down the hallway.

"The restroom is over there, and this is the main room."

I had just gotten a glimpse of the bathroom when the sound of a video game caught my attention. Sitting on the couch was a boy, somewhere in the ten-to-twelve range from the looks of it. His hair brushed against the collar of his T-shirt, which looked sort of grungy. He was wearing pajama bottoms. It was around eleven in the morning. And, last I checked, I think it was Friday, so that would mean it was a school day. Maybe he was home sick. That scowl and obsessive video game concentration didn't exactly make him look well.

"This is my son, Ichiro," Mrs. Kanai said proudly, as if she'd just presented the next emperor of Japan or something. "Ichiro-kun! Say hello."

"Nice to meet you," I said automatically.

His eyes didn't even flick my way.

Mrs. Kanai sighed, then shot me an apologetic look. "He's shy," she said.

I nodded. *Whatever.*

"When's my lunch?" the little emperor said, still not looking at us.

"Soon. Did you want noodles? I got the noodles you like," Mrs. Kanai cooed.

He grunted, which I supposed meant yes. Mrs. Kanai was obviously overprotective, and if the kid was shy, then I was a toadstool.

Mrs. Kanai then led me to the opposite hallway. "These are the rooms. You'll be sharing a room with Yukari. We've put another bed in. It will be a little cozy," she said.

I knew I'd be sharing a room, so I wasn't too freaked out. But when she opened the door, it was practically pitch black.

"Maaaaaaa," a voice screeched out.

I took a step back.

"Yukari," Mrs. Kanai said, with a touch of sternness that would've scared no one, "Risa-san is here. She needs to put her things away."

"I'm trying to sleep!"

The creature who was apparently Yukari was swaddled in bedding. The room looked like a tornado hit it—a lot like my room used to look in high school, actually. Now that light from the hallway was filtering in, I could see posters—pretty-looking Japanese boys in pop bands, Hello Kitty.

Holy Crap. Welcome back to prepubescence.

Between Yukari-the-lie-abed and Ichiro-the-video-game-king, I was wondering what sort of house I'd just signed on with.

"You can put your things in this dresser," Mrs. Kanai said, her voice soft, so as not to disturb the sleeping princess. "And this will be your bed. There is a laundry down the street. I can take your clothes there, if you like, with the family's clothes. And I will have lunch ready in an hour."

"*Arigato gozaimasu*," I said, which is thank you for doing something for me . . . more polite and enthusiastic than *domo arigato*.

She smiled, shaking her head.

"Shut the door!" Yukari growled.

Mrs. Kanai jumped, startled, then sighed. "I'll start lunch," she said, then hastily retreated, shutting the door behind her and plunging me in darkness.

I leaned against Godzilla Bag, waiting for my eyes to adjust. There was a little light coming in from around the window—apparently Yukari had invested in blackout shades. I rolled the bag toward the dresser, wincing when it thumped.

"Grrrrrr," Yukari said menacingly. I got the distinct impression she was telling me to knock it off.

Jet lag washed over me. This was supposed to be my haven. Perry said Yukari was nice, and her family was going to help me get used to the city. So far, I'd been lost, disoriented, and now I was in some kind of weird alternate universe where the kids seemed to run the show. My nana would kick Yukari's ass if she mouthed off that way. Heck, *my* mom would've swatted my butt if I'd still been in bed and yelled at her to shut the door. So much for that whole image of Japanese discipline, I thought, thinking I'd have to drop my mom a note. When I could get some paper and pen and could bloody well turn on a light without Princess getting on my case.

Well, strike one for Tokyo. Still, I wasn't here to become chummy with the natives, and while it would've been really nice to have a host family that I could feel a part of, it wasn't necessary. It was a place to stay. I'd get along better once I was at the job.

I hoped, anyway.

I felt around for my twin bed. A futon, I noticed . . . it lacked the "give" that my quilted cushion-top bed at home had. I wasn't going to think about that, wasn't going to think about my family, wasn't going to think about Ethan, or any of that. I was just going to get some sleep.

It wasn't a great start, but it was a start.

January 9, Monday

So far, Tokyo was, metaphorically speaking, handing me my ass.

I was dressed in what I figured were work clothes, the same thing I usually wore to the office at Philson's Semiconductor: a pair of navy slacks, gray silk blouse, black sweater, which I figured would be less nerdy and trying-too-hard than the navy blazer that went with the slacks. I had my suede jacket on, too, since it was cold out. Not that you'd know that, staying at the Kanais'. They had to have had the heater cranked to eighty-five degrees—Fahrenheit, that is. I had no idea what the Celsius conversion rate was. I guess I ought to find that out at some point.

I was on the train, crammed in with a bunch of other morning commuters. Men outnumbered women, from the looks of it, and everyone had that business-suit look about them, although several women were wearing dress suits with hooker boots, I swear to God. Probably expensive hooker boots, at that. I noticed that several people were leafing through manga magazines. There were no cell phones ringing, no loud music, or even loud headphones. I was standing because there was no room for me to sit, but so far I hadn't been pinched, or fondled, or anything else creepy that I'd heard about—you know, the horny business guy who would use the excuse of a crammed train to cop a feel. It's a good thing, too—after the times I've taken the New York subway, I'm sure I would've beaten any little perv into a pulp. I was a little grumpy, which only added to that sensation. I was still running at a severe sleep deficit, what with the remnants of jet lag and my new roomie Yukari's vampire habits. The girl partied all weekend, coming in at four or five in the morning, every morning. My internal clock was all out of whack.

The little screen on the train said KANDA, which was my stop, and I headed for the door, swimming against the stationary commuters. I prayed I'd get out in time and made it just before the door closed, feeling pretty proud of myself. *Ha, Tokyo!* Score one for me!

After floundering around with the directions I'd been e-mailed, I was finally standing in front of a medium-sized black-glass office building. It looked, well, like any other office building I'd ever seen, maybe even a little shabby by those standards. I don't know what I was expecting. This part of Tokyo, Kanda, was fantastically nondescript, other than the fact that it was the publishing center of the city. It still baffled and amused me that there was a center for everything in Tokyo—and everything pretty much in its center. There would be no stragglers of publishing, like a manga publisher in Shinjuku, any more than there would be an electronics manufacturer in Kanda.

I doubted the Japanese would stand for the disorderliness of it.

It was time for me to collect my prize: to go forth and start my internship. Stacy and Perry would be very proud of me, I thought. Ethan would be amazed, if he had the time.

I entered the lobby, catching the elevator to the seventh floor. The doors opened onto pandemonium, a cacophony of voices exploding out from a doorway. I stepped into the "foyer" in front of the elevator, only to be visually assaulted by a larger-than-life cardboard cutout of a manga girl, with huge saucer-round eyes, even bigger tits, and a thong bikini, brandishing some kind of intricate laser sword.

"Kimono Avenging Angel Die!" the title said, beneath the cartoon-girl's stiletto-clad feet.

Apparently, this was one of the new monthly comic characters coming out of Sansoro . . . and from the looks of the promo piece, one of their better sellers. It was a little intimidating, I had to admit. Next to this girl, I felt so flat I was practically concave.

"Ohayo gozaimasu!"

I quickly looked away from the cardboard to see a young woman, staring at me with a helpful smile. She looked nothing like Miss Kimono Avenging Angel Die, thankfully. She was wearing high-heeled boots, a long brown skirt, and an off-white sweater. She was standing pigeon-toed, I noticed—there was something about that over here. "Can I help you?" she asked in Japanese.

Showtime. *"Ohayo gozaimasu,"* I responded with a slight bow. "My name is Lisa Falloya. I'm the winner of the—"

I was interrupted by a small squeal and her impossibly bright smile. Nobody could possibly be happier at being introduced. "Risa-san! Yes, yes, we've been expecting you. And right on time! Would you please follow me?"

Like I could say no to that much enthusiasm. I followed her, ignoring the pounding of my heart as I entered the din.

It was like a scene out of *All the President's Men* or some other seventies movie pressroom. There were clusters of metal desks, with men seated all around the surface—something like six or eight guys to a group, from the looks of it. Each man had a one-foot-square surface of work space on the metal expanse. And that work space was bounded not by cubicle walls, like I was used to, but by piles of paper—sheaves of manuscripts, drawings, manila folders, and envelopes. It was like they'd used clutter as building material. On top of all that was a display of enough toys and knickknacks to fill a Toys "R" Us. It was enough to make a minimalist pass out.

Then there were the guys themselves. Editors, I assumed . . . although instead of Woodward and Bernstein types, they all looked like video game–playing dorm inhabitants. They wore jeans or slacks and T-shirts, with all sorts of slogans and cartoon characters. They drawled casual insults at one another. Those that weren't yelling across the room were hunched over drawings, making notes in blue pencil.

It was almost as intimidating as Miss Kimono, actually.

It took them all a second to notice that I was there, but the minute they did, it was as if someone had cut a fart in church. The room went suspiciously, almost notoriously, silent. They all stared at me, and in my business-casual attire, *and* being a woman, I felt distinctly out of place.

My guide just shot me a smile over her shoulder. "This is the editors room," she said, and then continued to shepherd me toward a conference room. I smiled at the guys, who didn't respond, then I hastily followed the girl.

"I'll get them," she said, not expanding on who "them" were, and left me to sit at the broad table. I toyed with the handle of my small leather portfolio, holding my contest-winning manga entry. It had been a pain to carry on the train, and maybe it was overkill, but I didn't know what this meeting was going to be like. I figured it was better to be prepared.

After a few minutes of getting more and more stressed out with each tick of the oversized, classroom-style clock, there was finally a knock at the door. Before I could think of something to say, two men entered the room, along with my guide.

The first man was older, about five foot seven, and a little stocky, wearing what looked like an expensive suit over a singularly ugly striped shirt. He wore a tie. He smiled broadly, too, as if he'd never been more overjoyed to see anyone in his life. "Risa-san," he said, warmly. Then he pulled the business-card trick. He bowed slightly, offering me his business card with both hands.

Thanks to my mom, I knew the drill. I bowed back, taking the card with both hands and making a big show of studying it, as if I'd never seen a business card before, much less one as fine as this one. Yes, that seems weird, especially since, in Japan, most of their business

cards invariably looked the same—no neato logos, no foil or emboss-
ing, or even color. Straight-up vanilla jobs, these business cards, and
this was no exception: black and white with a plain typeface. The important difference was, this told me his name: Kugaro. And his title,
head of marketing, Sansoro Publishing.

I looked at the other guy. He was maybe five-four, slender, with a
lot more style . . . a black turtleneck under a charcoal gray pinstripe
suit with a black pocket square. He looked like a lounge-singer-pimp
version of Mr. Spock. He handed me his card with both hands, and
I started to do my "wow, a business card!" routine when he surprised
me by sticking out his hand, offering me an American-style handshake. I didn't even have time to read his name.

"Lisa-san," he said, with a relatively slight accent, pronouncing the
"L" and everything. "It's so nice to meet you. Let me be the first to
congratulate you—you're the first American to win our manga contest. We were so pleased!"

I shook his hand, even though his grip was a little loose and tentative. Obviously, he was trying to be American-friendly, but the physical contact thing was still a little unpleasant. It was unseemly to
them, to invade a person's personal space that way. I let go quickly,
and he looked relieved.

"Did you have a good flight?" he asked easily. "Won't you sit
down? I'm sure we can get you some green tea. You must be tired.
When did you arrive?"

"Tea would be great," I responded, watching as my girl-guide
rushed off, no doubt to fetch tea, which made me feel a little guilty.
"I got into the country a few days ago."

"Are you well rested?" Kugaro asked, his broad smile turning into
a dramatic look of concern.

"Yes, yes, thank you," I answered. I realized I was starting to nod
like a bobble-head doll, and quickly sat up straighter.

We all looked at one another, silently, after that. I wasn't sure what I was supposed to do. I got the unnerving feeling that neither did they.

It wasn't a good start.

"I'm eager to get to work," I said. Awkward, but at least it might get us in the right direction.

"Yes, yes, of course," nameless Spock guy responded.

And again, silence.

"So perhaps I could get an outline of what I'll be doing during my internship?" I finally threw out.

Kugaro and the nameless guy exchanged a startled look. "Would you like a tour?" Kugaro said instead.

Hmm. Maybe I'd said something wrong.

The girl came in soundlessly, and a cup of tea materialized in front of me. I said thank you and took a sip. The thing was, I didn't really like green tea—it was too bitter, and this stuff was way too hot. I winced after burning my lip a little.

"You've probably seen the boys' adventure manga section," he said. "You'll be in the *shojo* manga section, for the girls' stories. We generally have more women working there."

I nodded. My own manga was more adventure than love story, but I got the gender thing. Besides, after the scene I'd walked through to get to the conference room, I would probably feel better with something a little less fraternity-themed.

"Why don't we show you those," Mr. Spock said, standing up. Kugaro looked relieved. I stood up and followed them out, leaving my bitter tea behind. The girl followed the three of us.

The guys were quieter, I noticed—maybe because Kugaro was there, and he seemed like more of a higher-up than I realized. I got the feeling Mr. Spock was in PR—he felt like my liaison or something, and was obviously the showman. We walked through a narrow hallway into another room. This room was quiet already, I couldn't help but notice. They had the same metal-desk setup, but each square-foot "cubby" was populated by a woman working industriously and silently. Strangely, it wasn't any more comfortable than the boisterous guys' bullpen. If anything, it felt Orwellian.

"This is where you'll be working," Mr. Spock said, with a sweeping arm gesture. "This is where we produce some of our finest manga. For example, *Sweets and Candies*, or *Robot Lover*—"

He was interrupted by a loud, brash voice. "Who's talking out there?"

We all turned to see a man exit from a small office, looking peeved. He was maybe five foot even, if that, and his face was wrinkled and gnarled. He looked angry at the interruption—probably at any interruption. He was wearing a tie, too, over a shirt as wrinkled as his expression.

"Akamatsu-sensei," Mr. Spock said, bowing slightly, and I realized that this wrinkled guy might not be a big exec or anything, but he obviously had a lot of juice. "We would like you to meet Lisa Falloya, our new intern."

"Intern!"

Now wrinkled guy—Akamatsu, and somebody important from the "sensei" suffix—stood in front of me, surveying me with deep-set eyes. He gave "scrutiny" a whole new definition.

"Risa-san is the contest winner," Kugaro added.

Now the guy scowled. "Contest winner," he said. "Useless! Just a bunch of publicity nonsense. And an American?" His derisive tone said volumes.

I guessed I wasn't going to be getting the guy's business card any time soon.

He looked at me. "Have you worked in manga before? Have you done artwork, editing . . . have you worked for anyone?"

Startled, I glanced at Mr. Spock and Kugaro, who were both looking chagrined. "Uh . . ."

"What did you do before you came here?"

"I worked for a semiconductor company," I stammered.

He rolled his eyes, then squinched them. I thought he'd scrutinized me before. Now it was like he was trying to pin me with his glare.

I looked back. I tried not to blink.

Finally, he shook his head, dismissing me completely. "Semiconductors," he spat out. "American!"

He stalked back to his office, shutting the door. At least he didn't do anything as cliché as slamming it shut, but still, the message remained.

I looked at Kugaro and Spock, who were looking at each other.

Finally, Spock cleared his throat. "Why don't we take you out to lunch?"

"Yes. We were planning on taking you out to lunch," Kaguro said, his voice hearty enough to imply *well, thank God that's over with!*

"It is a short train ride," Spock continued, gesturing me away from the room. The women at the desks, I noticed, had looked up to witness the spectacle of their boss ranting, but they had just as quickly snapped back down to their work. I got the feeling they were used to the ranting and were probably glad that a stranger was drawing his ire.

"All right," I said, feeling a bit railroaded.

"And then, later, we'll give you the rest of the tour . . . the production office, where we lay out next month's editorial." Mr. Spock was in full, smooth, PR-recovery mode. "Actually, I think we might even have a T-shirt in your size."

"A T-shirt!" Kugaro enthused. No fool, Kugaro.

I sighed. So the bottom line was, I was going to be working for a wrinkled little peanut of a fascist for a year, in this silent, gray, cubicle-prison.

On the plus side, I was getting free lunch and a T-shirt.

Score one for Tokyo, I thought, and followed them out.

CHAPTER 3

January 14, Saturday morning

I WAS AS CAREFUL AS POSSIBLE, TRYING TO BE QUIET USING THE Kanais' phone. I couldn't sleep. I had been awake for the past hour and a half, waiting for when I could make the phone call. Mrs. Kanai said it was all right to use the phone, I'd just pay them back. (She didn't say that last part, but I assured her I would.) It was Saturday, for pity's sake. So I went into the kitchen and shut the door behind me—it was a frosted glass, but it looked like those rice paper screens they always show in traditional Japanese houses, on the Travel channel or something. I hoped I didn't wake anybody up.

I called Stacy, and she got it on the first ring. "Hello?"

"Stace," I said. "Man, it's good to hear your voice."

It took her a second. "*Lisa?* Wow! How's it going? How are you doing? Tell me everything!" And before I could tell her everything, she added, "Wait a minute. What the heck time is it over there?"

I glanced at the microwave. "It's about four forty-five in the morning."

"Oy. Jet lag, still?"

I made a miserable little mumble of assent. "Among other things."

"Oh." A pause. "I take it you're having some trouble adjusting."

"To put it mildly," I said, trying not to simply buckle under and start sobbing my troubles out in true dramaholic fashion.

"Is the host family nice?"

I didn't see any shadows out there, indicating that somebody was up, but the whole place was quiet as a tomb. I dropped my voice. "It's different," I said, trying to put as much inflection as I could in that little phrase.

"What's Perry's pen pal girlfriend like?" This was asked with a giggle.

"Party girl," I replied, with a giggle of my own. "I rarely see her. She's either sleeping or she's out."

"Sleeping or out? What does she do for a living?"

"Nothing, from what I can tell," I answered.

"How about the folks?"

"They're nice enough," I said. "Father works some crazy hours, seems like he's in the office all the time. Mrs. Kanai is pretty nice. She fixes me food if I'm here." I thought about adding that I didn't necessarily know what food she was cooking at any given time, and I'd eaten several mystery meals since I'd gotten here. I took to leaving when I could, and she didn't seem to find it rude.

"Anybody else?"

"A kid brother. I can't even begin to describe him," I said. "He's twelve, and he doesn't go to school. And because of the laws here, they can't force him."

"What, there's no truant officer?"

"Apparently not," I said. "He stays home all day and plays video games. I swear, I can't believe his eyes aren't bleeding from the hours he spends in front of the TV."

"Crazy," Stacy said, and I felt a little better. Somebody understood, finally, what I was going through. Before I could go into full commiseration, however, she moved on, "But hey, that's not why you're there, anyway. How's work going?"

I sighed.

"Crap," she said, picking up on it immediately. "That bad, huh?"

I quickly filled her in on my teeny little desk space, the frat-boy atmosphere of the guys' side versus the prisonlike quiet of the girls' side, my overbearing future supervisor Akamatsu. I was letting my voice raise ever so slightly with the retelling. "This place is so nuts," I said, finally. "I don't know what I'm doing here."

"Yes, you do," Stacy said, and her voice was a little less gentle. "God, Lisa, I know that you're homesick and all, and I know that you hate traveling, and blah blah blah. But you've only been there a week. You can't say you're going to pack your bag and come home after a week. Please!"

I winced. This was not the comforting call home I was hoping for.

"You're in a foreign country, you're doing something people only dream of doing," she said, sounding part inspirational speaker, part bitch-slapping drill sergeant. "And you're going to whine because you've got a tiny desk and you're doing grunt work?"

"Saying that I'm whining seems a bit harsh," I said.

"Perry would be even worse, and you know it."

I mentally scratched him off my to-call list for the day. "Well, I was just looking for a little sympathy." I didn't mean to sound quite that offended, but damn it, I was.

"You were looking for a lot of sympathy, and you were looking to lay the groundwork for leaving early," Stacy said. She might've been right. "Don't do it. You've got this great opportunity and if you come home early, I swear to God, Lise, I will kick your butt myself."

Stacy was now speaking in her very best Mad Mom voice, one she used on her son just before a "time out." I knew she was serious.

I allowed myself one last sigh. "Okay, okay. No need to get militant. I was just looking to vent, and now I have."

"So what are you going to do today?" She was all brightness and perky fun again, the moment abated. "What have you seen? You have to have done something fun."

"Well, I stayed at a Love Hotel," I said, cracking a small smile. "Totally accidental, but . . ."

She squealed. "Spill!"

So I told her my adventures in the red-light district, and she howled with laughter, which made me feel a bit better. "But that's the extent of my sightseeing," I said.

"Well, there's part of your problem right there," she told me. "If the job sucks, and the host family's weird, you need to look at it as one long vacation. Go out, check out the sights. Don't just hole up in your little room."

"Half-room, technically," I said, thinking of my roommate Yukari.

"Half-room, then. I know you. If God gave you a one-week vacation in Heaven, all you'd be able to tell me was how room service was and what books you read." Her comments were all the more scathing because I knew she was right, and she was relentlessly cheerful about it. Yikes. "So don't blow this. I'll call you next week and I expect to hear a full report on something cool you've seen."

She meant well, I knew that. Hell, she was probably right. I don't know why I needed my friends to keep goading me into stuff that I knew I ought to be doing, but there it was. "Okay. But I'll call you— I don't know if the phone ringing would bug the Kanai family, and I'm trying to stay on good terms here."

"All right. Take care of yourself, *have fun,* and I'll be expecting that call."

We said good-bye and I hung up, feeling a little bereft. Even getting chewed out by my best friend was better than being lonely and self-indulgently woeful by myself.

I opened the sliding door and let out a little surprised yelp before I could stop myself. Mr. Kanai was standing there, dressed for work. He looked at me apologetically.

"I did not mean to scare you," he said, as if it were some terrible grievous fault of his, that he startled the strange woman renting one of his rooms at five thirty in the morning. "I just wanted to get a little breakfast before going into the office."

"You're going to work?" I couldn't help it. I was still a little loopy from the sleep deficit, and I suddenly had a terrible feeling that I'd gotten one of the days wrong, and maybe *I* should be getting ready for work, too. "I thought it was Saturday."

He smiled gently. "It is Saturday."

"Oh." I waited for him to say something, but he acted as if it was self-explanatory, so I hastily got out of his way. "I'm sorry," I added. "I didn't mean . . . I was just calling home." I paused a second. "Of course, I'll pay for the call." The long-distance bill would probably be horrendous.

"Please, don't worry about it," he assured me, and I felt even more guilty. I really needed to get a cell phone. This was nuts.

He went about making his breakfast, making no attempt at conversation, so I crept out of the kitchen—and promptly ran smack into Yukari.

Yukari after a night of clubbing was a gloriously disheveled sight to behold. She was wearing a neon pink silk jacket, one of those brocade-looking ones, trimmed in marabou. She wore a white T-shirt under it that said "Happy Moonbeams" in red glitter. Her skirt was brown suede with a border of matching brocade, and she wore brown boots that went up to her knees. Her makeup by this point was wrecked, and her hair had pink streaks in it. She looked vaguely hung over.

"Oh, you're up," she said, or something to that effect—she was mumbling, or maybe slurring.

Her father heard her, and he stepped out of the kitchen to send her an inscrutable look. She didn't counter, although she didn't look him in the eye, either. It wasn't outright rebellion. It was more like defiant ignorance.

You could feel the tension that churned up in Yukari's wake. I needed to get back in the room and try for a little more sleep before she started seriously cutting z's. For a girl who looked like a fragile porcelain doll, she could snore like a lumberjack. Besides, Mr. Kanai hadn't left the doorway but was still staring at Yukari's receding form. It had to be tough. In another century, he could've beaten her. Hell, some people still lived in that century. But she was determined to do her own thing, and he was obviously way too family-conscious to kick her ass out. But love and frustration were obviously warring.

I didn't stick around. I headed for the room. While crossing the living room, I felt a quick kick in my hip and spun around. "What the hell?" I yelled, in English. It wasn't a gentle kick.

I saw Ichiro's sleeping form, sprawled out on their white couch. He was wearing the same clothes he'd been wearing the past three days. He was asleep, with the controller to the video game still in his hand. I imagine Mrs. Kanai must've shut the TV off when he first nodded off. I stared at his face, trying to determine if he was still sleeping or if he'd kicked me on purpose. Then I looked back at the kitchen.

Mr. Kanai shot me another quick look and then disappeared. I heard the rustling of utensils. He wasn't going to apologize for his son. He wasn't even going to acknowledge his children's behavior.

No wonder he's hauling his ass into the office at five thirty on a Saturday.

I went to bed. Yukari had beaten me to it, dumping her clothes in a pile on the floor. Her blankets buried her like an Indian mound, so I heard only the muffled rumblings of her presnoring. Damn it.

It was this, or wander the streets of Tokyo at six in the morning.

I crawled into bed, taking an extra pillow and putting it over my head. Out of sheer exhaustion, or possibly self-defense, I fell asleep.

January 15, Sunday

I slept in until about nine o'clock in the morning, thanks to the fact that Yukari never came home that night to wake me up with her ritual of stumbling in drunk and turning on lights or knocking things over. I felt a little better rested, which was nice. I could hear Ichiro playing his video games, and whatever Mrs. Kanai was cooking for breakfast smelled . . . hmm. It smelled. I had no idea what it was, but it was probably one of Ichiro's favorites. I got cleaned up and dressed and then snuck out like a thief, ignoring Ichiro's wanna-be Clint Eastwood squint at me as I crossed the living room.

So far, my sojourn in Japan wasn't really a bunch of giggles. Between the Kanai household, and the job, and the culture shock, I was feeling pretty puny, but I knew I couldn't call Stacy or Perry, or even Ethan, looking for sympathy. And I certainly couldn't call my family, since they'd more than likely tell me to simply break my contract and come home—they didn't know why I was over here at all, and I know my nana would've come over here physically to collect me if she didn't hate traveling so much. (And if she wasn't so pissed off that I ignored her advice and flew off for a year anyway. The only thing she liked better than a searing scolding was a good, guilt-inducing "I told you so.")

But Stacy had a point. I was in Tokyo for a year. Stacy was stuck. Perry was drifting. They both would've given their right arms to do what I was doing, and here I was, whining and bitching. Granted, it was more *their* idea of paradise than mine, but I really enjoyed manga, and I had a shot at working with stuff I loved for the next year. Most people couldn't say that. And whether I liked to travel or not, I was *in Japan.* I might as well see some of it.

Besides, Stacy wasn't kidding. She was expecting a report in the next week on some cool thing I did. I was going to be lame enough if I went home and didn't do anything in Japan except hang out with my crazy host family and get chewed out by a Japanese editor who hated the fact that I was an American ex-semiconductor worker. She'd ride me every single week until I got home if I didn't change matters immediately.

I got breakfast at one of the American-style cafés, just coffee and one of the best croissants I'd ever eaten. Then I decided to brave the train system, looking carefully over the maps and the tour book Stacy had given me as a gift. After hearing Gwen Stefani make such a big deal over it, I decided I ought to see Harajuku, of Harajuku Girls fame. I'd read about it in the tour book, too, and Sunday seemed to be the day to people-watch.

I was lucky—only two wrong trains later, I finally made it to Harajuku Station. It was a sight to behold, I have to admit. Tons of Japanese kids, packed into one walking-only alleyway that was lined on both sides with clothing stores. And all the stores were targeted, obviously, at the Harajuku Teen. There were thrift stores that held everything from poodle skirts to simple flannel shirts. I guess grunge might be making some inroads. There were also "cheap" clothing stores, sort of like a cross between Forever 21 stores and 99-cent stores back home . . . you could get a skirt for the equivalent of five bucks, even though I doubt it would last more than two washings.

The kids themselves were like something out of a sci-fi novel, like *Neuromancer* or *Mona Lisa Overdrive* or, for that matter, something out of my beloved manga, which made me smile. Their hair was dyed all shades, from baby blue to electric purple. There were the requisite Goth kids, which was sort of comforting. Goth was recognized the world over as being a universal expression of being young, depressed, and angst-ridden enough to wear black lipstick. I smiled at one girl, remembering my own brief flirtation with the period. She didn't smile back, and as a Goth, I didn't expect her to. More strange were the young women dressed as Alice in Wonderland, complete with sky blue dresses and white aprons . . . and their counterparts, some kind of Strawberry Shortcake knock-offs, in pink dresses, usually with hair dyed a raspberry red. Other young women and men were dressed like installation art pieces, in fashions so complicated as to be completely useless, such as loose-knit sweaters that hung off their bodies like sacks, with sleeves that went down past their knees, or knee-high platform moon-boots that made them tower seven inches taller than they were. It was a spectacle. The kids looked pretty surly, too, as if daring someone to start shit for the way they were dressed.

Of course, in seven-inch platforms, you'd better know some pretty intense kung fu, I thought, grinning. Because it would be easy to get your ass kicked in those things. Of course, in Japan, the likelihood of that happening was somewhere between slim and ridiculous.

I decided to wander into a shoe store—Stacy had a thing for shoes—and was sidetracked by the fact that it wasn't actually a shoe store. It was a *sock* store. I knew that the Japanese have a foot fetish of sorts, but I had mostly seen the hooker-boot phenomenon in action. This was different, more geared to teens. They had pinup pictures of young girls modeling the latest foot fashions. They were seriously into toe cleavage, I noticed. They also had socks that went under other socks. And they had lace-up socks, lingerie socks, bondage socks, and ballet socks. Then I saw the "fat socks" that I'd read about, strictly the province of teen girls. They were like leg warmers: huge, thick knits, scrunched down to make the calves look enormous. I had joked about that with Stacy, I remembered.

"Why would they want to make their legs look fat?" Stacy had commented.

"They're not," Perry said, authoritatively. Of course, he was the authority on teenage Japanese girls. "They're trying to make their legs seem abnormally skinny. The fatter the sock, the skinnier the leg looks."

"Wait a second," I'd said. "You mean, they're actively *trying* to have chicken legs?"

"Apparently," Perry said. "Hey, it's fashion, okay?"

I smiled at the young girl working the cash register, shaking my head at her offer of help. Perry would go nuts on this street, I thought. Hell, after a day with all the Japanese kids, he might never come home.

I kept on walking, heading down the street, window shopping. It felt weird, and somewhat lonely without Stacy or Perry to make little giggling comments about the things I was seeing. I made as many mental notes as I could, but it wasn't the same as seeing something at the same time and sharing it. This was a big part of why I don't like traveling by myself. It seemed like such a waste, just to see it myself, with my wall of travel-numbness.

Suddenly, I felt the overpowering urge to connect with my old friends, to remind myself that I wasn't quite so alone.

At the end of the long alley was a gallery-type thing that boasted an Internet café on the roof. It was too late in the day to call home, I realized, and at any rate, I wasn't going to go back to the Kanai house to brave a phone call. So I figured I'd grab some lunch and send some e-mails. It wasn't as good as actually talking to someone, much less actually *seeing* someone, but the sense of connection would hopefully tide me over.

I entered the glass building, taking the decorative (and I almost doubted usable) elevator up to the top floor. The café looked a little ritzy, but I had cash and a burning desire to spend. I stepped in. There were a few other gaijin, I noticed, feeling immediately comforted. In the absence of friends, it was good to be around other foreigners.

The waitresses were wearing low-slung hip-hugger acid-washed blue jeans with studded belts and white T-shirts with black happy faces on them. They looked bored and fashionable. I must've wandered into the Japanese version of the Model Café or something. They didn't notice me for several minutes, not because it was crowded—there were several empty tables.

I was tired, hungry, lonely, and having less and less fun on my little outing. I'd been in Japan long enough not to have jet lag, but that's what it felt like.

Finally, a waitress came up to me, her eyes coolly appraising beneath blond-streaked bangs. She said something quickly in Japanese, and I didn't catch it. I stared at her. "*Sumimasen?*" I said, feeling awkward. "Pardon me?"

She repeated it, a little slower—and I swear to God, I couldn't make it out for the life of me. My Japanese had been managing pretty well, all things considered, so this felt horribly humiliating. Finally, I broke out in English, hoping that would help. "I'm sorry," I said. "I'm having trouble understanding you. Could you please speak English?"

At that point, she blinked, and then smiled at me—more of a smirk, really.

"I said," she said, with deliberate slowness, "are you here for lunch?"

And that's when it hit me. The reason I hadn't understood her. She had pegged me as a gaijin from the moment I had walked in the door—and she'd *spoken English*. Heavily accented, admittedly, but she'd tried. And I hadn't picked up on it at all.

I felt heat flood my cheeks. She must've been insulted, and now she must be thinking I was some kind of submoron. "I'm so sorry," I said, bowing a little, feeling utterly humiliated. "Yes, I'm here for lunch, and to use the Internet."

She led me to a table and put a menu down in front of her. "English on this side," she said, with that exaggerated enunciation, hammering the point home.

"Thanks," I muttered, and bowed my head over the menu, not even looking at her face. Then I remembered what I was doing there and cleared my throat. "Oh! Excuse me. I need to send an e-mail."

She looked at me like I was *really* stupid. "It's an Internet café," she said, as if I somehow didn't realize it. "Go ahead. Use any of them."

So much for the legendary Japanese helpfulness, I thought, creeping over to one of the open laptops. I got the feeling this wasn't the sort of story Stacy was looking for.

Score two, Japan.

If this kept up, I was going to be toast, in either language, way before my one-year contract was over. And a small part of me realized that there was no way I was giving girls like Miss Bleached Bangs the satisfaction of grinding me down.

January 16, Monday

Back at work after my Harajuku jaunt, I was still thinking about my current dilemma. If I was going to tough it out here, I might as well make the best of things. And since work was the heart of why I was here (and the heart of Japanese culture—that is, to everybody but freeloaders like my roomie Yukari), I figured the best way to start was to focus on getting to know some of my coworkers. If I could make my time at Sansoro that much more comfortable, it'd make the rest of my life easier. And it was just a year. Look what Ethan was putting up with for three plus years, going for his MBA. Yeah, I'd need to suck it up and just get this done.

I sat at my little desk-section, with my piles of blue-lined drawings and recently inked comics that needed the underlying pencil erased.

To my right was one assistant, Satomi. She had that brown-to-black hair that was almost definitely dyed. She was wearing a biscuit-colored sweater and a long black skirt with the requisite heels, although the heels were something workable. She was working hard on something, although the pile of paper that marked her boundary of the desk from mine was high enough that I couldn't see what she was working on so industriously. To my left was Sakura. She had darker hair, but there was obviously a burgundy wash over it that shone almost purple in bright light—not that we got a lot of bright light in this fluorescent place. She was wearing a gray sweater that could've come out of Satomi's closet. She was also focused on her work like we were taking the SATs.

I called them the S-girls, mentally, because it was easier. In the middle of the desk was a partition and the requisite stacks and stacks of crap that had been left there: bundles of old manga projects, paperwork, God knew what else. I couldn't see the women "associates" of the editorial staff who shared the opposite side of the desk. It was like the Berlin Wall or something. Our side of the room, the female side, was much quieter than the boisterous "boy" side of the room, I noticed. No watercooler chat or "did you catch *Desperate Housewives*?" or anything.

Obviously, this made getting to know my coworkers a bit more challenging. Especially since I'm not exactly the most outgoing girl by nature.

Come on, Stacy and Perry would be egging you on right now, I coached myself. At the very least, I didn't need to be reamed again by Stacy, who I knew hated her job at the semiconductor plant and would probably have had every single one of her coworkers over for coffee by now. I needed an in. Jeez, how did you ask somebody to be a friend, as an adult?

That sort of thing stumped me at home, too, actually. Which was probably why I still had the same two best friends from high school.

I looked down at my stack of pencil drawings. Maybe I could just start with something work-related. I leaned over to Sakura. "Excuse me," I said, hesitantly.

Her head bobbed up immediately. "Yes?"

"I was wondering . . . who is this artist? The work looks familiar, and it's beautiful, but I can't place it." There. An opening. And a way to talk about manga, which I could do for hours with strangers at the Comic-Con, so no worries there.

She glanced around, as if trying to make sure nobody heard me. Since the guys were yelling over some dirty joke one of the editors told, I didn't think anybody heard me, although I wasn't sure what all the secrecy was about.

"That's one of our greatest artists," she said, in a low tone. "That's Nobuko-san's work. You've heard of her, I'm sure?"

Actually, I wasn't as familiar with any artist named Nobuko, but from Sakura's reverent tone, I got the feeling I was supposed to be, so I nodded. "I haven't seen a lot of her stuff, though," I added, to explain why I hadn't recognized her right away. "So she's one of our artists?"

"She is our best *manga-ka*," Sakura said, and now her voice held almost a tremor of fear. Okay, *weird*.

"I thought, well, then, why doesn't her *assisto* erase the pencil drawings?" I asked, genuinely curious now. If she was that big, she probably had a team of flunkies, drawing and cleaning up for her. So why was I, an editorial flunky, doing the artistic flunky grunt work?

Her eyes widened, and I felt a hand on my shoulder. I turned, to see Satomi shaking her head and also glancing around.

Apparently I'd broken some kind of schoolyard rule: taking the name of Nobuko in vain, or something.

"I can do it, if you don't want to," Satomi whispered. "It's not that bad."

"Oh! No, I'm not complaining," I quickly whispered back. "I don't mind, really. I just figured she'd probably have a huge group of assistants to help her out. Because she's so good, and, er, famous," I said. "But I don't mind doing this. This is what I came here to do, after all." I tacked on a weak laugh at the end that didn't help.

Man, you're really winning them over now!

Sakura grinned, I noticed, even though Satomi still looked a little scared. "She only has a small staff," Sakura explained, her voice so low a librarian would have trouble hearing her. "Only one *assisto* at a time, and that person is responsible for doing a lot of background drawing and inking. At the same time, Nobuko-san has many deadlines . . . many projects. Because she is special, we have agreed to pick up some of her artistic duties." She shrugged. "At least it's just penciling."

"I tried inking once," Satomi added. From the tone of her voice, it apparently had been a fiasco.

Now, I was getting somewhere. "I'm sure there are tons of things I ought to know about," I said slowly. "I feel very strange here, and I don't want to make any mistakes."

"You'll be fine," Sakura said, and her smile was very comforting.

"I'll help you out," Satomi added.

"Can I take you two to lunch?"

They looked puzzled, almost a little shocked.

"I'd love to talk about the company, get my bearings," I said, trying to emphasize the business side of things. I guess asking people to lunch wasn't really done here. They were looking at me like I'd just asked them to participate in a lesbian orgy, or something. Yikes!

They looked at each other, silently communicating in the way that only people who have known each other for years seemed able to do. Sakura shrugged again, and Satomi looked doubtful.

"I would be happy to have lunch with you," Sakura said, almost defiantly, albeit still in her quiet tone of voice.

"I brought a lunch," Satomi said. "But I will go to lunch with you, as well."

I didn't want her to think I was taking her hostage, or anything, but it seemed like a good idea. I'd warm her up over some udon noodles or something and get to know her a little better. Sakura seemed more open. "All right. What time . . ."

"What are you whispering about?"

Sakura and Satomi froze like rabbits. I was dumb enough to turn around.

It was our supervisor, Akamatsu. He was standing there, all five-foot-nothing of gnarled, rumpled irritation. He was wearing an olive green corduroy suit with a brown-and-sage-plaid shirt that didn't go with his blue tie. His sparse hair stood out at odd angles from his head. He looked like a cross between Yoda and Charlie Brown.

"I was just asking a question about this artist," I said, and I swear I could feel the tension coming off the S-girls in waves. "Nobuko-san is so very talented." I hoped that didn't come out as suck-up as it felt.

He grunted, a sort of "tell me something I don't know" sound. "The editorial team is too far behind to sit here gossiping," he said. "When will you be done with the pencil lines?"

I looked at the stack of papers. "It shouldn't take me too long, Akamatsu-sensei," I replied.

"That's not an answer, that's an evasion," he pointed out, and crossed his arms.

Maybe it's because I lack the Force, Yoda-san, I mentally quipped, but I didn't think he'd get the reference, and if he did, I bet he'd be really pissed, and I didn't want a gnome on a power trip getting on my case. Besides, Satomi would probably have a nervous breakdown on the spot.

"By tonight," I answered, optimistically.

He looked at the papers, then looked at me, as if he couldn't believe I could possibly get the work done on time.

I may not be the best traveler in the world, I may whine to my friends, I may not be up for new places and taking big chances, but the one place I am confident, generally, is in my work. I don't mess around when it comes to work. I will stand up and talk about things when it's work-related. Basically, when I'm in a job, I'm the shit. That sounds cocky and ridiculous, considering, but it's a family thing. My brother's the same way.

He snorted. "I want it all on my desk by six o'clock tonight, then," he said.

I nodded. If I had to erase until my fingertips bled, I'd do it.

"Which means," he added, in an offhand way, "that you won't have time for lunch."

Damn it. He was right—and it meant that he'd overheard at least part of my conversation with the S-girls. Satomi went white as a sheet.

"Of course, Akamatsu-sensei," I said, through gritted teeth.

"And if you get this done," he said, and I wasn't sure if I was imagining the emphasis on *if*. I probably wasn't. "If you get this done, I suppose I will have to find more challenging work for you."

"I would be happy to," I replied, pulling a Stacy overly perky response on him and smiling vacantly. *Bring it on, Yoda.*

He grinned maliciously and then stomped away, breaking up a paper fight on the boy's side of the room. "Get back to work!" he barked, and they settled down.

"Sorry," I whispered to the S-girls. "I guess we'll have to reschedule lunch for some other time."

Sakura nodded. Satomi stared at her desk like her life depended on it. Neither said anything, and I felt depressed. So much for making friends here.

About ten minutes later, Sakura passed me a note. Just like in sixth grade. I opened it, and it took me a few minutes to translate it—my written Japanese really did suck.

Don't get Akamatsu-sensei mad, the note read. *He can be very unpleasant if he is angry at you. And we may not be able to have lunch for a while. We will all be too busy.*

Damn it. I nodded to her, although she never looked at me, and then I started erasing, quickly and carefully, determined to make the deadline. I got the distinct feeling I had somehow gotten the S-girls punished somehow. Even if we did have time for lunch, they might not want to be seen fraternizing with me, especially if my buddy Yoda was going to put them on some sort of shit list for it.

Swell. Just swell.

I almost tore the paper, I was erasing so hard. I focused again, determined.

There is no way I'm lasting here for a year, a traitorous voice inside my head murmured.

I was starting to agree with it.

January 19, Thursday

WHEN DEPRESSED AND IN A STRANGE COUNTRY, THERE IS ONLY
one place to hit, to feel better, to feel normal, to feel *American.*

That place is Starbucks.

I knew Perry would probably have several nasty things to say
about my chosen antidepressant. He's virulently against "corporate
coffee," and he sees going to Starbucks as selling out. He'd rather
drink instant coffee and "stand up to the man." He's sort of diehard
that way. Stupid, too, but I don't rub that in.

The thing is, you really don't go to Starbucks for the coffee. I
mean, I'm no coffee connoisseur, necessarily. I can't take a sip of something and say "ah, a piquant blend of Arabica and Java, nice acidity
with full body." I like my coffee drinks like I like my alcoholic drinks:
sickeningly sweet to the point of frou-frou, comfortingly girly. I want

a drink that a man would be vaguely embarrassed to order. That's my idea of comfort. And I like knowing that no matter what city I'm in, I can look for that damned green awning and know that there will be a place that plays innocuous music with tasteful decorations and, for a minute, I can drink my highly caffeinated, sugar-overdose beverage and read a book and feel right at home.

After my run-in with Yoda the Supervisor-Nazi, as I was calling Akamatsu, and after two weeks with the Kanai family, I figured I deserved a little shot of American corporate coffee, damn it. I wanted to feel normal. And I sure as hell wasn't eager to go home. There was a Starbucks right by the subway station that was near the Kanai suburb; I'd passed it several times now and hadn't gone in. Now was as good a time as any. I figured it would become a habit.

I walked in, and they were playing something sultry and English, probably Billie Holiday from the sound of it. It smelled like dark-roasted heaven, and for a second, I felt completely Zen.

I walked up to the counter. The barrista was Japanese, with short chin-length hair and a good deal of makeup. She asked me what I wanted.

"Venti Caramel Macchiato, please," I said. I could even order drinks in the same sizes, with the same descriptions, as the beverages back home. *Ahhhhhh.*

She nodded, and gave me change. I don't know why faux Italian would make me feel more American, but somehow it did. I waited like the other patrons, and they called my order. Then I went to the second floor, where there were the usual tables, people murmuring to one another, people reading books or looking over paperwork. I took a seat at the "bar" that faced the window, looking out on the teeming stream of commuters below, all heading home.

I took out my last English-language book, *Pattern Recognition* by William Gibson. I'd read everything else I brought with me, just to pass the time in the Kanai house. I'd been saving this. Now, I took the lid off my Caramel Macchiato, letting the sugary heat soothe my senses, and I cracked open the book.

I got about a page down when a bunch of giggling kids distracted me. Annoyed, I looked over.

There were a gaggle of high school kids . . . Americans, from the looks of them. Maybe about five of them, three girls, two boys. White, maybe Latino. They were staring at everything and whispering too loud in English.

"Thank *God* for Starbucks," one girl said, in that stage whisper. She didn't have a distinctive accent, so I pegged her for California. They all spoke like newscasters, anyway, with the slightest lazy drawl or that giggling wanna-Valley speak. Ethan was from California; I remembered from the girls I saw when we visited his parents.

"Oh, I *know,*" another girl quickly affirmed. Apparently the first girl was the Alpha Female, a shoulder-length blonde wearing a Baby Phat getup and a down jacket. This girl, the first runner up, was wearing a cutesy T-shirt that said "Vote for Pedro" on it. Gag. She was a brunette. The third girl was a redhead. They looked like preteen Charlie's Angels. "Do we even know what we were eating for dinner?"

"I didn't eat any of it," one boy, a lanky guy with sandy brown hair, said. He was dressed the way almost all teen boys seemed to dress: oversized jeans and a big T-shirt. He was slim, so he swam in his clothes, and his jacket looked like a tent on him. He was wearing a baseball cap: the Dodgers. Yup, Californians. Who would cheer for the Dodgers that didn't have to?

"I did," the other boy said. He looked Latino, as did the brunette girl, now that I thought about it. He was shorter, stockier, a pitbull to his friend's greyhound. He was grinning. "I didn't mind."

"You'd eat anything disgusting. You could be on *Fear Factor,*" Alpha Female Blonde said with disdain.

He had bought a cookie, which he quickly took a big bite out of and then chewed. "Aaaagh," he said, opening his mouth and showing the half-masticated pastry.

"Eyew!" This from the brunette.

"Nasty," the redhead agreed, but her giggling ruined the effect. The lanky guy simply nodded approval.

I glanced around. I couldn't help but notice the other patrons, sending looks of distress and disapproval over to the table of teens. I'm sure that Japanese teens were probably more rambunctious than their elders—at least, they were probably more of a pain in the ass, if Ichiro was any example. But there seemed to be a social contract, as it were, that there were some ways you didn't behave in public. You behaved like everybody else. I got that from my mom, years ago, and I had enough of it to get by here. Now, watching these teens, I felt all my happiness at feeling "American" leach away. Not that I was ashamed to be American, of course. But seeing these kids act like they could be as crude and idiotic as they wanted, act like they *owned* the joint, while never even noticing how they were affecting other people . . .

Well, it was ruining my sugar buzz, for one thing. My Macchiato was getting cooler as my own temperature rose with anger. There's a reason they call us ugly Americans. These idiots were a textbook definition.

They saw another man staring at them . . . at the blonde, particularly. Natural blondes are like rock stars here, according to urban legend, and I could see this guy was just short of drooling. The Alpha shot him a look that she'd probably perfected from years of skanks drooling after her: an acknowledgment that, yes, she really was that fine . . . and a look of freezing scorn, that added *and there's no way you're getting any of this, sleazoid.*

The man quickly rustled his newspaper and buried his head behind it.

"What?" the lanky kid asked a couple of Japanese women, who had also been staring . . . probably because he had his feet up on another chair. They hastily looked away.

I burned with shame for them, and anger at their hostile obliviousness. They'd officially ruined my Starbucks experience. I got up, dumping the stuff in the trash. I didn't want to rush home to the Kanai house, but this place wasn't going to be a refuge tonight. I decided to hit the bathroom before I left, knowing that when I got "home," Yukari would've taken up residence in the bathroom so she could get ready for her night out.

"You know," the redhead said, "she looked like she understood English."

"She" referring to me, I think. I pretended not to hear her.

"So?" The shorter guy sounded unimpressed.

Assholes.

I closed myself in the bathroom, still steaming over their whole attitude. Why even bother traveling if you were going to act like the whole place was just a suburb of the States? If you were going to go to just shit on everything and try to block everything out, why even be there at all?

Of course, this is something that Perry would say you were doing . . . going to a Starbucks.

I sighed. My conscience, annoying though it could be, was right. I wasn't exactly blameless in this scenario. They might be acting out, but I was doing the exact same thing, only the passive-aggressive brand of it.

The bathroom at Starbucks was plush, more so than any bathroom I'd been to back home. It was an ultra-deluxe model, with a space-age-looking faucet and soap system, and one of those toilets that I'd read about: heated cushioned seat, the works. I couldn't believe they'd have something like this in a public place. Of course, if the ugly Americans out there saw something like this, they'd probably push every button, clog the toilet with paper towels, trash it, and then leave, complaining that the whole thing was "too damned complicated to be a bathroom."

I went about my business. I wasn't going to be an ugly American anymore. So my host family was weird. So my job was trivial. I was in *Tokyo,* damn it. I didn't have to bitch and moan for a year. There were lots of cool things to see and do, and I wasn't going to just turn up my nose and order McDonald's for my entire trip. I was going to be an adventurer.

I was about to clean up when I suddenly had a bad realization.

I might be a mighty adventurer, but I couldn't figure out how to flush the toilet.

There was an electronic control panel with six buttons on it, around where the handle ought to be on a "standard model" toilet. They weren't in writing but had little helpful pictures to explain the function of each. I saw one that looked like a hose—I was assuming bidet, and the last thing I wanted was to get sprayed in the face because I pushed the wrong button while standing over it. There was one that had, I swear to God, a music note.

What? Does it have a radio, too?

The longer I was in there, the more embarrassed I felt. I couldn't just walk out, not without having this resolved. Even if it meant bidet fountain and all sorts of bad things.

So I pushed one that looked like rushing water. What else could it be, right?

To my horror, it didn't. What it *did* do was play a really loud, really amplified sound of a toilet flushing. Apparently, they were self-conscious enough about the sound of bodily functions that the sound of a toilet flushing was preferable. Of course, it also left no question of what the practitioner was actually *doing* in the bathroom.

"Oh, hell," I muttered, and quickly hit other buttons. I hit the right one, finally, and washed up.

When I emerged, none of the Japanese people were looking at me. The Teen America contingent, however, were staring.

I walked down the stairs with as much dignity as I could but not without hearing the Alpha Female say, "What do you think she was *doing* in there?"

Their hyenalike laughter followed me out the door.

January 30, Monday

Well, it's been less than a month, and I'm already being called into my supervisor's office. That has to be some kind of record. Back home, the only reason I'd be called into my boss's office would be to get a performance evaluation (which was usually positive if boring), or to fill my boss in on what happened while he was on vacation (also usually positive and boring).

I got the feeling that my buddy Yoda didn't have the S-girls tell me to meet him in his office to give me an "atta-girl," that much was obvious.

I knocked politely. *"Hai!"* he grunted, and I walked in.

Yoda's office was a mess—surprise, surprise. There were papers everywhere, in towering piles that were taller than either of us. God help the man if there was an earthquake, I thought, then suddenly realized that if there was one now, I'd be the one squashed by a leaning column of bond paper. I sat on the edge of my seat, as if that would somehow help.

"Risa-san," he said, his bushy eyebrows beetling as if he were communicating with them alone. "I told you I'd find more challenging work for you to do, after you finished the pencil work I asked."

I nodded. "Thank you," I said, for lack of anything better to say. Maybe this wouldn't be so bad, after all.

"But before I give you work, I need to know what you think you're doing here."

Scratch that earlier observation.

He looked almost crafty, although still fierce. I don't think the guy ever looked just happy. "You're the winner of a contest. You've only got a year here. You're an intern."

"Yes," I said, not sure where he was going with this.

"So, what did you think you'd be doing, if not erasing pencil marks?"

Aha. "I don't want you to think— I didn't expect to be doing anything in particular," I said. Was he pissed that I was ungrateful? That seemed like a Japanese thing to do—at least, it was the sort of thing my mom would probably take me to task about. Which was why I hadn't called home and complained to her. "It's an honor just to work here," I said, again hoping that didn't sound too kiss-ass.

He nodded, of course it was an honor. "We have an editorial shortage right now," he said. "Do you know what editors do here?"

I shook my head. *Now* we were getting somewhere.

"A lot of what we're working on are manga translations of written material," he said, and his tone was still sharp, like he couldn't believe he had to actually spell it all out for me. "So an editor would be responsible for reading the original work and making sure that the *manga-ka* was correctly interpreting what was going on in the story. Getting the nuances correct, getting the emotion across. Emotion is the most important part of these stories, since they're *shojo,* geared to young women. Do you understand?"

I nodded. At least, I hoped I'd gotten the idea right—my Japanese wasn't that great. "So, you want me to read some original work?"

His eyes widened. "Of course not!"

Whoops. Missed the call on that one.

"Once the artist gets the initial sketches correct, the editor is responsible for making sure they are in good shape for the printer," he said. "That includes making sure they are inked properly, that they read properly, that the type is legible, and that everything is in order. That is why you have been erasing pencil lines for one of our most prestigious artists."

I nodded. No problem there.

"This artist needs one more *assisto*," he said. "You have some artistic ability, as can be seen from the manga you submitted to win the contest."

I smiled, feeling a warm glow in my chest. I nodded again and looked down, in case it was too immodest to feel happy about the compliment.

"Still, you're not good enough to be a *manga-ka*," he said, stopping the warm glow in its tracks. "You do have a good sense of story, however, and you seem to have a good sense of interpreting scenes."

I didn't say anything, not even thank you.

"So . . ." And he leaned back in his chair, like an evil mastermind plotting some grand scheme of destruction. He did everything but steeple his fingers. "What I am going to do is have you work with Nobuko-san's *assisto*. Her name is Chisato-san. She is a nice woman, but she hasn't done anything particularly ambitious. Nobuko-san is under intense pressure with several different deadlines, so she has agreed to let Chisato-san take the lead on one small short story in particular. Chisato-san knows the style, she's done drawings. She will need some guidance. And the story needs to be done in two weeks."

My eyes must've popped wide open, because he scowled at me.

"Is that going to be a problem?"

"How long is the story? And how many manga pages does it need to be?"

"It's not that long. It's running in one of our magazines," he said, which meant that it was maybe twenty pages, I assumed. That wasn't that bad. Tight, a lot of work, but not that bad. "If she's going to be a *manga-ka*, she'll have to learn to work to deadline. And so will you."

"It shouldn't be a problem," I said, with all the confidence of someone who has no idea what she's promising.

His phone rang, and he said, "Please excuse me," with a little half-bow. Scowling or not, he was still polite, which was nice. He answered the phone. I stood, wondering if I should give him some privacy, since he didn't look my way. He was speaking rapidly. "She is? I wasn't expecting her. No, of course. Send her in. Thank you."

He looked at me. "You're in luck," he said, although his tone of voice didn't sound like I'd won anything, as it were. "Nobuko-san is here, herself. You should meet her."

I nodded, and then swallowed hard. From what the S-girls had said, this woman was just short of the Devil himself.

Oh, goody. Because what I really lacked over here was more challenges.

It was interesting to see Yoda get ready quickly. Apparently Nobuko-san made him nervous, too. He straightened his tie, then gave me the evil eye when he noticed I was looking at him. I made sure I wasn't smirking. He put his coat jacket on and tried hastily to derumple himself. He wasn't very successful.

The receptionist walked in, and I could see the tension on her face as well, which was weird since she was usually placid as a statue. She made a Vanna White–style gesture to Yoda's office and then beat a quick retreat as soon as the infamous Ms. Nobuko walked in.

"Akamatsu-san," Nobuko said with a short bow. "So nice to see you again."

"I wasn't expecting you, Nobuko-san," he said, returning the bow. I remembered that they weren't big on any physical contact here—not the handshake that was the office prerequisite in the States and certainly not a hug, although Nobuko's tone was very cordial. "But it's always nice to see you," he added, as if she might misinterpret his comment.

She wasn't what I was expecting, either. She was five feet tall, maximum, and looked to be in her early fifties but trying for her thirties. She did a pretty good job pulling it off, too: she wasn't trying too hard, she just looked well preserved and stylish. Hell, she looked like a friend of my mom's, someone to carpool with. Not the demon everyone was nattering on about.

She turned to look at me, and she smiled. "Is this our contest winner, then, Akamatsu-san?"

He nodded. "Risa-san, this is Nobuko-san."

"Pleased to meet you," I said, with a polite bow.

Nobuko handed me a card, with both hands. I returned the favor. Nobuko's card looked expensive and only had her name on it—no contact info or anything, just a drawing of a woman's face. Either really arrogant or really impressive, I guess.

"Risa-san is going to be working with your *assisto* on the short story," Yoda said.

Suddenly, the happy carpool mom thing was pulled away for a second, when Nobuko frowned. "Really?" she said, in a tone that better suited something more stringent. Something like "What the *hell*?"

"You yourself said that Chisato-san needed more help," he said.

"Chisa-chan just needs to work harder," Nobuko said with a negligent shrug. "I'll have another talk with her."

Yoda took a deep breath, as if he was steeling himself to jump off a high dive or something. "Honestly, Nobuko-san, it would be a great favor to me . . . to Sansoro . . . if you would allow Risa-san to work on this project. She shows great promise, and the other editors are already working on projects that are almost completed. Since Risa-san is the contest winner, we want to give her something a little more high profile."

I stared at Yoda for a second. *You're lying your butt off!* I felt proud of him, actually. I wouldn't have thought such a suave cover-your-ass move was in his repertoire.

Nobuko studied him, too, trying to determine if he was pulling a fast one. He really didn't look like the fast-one type. "Of course, to help Sansoro," she said. "At least it isn't a very important assignment. I wouldn't want someone new ruining a project."

Okay, so much for the vaunted Japanese politeness. I kept smiling anyway, although I'm sure my eyes went a bit flinty.

Yoda quickly and effusively thanked the woman. Of course, she was right. I was new, there was a chance I could screw it up. I should've felt better. Especially since I didn't really want to be there in the first place. But I'd stay long enough to get this project done, that was for damned certain. No way was a midget Nazi *manga-ka* going to intimidate me.

February 14, Tuesday

I listened to the phone ring. I'd finally gotten a cell phone. This was my first international call on it, and I hoped that it worked.

"This is Ethan Lonnel," I heard the familiar voice say.

I smiled, although it was all I could do not to burst into tears. "Happy Valentine's Day," I said, in a small voice.

"Lisa." Just hearing him say my name like that made it worth it. "Wow, I almost didn't answer the phone—Caller ID was so weird. How's it going?"

"I've survived over a month," I said, trying not to be unreasonably proud of myself. "I miss you a lot, though."

"I miss you, too, baby," he said, and I curled up on my chair, glad that the S-girls weren't in yet. "Fortunately, life has been so damned hectic I don't have time to think about it all that often."

"I've got some time," I noted.

"Really? I would've thought that taking in the sights and working at your . . . what's it called? The comic publisher."

"Manga publisher," I corrected. He never got that right—mental block.

"Yeah, I would think they would be keeping you busy."

"Actually," I said, looking over at the proofs I had of the work Chisato and I had done for that short story, "things are picking up over here. At least they're giving me real work instead of just busy work."

"For an intern? I'm surprised they let you do anything other than fetch coffee!" He laughed—he'd done a ton of internships during his undergrad years, apparently. "But this is great, sweetie. And have you seen much?"

"Not a lot. Harajuku, that's about it." It sounded lame; here I'd been there a month and all I'd seen was one street? "I've been meaning to window shop on the Ginza, though. One of these days."

"Doing anything to celebrate Valentine's?"

"Just missing you," I said, not caring if it sounded sappy. This was the first Valentine's Day we'd spent apart since we started dating, and he was the first boyfriend I'd ever had who actually did stuff to celebrate it. He'd usually take me out to dinner, maybe get me flowers. It was nice.

"I'm sorry I didn't get you anything this year," he said, as if he suddenly realized it. "I've been so—"

"Busy," I finished. "I know. It's no big deal. Besides, if you sent something, I'd probably feel so homesick and miss you so much, I don't know what I'd do."

"You sound better," he said. "Usually you're tearing your hair out. So hey, you must be getting used to the place, right?"

I thought about it. "It's different," I said. "And I am here for the whole year, anyway."

"We'll see about that," he said cryptically. "But it's good that you're over there now, anyway. There was a blizzard, can you believe it? It's freezing out here."

"It's been cold here," I said, but I knew it was nowhere near what upstate New York could dish out. "But yeah, you're right."

"And you know how much you hate driving in the snow."

He was trying to give me a pep talk. I appreciated it, sort of. But considering I was calling because it was a romantic day and I missed him, I have to admit I didn't appreciate his rah-rah "aren't you glad you're somewhere else" speech. No matter what his rationale was.

"I really do wish I was with you," I said emphatically.

"I told you, I miss you, too," he said, although there was a little crispness in it. "But I have to say, you wouldn't believe the amount of work I've been able to get through without—" He stopped. "You, er, being here."

"God, you can't get more romantic than that," I said, feeling pretty crisp myself.

"Don't get that way. You know what I mean."

"Yeah, I know." I focused on being the understanding girlfriend. It wasn't his fault it was his last semester. Besides, it was only temporary. "I have to go . . . ton of work, you know how it is."

He paused, then sighed. I knew the sound. It was his "well, there's nothing I can do, so I'll just let you sulk" sigh. This wasn't really how I'd planned for this phone call to go.

"I love you," I said, meaning it and trying to take the edge off the previous portion of our conversation.

"I love you, too," he said. "I'll e-mail you soon."

"Okay."

I hung up, and then put the phone in my pocket. *Happy frickin' Valentine's Day to me,* I thought. At least I had the short story to finish up, and then Yoda said he'd have more work for me.

The S-girls came in, slightly late, which was unusual for them. They were also laden down with big brown bags, another abnormality. "What's going on?" I asked quietly. We still hadn't really been fraternizing—I wasn't sure why, but I'm pretty sure Yoda said something to them about not getting too buddy-buddy with me. That could've been paranoia, but I wouldn't put it past him.

They put their bags down on their chairs. "It's Valentine's Day," Satomi said to me, as if it were obvious.

"Yes, I know," I replied. "But . . . what's in the bags?"

Satomi looked at Sakura, who looked embarrassed for me. "It's a custom in Japan to give chocolate on Valentine's Day," she said.

I suddenly saw that they had brought in huge bags of chocolate, in cute little wrappers—little individual baskets, from the looks of it. Each basket was tiny and maybe held five Hershey's kisses or the equivalent. They had little tags on them.

Oh, crap. It looked like they'd each bought chocolate for the entire office.

"I didn't get you anything," I said, immediately feeling guilty. Not that I knew this was a custom, but I should have, and I hate getting gifts from people without having anything to return. Call it a family custom—Nana Falloya would be appalled at my lack of foresight.

Sakura laughed. "No, no . . . it's not for women."

I sat back, surprised. Well, at least I wasn't getting anything that I couldn't return. But then . . . "So who is all of this for?"

"It's a custom that the women in the office get chocolate for the men in the office," Satomi explained further. "That's the tradition."

"You got chocolate for all the guys?" I looked—that was a hell of a lot of chocolate. The guys were already starting their early-morning loud joking ritual on the other side of the room. "Why didn't you guys just pick one name out of a hat or something?"

Now both S-girls looked at me like I was insane. "It's not that many," Sakura said. "And . . . it's a tradition."

I knew they took their traditions seriously over here, but this seemed a little nuts. "Okay," I said, still sounding dubious.

"Besides," Sakura added, "it would look odd if you only got chocolate for one man, you know?"

Putting it that way, yeah, I could understand the blanket chocolate policy. "Seems like the guys are the lucky ones, since they get all the gifts and they don't have to give anything," I remarked. "That's a little unfair, isn't it?"

"That's what White Day is for," Satomi said. "That's March fourteenth. The men will give us candy then."

"Oh." There it was. Nice and fair.

I looked around. "Oh! I didn't get anything for *anybody,* though. Will that look bad?"

Sakura looked at Satomi, who shrugged. They had their own telepathic language, I swear.

"Don't worry. You're American," Satomi said, in a patronizing tone. She might as well have said *you're mentally challenged.* "I'm sure they'll understand."

"I'll go out at lunch and get chocolate," I said, resolved. "I should be done with this short story by then."

"You don't have to," Satomi said. "You're a foreigner. No one expects anything from you."

I sensed a double meaning there. "I'm half Japanese," I pointed out.

"Exactly," Sakura added brightly, as if I was agreeing with them.

Whatever. I let it go.

I have to admit, I was getting a little sick of everybody trying to help me out and make me feel better by remarking on something that I already felt lame about. First Ethan trying to pep me up for not being with him for Valentine's Day by pointing out he was better off without me, now the S-girls trying to cover up for my rudeness at not buying candy by emphasizing not only my ignorance but the fact that I simply wasn't one of them. I know, I know, nobody probably meant it that way. But that's how I felt.

I heard someone clearing his throat, and I turned. I knew it wasn't Yoda—throat-clearing wasn't his style.

It was one of the editorial staff. Satomi and Sakura handed him baskets, which he took with a large grin and an appreciative bow. He looked young, maybe early twenties, although that sort of thing was hard to gauge. He had hair that was a little straggly, hitting the back of his collar, his bangs flopping in front of his wire-rimmed glasses. He was very thin. He was wearing a pair of jeans, sneakers, and an Adidas track jacket similar to what Uma Thurman wore in *Kill Bill.*

"Risa-san?"

"Yes?" I said, already feeling bad that I couldn't add to the guy's stash. I was definitely cleaning out the convenience store at lunchtime!

"I was wondering . . ." He glanced around, looking embarrassed. "I would love to talk to you. About American comics. Sometime . . . maybe I could take you to dessert or coffee, so we could discuss it?"

I stared at him. Then I looked at Satomi and Sakura. Apparently I wasn't in on the telepathic wavelength because I couldn't get any expression from them, no idea what was going on.

Was this guy asking me out?

"I, er, I need to think about it. Akamatsu-sensei is keeping me very busy," I added, apologetically. "But I will see what I can do."

"Thank you. Thank you very much," he said, and he blushed. Swear to God *blushed.* Then he backed away, almost dropping his chocolate in the process.

I looked at the S-girls, and they didn't say anything, they just smiled.

Damn it. The one romantic thing that happens to me on Valentine's Day, and it's from a stranger. Wouldn't you know it?

February 19, Sunday

IT WAS MIDNIGHT. YUKARI WAS OUT, AS USUAL, AND MR. AND MRS.
Kanai were asleep already—considering the crazy hours that Mr.
Kanai worked, that wasn't a big surprise.

Beep! Beep-beep! Poiiing!

I gritted my teeth and tried to bury my head deeper into the pillow. The twin-sized futon wasn't necessarily all that comfortable to
begin with, and with the heater blasting, the room was hotter than
hell, so it wasn't like I could burrow under the comforter. And there
was Ichiro, playing video games with the volume up way too high.

I am going to kill that kid.

In the month plus that I'd stayed with the Kanai family, I still
hadn't gotten a bead on Ichiro, and I was pretty sure he'd taken an
instant dislike to me. I know, I know, paranoia again. But the kid

really did seem to have some kind of beef against me, for whatever reason. He would sit there, camped out in the living room like it was his own private fiefdom, with his PlayStation or Xbox setup taking over the coffee table. He'd sit on the floor, slurping noodles and watching cartoons if he wasn't playing games, but those breaks were infrequent. He would scowl at whoever crossed his path with that deep, preteen angst grimace, as if daring you to say something. It was annoying. My mom would've put him through a wall by now, I'd think. As irritating as my own brother was, back when he was a teen, he was never quite this bad.

The thing was, now that Chisato and I had successfully completed the short story, Yoda said that he was going to have another project for me to work on with her. I hadn't met Chisato yet, and fortunately I hadn't run into Nobuko again, either. I don't know what Nobuko's reaction to the short story was, although I guess her name was still on it despite her barely contributing to it, from what I could tell. Yoda was very clear, though: I was supposed to come in early on Monday, and he'd go over my next assignment. I got the feeling it was pretty important. It was actually fun to work on the short story—I'd gotten the familiar rush that I used to at work, when you planned something out and saw it actually accomplished, saw it *finished*. In this day of corporate paradigm shifting and all kinds of other bullshit, it was nice to see something checked off as complete. And I'll have to admit, as far as being the token foreigner intern, despite being half-Japanese, it was nice to feel helpful.

Poonk poonk poonk! Beep . . . Brrrrreeep!

I sat up in bed, on low boil. I needed to get some sleep. It had taken me two weeks to finally get used to the time difference, and I was feeling a little more competent, although I wouldn't go so far as to say I felt at home. And here was Little Lord Video, blasting his video games with complete disregard for the rest of his family.

I just needed to be polite but firm. Let the kid know.

I pulled a robe on over my favorite pajamas, the black ones that said "Can't sleep, the clowns will eat me." I figured a robe made me look like more of an authority figure. I padded out into the living room.

There he was, ensconced on a pile of pillows, his hair sticking out like a shrub. He was staring so hard at the television screen he wasn't even blinking, and I could hear the frantic tapping of his thumb against the buttons of his controller.

"Ichiro," I said. "Sorry, Ichiro?"

He didn't acknowledge me. Maybe he didn't even register that I was there—I don't think I'd said two words to the kid, and I certainly hadn't called him by name.

"Ichiro," I said, a little louder and more forcefully.

He shot me a quick, irritated look. *"Hai?"* he barked.

"I have a big day at work tomorrow—a big week," I said. Not that he'd necessarily understand or give a crap about my priorities, but at least it seemed like a valid excuse. "Could you please turn the television down a little? I'm having trouble sleeping."

Now he paused the game and turned to stare at me. "What?" he asked. He sounded astounded.

I gritted my back teeth. It wasn't as if he was my kid brother—or my kid, for that matter. So I couldn't yell at him for taking such a rude tone of voice. "I'm sorry," I said, as gentle and soothing as possible. "It's just . . . my room's right over here, and the television is kind of loud . . . could you please turn your game down a little bit?"

Now he stared so hard that his eyes were huge. I really wished he'd blink. He looked like a fish or something, with his eyes bugging out like that.

"No!"

Now I stared in disbelief. He actually yelled that—a full-on, completely filled lungs scream, like I'd gone at him with a knife or something.

"Wait a second," I said, putting up my hands to placate him . . .

or protect myself, if it came to that. He really did look pretty wild-eyed.

"You can't tell me what to do!" He stood up, knocking over a bag of chips and a bunch of Kit Kat wrappers. "You're not my family!"

"It's not like you listen to them, either," I pointed out, unable to help myself.

"No! *No! Noo!*" He was jumping up and down, throwing a tantrum like a little kid. "Shut up! Get out of here! This is my place!"

At this, Mr. and Mrs. Kanai came out, looking exhausted and confused. "What's happening?" Mr. Kanai said in a gruff voice.

Mrs. Kanai rushed over to Ichiro. "What's the matter, darling? What is it? What's wrong?"

I wondered if maybe I'd misread the situation. Maybe Ichiro had some severe emotional issues or some mental instability that I'd inadvertently tripped off. I thought it had just been teenage rebellion and sloth, but obviously I'd guessed that one completely wrong. "I'm sorry," I said to Mr. Kanai, since Mrs. Kanai didn't even look at me. Ichiro was still half-yelling "no no no" and she was offering her usual comfort, making him some sort of meal.

"What happened?" Mr. Kanai repeated.

"I have a big week at work," I said, now feeling heartless *and* lame. "So I came out to ask if Ichiro could please turn the television down a little bit, because I was having trouble sleeping."

Mr. Kanai looked at Ichiro, who had finally calmed down with the offer of some ice cream. Ichiro looked at me triumphantly. Mr. Kanai just looked sad.

"We are sorry that you are having difficulty sleeping," he said, in solemn tones. "I should have realized. Of course, we'll do something about that."

I swallowed hard. God, this was painful. "If you could just . . ."

He looked quickly at his wife, who had brought out a huge bowl of chocolate ice cream and handed it to Ichiro. "We'll trade rooms," he said to his wife, and she nodded.

"Whoa, wait a second," I said, when I realized what he meant.

"It's quieter in our bedroom. You sleep in there, and we'll sleep in your room," he said, his voice drowning in apology.

"We are so sorry," Mrs. Kanai said.

That was it? Ichiro was getting a big honkin' bowl of ice cream, and the two of them were going to cram onto one twin futon, just so I could get some sleep?

"No, no," I said, unconsciously echoing Ichiro. "Please, I couldn't put you out of your bedroom."

"It's our fault that you are having trouble sleeping," Mrs. Kanai said. "We must do something to make up for it."

I looked at Ichiro, who was smirking at me around his ice cream spoon. *Actually, it's that little bastard's fault,* I thought. Emotional problems or no. "I would feel terrible if you slept in this room. It will be fine. I'm sure I overreacted. Please, please go back to bed."

It took another twenty minutes of discussion, and basically being rude again on my part, to get Mr. and Mrs. Kanai to go back to their room, so I could go back to mine. Ichiro was still smirking. I got the feeling he didn't have any kind of mental aberrations. It was terrible, so help me, but I got the feeling he was just spoiled, and his parents were too confused and too kindhearted to do anything about it.

I went back to Yukari's room. It was now closing in on one thirty in the morning. I needed to be up in five hours to get to work on time.

I lay back down in bed. As soon as I threw the covers over myself, I could hear the television blasting again—louder, if possible, this time.

POOONK POONK BOIIIING!!!

I was going to have to do something about that kid. For the

moment, I just covered my head with the pillow until I could finally fall asleep.

February 20, Monday

So much for getting a good night's sleep, I thought. So much for *needing* a good night's sleep, to make matters worse. Here it was five thirty in the evening, and I felt as if I could fall asleep on the train again. I made a mental note to grab some coffee before going home so I didn't have a repeat of the Shinjuku Love Hotel incident. I had gotten sporadic sleep until five thirty that morning thanks to Ichiro's video game nonsense, and I had gotten to work early to find Yoda on the phone. I twiddled my thumbs at my desk for most of the day; I'd even offered to help the S-girls on a project, which neither had taken me up on.

Yoda had finally called me into his office after lunch. I was eager to find out what the new stuff was, but he was scowling, more than usual.

"Nobuko-san has gone over the short story," he said.

I nodded. "I think we did a good job," I offered. I wasn't sure if that was proper Japanese office politics—I know you're not supposed to toot your own horn—but I really did think that Chisato and I pulled it off. It had taken me longer to read the story since my written Japanese wasn't that good, but the translation seemed to work, and Chisato could draw her butt off.

"She thought it was . . . adequate," he said, and I got the feeling that "adequate" probably wasn't the word she had used. I also got the feeling that "adequate" probably was way kinder than whatever she'd used. "After all, her name is on the project, so she wanted to ensure that the quality maintained her high standards."

I didn't say anything. I didn't think there was anything *to* say.

"She did bring up one point, which I have to say I agree with." He sounded sour, like he'd just eaten a bug. "Your style of interpretation is very American. The comic came out looking much more American than Japanese."

I couldn't help it. I made a tiny little protest sound in the back of my throat at that one, before I could stop myself. I'd been reading Japanese comic books since I was seven years old, for God's sake. I knew an American comic book when I saw one, and I certainly hadn't been following that style! What, did she think I was taking a short romantic comedy story and turning it into *Batman*?

He did the fierce-eyebrow stare at me. "Did you have something to say?"

"No. Sorry," I said, looking at the corner of his desk. Man, that frosted me. But what could I say? She was Nobuko, artist extraordinaire. I was American Intern, aka Nobody Important.

"She thought maybe you should have more access to Japanese manga style before you take on another project," he said.

I waited, unsure what he was getting at.

"So I am pulling you off project work for the time being," he said, and his voice was as flat and toneless as a rock dropping. "I want you to read Nobuko-san's previous work, so you can get a better sense of her style and our style here at Sansoro. You should be better acquainted with manga before you try more editing."

I gulped slightly, blinking hard. I was pretty sure it was just because my eyes felt so sandy, after the lack of sleep, but I didn't want there to be any mistake. I had never cried in a boss's office before, and I certainly wasn't going to start now. "Of course, Akamatsu-sensei," I said, and I was proud that it came out completely toneless, too, not irritated or guilty or anything. I wasn't sure what I'd done wrong, besides being too American. Hey, maybe the guy was right.

He looked gruff and slightly confused. I guessed he didn't have many of these kinds of conversations. "You can still do pencil work, if you want," he offered.

I didn't necessarily want to, but if I didn't, then poor Chisato would be stuck with it, so I agreed. I went back to find my cubicle surrounded by copies of various books, phone-book thick in several cases. All of it was Nobuko's. On my desk itself was a sheaf of inked drawings that needed pencil lines erased.

It was only February, almost the end of the month, at that. I shouldn't really mind, I told myself. Besides, I'd gotten to edit one project. And he was probably right.

But deep down, I knew that Chisato and I had done good work. I'd even shown Yoda before Chisato inked it, and he'd made no noises about it being too American. So what the hell was really going on here?

Before I could go home, I turned to find that same young editor, the guy who had asked me out on Valentine's Day, hovering behind my chair. I yelped slightly and jumped, knocking over a pile of Nobuko manga. "Sorry," I said automatically.

He helped me collect the scattered comic books. "No, I didn't mean to startle you," he said. "I saw that you were going home. I was wondering if you might like to join me for some coffee? Or maybe some chocolate? There is a good chocolate café in Tokyo that you might like to try."

Chocolate. I didn't want to lead the guy on, but right now, the thought of some really good chocolate was like a promise from heaven, something that would take the sting out of Yoda's reprisal and the sleeplessness of Ichiro's power trip. "I would actually love some chocolate," I agreed, then quickly added, "but this is to discuss work, yes?"

He glanced around again, doing the sort of "I'm being furtive" look that was straight out of a bad spy film. "Yes," he admitted. "But we can talk more about it there."

I followed him, wondering what exactly I was letting myself in for. He didn't seem the type to make a blatant pass, honestly. And considering the fact that he looked like a strong wind would blow him over, I got the feeling I could beat the pulp out of him if he did try anything funny. Still, the worst would be him mooning over me or something. *Just focus on the chocolate,* I told myself. We didn't talk on the train or subway on the way over there, and finally he gestured to a small store-front at the bottom of a large glass office building. It said "Meiji Chocolate Café" and when he opened the door for me, it smelled heavenly.

It was pretty crowded: we stood and waited. "Have you been here before?" he asked.

I shook my head, already mentally cataloging how to get back here. This could become a safe haven, I thought.

"I'm glad you agreed to come talk to me," he said, and now that he was out of the office—and out of scared-rabbit mode—his voice was a little deeper and a little more relaxed. "I know, it was a little impolite of me to put you on the spot. But I really wanted to talk to you."

"Uh, okay."

The waitress finally seated us and took our orders. I ordered the dark chocolate profiteroles, which looked heavenly, and a cup of hot cocoa. Editor-guy just ordered the hot chocolate.

It suddenly occurred to me. "I'm terribly sorry," I said, "but . . . I don't know your name."

He blinked at that one, then laughed. "How rude! I'm Morimoto. I'm editor number nineteen, on the Shonen manga projects." He quickly opened his briefcase and pulled out a business card, giving it to me. I bowed, or at least tried to, since I was sitting down. I looked at the card. Nothing as simple, artsy, or arrogant as Nobuko's, I noticed. It had the Sansoro logo in the corner, and a bunch of kanji on one side, plus all his contact numbers. On the other side, the words and his name were in the simple hiragana, phonetically spelled out, so I had an easier time reading it. And damn it, the guy really *was* "editor number nineteen."

"I work on the boys' adventure projects, largely," he said. "We're doing quite well, but we could be doing better."

I stared at him. Coming from a Japanese person, this was tantamount to treason. You never badmouthed your company or its policies, and especially not to some gaijin like myself! I didn't know what to say, so I shut up until the chocolate got there. The first thing I did was take a sip of the cocoa, scalding my tongue slightly but feeling tons more awake than I did before I sat down. "Really," I said, as innocently as possible.

"I know. Sansoro is working on distributing more in the United States because that market is untapped."

I knew now that there was no way this earnest young guy was chatting me up and trying for a date. His eyes blazed with the light of a zealot. Here was an editor on a mission.

"The thing is, the Americans have been buying more of our *shojo* work, the girls' books," he said, and his frustration was obvious as he stirred his hot chocolate. I just ate the profiteroles—oh my God, *yum*. It was almost hard to concentrate on what he was talking about, in the face of all that dark, rich chocolate mousse and pastry. "I think part of the problem is that we need more of a blending of love story with manga action—mecha and robots and the things we're noted for, battle scenes, *and* American comic book sensibility."

"That makes sense," I said, taking a breather from my dessert. Now that sugar was coursing through my veins, I felt a lot more alert. "I have read some American comics, but I have to be honest, I've read a lot more manga."

"But your style is inherently American because you *are* American," he said, and he obviously meant it. "I saw the manga you turned in— the one that won the contest."

Now I was surprised. "You did?"

"Everyone did. I helped judge," he said. "I could see immediately that you touched on themes that boys and girls would enjoy. And you had the manga style, true, but it was obviously an American interpretation. I think you could go far in this business!"

I glowed. I couldn't help it. After hearing Yoda put me on reading and erasing detail, after dealing with Nobuko, it was nice to hear somebody say they thought I might be good at the job.

"I am working on a project," he said. "It would be targeted for America. It is very . . . risky. And very secret. I need another editor's help on it, and then I need to run it by Akamatsu-sensei."

I stared at him, finishing the last of my profiterole. I got the feeling I was going to need it.

"This is where I need your help," he said. "Would you be the other editor? And help me give the proposal to Akamatsu-sensei? We would need to be ready by May at the latest. That gives us plenty of time—although there's a lot of hard work in the meantime, getting the story ready, getting our argument ready. Can you help me?"

I didn't know the story. I wasn't getting a lot of sleep as it was. I didn't know how long I was going to stay in the country, at this rate. And I was just an intern, and one who didn't seem to be on the star artist's good side. I didn't know how much my being attached to the project was going to help this guy. I really ought to tell Morimoto no, or that I'd think about it.

"Sure," I heard myself saying.

He smiled widely, obviously relieved. There was no way I could say no. It would be like kicking a puppy. Now, the only thing would be staying to see if we could make some kind of a success out of this impossible dream.

February 25, Saturday

It was Saturday night, and I was crawling the walls. I'd managed to make excuses to stay out during the day, once I woke up—or should I say, once Yukari managed to wake me, coming in a bit drunk and then snoring loudly. I told Mrs. Kanai that I would pick up breakfast out, and then went sightseeing . . . more because I didn't want to deal with her trying to stare politely at me while Ichiro stayed camped out on the couch and Yukari snored. Mr. Kanai was, of course, at work.

I went to the Ginza, just as I'd told Ethan I would. Honestly, it wasn't much different from going into New York City to shop, especially if you were hitting a really ritzy part of Manhattan, say. Then, after a little getting lost and taking the wrong train, I wound up going to the Omotesando. That was actually close to where I'd been when I went to Harajuku, I just didn't know it. Think of it as a mall district, tailored specifically for teenage girls who had a lot of discretionary spending power.

The funniest part of the whole thing was the T-shirts that they sold. "Hysterical Glamour: Too Drunk to Fuck!" was priceless. I bought one for Stacy, even though she couldn't wear it in front of her son. (Or probably her husband.) I wished I'd brought my camera. There were even "Cali Girls," apparently the last die-hard remnants of a fad that had been popular a few years before. In one store, there was a young Japanese woman clerk, standing behind the counter. Her skin was abnormally tanned a dark burnt sienna color—I hoped for her sake it was the spray-on stuff—making the whites of her eyes pop out. She had dyed her hair blond with streaks of brown, or vice versa. Striped was probably a more accurate term. She was wearing a tiny tank top, despite the fact that it was February and pretty chilly. I think she was trying to be Malibu Barbie. I was hoping that was why the fad eventually died out.

After about two hours of window shopping and chuckling to myself over the weirdness of the shopping culture, including the Kinderwhore micro-minis, baby doll dresses with pictures of Care Bears on them, purses that looked like shoes, and shoes that looked like God knows what, I got bored. I ate at an Internet café, wrote to Ethan (who wrote me short e-mails like "exhausted from studying and work, gonna grab a bite, miss you." Which was sweet, I guess.) I also wrote to Stacy and Perry, having received my first K-tei cell phone bill, and man, was it a doozy. I figured I'd stick to e-mailing when I could.

Still, after all that, *and* a trip to Starbucks—after making sure that any Americans seemed harmless—I wound up back at the Kanai house by six o'clock. That meant early enough to have a really painful dinner with Mr. Kanai, who was home just long enough to eat and change before going out with some work buddies; Mrs. Kanai, who had created her usual sumptuous feast; and Ichiro, who was deigning to eat at the table instead of the TV because his mother had begged him. He made faces at me all during the meal. I have to say, I'm not even sure what the meal was, so his little display really wasn't helping matters any.

Now it was eight o'clock and I was still bored. I couldn't watch TV. There was a small set in Yukari's room, but it had what I guess was basic cable over here, so no American movies or television programs. I missed hearing things in English. The shows they had here were a little too weird for me. For one thing, their game shows all seemed to involve food. Not like *Fear Factor,* where you had to eat maggots or something, although I know they had some wicked game shows that made *Fear Factor* look like *Hollywood Squares.* It was more like a regular game show, where all of a sudden, everybody decided to sit down to a meal, remarking specifically on how delicious the food was. It was like interrupting *Jeopardy* with a quick visit to Paula Deen's kitchen.

Of course, leaving Yukari's room was worse. It meant dealing with Ichiro, who was almost out to get me lately, or sitting in the kitchen with Mrs. Kanai, which, as I said, was awkward. Still, I had to do something.

Yukari was in the bathroom, putting on her makeup for her night out. I went to the kitchen, ignoring Ichiro's malevolent glare as I quietly made my way there. "Excuse me, Kanai-san," I said, as tentatively as possible.

She looked at me. "Yes? Did you need something? Was dinner all right?"

"Dinner was wonderful," I said, although I really didn't remember much of it . . . or was trying not to. "I was wondering, is there any place to go around here? You know, at night?"

She stared at me, as if she wasn't sure she understood my question. "For what?"

"Just a social thing," I said. "You know. Maybe a movie theater or something?" Although it occurred to me that watching a movie in Japanese might not be the best thing, either.

"You want to see a movie? We have a lot of movies," she said, although even as she said it, it occurred to her that Ichiro the Couch Commando would probably not be amenable to giving up the television for the gaijin intruder. "Of course, I'm sure there are theaters nearby."

"I don't mean to cause any problems. I was just a little restless and wanted to get out a bit." I hoped that didn't sound rude. I really didn't mean it to be. I suddenly felt bad for all those foreign exchange students I'd ever been around in high school. Hell, it wasn't their fault nobody could understand them. They had to be bored all the time. And odds were good their host families were a bit freakish, as well.

"Do you mean, you wanted to go to a bar? Get drunk?"

Now I stared at her. What sort of person asked that? "Excuse me, I was wondering where I could go and get drunk. Know of any good places?" What the heck sort of person did she think *I* was, if that was her question?

"Uh," I responded, really not sure how to field that one.

"What have you done so far?"

"Really not much of anything," I said. "I haven't gone out much at all, which was why I thought . . ." I took a deep breath. "I'm sorry, I don't mean to be any trouble. I'll go out and . . ."

And what? Troll the streets?

"Wait a second," she said, gesturing to me to stay put. Then she went to the bathroom and rapped on the door.

"Whaaaat?" Yukari said, opening the door. Half her eye makeup was on, and she looked irritated.

"Risa-san wants to go out," her mother said, and I could've smacked myself for not seeing this coming.

"So?" Yukari's response was also pretty typical.

Mrs. Kanai looked at me, to see if I'd heard it. I pretended to be engrossed in Ichiro's video game, as if I couldn't hear what she was saying to her daughter.

"She is the friend of your friend," her mother said. "You are the reason we brought her in here in the first place."

"But not the only reason," Yukari said, and her voice had a hint of sulk to it.

"She is bored, and I don't blame her. You go out. She should meet your friends."

I didn't look, but I could sense Yukari looking at me, sizing me up. "I don't know," she said. "She's so old."

I gritted my teeth but still didn't look. So she was twenty-one. I guess when I was that age, anybody who was twenty-nine seemed pretty ancient to me, too. And it wasn't like I'd been a big party animal, even then. For all I knew, people who lived like she did generally didn't survive to twenty-nine. Did I really want to . . .

I was too deep in my thoughts and didn't hear her walk up to me. "Do you want to hang out with me and my friends?"

It was jarring, to have the question from Yukari in her half made-up state. She looked like Two Face from *Batman,* normal on one side, almost maniacally tricked out on the other. "Uh . . ."

I glanced over at Mrs. Kanai. She had her arms crossed. I had no idea what she'd come up with if I said no.

"Sure," I finally agreed. "Thank you so much for inviting me. I hope I'm not imposing."

She rolled her eyes at me, in the fashion of all teens and college kids. I guess some things are universal. "I'll be ready in a minute," she said, which I knew from experience meant closer to half an hour. Then she shot me a quick once-over. "You're not wearing that," she added. It wasn't a question. It was a statement. Practically a declaration.

"What would you suggest I wear?"

"Look more like me," she said, then went back in the bathroom to complete her transformation.

She had been wearing a short red plaid skirt over white tights that had glitter woven into them somehow, with a pair of leg warmers, over a pair of high heels that had massive toe cleavage. Topping that was a pink angora sweater of some sort and a suede jacket trimmed in purple faux fur. There was no way in hell I was wearing anything like that, even if I owned it.

I went back to the room and pulled out my suitcase, looking for "party suitable" gear. I had the "Too Drunk to Fuck" shirt I'd bought for Stacy over in Harajuku, so I pulled that on, even though it was a little big on me. Then a skirt that was just over the knee . . . but that looked lame, a cross between pajama party and business meeting. I was about to give it all up and pack it in when she came back in the room and burst out laughing.

"No, no, no," she said, then sized me up. "You're a little big, but I might have something that—"

"*No!*" I said hastily, backing away. Then I added, "I'd hate to stretch out your clothes, you're so tiny."

She seemed to buy that, or at least saw it as an acceptable excuse. "Then let's see what you've got," she said. She finally settled on a pair of navy blue Lycra jogging pants with sky blue trim and a white hoodie.

"Those are my exercise clothes," I pointed out.

Then she told me to put my hair up in a ponytail, which I did. She put a few streaks of hair-mascara in it, in blue, and then shellacked me with some makeup. After that, I was talked into wearing a pair of spangly white leg warmers and my white sneakers, which were still reasonably pristine. I wore my leather coat over all of that.

I looked like . . . I don't know what I looked like.

"Now we're ready," Yukari said, and tugged me out the door. Toward what, I had no idea.

CHAPTER 6

February 26, Sunday

"ONE MORE DRINK!" ONE OF YUKARI'S MALE FRIENDS SLURRED, AS we walked down a nearly deserted street. It was about five o'clock in the morning, and it was pretty cold—not that we could feel it. Had to be about forty-something degrees (Fahrenheit—I still couldn't make the transition to Celsius) and the skies were that orange-tinge common to cities with too many lights reflecting off fog. The trains had stopped running at midnight: we were searching in vain for a cab, somewhere in the Hiro-o area, I believe.

Yukari was standing by my side, holding hands with one of her girlfriends who was also giggling and somewhere between tipsy and drunk. It wasn't that Yukari was gay, it was that weird little-girl thing. No one had tried for my hand yet, thankfully. I would've found that weird; I don't even really hold hands with Ethan.

"Did you have fun tonight?" she asked me.

I nodded. I really did have fun, although right now I was feeling all twenty-nine of my years, plus about six of somebody else's. I hadn't been out till morning in a long, long time.

"You were funny," she said.

We'd started out the night at one of those arcades in the Shinjuku area, away from the red-light district. I'd mentioned to Yukari that I'd stayed in a Love Hotel, and she seemed humorously scandalized— and then somewhat embarrassed, when she discovered that I'd stayed there by myself. I guess it was equal to saying you'd had a steamy encounter in a spa tub, but it turned out that you were just having a good time on your own. Even though I assured her that I was only crashing there because I was lost and tired, she obviously saw me as someone in need of social instruction. From then on, she introduced me to her friends as "Riri-chan" and treated me like a sort of pet, making sure I had plenty of drinks and ate plenty of candy. Apparently the combination of sugar and alcohol were what fueled the young Tokyo partygoer. We did sticker machines, then hit a tiny hole-in-the-wall bar somewhere, I forget the station. We did *nigorizake* shots for hours, and then listened to some truly horrendous karaoke. By midnight, I was pretty looped—I don't drink all that much, and I'd had enough to have beyond a buzz. I wound up singing "Proud Mary" with Yukari and her crew, messing up about half the words but at least getting the English right and having my own giggling crew of Tokyo Teen-plus Girlies backing me up.

Around two a.m. I slunk off to puke in an alley, and since then I'd been drinking water and dodging the winter pear *chuhai* Yukari wanted to keep buying me—*chuhai* being a cross between Fanta soda and Zima, in a rainbow of flavors.

"You're so cute," Yukari had said, and she and her friends had started planning a whole new wardrobe for me. By that point, I was tired, sore from throwing up, and ready to crawl into bed. Still, it was nice to be included, and they were nothing if not the soul of kindness. The girls told me about their lives. The guys didn't talk much, but that was pretty universal as well.

We caught a cab and dropped everybody else off before Yukari and I finally made it to our street. The violent turns and twists the cab took did nothing for my delicate state, and I prayed I wouldn't get sick again.

"I'm so glad you came out with us," Yukari said, oblivious to the roller-coaster ride of our taxi. "I should've thought of it sooner. After all, you are Perry-san's friend."

That thought brought a smile to my face. I couldn't help but wonder what she thought Perry was like. I mean, e-mail is great and all, but there's a whole lot of play between the written person and the actual person. "How long have you been pen pals with Perry?" I asked, curious.

She shrugged. "Three years or so, I guess."

So, since she was eighteen. I was so going to give Perry a ribbing for this when I talked to him again.

"He's nice. I have a lot of pen pals," she said, and that didn't surprise me a bit. "They're fun. Super-fun!"

It was like clubbing with a live version of *Sailor Moon*. Still, it wasn't annoying. If anything, it was more like falling into a cartoon world. Considering the surreality of five in the morning, it all seemed to work.

"You managed much better than I thought, too. For someone your age," she said. I didn't take it personally. As it was, I didn't want to admit she might have to carry me back to the house. "Too bad tonight was so dead."

"It was dead tonight?" With all those people? What the hell did "crazy" look like?

"I'll tell you what, you should come with us to club in Roppongi on Thursday," she announced, nodding vigorously. "That is *much* better. I mean, part of it is stupid, because there are so many gaijin, and the clubs can be tacky, but there is a lot of fun and dancing. Oh, you have to come!"

I made a mental note to count how many times Yukari used the word "fun." "I don't know, Yukari," I said, as we walked toward the house, and I realized she was waiting for me to answer her. "Thursday is a workday. I'll need to get more sleep."

She made a little noise of derision, somewhere between a squeak and a growl. It was sort of remarkable-sounding, actually. "You're not even really working there, are you? I mean, they're not paying you very well, and it's not like you can actually *go* anywhere. They won't hire you as a real *manga-ka*."

I stared at her, momentarily sidetracked from my overarching goal of getting to bed. "Why— What makes you say that?"

She shrugged, not realizing there was something of an insult in her words. "You're not Japanese," she said. "*Manga-ka* are Japanese."

"Well, they did look for an American," I said. A little defensively, I realized too late.

She didn't seem to notice. "They aren't really interested in more *manga-ka*. They're just interested in America."

I didn't know how to counter that, so I didn't say anything.

"Besides," she added, as we got to the doorstep of the house. "Perry told me that you were only going to be here for a year. He also doesn't think you'll get hired for anything else."

"Really?" I would *definitely* be having words with Perry.

"And he said if you did get offered a job, you wouldn't take it. So why worry about what they'll think? You can go to work tired," she said, as if that solved everything.

I was torn between being pissed at Perry and wondering if this slim little girl had ever held down a job in her life. Even something dumb, like babysitting.

Yukari opened the door, and we walked in. The TV was going,

but the sound was muted. Ichiro was still sprawled on the couch, hand hanging over, video game controller fallen to the floor.

"How did he get this way?" I whispered to Yukari, when we both got into the room.

"What, you mean not going to school? I don't know." Yukari didn't sound overly concerned.

"I mean, don't your parents worry?"

I didn't like Ichiro, but it still sat funny with me . . . a kid his age, not going to school, not doing anything but playing games at home. What would happen to him when his parents were old and couldn't work and take care of his butt anymore? It wasn't as if he was actually handicapped. Would Japan develop some kind of fund, or build nursing homes for video game addicts who couldn't handle their own lives? Would he become homeless?

Yukari was stripping down for the night. She took out a Handi Wipes and removed what was left of her smudged makeup. "I'm sure my parents would rather he was in school," she said reflectively, as if she'd never actually thought about it before or it had never come up. "But it's not like it was when they were kids. I mean, he could be top of his class, get into the right university, and then what? It's not like there are jobs all over the place." She bit her lip. "That happened to a cousin of mine."

"What happened?" I took off my party clothes, too. At least, being mostly exercise gear, they were comfortable. I watched as Yukari took off her shoes and rubbed her feet. Those heels had to be painful.

She thought about it. "He studied a lot, and got top marks, and got into a great university. We thought he'd go really far."

"Then what happened?" I had bad images: maybe he was pumping gas or cleaning septic tanks, which was what Grandma Falloya always told me I'd do if I didn't get my academic act together.

"He didn't get a job," she said.

"And then what?"

"Then he killed himself."

I stared at her. That was not where I expected that story to go. "My God. I'm so sorry," I finally said. "Was Ichiro close to him?"

"Huh? No. This was a few years ago, and Ichiro didn't really know him. I didn't even know him that well." Yukari sounded unperturbed by this. Which made one of us, I thought. "I'm tired. Good night, Riri-chan."

I meant to take some umbrage with the nickname, but I was exhausted, so I left it alone. "Good night, Yukari-san."

"We're friends now," she said, staring at me. "So call me Yuki-chan."

I smiled. Friends. It had been a while. And I have to say, it was nice.

I climbed into bed and shut off the light. Just before I could settle in, I heard Yukari say, "You're coming with us on Thursday, right?"

I smiled. "Sure," I said. Then I fell fast asleep.

THERE WAS a knock on Yukari's bedroom door, and the two of us groaned at the same time. I now understood why Yukari did that, actually. After only a few hours of sleep, and after a whole night of drinking, it was pretty hard to verbalize words, much less complex sentences.

"Excuse me," Mrs. Kanai said. "Risa-san? Telephone. For you."

"Thank you, I'll be there in a second," I said. It came out as unintelligible mush, so I repeated it. When she finally understood what I was saying, she nodded and smiled and quickly exited.

I pulled on a robe and headed for the living room, only to let out a painful squeak as the light hit my eyes. *Ugh.* It was maybe noon, if I was lucky. Maybe one o'clock. So I'd gotten, what, six or seven hours' sleep? I guess I shouldn't complain. Of course, I usually had eight hours of sleep at least, and that was stone cold sober.

Mr. and Mrs. Kanai were watching TV in the living room with

Ichiro, looking deceptively Norman Rockwell. I was surprised that Ichiro tolerated it, but he was eating a tin full of cookies, so I guessed they'd bribed him. The news report was talking about the advance of the cherry blossoms: the season was coming. Apparently it was big enough to warrant this kind of reporting, like it was a war front. "Cherry blossoms have been sighted as far as Osaka," that sort of thing.

I waddled to the kitchen and picked up the phone that was lying on the counter. *"Mushi-mushi,"* I mumbled.

There were peals of laughter on the other line. "Wow. You sound awful!"

It was Stacy. I grinned ruefully. "Not so loud," I said.

There was a pause, and now two sets of chuckles emerged. "Tell me you're not hung over," I heard Perry say.

"Tell me I'm not on speaker phone," I said instead.

"You're on conference, actually. I set up a three-way call," Perry clarified. "You *are* hung over, aren't you?"

"Just a little," I said, although now that he mentioned it, I had a fairly good headache shaping up. I needed to take something—I think I packed some aspirin, didn't I? No, I realized. I hadn't packed any meds, and antihistamines were illegal in Japan. I don't remember why, but I did remember not wanting to get arrested for bringing over-the-counter stuff. God forbid I become the big bad Advil dealer of Groverton, New York. "I partied a little last night with your friend Yukari. I may be recovering for a week. I'm not as young as I used to be."

"Partying, huh?" Stacy laughed, and even if it wasn't louder than usual, I winced. She sounded like she was chuckling through a megaphone.

"With Yukari?" Perry's voice had much more speculation. "So, what was that like?"

"She makes Paris Hilton look like a nun," I replied off the cuff, then closed my eyes. "But she's very sweet. I didn't mean that in a bad way. She just goes out all the time. I'm lucky I made the cut . . . to 'mob' with her and her posse of party people, as it were."

"Well, aren't we urban?" This quip from Stacy.

"Party girl." Perry's voice sounded dreamy, as if he was trying to picture partying with Yukari himself. "Wow."

"She may be out of your league, my friend," I said. "But you're welcome to try. And you've been e-mailing her since she was eighteen?"

Now Stacy's laughter turned to cackles, and while the noise hurt my head, I felt vindicated. I felt sure Stacy would give him hell, torturing him for me, as a sort of proxy. *This is what you get for not letting me know more about the host situation you set up, pal.* I should've felt bad, I suppose, but I didn't. Perry's affinity for young Asian girls was awfully stereotypical, racist, and if we didn't love him so much, I know I for one would be pretty grossed out by it.

"We're just friends," Perry said. "And she's way too young for me."

"Yeah, yeah, save it for the judge," I said.

"I was practicing Japanese with her," he grumbled.

"How come you never practice Japanese with guys?" Stacy pointed out, and now I laughed.

It was nice to joke with them again, even though I was seriously tired. Hanging out with Yukari was fun and all, but there was something about being with your best friends, the ones you've known for years, that made a big difference. I felt homesick all at once.

"I'm glad you guys called," I said.

"Are you feeling any better?" Stacy's asked. "Or do I need to administer a little more tough love?"

"No, no more butt kicking is in order," I assured her. "I guess it did the trick, by the way. I'm getting along much better. I'm sleeping—well, except for my bouts of partying," I added, causing Perry to chuckle again, "and I'm working on stuff. I'm even helping an editor with some special project he's working on. And now I've got a friend. So things are looking up."

"That's good." Perry sounded relieved, which was heartening. "Just another, what, ten months to go, right?"

"Thanks, Perry," Stacy said caustically. "Remind her of how long her stay is."

"Really, it's all right," I assured them. "I'm getting along okay. If I can just get some sleep today—and tonight, I guess—I'll be golden."

"Well, hang in there, and keep us posted," Stacy said.

"And tell Yukari I said hi," Perry added, causing Stacy to growl at him.

I laughed, said good-bye, and hung up. I felt better, and worse. Sort of a hodge-podge of emotion, really. I stumbled back to the living room.

The news was over, and the Kanai parents had retreated back to their bedroom. Which left Ichiro, with his latest video game of mayhem. He looked at me through slitted, almost villainous eyes.

I glared back at him. The guy was *twelve*, for pity's sake. I have no idea what his beef was with me, whether it was because I invaded his territorial bubble or because I was gaijin or because I simply smelled bad. But whatever his problem, I was getting pretty tired of it.

I went back to Yukari's room. She was back to cutting z's, but quietly for all that, so I was pretty sure I could get another hour or so in before getting up, eating, and then going back to bed for my full eight hours.

I was just settling in when I heard Ichiro deliberately turn up the volume. Whatever game he had, there was some bizarre music, like a Satanic circus or something. It sounded both outrageously chipper and menacing at the same time. I wondered if that was the intent.

I went to the door. After my little incident the last time, trying to get Ichiro to turn the volume down, I wasn't about to start up another ruckus, especially since it was the afternoon and, theoretically, he was well within his rights to blast that sucker as loud as it could go. But I glared at him.

He simply grinned back at me.

After a few moments of futile scowling, I turned back and went to my room. There had to be something that could be done about that kid, I thought. Too bad I obviously wasn't the one to do it.

February 27, Monday

Yoda must've gotten a missive from a higher-up, telling him to take me out to lunch and see how I was doing, because it certainly wasn't a typical thing for him to do. Everyone seemed a bit shocked that it was happening, actually. Lots of people packed lunches, like the S-girls, and while the guys sometimes went out to a noodle-house or something at lunchtime, it wasn't the usual social thing that it would be at, say, my old job. Especially not lately. Yoda had made it clear that deadlines were coming up and that we'd all better put our nose to the grindstone, although he'd used more appropriate Japanese Zen examples—if you could combine Zen and workaholism.

Yoda walked past my desk that morning, saying I could go to lunch with him, and that there would be a photographer; I guess they were doing some kind of press release, like "contest winner ecstatically happy while eating traditional food" or something. "Who else will be there?" I asked.

He was momentarily startled. Lunch itself was weird enough—he apparently hoped to get the "invitation" out without a lot of thought, and he'd just worry about the event when it happened. "Just you and me," he said, and then frowned, as if wondering if perhaps that wasn't enough people. "Maybe . . ." He looked around the table. I noticed the S-girls staring studiously at the desk. That stung a little. Was lunch out with me so terrible?

Then I noticed the way Yoda was staring, like he was looking for a volunteer for a firing squad. No wonder they were pulling their best Invisible Girl routines.

"Could Morimoto-san come?" I asked. Better to kill two birds with one stone, and Morimoto had been trying to come up with a way to approach our very scary boss. Lunch would be better than Yoda's office, where he had that intimidating, claustrophobic home court advantage.

Yoda looked surprised, then nodded curtly. "We will leave at noon," he said, and then retreated to his office and shut the door, obviously glad that the whole unpleasant thing had been arranged.

"You're going to take Morimoto-san to lunch with Akamatsu-sensei?" Satomi whispered to me.

"Well, yes," I said, wondering at her tone of voice. "Why? Is there something the matter?"

Satomi and Sakura laughed, their soft, almost swallowed chuckles. Sakura's eyes were bright. "Akamatsu-sensei and Morimoto-san don't get along," Sakura pointed out.

I closed my eyes momentarily. That would've been good to know about five minutes ago, before I'd opened my big trap. "Why?"

"Akamatsu-sensei thinks that Morimoto-san wants to be too Western," Satomi explained. "Morimoto-san has very big ideas. Big changes."

She could say that again. Suddenly, my decision to ambush Yoda with our little "American comic" project seemed more and more ill conceived.

"Is Morimoto-san . . . disrespectful to Akamatsu-sensei?" I asked, wondering if I was going to have a brawl on my hands or what. *And wouldn't the press photographer love that one.* Man, I really needed to do my homework before offering to help people!

Sakura looked scandalized. "Of course not, Risa-san," she said.

That helped a little. At about nine thirty, I took a break and walked over to Morimoto's space, over on the men's side of the room. Funny, how the sexes segregated, even though that wasn't really the point. "Morimoto-san," I murmured, bowing a little. "Could I speak with you for a moment?"

The other guys looked amused, but nobody said anything—at least, not with me there. He stood up and we walked toward the hallway. I thought I heard a few mutterings, maybe a guttural laugh, but I ignored it. I had bigger fish to fry here.

"Have you been thinking about the manga comic?" he asked, and he sounded all excited, like a six-year-old on Christmas Eve. "I've got some more ideas! I'd love to talk to you about them." He glanced around. "Although not here, of course."

"You said you wanted to run your idea by Akamatsu-sensei," I said. "Well, I'm supposed to have lunch with him, and I invited you along. This is your chance."

I didn't think it was possible, but he went pale. Hell, since he already was pale, he looked practically like a mint Life Savers—sparkling white with a faint tinge of green. "Today?" he squeaked.

"I saw the opportunity," I said, feeling even more like an idiot, "and I took it. I figured it could be a casual discussion. It'd feel impromptu. Just so you could get his take on things."

I could tell immediately that this was not how he planned on presenting his idea to Yoda. In fact, he'd probably prefer to stand in front of the metaphorical firing squad I'd conjured up earlier than sit at a table with Yoda and toss off a pitch.

"You don't have to," I said quickly.

He relaxed visibly.

"I'll just tell him that you had too much work and couldn't make it," I said, trying the excuse out loud.

"You already told him I'd go?"

I sighed, then nodded.

"I can't back out," he said, and suddenly I realized that my invitation was actually a trap, of sorts, for both of them. Yoda couldn't tell me no without seeming rude, and Morimoto couldn't turn me down without looking unreliable. If I was a more ruthless sort, I could really play the system. Since I wasn't quite so Machiavellian, I felt more like an asshole.

"Don't worry. It'll be painless," I promised, although I was fairly sure I was lying. It'd probably be at least a little bit painful for all three of us. I waited for noon with a sense of foreboding.

Yoda was wearing his rumpled brown cord blazer and usual plaid shirt/striped tie combination. Morimoto looked woeful in his bright blue windbreaker. We went to a *donburi* restaurant, which seemed fairly casual: the menu showed a lot of different pictures, and every dish was a meat or stew-type item, served over rice in a bowl. Yoda ordered for all of us. I barely noted what he asked for.

The photographer showed up a few minutes later, full of smiles. They were contagious, which was good, since all he kept saying was "smile!" "Pick up the menu . . . now smile! Happy! Fun! Okay, now pick up your teacup! Smile! How about the fork?"

Apparently, I was overjoyed at both eating and using cutlery. I would love to see how this press release turned out. Something like "American simpleton contest winner gets to eat noodles" with a picture of me grinning like an idiot as I poured Morimoto some tea and Yoda grimaced in the background.

I wondered for a minute if the photographer would stay and eat lunch with us, or if there was any kind of reporter along for some written stuff, but after snapping a few shots, he left us alone. Yoda settled down with his cup of tea and with the first platter of whatever they'd brought us. After he picked out his food, Morimoto offered to fix me a plate, which I appreciated. Apparently this was family-style eating, and I had no idea how many courses were coming. Morimoto finally fixed his own plate, and we sat there for a minute, surveying one another in silence.

Boy, could this get more awkward?

I cleared my throat. "Thank you so much for taking me out to lunch, Akamatsu-sensei," I said. "And thank you for allowing me to invite Morimoto-san."

Yoda grunted assent and started to eat his food.

I looked at Morimoto, who also started eating, never even looking up from the plate. No wonder he wasn't getting anywhere, I thought. He had great ideas, but he was terrified of Yoda. Not that I necessarily blamed him, but he'd approached me, and he was the one who wanted help with this. And, to be honest, I was pretty sick of doing busy work, especially now that I'd had a taste of working on a real project. Yoda might not like Morimoto's ideas because they were Western. He might not like *me* because I was Western. But if I was going to help Morimoto at all, I might as well jump in and test the waters.

Don't go to Hell for a quarter, as my grandmother would say. Although she never really meant it the same way I did.

"I became friends with Morimoto-san when I found out he liked American-style comics," I said, and I noticed that Morimoto had frozen like a mouse who had suddenly realized he was in front of a cat. "He has some fascinating ideas about new Japanese-American hybrid manga."

Morimoto choked.

Yoda made a snorting sound that could've been him slurping his soup. He looked at me, scowling. "Morimoto-san," he said, never once looking at the guy, "has a lot of wild ideas."

"Oh, good," I said, putting on my fake-bright, overly happy optimistic voice. "So you know the project he's proposing, the one with the adventure/love story that's made like a manga but has a lot of influences from American artists? I think it could sell really well. It'd be a great thing for Sansoro."

Now both men stared at me, with a mixture of shock and horror.

I had jumped in this far, and stupid or not, I couldn't think of how to back out of it. "It's a bit ambitious, sure," I said. "But I've been reading all the comics Sansoro has come out with. That was my assignment. I can already see previous story elements that have worked. I don't think it would be that much of a stretch."

I babbled on for a few more minutes, praying that Morimoto would jump in and save my ass. But he seemed content to let me prattle.

"So, what do you think?" I finally said, because I couldn't think of how else to "sell" the project and because I wanted to know if Yoda thought I was crazy or if he was simply sorry that I'd won the contest. I supposed he could fire me, I thought. But I'd just done press release photos. He couldn't fire me before that launched, could he?

"Interesting," he said instead, and my shoulders relaxed. Apparently I'd been pinching them with tension, practically pinning them together while I did my Pollyanna-on-speed version of Morimoto's comic book proposal.

Morimoto's mouth dropped open in shock.

"Still, I can only think of one artist who could pull off something of that scope, if you wanted it to be a big project," he said slowly. "Nobuko-san. She would be perfect."

Now Morimoto's mouth closed, and his shoulders slumped. I felt the same way.

"I wouldn't think this project would be viable unless she was involved," he said, crafty as a fox. "Of course, you could go ahead and ask her. You need to stop by her house to pick up her latest batch of ink drawings anyway, Morimoto-san. Why don't you ask her then?"

Morimoto visibly shrank. "I . . . would not want to impose," he stammered. Apparently Nobuko scared the hell out of him, too.

"Really? But you thought the project was so promising."

Yoda was toying with Morimoto, I could tell. And Morimoto was letting him.

I've always been a fan of the underdog. Maybe it's a New York thing, maybe an Italian thing, maybe just an American thing. But it pissed me off to see Morimoto's childlike enthusiasm just whirl down the drain.

"I could go," I said.

They both stared at me again. I was getting used to it.

"Well, all right," Yoda said, apparently floored. "But I don't want you bothering her."

"I'm sure you'll let her know I'm coming," I replied, knowing I was putting the onus on him. "And I promise to be brief."

They looked at me as if they weren't sure what they'd unleashed. Honestly, I wasn't sure what they'd unleashed, either.

March 3, Friday

SO HERE I WAS, FOLLOWING MORIMOTO'S DIRECTIONS TO THE LET-
ter, trying to figure out how to get to Nobuko's house. She worked
out of her home, which was relatively large and sumptuous for Tokyo;
she had her artist's studio in there or adjoining or something. Morimoto hadn't been all that clear.

It was really stupid of me to volunteer for something like this, all
things considered. If I was still working at the semiconductor plant,
and a secretary came up to me with a great new system for ordering,
say . . .

I sighed. I'd listen, actually, even if the person who came up to me
was a secretary. Hell, that was how I got out of the secretarial pool to
begin with. I'd been typing all these memos for higher-ups, and the
solution seemed right there, so I'd asked my primary boss why things

weren't done differently. I'd gently pestered for a couple of months. My mom said I inherited that from my dad. Apparently, that was how he got her to agree to marry him.

I was counting on the Falloya Charm—and the Falloya Persistence—to win Nobuko over. She hadn't been that impressed with me to begin with, granted, and I still wasn't sure why that was, but I was coming here with a new project and Yoda's blessing. I wasn't completely without ammunition.

After the usual half-hour of scouting around and trying to figure out the numbering system—at least I didn't have to hijack a neighbor to get where I needed to go this time—I finally got to Nobuko's house. It was an actual house, it turned out, not a condo like the Kanais' place. It wasn't a palace or anything, but having lived in cramped quarters and seen how every square inch of space was used over here, I figured she had to be pulling down some serious money. They said *manga-ka* were like bestselling authors over here. I mean, they *were* bestselling authors, technically, but they were more like Stephen King or Tom Clancy: you recognized their names, they made a boatload of cash, and they were sort of celebrities. Not as flashy as actors, say, but more impressive than screenwriters or CEOs. I was definitely in over my head.

I knocked on the door, and after a few minutes, a young woman opened the door. My first impression was one of fear—on my part and her part, I'd imagine. She had long straight black hair that fell past her breasts and obscured most of her face. She looked like the scary daughter out of that movie *The Ring*. She wore a shapeless pair of pants and a light blue smock-thing that was smeared with ink from the looks of it.

"I'm sorry," I finally stammered out. "I'm looking for— Is this the house of Nobuko-san?"

The girl nodded. Her eyes didn't bug out. If anything, she had a tough time actually meeting my gaze. She stayed silent.

"I'm from Sansoro," I said, deliberately gentling my voice, like she was a skittish dog or something. "Akamatsu-sensei sent me. I was hoping I could speak with her."

It took a minute for the girl to process this. Obviously the publisher's name meant something to her, but she kept glancing over her shoulder down the hallway. I knew that look. I'd seen secretaries get that look when you asked to bother their boss, and they knew that even though it wasn't their fault, they would probably catch hell anyway.

"I will tell her you are here," she finally said, although her tone was dubious. "May I have your name, please?"

"Lisa Falloya," I said, and her eyes widened, because I'd used the American pronunciation. She wouldn't be able to tackle those *L*'s, I knew. "You can tell her Risa-san is here," I corrected. "The Sansoro intern."

The girl looked at me, and I knew that expression. It was the "are you kidding me?" look. I didn't blame her.

She shuffled off in her house slippers while I waited on the tile in the foyer. She hadn't offered me house slippers, so I didn't take off my shoes. I'd already learned the hard way after the whole dishonorable shoe incident at the Kanais'. At least that had served a purpose. I knew that Nobuko wasn't going to be all that thrilled I was here; I didn't need to further the problem by screwing up the shoe thing. I got the feeling she'd be looking for ways she could call me out for being incompetent.

After what seemed like forever, Nobuko finally accompanied the girl to the hallway. She was dressed impeccably, a distinct counterpoint to the girl next to her. I got the feeling I hadn't interrupted her drawing. She was dressed as if she had just come back for a breakfast meeting; she wore a Western-style suit and had makeup and jewelry on. She studied me sharply. I was glad I'd dressed up a bit myself. I bowed politely.

"Nobuko-san," I said. "I appreciate your meeting with me on such short notice. I believe Akamatsu-sensei mentioned I would be stopping by."

She frowned. "What do you want?" Her voice was clipped and curt.

Or maybe Yoda hadn't mentioned me. Great. Just swell.

"Akamatsu-sensei has a new project in mind, and he thought I should discuss it with you," I said, leading with his name first, since obviously she saw me as somewhere between an assistant and a panhandler.

"You want to discuss a project . . . with me?"

Oh, God, this wasn't a good idea. Still, I'd gone this far. "It would be a tremendous help to me," I tried, hoping that, if I framed it as a favor, like a student asking someone famous to help with a class project, she wouldn't be insulted. It wasn't far from that, actually.

She crossed her arms. I still hadn't been offered alternate footwear, so I guessed I wasn't staying. It was here in the hallway or nothing.

"Sansoro wants to broaden its efforts in the United States," I said. "You mentioned that my style was very American, and Akamatsu-sensei agrees. A project has been proposed that would be a hybrid between American comics and manga. Akamatsu-sensei thought that there would be no one better to draw this than you, and he sent me to discuss the possibility with you."

She smiled, and for a second she looked completely benign. Almost friendly. Apparently, that "supplicant begging for a favor" tack was the right one to take, even if it did smack of sucking up.

"I'm afraid Akamatsu-san has sent you here to waste some of your time," she said, in that friendly tone of voice. "He knows exactly how busy I am, and he also knows that I don't discuss new projects. I develop new projects—all my books are my idea."

I frowned. That wasn't true; I'd read enough of her books to know that most of them were adaptations of other books. And all those books were already owned by Sansoro. "Perhaps he believed I might be able to persuade you," I ventured. "Also, this is something completely different from what you've been doing. Maybe he just wanted to see how you felt about trying something this challenging."

If sucking up didn't work, I figured the old "or are you too chicken?" threat was worth a shot.

Her eyes narrowed. "I am completely overloaded," she said. "My deadlines are insane. I can barely keep up as it is. Akamatsu-san knows I don't have the time. You can tell him that. And now I must work. I am afraid you'll have to leave."

I sighed. "I am also supposed to pick up your latest batch of inked drawings," I said. Obviously, the meeting was over.

"Chisato-san!" Nobuko snapped.

The girl with the long hair had been standing off to one side, and she jumped like someone had goosed her. *"Hai!"*

"Bring this woman the drawings and show her out." With that, and without even a good-bye, Nobuko left the foyer. She didn't even look over her shoulder to see if Chisato jumped to do her bidding, probably because it never occurred to her that Chisato wouldn't.

I bet it never occurred to Chisato, either, since she fled the foyer like she'd been set fire to. After another few minutes, she handed me a package, wrapped neatly in brown paper.

"Thank you, Chisato-san," I said. I felt bad for her. I felt bad for anybody who had to put up with that bitch on a daily basis, actually.

Chisato nodded, then looked like she was going to say something, but Nobuko's piercing voice yelled "Chisato-san!" and Chisato simply bowed and left, not even bothering to see me out. I sighed and shut the door behind me, heading back for the train.

When I got on the train, I had a good twenty minutes before I got to the office again, and it wasn't crowded since it wasn't rush hour. I decided to take a peek at the drawings. I had seen her work before, but I couldn't for the life of me see what the big deal was.

The drawings were great. She'd obviously improved with age, or something, I thought, noting the shading, the facial expressions, the amount of emotion she could get in just a single panel. She might be a bitch, but she was a talented bitch.

Then, a single piece of pale pink stationery fell out. That wasn't part of the package. It was a note.

I picked it up. It was probably a note asking Yoda what the hell he was thinking, sending a snot-nosed intern to her house to bug her about a pointless project. But as I struggled to translate the note, I realized it wasn't for Yoda.

It was for me.

And it wasn't from Nobuko. It was from Chisato, the scared assistant. She'd obviously scrawled it hastily, probably scared she'd be discovered—like a hostage trying to get word out about her captivity.

Risa-san . . . I did these drawings. I am interested in this project. Can we discuss it? Please call me.

I stared at the note, an idea brewing. Maybe we had something here. Only one way to find out.

March 9, Thursday

It was maybe the weirdest office party I'd ever been to. Cherry blossom season was in full effect, and there was a big celebration— the whole office was shut down for the day. I was an intern and low man on the totem pole, so I'd gotten up early that morning to accompany the Sansoro janitorial team down to a big park over by Ueno. It was about six thirty in the morning and still crisp with cold, but the sky was crystal clear and it promised to be a beautiful day. Other people were already in the park, and they were all doing the same thing: laying huge swaths of blue or green tarps out on the various lawns.

My job, as it had been explained to me, was to "stake out" the Sansoro spot for the annual Cherry Blossom Festival viewing. People from the office would use our blue tarp as a central meeting area, bag check, and picnic ground. I was to secure the space, set up the tarp, and keep other people off it.

Basically, I was a combination security guard and paperweight.

I brought a book, since I didn't know how long it would be before my colleagues showed up, and I settled down on the cold tarp, making vaguely threatening faces at any one who eyed the large blue area I was in charge of. I wasn't a bouncer by any stretch, but I did my job.

I'd told Morimoto to come early, if possible. I was still intrigued by Chisato's note. I'd even called her on Sunday.

I'd let the phone ring, wondering if she'd even pick up, and when I heard her tentative "*mushi-mushi,*" I knew I had the right girl.

"This is Risa-san," I said. "I got your note. Is this a good time for you to speak?"

"Yes, it is." She sounded relieved. "I just got home from Nobuko-san's house."

"It's Sunday," I protested, glancing at my watch. It had been six o'clock, too.

"That's why she let me go home early," Chisato reasoned. "I would not have been able to answer my phone if I was there. I'm very glad that you called me."

She sounded like she'd just crossed the Sahara and I'd offered her a glass of water. "Um, so you're interested in working on American-style comics?" I said, giving her an opening.

There was a pause. "I . . . am not very familiar with American-style comics," she said. "But I'm sure I could learn. It sounded very interesting."

Of course, there was no way she could know that. I hadn't even been able to give any details to Nobuko-san, much less her assistant.

I think I knew what was going on, though. "Your note mentioned you do a lot of the drawings for Nobuko-san," I said carefully.

Another pause. "I am not— Nobuko-san is a fantastic artist. I can only hope to one day follow in her footsteps," Chisato said, with equal caution.

But . . . There had to be a "but" at the end of that sentence. Still, her cultural sensibilities would not let her badmouth her boss, even if she was working for the demon artist from Hell.

"I simply thought that if she was not interested in the new project, and they were looking for an artist, I might be able to volunteer."

Her voice betrayed none of the desperation her quick escape note had reeked of. I knew better. "If Nobuko-san is under all these deadlines," I said, "doesn't that mean you are very busy, too? You are working on weekends, and working very late. Would you have the time for an extra project?"

"I am sure I could handle it. I would try very hard," she said quickly. Which meant she'd probably forgo sleep. I got the extreme visual of an animal trapped and biting off her own leg to escape. Chisato was a woman on the edge. She was taking a huge risk, working around Nobuko to angle at this chance.

"I'm just an intern," I said, not wanting to get her hopes up too much. I was feeling sort of jerked around by Yoda, so I didn't know if he was set on Nobuko or just wanted to put me in an untenable situation so I'd stop championing these harebrained projects. "I don't know if this project will get off the ground. But I'm very interested, and I think it could be a big success. I still need to discuss it further with the editor pushing the project and with our supervisor, Akamatsu-sensei. I can be sure to bring your name up as a potential artist. How long have you been drawing?"

"For five years," she said.

"Five years?" I repeated. "And you've been working with Nobuko-san this entire time."

"Yes," she said, and that soft word spoke volumes.

Jesus, kid, you don't just deserve your own job, you deserve a purple heart or something!

"Have you ever been offered a project before?"

She made a little sound that could've been a sigh or possibly just a tiny wordless prayer for patience. "No," she said.

"Why not?"

"Nobuko-san does not think I am ready yet."

And there it was, why she had decided to slip a note to the American intern who probably didn't know any better. After all, I'd been dumb enough to bug Nobuko in the first place, hadn't I?

When I hung up, I told her I'd get back to her; I was determined to help the girl. Which made me dumb, but at least sort of heroic about it.

Morimoto showed up at our blue tarp at around eight. Other people were slowly trickling in, but I got the feeling that, since it was a holiday, they would probably sleep in a little bit. The cherry blossoms would be there all day, after all. He walked right up to me.

"Good morning, Risa-san," he said. He was wearing his usual, jeans and a sweat jacket, only this time he had a matching bright blue fleece jacket over the ensemble to ward off the cool morning air. "I'm sorry things did not go better with Nobuko-san. Akamatsu-sensei mentioned that the project would not work." Morimoto sounded very glum about the whole shebang.

"Yeah, well, about that," I said, glancing around. The other guys from the office who had shown up early were apparently too busy getting ready for a tailgate kind of extravaganza to eavesdrop on our conversation. They were bringing out a wide range of coolers and even a small table. "Does the project really *need* Nobuko-san?"

His expression was one of utter mystification. "Akamatsu-sensei said she was the best artist for the project," he said, with a note of both frustration and finality.

"But why?"

"Because . . . because Akamatsu-sensei said so," he repeated, as if I was a small child who couldn't grasp the concept.

"Because of her style or her name?" I pressed. "If it's for her name, well, I don't think that a small project really deserves her attention. That's like killing a fly with a sledgehammer."

Now he was the one who seemed unclear on the concept, like I'd suddenly switched languages to Latin. "Killing a fly?"

"I simply think that a smaller artist, even an unknown, might be better for a small experimental project," I argued. Of course, it was easy to argue with Morimoto—he had all the aggression of a teddy bear. It would take years for him to develop a scowl and a tough persona like Yoda's, and that was assuming the guy even had it in him.

"An unknown artist," he repeated dubiously.

"You guys use unknowns all the time in your manga volumes," I said. "You're always working with new talent."

"Yes, but for the American market . . ."

"I hate to break it to you," I said, and I glanced around to make sure the cooler guys were still engrossed in their preparations, "but in the States, Nobuko-san is not very well known."

He took a step back, shocked by the statement.

"So as long as the comic itself is cool, and we got some distribution." I shrugged. "Well, it's your project, but I think that it might be too early to abandon it altogether."

Morimoto sat next to me on the cold tarp, obviously digesting this new bit of intelligence. "Akamatsu-sensei sounded very definite," he said.

"He might just need a little persuasion," I said.

"And you could do that?"

I sighed. Morimoto would rather be in a knife fight with Harley-riding *yakuza* than have a face-to-face meeting with Yoda. Of course, I didn't have anything riding on it. And the thought of poor Cinderella-esque Chisato was enough to encourage me to brave the wrath of my supervisor.

"I could do that," I agreed.

"It might be worth it." Now Morimoto's trademark enthusiastic grin was back in full force. "It might be worth it, indeed!"

I nodded, feeling gratified.

"Well, that's enough business," he said, and he sounded much more ebullient. "Have you been enjoying yourself?"

"Uh, yeah. Sure." Enjoying myself? By being a human tarp holder?

His grin was broad. "There's nothing like the cherry blossoms," he said. "Absolutely nothing."

I looked around, finally noticing something besides the fact that I was playing security guard to a piece of plastic. The long, whitish-gray limbs of the trees were covered in lacy, pale pink flowers. Everyone seemed to be staring at them with wonder, laughing under them, partying almost with them. Even though they were there every year.

I found myself smiling back, really looking at the flowers, drinking in the party atmosphere.

They were really on to something with this cherry blossom thing. I wondered if there were cherry trees in Groverton, and if there were, if anyone enjoyed it as much as the Japanese did.

As much as *I* did, right that minute.

March 10, Friday

I was in a part of Tokyo I'd never been in before. I was with Yukari and crew, so I had just followed the crowd from the Shibuya station and didn't really register which stop we were getting off at. It was sort of like Shinjuku—the same eight-story-high displays on the sides of the skyscrapers, projecting music videos and ads. We were in another arcade. I was going to meet Chisato, outside of work. She wasn't getting out of Nobuko's until nine or so; I had an hour to kill.

"Riri-chan! Come on!" One of Yukari's little giggly friends tugged at my hand, dragging me toward a photo-sticker machine.

"Uh." I winced at the nickname, but since it was a sign that I'd been accepted by the posse, I couldn't really complain. This little girl (she had to be eighteen at the very oldest) was named . . . God, I couldn't remember her name. I think I called her Red because her hair was dyed a bright, Ronald McDonald red. She looked like an Asian Raggedy Ann. She practiced English with me more than the rest of the crew.

"Pick!" She had already put money into the machine, and now there were a series of backgrounds: a cartoony moonscape, a bright meadow, a beach, a snowscape. I picked the moon and the beach. She giggled loudly, covering the perfect "O" of her mouth with both hands as she did. Then she grabbed my hand again and dragged me into the booth.

"Smile!" she instructed, and promptly started mugging for the camera. Feeling foolish, I grinned, then started to make funny faces. I mean, I didn't want to be a stick in the mud, and Red was obviously having a blast. A TV screen showed us what the pictures looked like, after we took them. Red looked like a cartoon; I looked like an idiot. But it was still cute. Then she dragged me around, back to the screens, and we got to draw on the photos with a light pen, stamping little motifs. We split them evenly. In the end, we got a sheet of stickers. She promptly stuck a small one of the two of us against the lunar landscape on her K-tei, showing me proudly. I was just about to do the same when my K-tei rang, startling me.

"Excuse me," I told her, and she quickly made a "no problem" gesture and grabbed another girl for another go-round in the sticker booth. *"Mushi-mushi?"* I asked, thinking it must be Chisato.

"I'm never going to get used to that," I heard Ethan laugh.

I smiled. "Hi, sweetie. I wasn't expecting your phone call."

"You weren't?" He was obviously surprised. "But it's our anniversary!"

I winced. I'd forgotten our anniversary? Oh, how much did *I* suck? "I completely spaced on it," I said, feeling guilty.

"Well," he said, "there is the whole time/date difference. It's only six a.m. here, after all. And it's, what, nine o'clock at night there, right?"

I thought for an awful moment that I'd messed up the date, too. Since there was a huge time difference, he was usually a day behind me. If I'd missed the day entirely, that would've been too awful for words. "Yeah, there is the time difference," I said. "I'm so sorry."

"Don't sweat it," he said, even though he did sound a little annoyed. "I'm lucky I remembered it. My mom asked if I was sending you anything." Now he laughed. "I sent you an Amazon gift certificate, by the way."

His usual last-minute gift. The feelings of guilt receded. At least I wasn't the only one who wasn't romantic. "I just feel as if time has stood still around here; I lose track of months," I said. "I can't believe I've been here over two months already."

"You certainly sound acclimatized," he agreed. "What's all that noise? Is that kid still blasting the TV?"

"No. Well, yes, he is," I said, thinking of Ichiro's passive-aggressive campaign. "But no, I'm not in the house. I'm at an arcade with some friends."

"An arcade?" He sounded amused. "What, are your friends twelve or something?"

I glanced around. Everything was in bubble-gum colors: ice blue, cotton candy pink, lemon drop yellow. And nobody that I could see was under the age of, say, seventeen. "It's sort of hard to explain."

"Fun for you," he joked. "Man, you must be dying to come home."

"Actually, I'm having a good time," I said, and realized as soon as the words left my lips that I really was. "Besides, it's not all fun and games, as it were. I'm out waiting to meet with somebody for a work project."

"Kinda late, isn't it?" He sounded concerned . . . and a twinge suspicious.

I shrugged, then realized he couldn't see it. "She works hellish hours," I explained. "That's part of why we're meeting. I'm trying to get this project together so she can escape from her psycho boss."

"Oh." Now he sounded relieved. I wondered if it was because I said "she," as opposed to "he." He probably wouldn't love me meeting Morimoto at night, even if it were in the equivalent of an adult Chuck E. Cheese. Of course, if the tables were turned, I probably wouldn't love—

I stopped myself. He had female study partners before, that he'd met late at night. And yeah, it had bugged me a bit, but I hadn't said anything. Had I?

I shook my head. "I miss you," I said instead. "And I'm glad you called for our anniversary."

"I get up this early anyway," he said, "to get a jump on work, so it wasn't any trouble."

"I still appreciate it." I saw Chisato walking in, looking as if the noise and flashing lights of the arcade were overwhelming her. "Damn it, there's my artist. I have to go, sweetie. I love you."

"Love you, too," he said. "Don't work too hard, okay?"

"Hey, that's my line." In our entire three years together, I couldn't remember him ever saying that to me, although I remembered saying it tons to him. I cradled the phone against my ear for a minute. "I really do miss you."

"I know. But you'll be home soon enough. Talk to you soon."

He hung up, and I tucked the phone in my pocket, walking up to Chisato. "I'm glad you could make it," I said to her. "Was it difficult to get away?"

She smiled broadly at me, if a little shyly. "I was nervous all the way here," she said. "I am glad you called me."

I smiled at her, then I motioned to Yukari, who had just finished playing the Claw game, the one where you try to get a stuffed animal. She was proudly displaying a sherbet-colored elephant. She came over. "See what I won?" she asked.

I admired the elephant, then introduced Yukari and Chisato. Chisato stared at Yukari, who was dressed in an electric blue mini-skirt, matching blue knee boots, and a silver halter top under a knee-length purple leather coat. Chisato was wearing her usual uniform: slacks, low shoes, and a shapeless gray shirt. Yukari gave Chisato a casual greeting, then looked at me.

"I need to talk to Chisato about a project for work," I said.

"Okay. But you're still going drinking with us later, right?" It was not a request but a demand.

I nodded. "Sure thing, no problem."

"Text me when you're done, we'll make sure you don't get lost!" With that, Yukari gathered her whole crew and they meandered down the street, toward a karaoke place. The bar would be the next stop.

"Have you eaten?" I asked Chisato.

She stared at Yukari's disappearing form for a minute, then realized I'd asked a question. "No," she said. "But it's okay, I'm not hungry."

Jeez, Nobuko wouldn't even let the poor girl eat. I lied and told her I was hungry, and we stopped at a Happy Burger nearby. I had eaten there before and knew that I could polish off a Happy Burger, no matter what state of satiety I was in. They were roughly the size of a White Castle burger, no larger than my palm. Their fries were nothing to write home about, either. She got two burgers, at my insistence, and nibbled at them, obviously feeling a little awkward. Still, her stomach had started growling the minute we walked in, to her embarrassment, so I didn't feel that bad about strong-arming her.

"So," I said, after inhaling my own tiny Happy Burger, which was more like a soy appetizer than fast food, "you want to be a *manga-ka* instead of just an *assisto*."

She choked on a fry. "I'm not ungrateful to Nobuko-san," she said hastily.

"Nobody's saying you are," I assured her. "I'm just sure that after five years, you're more than ready to tackle a project of your own. And since you approached me, I figure you agree with me."

She looked torn and paid way too much attention to methodically chewing her Happy Burger, buying time for the right answer. She finally stared at my face. "You're not Japanese." It was said tentatively enough to be a question, but I got the feeling it was a statement.

I sighed. "I'm half-Japanese," I corrected.

She nodded, as if I'd said "yes." "Being from America, you do things differently. You . . ." She paused, as if her mind had gotten caught on a snag. "Put yourself . . . forward?"

She said it like it was some kind of dirty habit, like swearing or picking your nose in public.

"Something like that," I said, although I felt a little dirty admitting to it.

"I have always wanted to be a *manga-ka*," she finally said in a rush. "I apprenticed with Nobuko-san out of high school. I did little amateur manga when I was in high school. It's what I love." She looked down at the table, as if ashamed. "When you talked about the new project, I thought it would be fantastic, and fun. And if Nobuko-san does not want it . . ."

She didn't finish the sentence, so I did. "You do."

She looked at me, heart in her eyes. Her enthusiasm reminded me of Morimoto actually. "Do you think— Is it possible?"

I leaned back. I should not get this little girl's hopes up. I was just an intern. God knows, I wasn't really responsible for anything.

"I'll certainly try," I said. And from the look on her face, I guess I might as well have said "yes."

CHAPTER 8

March 14, Tuesday

I WENT INTO YODA'S OFFICE, AT HIS REQUEST.

"Did you finish the pencil erasing that I left on your desk?" he asked brusquely, without even a hello. He was drinking strong green tea—his whole office was permeated by it.

"Yes, Akamatsu-sensei," I said, putting the sheaf of drawings down on his desk. "I also helped Satomi and Sakura with the Goth Lolita project they were working on."

His eyebrows jumped up. "Why couldn't they do it for themselves? What help did they need from an intern?"

I didn't want to tell him that I'd basically pestered them into letting me help with something—I was between projects and I had no work to do. The last time I'd asked Yoda for something to keep me busy, he'd had me sweep the break room. And I'd done it—it had taken about ten minutes. By the time I went back to his office to ask for another task, he scowled at me and told me not to bother him.

"They were both trying to make deadline on two other projects," I said. "They just needed someone to make sure that the lettering was all right, that the rough sketches that were coming in on the second in the Goth Lolita series were equivalent to the first version. I didn't approve of anything or work independently," I quickly added, since he looked peeved. "I made a few suggestions, but Satomi and Sakura made all final decisions."

"Really?" He got up and did his slow scurry to the door. His walk wasn't very fast, but it gave the impression of quickness. "Satomi-san! Sakura-san!"

They showed up like they had beamed into his office. "Yes, Akamatsu-sensei?" Sakura asked, as they both snapped a fast, casual bow.

"Did you give work to Risa-san?"

They looked at me as if I'd betrayed them. I certainly hadn't meant to. "She was eager to learn, so we let her look over a few things," Satomi said slowly. "She did nothing substantial."

I chafed at that a little bit, but I could see where she was coming from. I mean, I did bug them to let me help, but I could also see they were severely backlogged. Once I'd convinced them that they couldn't possibly get in that much trouble, they'd seemed relieved to get the menial work of letter-checking and whatnot out of the way. They were already glad they didn't have to erase pencil marks. Still, here they were, called up on the carpet. I probably wouldn't want to admit anything to Yoda, either, in his present mood. Especially if I was working here for more than my one-year stint.

"Akamatsu-sensei," I started to intercede, not wanting to make matters worse. He glared me into silence.

"Why didn't you just refer her to me?" he asked them.

"Ah"—they looked at me—"she had already spoken to you."

"And what did I tell her?"

Sakura looked sublimely uncomfortable. "Ah, you told her not to bother you."

He made a startled little step back at that one. "Oh. Yes. So I did." Then he turned to me. "That did not mean you should bother your coworkers."

"There's a ton of work out there that needed to be done, and they are both . . ." I searched for the Japanese word but wound up using the English. "*Swamped.*"

All three of them stared at me, not comprehending.

"They have too much to do," I explained. "There is work enough out there for five editors, not just Satomi and Sakura."

Now he was pissed at me, I could tell. Satomi and Sakura were looking at me with both sympathy and horror. "Are you telling me how to run my department, *intern* Risa-san?"

I sighed. "No, of course not, Akamatsu-sensei. I wouldn't presume."

"On the contrary. You seem to presume a lot." He turned back to the S-girls. "You can go back to your desks."

They looked happy to do so, although Satomi sent me one last woeful look over her shoulder before retreating. Yoda shut the door on them, then turned to me, arms crossed. "What am I going to do with you, Risa-san?"

I sighed. "I'm sorry, Akamatsu-sensei. I'm American. This is how we act." Actually, I'm pretty sure lots of other Americans would have just shut up and waited for work, but hey, with any luck, Yoda didn't know that.

If people were going to keep saying I wasn't Japanese, it was time I started using it to my advantage.

He sat down, looking more tired than pissed, which I was grateful for. "What you perhaps do not realize is . . . this job you have . . ." He ran his hand through his hair, making it stick out of his head at crazy angles, like a Troll doll. "It's an internship."

I knew that. "Yes, Akamatsu-sensei."

"It was very good publicity for the company." He looked at me, solemn, as if by merely staring he could make me understand.

I think I did. "You mean . . . you never really intended me to do much work at all."

"You do not have the background," he said apologetically, not contradicting my statement. "You do learn quickly. And you have a good deal of energy. You have done things without complaining. Those are good things. But you are taking on a great deal. And I don't know whether that is a good idea or not."

The Morimoto project. That was what he was talking about, I was sure of it. After my little Happy Burger with Chisato, I really didn't want to back down.

"I can be less visible on the projects if that would make things easier," I conceded, rather than saying I'd stop altogether.

He smiled a little. "You don't quit, do you?"

"Of course not," I replied.

"You are so very American." He shook his head. "Morimoto-san has been doing the work of—how did you put it?—five people, since we spoke about his little side project. I have not seen him work like this ever. I am assuming it is your American influence. Either that or he is trying to ensure that I am on his side when he proposes what he does to my superior, Tanaka-san."

I smiled, feeling more comfortable. "Morimoto-san's idea is a good one," I repeated. "I think it could go over very well."

"I have watched him. He has many innovative ideas. And he works hard. I never suspected that he would be someone who would bring good things to Sansoro, however." He said this as if it was a bad admission. "It is interesting now to see what is happening. Also,

Satomi and Sakura never talked to me quite as much as they do now."

I wasn't sure if he was pleased or displeased about that little news bit, so I didn't say anything.

"You are having a strange influence on my staff, Risa-san," he said finally. "And it has puzzled me for the last few months. I have not been sure how to handle you."

I realized that, more than likely, he was talking about firing me. Which was bad. I held my breath, finally understanding why so many people in the office were terrified of this short, rumpled old man. I wasn't afraid of him, but I'd been much more forward with him because I didn't feel as if I had anything to lose—I wanted to go home, I was tired and heartsick from being so far from Ethan and my friends, and I was just doing stupid busywork. But now I had a chance to do stuff I liked, help people I liked, like Morimoto and Chisato. And thanks to Yukari, I had a social life that I'd never experienced, not even in high school or college.

I suddenly had a lot to lose, I realized.

"There is a trial clause in the agreement you signed," he said, and I felt cold chills despite the ninety-degree heat blasting from the heating vent. "If Sansoro feels you are not working out, we are within the contract to send you back to America early."

I swallowed hard. The document to work here had been fatter than escrow paperwork, and I hadn't paid a lot of attention to the niceties. I guess I should have.

"But we are people of our word," he said. "And besides, as I've said, you have had an interesting influence on my staff."

"Thank you," I said, feeling some of the circulation return to my extremities. I'd been clutching the chair so hard, I didn't realize my knuckles had gone white.

"You will need to learn to work with me, Risa-san, not around me," he said bluntly.

I nodded. "I will work with you, Akamatsu-sensei. Thank you for giving me the opportunity."

He nodded back, then said, "You may go back to your desk now."

I got up, my knees feeling slightly shaky. I hadn't expected it to feel like this. It was nearly impossible to get fired at the semiconductor plant; we'd often joked that the only way to get canned was to bring a gun in, and even then, you'd get a verbal warning first. Here, I had figured I only had a one-year internship, so it wasn't a real job. But now it felt very, very real. And I'd gotten my verbal warning.

I turned back to him. "Uh, Akamatsu-sensei?"

Since he'd already dismissed me, he looked up, mildly irritated. "*Hai?*"

"If I'm going to be working with you," I said, tentatively, wondering how to broach the subject, "does that mean I can stop by your office to discuss things? The project is going to be moving fairly quickly soon—"

He stared at me, his eyes going buggy, then he burst into short, barking gasps of laughter. I flinched, unprepared.

"Americans," he repeated, shaking his head. "Go sit down, Risa-san. Oh, and here." He reached into his desk and produced a small cellophane bag with a picture of Winnie the Pooh on it, filled with what looked like small, jelly-filled marshmallows.

"Thank you," I said, mystified.

"Just go sit down," he said.

I went back to my desk, still mulling over my near miss, when Morimoto walked over. "This is for you," he said, smiling, and handed me a small box of chocolate. He had already done the same for the rest of my desk crew—I could see matching boxes all over the place.

"Thanks," I repeated. "Uh, what's it for?"

He laughed. "It's White Day. The girls give us candy on Valentine's, so we need to return the favor. March fourteenth. White Day."

"Oh." It made a lot of sense, actually. I wondered how long it would be before Hallmark and Hershey's picked up the idea. "So that explains this."

Morimoto saw the bag of marshmallows, and his eyes widened. "Is that—" His voice dropped to a conspiratorial whisper. "Is that from Akamatsu-sensei?"

I nodded.

"Wow. He never gives candy to anybody."

I smiled. Maybe, hopefully, my job wasn't quite so precarious after all.

March 30, Thursday

I was starting to burn the candle at both ends. I think I finally understood how Ethan felt, being burned out by work and then school and studying. Not that I was terribly worried about the work itself, but Akamatsu-sensei had authorized the S-girls to give me a little more to do, and I was doing everything I could to learn more about the job. Then there were my training and planning sessions with Morimoto and Chisato, who were getting along like a house afire, when we could all meet face to face. (Chisato's slave hours didn't permit a lot of outside time, we discovered.) And then, of course, I didn't want to abandon my new friend Yukari and her crew. I was averaging maybe five hours of sleep a night when I was lucky.

I knew I couldn't go on like this indefinitely. Still, all things considered, I was only here for a year. And all my friends, and even my boyfriend, had mentioned that I needed a bit more adventure.

So here I was: adventure central.

Tonight, I'd only been out with Morimoto and Chisato, thankfully. We'd spent the first part of the night in a Starbucks (my new headquarters) and the rest of it in a bar down the street. Morimoto lived in Shibuya as well—with his parents, I got the feeling. Chisato lived near Ueno. It was eleven o'clock, and she still had time to catch a train. I had a few qualms about her going on public transportation all by herself at night. She couldn't have looked more vulnerable if she had had five-dollar bills pinned to her and a hat that said "please rob me." However, she assured me that Tokyo was one of the safest cities in the world, if you were careful. And besides, she'd worked much later hours for Nobuko in the past.

We *really* needed to get her a new job.

Since I wasn't out with Yukari, I went to the apartment, using the key they'd given me. I walked in quietly. Yukari, for all her drunken giggling, managed to come home at four in the morning and not disturb anybody. Not even me, lately, although maybe I'd gotten used to her. I didn't have her stealth, though, so I was being extra careful. If I was lucky, Ichiro was asleep on the couch, the Kanais were already conked out (prepping for their early morning), and I could just cruise back to my room and get some dedicated hours of deep REM sleep before Yukari came home.

I heard voices and knew I wasn't lucky. The voices did not come from the TV, either, although that was on. I realized that the volume was turned down a bit, and Ichiro probably was asleep. One out of two wasn't bad, I thought, and slowly crept toward the bedroom.

"At least we have Risa-san," I heard Mrs. Kanai say.

I froze involuntarily. I had no idea what they were talking about, but if they were touting me as the Great White Hope for something, then the situation had to be pretty dire. For the most part, I thought they'd just blocked out the fact that I was there.

"I am not happy that we have to charge rent and let a stranger stay here with us," Mr. Kanai said, with a heavy huff. "And we are not getting very much from her."

They could say that again. I was getting a great deal, and I knew it. I didn't realize they were in financial straits, though. I just thought that Perry had set the matter up, and Yukari had forced them into it. They always seemed embarrassed when I paid them.

"How bad is the cut in pay?" Mrs. Kanai asked.

Pay cut?

"It could have been worse," Mr. Kanai evaded. "Poor Oki-san was asked to leave entirely. For the good of the company."

I don't know if he was deliberately being bitter or if he always sounded that way; I'd just never had a long conversation with the man.

"We will manage," Mrs. Kanai said, and to her credit, her voice only shook a little.

I realized they were deep enough in their conversation that they'd never notice my intrusion. I just had to creep to my room, or rather Yukari's room, and close the door as quietly as possible. That would be the smart thing to do. But I felt drawn into the conversation simply because I wanted to know what was going on. If they were in that much trouble, I ought to pony up more for rent, at the very least. Although then they'd know I was eavesdropping, and I get the feeling Mr. Kanai would rather bite off his own arm than admit they were having trouble, especially since he was the only breadwinner. He'd lose face something fierce . . . and to a gaijin, no less. Maybe I could do something else. Buy groceries? No, that was Mrs. Kanai's domain, and she'd probably be hurt if I poached on her territory.

Maybe I could subsidize Yukari. Lord knows, that girl had to be expensive to maintain.

"If Yukari got a job, perhaps . . ." Mr. Kanai said. Like he was reading my mind!

"I don't want to force Yukari into anything," Mrs. Kanai said. "The job market is very difficult right now."

"I am well aware," Mr. Kanai said.

Mrs. Kanai fell silent. No doubt that's why Mr. Kanai took the pay cut. Getting laid off, especially at his age, was tantamount to death. Especially in a culture that thought going to school and getting a good job with a good company was your guarantee for life. If you became a Sony man, you died a Sony man. Nowadays, no matter whose man you were, you could become an unemployed man pretty damned quick. And you'd just die broke.

"Perhaps she could get a job," Mrs. Kanai finally agreed. "Should I speak with her?"

"Perhaps that would be best."

I got the feeling Mr. Kanai and Yukari probably didn't have a lot of heartfelt conversations.

Another lull, this time just out of sheer despondency, from the sound of it. They were safely in the kitchen. I decided it was past time I headed back to my room. I turned, only to see Ichiro staring at me from the couch.

"What are you doing?" he asked in a loud voice.

He'd obviously been awake, and also listening to the conversation, for some time. He grinned maliciously at me as he yelled. I tried to shush him, and I headed toward my room.

"You were spying!" he yelled.

Mr. and Mrs. Kanai came out of the kitchen in a rush, just as they had the last time Ichiro had thrown a tantrum. "What is it?" Mrs. Kanai asked. Mr. Kanai only looked at me, as if trying to ascertain how much I'd heard, how much I knew.

"I'm sorry," I said, opening the door to Yukari's room. "I didn't mean to disturb everyone. I was just late getting in, that's all."

"You were listening!" Ichiro squealed.

I glared at him. *You little narc.* "I only heard a little of the conversation, nothing much really."

Mrs. Kanai looked at the floor, blushing a little, her lip trembling ever so faintly. Mr. Kanai's forehead furrowed into long worry lines.

"I was more concerned with trying not to wake up Ichiro," I said, spur of the moment.

"No you weren't!"

I stared at him. "You were asleep," I pointed out, "and also didn't hear anything except my being clumsy, right?"

He started to open his mouth, and then shut it, realizing that he, too, had been eavesdropping. Of course, if they weren't going to punish the kid for ditching school altogether and for acting like a brat of *Charlie and the Chocolate Factory* proportions, then I don't know what he was scared of. But he took one look at his father, whose unhappiness was etched into his face like acid, and I think he realized this was one time that his father might actually dish out some punishment, just to get rid of some of the pain of embarrassment.

"You were clumsy," Ichiro finally said. "And . . . and you woke me up. And you were being sneaky!"

"I'm very sorry," I repeated to the Kanai parents. "It won't happen again."

"It's nothing," Mrs. Kanai said, grasping eagerly at the falsehood.

Mr. Kanai didn't even acknowledge my statement. He just turned and went back to the kitchen. After one last glare at Ichiro, I retreated to the bedroom. This had "bad" written all over it.

CHAPTER 9

May 5, Friday

"HAPPY BIRTHDAY, RISA-SAN!"

"Yuki-chan, you shouldn't have," I said, and part of me really meant it. I was wearing a pink minidress, Yukari's idea, and a little plastic tiara studded with rhinestones. Yukari's whole crew was there, as well as Chisato and Morimoto. I was starting to suspect those two were becoming a couple, which was very cute. Chisato was actually pulling her hair back from her face, and without the horror-movie 'do, she was very pretty. It reminded me of Nana Falloya's constant admonitions to pull my hair away from my own face. "You've got such a pretty face! Why do you keep hiding it?"

Yukari had booked a table at an Italian restaurant, just off the Ginza. I prayed that everyone was contributing financially, including myself. After the discussion I'd overheard between Mr. and Mrs. Kanai, I really didn't want Yukari telling them she'd blown an unreasonable amount of money on the gaijin renter they hadn't even wanted.

"Are you having a good time?" Yukari asked me as they served the first course. "I picked Italian food because I figured you'd be home-sick."

The restaurant was under the train tracks, in a sort of "restaurant row" that included a Mexican cantina and a "real American" burger joint. This place was called Il Bellagio and was very upscale—no red-checkered tablecloths or candles stuffed in Chianti bottles, which I'd seen plenty of at home. Maybe red-checkered cloth was against the Japanese aesthetic. Their one bow to Italian-American influence was the large black-and-white pictures of movie stars, like Sophia Loren and, of course, Frank Sinatra. Some things never changed, and, oddly, the very kitsch quality made it even more endearing.

"It's wonderful," I said. "And I'm much less homesick since you became my friend."

She beamed at this and then got drawn into a conversation with the people on the other side of her. It was true: since I'd made some friends, it was a lot easier to be so far from home. That, and work.

"Thank you for inviting us," Morimoto said, smiling at Chisato, who blushed.

"Well, you're my friends, too," I pointed out, "not just people I work with." Then it occurred to me. "Wait a sec. Don't get me wrong. You are my friends, but I thought people at work here usually hung out all the time. You know, hit the bars, stuff like that."

Chisato shrugged. "I certainly don't."

"Well, no, I guess you wouldn't," I agreed. Somehow, I couldn't see Chisato and Nobuko pub-crawling and doing shots together. I looked over at Morimoto. "What about you? The guys are so rowdy, I figured they must go out drinking all the time."

"They do," Morimoto said. "I go sometimes and try to keep up. I'm not much of a drinker."

That would be a bad thing, a way to lose face, as it were. One more thing that separated him from the rest of the staff.

They brought us our food. Almost everybody had ordered some kind of risotto or seafood, I noticed. I'd ordered the fettuccini alfredo because I'd missed real pasta and real cheese. It smelled heavenly.

"So, what are you going to do when you go back?" Yukari's friend Red asked me.

"Um, I'm not sure," I said. I hadn't really thought that far. If I'd gone back in January or February, it would've been obvious: begged for my old job back and kept out of Ethan's way until finals were over. Easy enough, in theory. Now . . . "I'm not worrying about it, though. I'm sure something will turn up."

Knock on wood.

They seemed impressed by my nonchalance; well, Morimoto and Chisato seemed impressed by my nonchalance. I got the feeling things didn't just "work out" for them all that often. Yukari, on the other hand, was a walking infomercial for the Hakuna Matata way of life. I don't know that I'd seen her worried about anything.

"Oh," I said. "I'm probably getting married."

Suddenly, there was a chorus of cheers, and I blinked for a minute.

"No wonder you're not worried," Chisato said.

I stared at her. "No," I corrected hastily, "it's not like that."

"Does he have a good job?" Red asked. Red apparently didn't have issues with privacy. At least, not other people's privacy.

"Um, yes," I said. "But he's going to interview for a better one when school is over."

"He's just graduating?" Now Red was grinning. I realized she thought I was robbing the cradle. Morimoto looked startled. Yukari just shook her head.

"Younger men are so pointless," Yukari pronounced with some authority. Since she was twenty-one, I had to assume any experience she had with younger men bordered on the illegal. Besides, her type ran at least ten years older.

"He's finishing business school, not university," I clarified. "Grad school, you know?"

"Oh," Red said, and her eyes gleamed. "So he'll be making a lot of money! Aren't business school people in America making a lot of money?"

"I, er, think so." This was getting disturbing. I wondered if Red's next question was "Does he have a brother?" Not that I suspected any of Yukari's crew of being eager to settle down.

Somebody at the other end of the table, one of Yukari's guy friends, made a low, snide-sounding comment. All I caught was something about a dog. I looked at Yukari, trying to figure out what the hubbub was.

She glared at him. "She is *not* a 'barking dog,' Tetsuo-san!"

Ooh. The guy in question straightened, putting his hands up defensively. "I didn't mean anything—"

"What's a barking dog?" I asked Chisato quietly, as Yukari and the guy argued. It didn't help that Yukari was about one sheet to the wind and working on her second.

Chisato shook her head. "It's just— It's a career woman, or a woman who says she's interested in her career, and then when she gets a proposal she throws it all away because all she really wanted was to get married."

I looked at the guy, the feminist in me utterly appalled. I didn't know any women like that. Of course, I didn't know many couples who could afford to live on one income, either, now that I thought about it. I wondered if it was feminism or practicality.

"I'm not giving up my career," I said to the guy, realizing that a little of my bravado was the Asahi beer from the bar we'd hit before the restaurant.

"I'm very sorry," he said. He obviously didn't want to get on Yukari's bad side. With good reason.

"That's fine. Let's just enjoy dinner."

Another round of "Happy Birthday!" followed, and I dug into my pasta, determined to have a good time, stay in the present, and worry about the career, the marriage, the whole nine yards later, when it happened. For now, it was just like being at home with the Falloya clan, having a big meal, joking, talking, and even squabbling.

I realized my pasta was abnormally chewy, even though the alfredo sauce was passably good. I stirred around with my fork.

There was octopus in my pasta. I mentioned it to Yukari.

"Of course there is," she said, puzzled at my comment. "Wait. How do you normally eat it? Is it different?"

"No, this is great," I said, taking a big bite to reassure her that it was fine, and I kept eating.

Okay, so it wasn't exactly like home. But still it wasn't bad.

May 6, Saturday

It was Saturday morning, in Yukari's room. I had the joint to myself. She was staying over at a friend's house. I got the feeling that her parents thought the friend was one of her Giggling Girls, but I knew that Yukari was actually staying over at a pen pal's hotel room. A male, American pen pal. I'd met him on Thursday. He seemed nice enough—a sort of Perry clone, pale and thin. He didn't seem to have dangerous intentions, but I made Yukari tell me the hotel name and room number and I carded the guy. He seemed offended, and Yukari was terribly embarrassed and tried to laugh the whole thing off as a joke, but I figured it was better to be safe than sorry. I didn't want to be the person to rain on Yukari's parade, but I wasn't going to let her get murdered in some stranger's hotel room, either.

It was probably just as well her parents didn't know what her life was like. Both of them would've gone completely gray by now if they did. I knew just being her self-appointed watchdog was giving me a couple of gray hairs. Also, it made me really wish not to have daughters, although then I'd look at Ichiro and reconsider giving the whole child-rearing thing a miss altogether.

At any rate, I used my K-tei and my rare privacy to give Ethan a call. His graduation was coming up in a month, and I needed to tie down some details. Of course, he was probably going to be able to talk for only a minute, probably deep in the muck of finals. Still, I didn't mind. I really did understand that he was busy, for one thing. And the fact that my own life had picked up in busyness helped. I didn't feel so needy, and I didn't crave his connection quite so much.

It was sort of nice, actually.

"Hello?" He sounded clipped and frazzled.

"Hey, sweetie," I said, settling against my bed, propped up by pillows, feeling downright decadent. "I missed you."

He paused for a minute.

"You know who this is, don't you?" I said, going from sweet to offended in under five seconds.

"Jeez. Lisa, I'm sorry, baby. Of course I knew it was you. I just had to switch gears," he said, laughing. "I miss you, too, by the way. Here, let me close this book."

"I rate a book closing!" I joked, just trying to lighten the mood. "Well, that's news. How's it going?"

"Finals," he said, just as I predicted. "I can't believe how ball-breaking they're being this semester."

I made sympathetic noises. "How are you holding up?"

"I've been better," he admitted, and his voice sounded ragged. I bet he wasn't getting enough sleep. Still, he probably only budgeted five hours a night because he needed every other spare minute to study or work, and he stuck to a plan like it was carved in marble. We'd really need to negotiate that if we got married, I thought.

When, I quickly corrected myself, shocked that I'd gotten that wrong. *When* we got married.

"At least now I can see an end to all of it, you know?"

"End to what?"

"Finals. This crappy job," he said, and for the first time, I heard longing in his voice. Usually he was such a trouper, he could be a poster child for model prisoners of war. Now, he was actively admitting that his life sucked. It was as close to whining as he was ever going to get, which strangely made me feel better—not that he was in a bad situation but that he was human enough to show it. "Once June comes and finals are over, it's just interviewing and getting the new job, and then just taking it easy for a while. I can finally see the light at the end of the tunnel, you know?" He sighed heavily. "I can't believe how long I've been going after this."

"You've worked really hard," I reassured him. "I could never do what you've done. I don't even think I know many—*any*—people who could do what you've done. Juggling a forty-hour-a-week job with demanding bosses and getting your MBA at night. Ethan, you've been running on fumes forever."

"At least I had a girlfriend who always had my back," he said.

I laughed. "It wasn't like it was that hard." Still, I felt warm and appreciated.

"You always understood when I was too busy to see you. You always took whatever time I could see you to sneak over and give me cookies you'd made or something. You're really amazing."

"Okay, now you're making me blush," I said. "What's gotten into you?"

"I just know that I couldn't get as far as I've gotten without someone as wonderfully supportive as you are," he said, and it was the most effusive I'd ever heard him. He really was a great guy, I thought, and I missed him more than I did the first week I'd gotten to Tokyo.

"Thanks, Ethan. You're great, too."

"We're going to be a great team when we get married," he said. "Don't you think?"

"Sure," I said, although I wasn't thinking of it in terms of team-work. It just seemed to make sense. We loved each other, we liked being around each other, ergo marriage.

"I know I can do anything with you there."

I didn't know what to say to that. I felt like I ought to reciprocate, but I didn't know what I could do, and as much as I loved the guy, I didn't really feel that my capabilities were all that different thanks to his presence. He was sweet; he was caring. But I wouldn't have characterized him as *supportive.* On the other hand, I hadn't given him anything to be supportive *about.* Hadn't he complained about as much, before nudging me to get my butt over here to Tokyo?

I sighed, rubbing at my temple. I was giving myself a headache. This was getting me nowhere.

"Well, I know that you've got studying and stuff to do," I said, my tone turning businesslike, trying to hide whatever weird mental loop I'd let myself get caught in. "I don't want to take too much time. I just wanted to solidify plans for your graduation."

"You're staying with me, right? In my apartment?"

I laughed. "My family wouldn't get *too* pissed at that," I said. "They're already complaining that I don't call enough. Apparently e-mail doesn't count."

"You can see them during the day," he wheedled. "Come on. I miss you."

I sighed. "You know how my parents are," I responded.

"You stayed over at my place all the time when you actually lived here," he pointed out.

"Yeah, but I had my own place, and they didn't know. Now, it'd be like I was flaunting the fact that I was living in sin," I said.

There was silence on the line for a second. "You *do* want to see me, don't you?"

"Of course I do!"

"Well, it doesn't sound like it."

I chalked up his bad mood to the stress and pressures he was under. "Let me see what I can do," I said, not wanting to get into a full-blown argument. "I'm coming home for about a week. I'm sure I can swing at least a few days."

He didn't sound happy, but he conceded. "Whatever you can swing. I haven't seen you in months, you know."

A quick, snippy part of me wanted to say "And whose idea was that?" but I didn't.

"How's it going over there, anyway?" he said.

"It's going a lot better," I said, my voice brightening. "It's still weird, but I'm getting some real work done at Sansoro, and I've made some friends. They even took me out to dinner for my birthday," I said, with a chuckle, and then told him the Italian restaurant debacle. He laughed, and it felt as if the rough patch was behind us.

"Speaking of birthday, did you like what I sent you?"

"You sent me a gift?" I asked.

Another pause. "You didn't get it? I wondered why you didn't send an e-mail or anything. I mean, I know you've been careful not to bug me during this semester, but it's not like you not to say thank you."

"It must've gotten lost in the mail," I wailed. "Damn it! Well, what was it?"

He laughed. "I figured you were probably missing real food, so I sent chocolate and peanut butter."

I didn't bring up the fact that the chocolate and candy over here rocked. It was the thought that counted, and I really was glad he'd remembered my birthday. "I miss peanut butter," I admitted.

"Well, you'll have as much peanut butter as you want. I'll stock the pantry before you get here," he said. "Love you, sweetie."

"I love you, too, Ethan," I said. "Feel better, okay? Don't let stuff get you too crazy."

He sighed. "Okay. Take care, and I'll see you soon."

I hung up and then wandered out into the living room. Ichiro was awake, surprisingly. His mom was working on the meals for the day. He was eating chocolate, I noticed. Not unusual, for Ichiro—Kit Kats were his breakfast of video game champions.

I looked down at the wrappers . . . and noticed a box. These weren't just the usual convenience store haul, I noticed. They were truffles.

Nah. He couldn't have.

I went into the kitchen, where Mrs. Kanai was making some sticky rice. "Excuse me, " I said, "my boyfriend sent me a birthday package with some food in it. Did any packages arrive?"

"I don't think so," she said. "Unless someone came while I was grocery shopping one day."

Well, that narrowed it down. But Ichiro was studiously avoiding looking at me, instead of sending me his trademark glare.

With a sense of foreboding, I went to the box of truffles and picked it up, ignoring Ichiro's yelp of outrage.

Swiss Alps Chocolate Shop, the box said.

Groverton, New York.

I spun on Ichiro. "You thief!"

He hissed at me, like a feral animal. Mrs. Kanai came out, rice spoon in hand. "What's happened?" she asked.

I showed her the box. "These are the chocolates that my boyfriend sent me for my birthday," I said, showing her the Groverton stamp. "Where's the rest of it, you sneak? Where's the peanut butter?"

"You're living in my house!" he yelled back. "It came here, and I got to it first. It's my right!"

I was way too pissed and way too tired of this kid's sense of entitlement to even let Mrs. Kanai's murmured apologies sway me. "You are a spoiled brat," I said. "You get away with murder. But if you touch any more of my stuff, I will make sure you're sorry!"

"What are you going to do?" he asked, looking at his mom with a sense of smug superiority.

"You just wait, pal," I said in English. "Try it again, and you'll *see* what I do to you!"

Mrs. Kanai put a hand on my shoulder. "I am so sorry! This is terrible. Ichi-kun, how could you?" she asked, her tone plaintive. "Of course, my husband and I will reimburse you for your loss."

"That isn't the point," I said, trying not to yell. It wasn't— Actually, yes, it *was* her fault, I thought. The kid was a beast and she was an enabler, and I had had it up to my eyeballs with the whole dynamic. "Ichiro needs to knock this off."

"Ichi-kun can't help himself," she said.

"Well, he'd better," I said. "Because next time—" I couldn't even verbalize what would happen next time. I'd probably create an international incident, but by God, that kid wouldn't be smirking. I frowned at him.

He growled at me. I growled back.

Mrs. Kanai looked scared of both of us as I shut Yukari's door.

May 15, Monday

It was a day of firsts. I'd never seen Morimoto in a shirt and tie before. I'd never been upstairs to the twentieth floor before—the super-exec stomping grounds. And finally, and perhaps most disturbing, I'd never seen Yoda nervous before. He was even grouchier than usual, although his suit was slightly less rumpled.

We were going to be discussing the "American Project," as Yoda was calling it, with Yoda's boss, a Mr. Tanaka. He was apparently a big muckety-muck, even if he wasn't on the executive board. I still hadn't quite figured out the organization chart in this place, and I doubt Yoda would've given me a copy of one had I asked.

Chisato had done a bunch of rough sketches; Morimoto and I had hammered out an outline of what the series could be and what the small first story would be. Yoda had prepared some kind of market research, I think. So we were as ready as we were going to get. Of course, I had no idea how these things ran; I'd never done anything remotely like it back at my old job. Did they just say "we love it" or "we hate it" or what? I wished we had Chisato there. First, because I would have loved for her to get more exposure, and, second, because it would've been comforting to have another woman there. As it was, I could expect no comfort from Morimoto or Yoda, who had their own issues to deal with.

"Akamatsu-san. I am glad we could meet."

Mr. Tanaka walked in, looking like a Japanese version of Ricardo Montalban, all gray hair, nice suit, and super-suave demeanor. He was very *GQ*, especially compared to Yoda's grumpy/frumpy demeanor.

Yoda and Mr. Tanaka exchanged bows, then Mr. Tanaka looked at the two of us remaining. Morimoto looked as if he was going to hurl. Instead, Mr. Tanaka and Morimoto exchanged bows, and Morimoto bobbled while handing him a card. "I've been interested in hearing about this project, Morimoto-san," Mr. Tanaka said, his voice casual. "Very interested."

Morimoto made some unintelligible noises. That didn't bode well for the oral part of our presentation.

Mr. Tanaka took Morimoto's incoherence in stride. I guess he got a lot of that from underlings. Then he looked at me. He had brown eyes, I noticed—not surprising. His smile was gentle, but those eyes were a little more mercenary. They didn't have Nobuko's open hostility or polite fuck-you quality, but I still knew he wasn't one of us, not necessarily.

This was going to be a bitch, I could just tell.

"And Risa-san," he said, bowing. I returned the bow and kicked myself for still not having business cards. "I must say I was surprised to see our intern was a part of this project, but at the same time, I'm not surprised. After all, we ran the contest specifically to get the attention of the American market, and your contest entry itself was charming and much more American than anything we would've published."

"Thank you," I said. "I've been learning a lot since I've been here, and I'm excited to be a part of this—"

"She's just been assisting on this," Yoda interrupted, glaring at me. He had pretty much told me not to talk during this whole thing, but I thought he meant just during the presentation part. Apparently he meant not to talk at all. I took his cue—this was too important to Chisato and Morimoto for me to mess it up because I didn't know proper etiquette.

We all sat down at the long cherry conference table. The walls were fabric, I noticed—they looked like a sand color with swirls of dove gray and seemed to be made of brushed silk, which seemed strange to me. Still, it looked very impressive. A secretary came in and poured each of us green tea in a delicate porcelain cup with a single cherry blossom painted on it. Now I was starting to get as nervous as Morimoto and Yoda. This was more formal than anything I'd ever seen. Of course, I'd been in staff meetings where supervisors had been fairly blunt. Factories were like that. I couldn't imagine my old boss having our receptionist pour tea for people. Getting coffee in Styrofoam cups was usually a signal of some kind of celebration.

"So, tell me about this project," Mr. Tanaka finally said, after we'd all taken a few sips of the tea.

Yoda sent one last glare at me to remind me to shut up, and for once, I did as I was told. He launched into his idea: a little launch, just a small side project, experimenting with the story. He then turned it over to Morimoto, who stammered and stuttered his way through presenting our story line. It was all I could do not to correct him or jump in, but Yoda was watching me like a hawk, and it would probably be professionally humiliating for Morimoto to be corrected by an intern/assistant, so I stayed silent. Finally, Morimoto showed the sketches that Chisato had drawn. Even unfinished, they showed a great deal of energy. She really was brilliant. If nothing else came of this, I hoped she'd break out as a result.

Mr. Tanaka stayed silent, too, throughout the presentation. Morimoto still looked green around the gills, but at least it looked like he'd be keeping his lunch. Yoda was scowling so hard, you could barely see his eyes for the folds in his forehead. It was as if his face had imploded. They waited for some sort of feedback. I was on the edge of my seat.

"Intriguing," Mr. Tanaka finally said, and I swear I saw Yoda let out a breath of relief. "The story line would need adjustments, of course. But I like setting the story someplace other than Japan. And I think there is a lot of potential here."

I smiled broadly—I couldn't help it. Success! Finally! I'd never felt a rush like it before, certainly not at the semiconductor plant.

"There is only one question I have," Mr. Tanaka said, putting my glee on hold. "Who did these drawings?"

Yoda looked at Morimoto, whose mouth was moving like a fish but no words were coming out. "This is a new artist, a relative unknown, working on spec," Yoda explained. "Her drawing style fit the direction we wanted to go. She can draw both traditionally and in a more unconventional vein."

"I see that. Her drawing is very good." Mr. Tanaka paused, as he flipped over a few more pages. "Excellent, actually."

"Her name is Chisato-san," I said, and Yoda growled at me. Well, it was his own fault. Chisato had to break out somehow, and if her name didn't get around . . .

"That doesn't sound familiar," Mr. Tanaka said, "but my question is, are you set on working with her?"

Now my stomach fell. I saw the project as a package deal. It was stupid and showed my inexperience, but it never occurred to me that they might just take the idea and hand it over to someone else. Another artist. Hell, I supposed they could move it to another person on the editorial staff.

I knew I was expendable. I didn't want anybody else to be.

"Did Tanaka-san have a different artist in mind?" Yoda said, his voice deceptively mild.

"I was just talking to one of our artists the other day, about just this sort of project," Mr. Tanaka said, in an equally mild voice. "I promised to keep my eye out for any opportunity."

I had a bad feeling about this. So apparently did Morimoto, who sat up straight in his seat, like someone had tied him to it.

"I was surprised at the request, since she's quite busy, but can you believe Nobuko-san would like to try an American/manga hybrid?" Mr. Tanaka really did sound stunned. "She's so big named, so established, and yet she's willing to take this big a risk. It's very admirable."

"Very," Yoda said, his expression showing nothing. Morimoto just went white as a sheet.

"She was actually surprised she hadn't been offered a chance at it to begin with," Mr. Tanaka added, with a note of reproof.

"But—" I started. Yoda shot a look at me that would've frozen the teapot in front of us. I shut up.

"I wouldn't dream of wasting Nobuko-san's time with so small a project," Yoda said, and his own diplomacy shocked the hell out of me. He went from grumpy troll to car salesman in a matter of five seconds. I stared, unable to believe the transformation. He was even smiling.

"I think a small project would be a safer way to test our idea,"

Yoda said. "See if it even works. Nobuko-san is so busy with so many award-winning projects. Maybe after this experiment, if it is successful. Maybe then she could do something on a larger scale."

Mr. Tanaka nodded, processing Yoda's argument. Then he shook his head. "Nobuko-san was very persuasive. And if she's involved, well, I think we could take it on a larger scale. Why waste her talent, as you say?"

Yoda gritted his teeth but nodded.

"What editorial team did you have in mind?" Mr. Tanaka said, as if the team he'd be replacing wasn't in the room hearing him say they'd be getting the ax. Morimoto looked at me, his expression one of utter misery.

"Morimoto-san is very competent," Yoda said. "And we still think the project should be small. I would not want to take resources from the rest of the team . . . at least, not yet."

I sighed. At least Morimoto had been saved.

"And Risa-san will continue to assist, of course," Mr. Tanaka said. "That will be a good publicity angle, as well: our American, helping with an American project!"

I grinned, even though I felt like some kind of token—the token American, a combination pet and mascot. Ugh.

"I will let you coordinate things with Nobuko-san, then," Mr. Tanaka said, getting up. The meeting was over. "It was nice meeting you all."

We filed out and went back downstairs. Morimoto was shaking.

"Why would she do that?" he asked Yoda. "She said she wasn't interested. We approached her—Risa-san approached her—and she said no!"

Yoda was grumbling under his breath.

I thought about it. "Maybe . . . maybe she thought if it got this far, she didn't want us to be successful without her," I said. It sounded plausible.

I didn't believe it, but it sounded plausible.

"That could be it," Morimoto said, sounding vaguely cheered.

"Or maybe she didn't want Chisato leaving her," I added.

Morimoto blanched.

I looked at Yoda, who didn't say anything. He just looked at me, shaking his head.

I got the feeling that Nobuko might've had something even more nefarious in mind, but hey, I'm paranoid that way. All I knew for sure was that Chisato was screwed, and we'd just gained a Nobuko-sized stone around our neck. I had no idea how we were going to get out of this one.

I did know that work was about to be a lot less fun.

May 17, Wednesday

"I DON'T KNOW WHAT I'M GOING TO DO," CHISATO SAID. AT LEAST, that's what I think she said. It was hard to hear her over the noise of the amusement park. It was warm, getting hotter as spring slowly slid into summer. The place had a country-fair-like feel to it.

I knew it was a bad place to meet with her, all things considered, but Yukari assured me that if an amusement park couldn't lift Chisato's spirits, then nothing could. I got roped along. I now realized Yukari simply wanted to go to the amusement park, one of the oldest in the city, sort of an Atlantic City boardwalk on steroids.

Chisato was not cheering up. Although, as Yukari said, I got the feeling that nothing could.

"You tried," I said, knowing that was a piss-poor balm, and then I handed her some carnival food. There's a thing in Japan: you're not supposed to eat outside. Or if you are going to eat outside, you need to sit down somewhere, like a picnic area or something, some makeshift table or bench. No walking with your burger, grabbing a quick fry on the way somewhere. It was considered uncouth. The only exception to this rule was fair-style food, which was pretty much the same as our idea of carnival food, all things considered. I had bought her a funnel cake, for lack of a better term: a fried dough cake, although in Japan it was filled with red bean paste. She smiled weakly and accepted it, biting into it without thought. I was forever trying to feed this girl, I thought. She definitely looked like somebody needed to take care of her.

"It wasn't your fault that Nobuko-san decided to step in and muck things up," I said, causing her to gasp a little and consequently choke on her funnel cake.

"I shouldn't have overstepped my bounds," Chisato said. She was wearing her usual drab clothing. That would be the other thing: not just fattening her up but tricking her out, as it were. I'll bet Yukari and a credit card could go a long way toward making Chisato a force to be reckoned with. "I shouldn't have even asked you for the opportunity. They will promote me, eventually. Nobuko-san knows that I am a big help and that I have talent."

"She definitely knows you have talent," I said sourly. Hell, I would bet that was the main reason Nobuko had gone to the lengths she had. She didn't want to lose her workhorse—or worse, be outshone by her little *assisto*. It was a dangerous situation.

"Anyway, I appreciate your helping me," she said and took another tentative bite of funnel cake. "You've been so nice . . . bringing me out with your friends, buying me food."

I sighed. She sounded like a beaten dog. It was obvious she'd already given up the fight.

For a second, I felt sad for her and incensed on her behalf. In weird ways, she reminded me of myself. I mean, I had the Falloya stubbornness in spades, no question. But that stubbornness was usually used to keep me where I was. I didn't want to go for supervisor at the plant because I didn't want the responsibility. I didn't want to travel because it made me uncomfortable. I was used to arguing and digging my heels in when I didn't want to do something. It was a neat change to use my genetic tenacity toward something I actively *wanted*.

Chisato didn't have my stubbornness, that much was obvious. But she did have a natural proclivity toward staying where she was, and that was scary. I hadn't loved my job, but it hadn't occurred to me to look for anything better; I was where I was, and that was that. Now I was becoming a little Ms. Gordon Gecko, getting involved in office intrigues and corporate politics. And I was dragging Chisato with me, for her own good, because I knew if I didn't, she'd be miserable and in exactly the same place in ten years.

I suddenly forgave Stacy, Perry, and Ethan for all their pushing. *I need to call them or write a note, or something.*

"Risa-san?"

I saw that Chisato was giving me a curious look. I'd blinked out there for a minute. "I'm sorry," I said, tugging her toward another food vendor. "I was just thinking."

They were selling flavored ices. I was thinking of the funnel cake as dinner, and now Chisato and I could use some dessert. I bought a lychee-flavored ice and bought Chisato a cherry-flavored one. She protested for a minute, then accepted it, and it seemed to make her a lot happier.

"You can't just give up, Chisato," I said, around a mouthful of the sugary ice. "You're brilliant. Tanaka-san was very impressed with your drawings."

Her eyes went round, like a little kid's. "Really?"

"You bet." I sighed. "If Nobuko-san hadn't butted in, I think you really could make your name with this one."

She looked dreamy for a minute, then shook her head. "Nobuko-san would not be happy. She will not like losing her only *assisto*. She has been through so many—she says it's hard to find someone compatible."

I grimaced. Read: someone docile and browbeaten enough to put up with her shit and not look for another job or try to strike out on her own.

"Well, did any of her other *assistos* move on to new projects?" I asked.

Chisato thought about it, biting her lip. Then she shook her head. "Nobuko-san said they didn't have the gift."

"I'll just bet she did," I muttered darkly. "Listen, Nobuko-san might've taken this project over, but you'll still be doing key drawings. At least Tanaka-san knows your name now. The important thing will be making sure they know you contributed. Then we'll be able to leverage that exposure and start to convince them that they've got a good artist on the rise."

I was excited by the prospect. It was, I don't know, strategic and exciting, like we were spies or something. Besides, it would get Chisato closer to her dream and closer to where she deserved to be. I was all about that.

"Why are you helping me?" she asked, genuinely mystified. "This seems to mean more to you than it does to me." Then she smiled shyly. "Almost."

It was the most straightforward I'd ever heard Chisato speak, which was good. Still, she had a point. I was getting pushy. I thought again of Stacy and Perry.

"You're my friend," I said. "At least, I consider you my friend. I don't mean to pressure you."

She gave me a small smile. "You are my friend."

That was comforting. "I want my friends to do well," I said. "I hate to see people trapped, especially by bullies. I hate to see people not get what they want." I thought about all the times I'd done things to help Ethan: picked up his laundry when he was too exhausted from working and going to school, or cooked him meals and dropped them off. Or offering to babysit Stacy's baby, Thomas, when she and her husband were exhausted. "Helping's just in my nature. But if I'm pushing, please tell me. I don't really want to force you to 'improve' if that's not what you want." I knew what that was like! "Everyone has to go at their own pace. Usually, I'm slower than most. I don't know what it is about being over here, but apparently something in the water is making me ambitious."

I meant it to be a joke and I laughed, but she nodded as if I'd made a profound insight.

"You are also doing what you're meant to do, Risa-san," she said seriously. "I don't know what you did in America, but you are a very good editor. I have worked with several—Nobuko-san gets a new editor every six months to a year—and I have never worked with one as insightful as you. Or as willing to help." She smiled then. "You have no idea how helpful that is."

Considering the poor kid was doing everything on her own, I could just bet. "Half the time, I don't know what I'm doing," I admitted. "Still, erasing pencil lines isn't brain surgery. It's not that hard."

"But you didn't mind," she repeated. "And you thought of other things to do to help. You're having fun, aren't you?"

"More than I have had at any other job in my life," I said. I couldn't believe how true that was until I said it out loud.

"So, when you go back to the United States, what are you going to do?" she said, echoing Red's question from my birthday.

I swallowed hard. It was getting harder and harder to evade that question. At the same time, a new idea had been hatching, nascent still but insidious.

I could keep doing what I'm doing.

It would take negotiation. It would also mean leaving Groverton, and that would complicate things enormously.

"One thing at a time." I evaded. As nice as it was to have a friend in Chisato and even Yukari, I didn't feel either of them were really close enough to me to trust with that kind of discussion. It was times like this that I missed Stacy. Even Ethan would be too much of a problem-solving guy to be able to really get the emotional ramifications of changing your life radically.

Chisato smiled. "It's easy to change someone else's life," she said quietly.

I realized it was a wry observation, and I smiled back at her.

"Speaking of changing someone else's life," I said, clumsily changing the subject, "I think my next plan is getting you into the office. There's someone you need to meet." I chuckled at the thought. "His name is Akamatsu-sensei."

She gasped. Morimoto must've told her some horror stories. "Morimoto-san's supervisor? Why would he see me?"

"Because I'm going to ask him to."

May 19, Friday

It was the end of the day, and I needed to talk to Yoda.

I'd been mulling over how to approach him since I'd hung out with Chisato at the amusement park on Wednesday. He knew her work. He knew who she was, in theory. But you'd have to have a heart of stone not to be moved by Chisato's plight once you got a look at her little woebegone face, and as mean as Yoda liked to pose, I knew his type. He was a burned marshmallow: dark and forbidding and crusty on the outside, sure, but sweet and utterly mushy on the inside. All I needed to do was get those two in a room together, and he'd see why I was pushing so hard.

I decided to remind him I was taking a week and a half off in June for Ethan's graduation. That was a good excuse, and then I'd bring up the Chisato thing, see if there was some way for them to meet while I was gone, maybe. Morimoto probably wouldn't be a huge help in that arena. I don't think he wanted to meet with Yoda privately if he could help it, much less introduce his new girlfriend.

Well, I'd just have to see how it'd go.

I waited until the S-girls left, then went to Yoda's office and knocked on the door.

"*Hai!*"

He sounded crabby. Not a great sign. I let myself in anyway.

He had his suit jacket off and his shirtsleeves pushed up, and his tie was askew. His hair was sticking up like a haystack. He looked like a poster for the harried executive at work. I almost cracked a smile, except he looked over at me, and I knew he wouldn't find it amusing. "Excuse me, Akamatsu-sensei," I said, keeping my tone mellow.

"What are you still doing here?"

Definitely not a promising sign. "Is this a bad time? I can talk to you tomorrow, if that's better," I said, trying to sound as conciliatory as possible. I wanted a favor from him, it wouldn't do to ask while he was in a bad mood.

"No, no. What? Do you need more work or something?" His eyes narrowed. "Or is it to talk about your big 'project' with Morimoto-san? Because I'm leaving that in his hands. He's going to have to meet with Nobuko-san and figure out how to make it all work."

Oh, hell. I hadn't heard about that. I needed to talk to Morimoto, too, before I left. "There was a little personal business I wanted to discuss, actually," I said quickly.

"Personal?" He looked as if the word made his skin crawl.

"I just wanted to remind you that I would be gone for a week and a half, starting June seventh," I said, figuring that was just polite. "Then I wanted to—"

"Wait. You're leaving?" He sounded appalled. "But you're an intern! You don't get vacation time! You just got here!"

"Uh . . . ," I floundered. "It was part of my acceptance of the internship terms. My boyfriend is graduating from business school, and I promised I'd come home," I said. "I haven't been home for five months."

His expression clearly showed no sympathy. "You've only been with us for five months," he pointed out, "and you're already wandering off for long travels. This doesn't look good at all, Risa-san. It doesn't show *loyalty*."

"But I already promised," I said. "I booked the tickets back in February. Sansoro knew that I needed to— It's built into my contract," I pointed out.

He harrumphed speculatively. "That's why you'll just stay an intern," he said.

"I didn't realize I had a chance at anything else," I shot back.

That was lippy, I realized, aghast. He stared at me, his face torn between cruel amusement and irritation at my insolence. "You're from America," he said, in a slightly mocking tone. "From what I could see, from your behavior with myself and Nobuko-san and Tanaka-san, why, I thought you'd be running the place in the next year or so."

I could feel my cheeks blushing at that one. Had I been that big a pain in the ass?

"You have the ambition to start these wild projects and to get other people on board with them. You stir up trouble," he said sharply. "And then you leave for two weeks—"

"A week and a half," I corrected weakly, as if those few extra days would help matters.

"A *week and a half*," he emended, "and you expect people to see you as serious?"

What was he asking? Did he want me to just cancel everything, cancel seeing my fiancé achieving the goal of his life, simply because it would look bad and people wouldn't take me seriously?

"They're not seeing me as serious now," I said.

"This won't help!"

I sighed. "I appreciate your advice," I said, keeping my voice steady and not being snotty, like when people say "we value your feedback" but really mean "shut the hell up."

"Yes, but are you going to take it?"

I bit my lip for a second, so no quick, nasty quip could leap out. I took a deep breath and counted to ten. "You yourself told Tanaka-san that I was simply assisting on this project," I said. "As far as anyone is concerned, all I am is the American intern, the gaijin flunky."

His eyes narrowed. "I would not put it that strongly."

"But you have," I said, not caring if it was insolent or not. "And the bottom line is, from what I can see, I don't have a future at Sansoro. I am a publicity item. And while I am excited about Morimoto-san's project and I want to help Chisato-san, I also have a life waiting for me. My boyfriend, my family—they are also important."

He didn't say anything, although his scowl ironed out a little bit.

"So I'm going to go," I said. "If that is a problem . . ."

I let it hang. I had no idea how to rectify it if it was a problem.

I stood in front of his desk, and he sat, studying me. It had all the feel of *High Noon*.

Finally, he caved. "Go on your vacation," he said. "I'm sure we will manage without you somehow, for a week and a half."

Ugh. That was not how that was supposed to go, at all. I nodded. Then, figuring I had nothing else to lose, I said, "There is one more thing."

He let out a short, barking laugh. "What now?"

"I would like you to meet Chisato-san," I said.

"Why?"

"Because she is brilliant," I said.

He grunted. "I've seen her work. She's not bad."

"She's a hard worker. She's enormously loyal—she's worked with Nobuko-san for five years," I said, and I saw that that did impress him. Nobuko-san went through employees like toilet paper. Almost literally.

"I still don't see why I need to meet her."

"She could use some guidance," I said. "I don't have the experience to help her, and it would mean a lot if she could talk to you about the business."

I was making that up. I mean, I'm sure it would help her, but I'm also sure she'd probably shut up like a clam in the face of the Great and Terrible Akamatsu. Which, with any luck, would only endear her to him more.

Here was hoping, anyway.

"So, you're asking for a favor," he said. "On top of leaving for vacation."

"Yes." I grinned. "Some nerve, huh?"

He stared at me, startled. "Americans," he muttered.

"It would mean a lot. I think she's got great talent, and she just needs a chance." I looked out the door, making sure no one was listening. "And you know Nobuko-san won't give her that chance."

"That is disrespectful," he said sharply. "Nobuko-san is also a brilliant artist."

I didn't add anything. It was disrespectful to talk about her in such a way, without her being there to defend herself. At the same time, I knew he realized it was the truth. Chisato would be buried by the woman if somebody didn't rescue her.

He sighed. "I don't want to anger Nobuko-san by making the whole thing seem on the sly," he said. "I will tell her I'm interested in meeting Chisato-san and seeing how far along she's progressing. I do not want to meet in anything secretive. It would not be right."

I winced. Apparently I was just doing things really wrong. "If you think that would work," I said, not adding *if you think that wouldn't hurt her more.* I wondered if Nobuko would retaliate if he even asked.

"Are you sure you want me to do this?"

Apparently he'd thought of the same thing. But if he wasn't going to meet with her privately, hell. Maybe he could save her.

"Let me talk to Chisato-san," I said. "But I appreciate your offer. And I certainly don't want to do anything to offend anyone."

"Of course not," he said. "Why start now, yes?"

I realized he was joking. Sort of. It would be good to go home and clear my head of all this stuff, I realized. I was getting pretty mixed up.

June 8, Thursday

I felt like an alien in my parents' home. I hadn't lived there since I was, what, twenty, but I visited plenty, so it shouldn't have felt as strange as it did. I'd gotten in, and they'd picked me up at the train station in Poughkeepsie, which wasn't far away. My mom had asked how I liked Tokyo, stuff like that. My father claimed that I'd lost weight (with that undertone of worry that I loved about him). I'd slept on and off, trying to ride the waves of jet lag that came with the territory. Still, to wake up and smell Dad's brewed coffee, to not hear video games . . . hell, even getting used to the absolute silence of a small-town night was weird, after Tokyo's din and Yukari's persistent snoring.

Now, it was about eleven o'clock, and it was time for me to have a meal. I wasn't going to even bother labeling which meal anymore. If I wanted a hamburger at seven in the morning or scrambled eggs at eleven o'clock at night, I would just go with it.

About half an hour later I was fixing frozen waffles with peanut butter, bananas, and honey when Stacy and Perry stopped by. I let them in, and for a second it felt eerily like high school, when they'd stop by during the summer. Still, there were some differences. The slight bulge in Stacy's stomach being the first one I noticed.

I gestured to her. "You look different," I hinted, crossing my arms.

"I've been working out," she deadpanned. "You're cooking. You're not eating meat, are you? I've been having trouble with meat."

"So you *are* pregnant," I said. "Don't worry, I'm just making, er, elevensies. Frozen waffles."

"That sounds good," she said.

"I'll make you one," I promised and led them both into the kitchen.

Perry looked pretty much the same. He was wearing his work uniform: blue cotton polo shirt, with the logo of his computer repair company on the pocket, and a pair of khakis. He did look eager, though. "Tell me you brought pictures," he said.

I shook my head and then laughed at his crestfallen expression. "I'll e-mail you some from my phone," I answered, to try and cheer him up. "With everything going on, I really didn't have the time. And I never think to take pictures. You know that."

He nodded, although he still looked pretty disappointed.

Stacy sat down heavily in a chair at the kitchen table, with Perry flanking her. I gave her one of my waffles and popped two more into the toaster. She ate it slowly, carefully, as if unsure of its staying power.

"Morning sickness kicking your ass, huh?" I asked.

She nodded. "It wasn't this bad with Thomas," she said. "Roger's counting on that meaning it's a girl. I just found out last month."

"And you didn't tell me?"

"I tried calling you," she said, "but it's been crazy. I've been trying to get them to hire somebody else at work, so I can get them up to speed before the maternity leave, but you know how they are. Morons, the lot of them. And they still haven't filled your position. Keep claiming 'budget cuts' and 'hiring freeze.' It's ridiculous."

I ate my waffle and listened to her complain about the people we knew—people at work, my old boss. It was, again, odd, like it should've felt more comfortable but didn't. It was like watching a movie with the soundtrack off by a second. You could make out what was going on, but it was still slightly jarring.

"You're still jet-lagged, aren't you?" Perry finally asked. "You've got that spacey look about you."

I nodded apologetically. "It's only my first day. I figure I'll probably get fully acclimated just before I have to go back," I joked.

"Well, at least you don't look miserable," Stacy said, finally finishing up her waffle and refusing a second. "I thought you'd be kissing the ground, thankful to be home."

"I still plan to get a chocolate peanut butter milkshake," I said, "but otherwise I'm doing pretty well, I think."

"See?" Perry was practically preening. "I knew that once you sucked it up and quit whining, you'd get along fine. You just needed to give it some time. How's the manga gig going?"

"Well," I said, and briefly sketched out what was going on: Morimoto's grand plan, Yoda's help and interference, Nobuko playing evil stepmother to Chisato's Cinderella. It sounded like *As the World Turns* by the time I was done.

"Sorry," I finished. "That was probably as boring as vacation pictures. They're always interesting to the person who took 'em, but to everybody else . . ."

"No, no," Perry said, and Stacy nodded. "Actually, it sounds really neat."

But there was something weird in his tone. I looked at Stacy, trying to read her expression.

"You sound pretty settled in," she added. "Almost at home."

"Yeah, well, it took a while, and I still want to kill Ichiro at various points," I amended, "but I never had a little brother, so I guess that's probably pretty normal."

"You're getting into work mode," Stacy said. "I remember when you got that way at the semiconductor plant. They still miss you." She paused a beat, then studied my face as she said, "They've completely screwed up your ordering system, you know. And that project you were working on, for the bond orders and the clearance protocol? Scrapped."

I felt a little pang at that. I was proud of what I'd done at my old job, even if I didn't love the position itself.

"It's going to take you forever to fix it," she said, sighing. "I don't even want to think of what state it's going to be in when you get back. You wouldn't happen to have any herbal tea, would you?"

"I'll look," I said, then started rummaging around in the cupboards for whatever tea stash Mom had hidden about. I guess I hadn't really thought about getting my job back, didn't think of it as a possibility. I'd been so immersed in just making it on a day-to-day basis in Japan that I hadn't thought as far ahead as December. "How far along are you, anyway?"

"Just two and a half months," Stacy replied, then made a thankful sound when she saw the orange spice herbal tea bag I held up. "That's great, thanks."

"Which puts you on maternity leave . . . when?"

"About end of December," she said. "I might take off a little earlier. If they're still being lame and haven't filled your position, they'd take you back in a snap. Even if they have filled your position, they'd be glad to take you back just because you know the job. Whatever new hire they pull on would probably be flailing around."

I thought about it for a second. "Well, December's a ways away," I said.

Perry and Stacy exchanged a look. "That's so not you," Perry said, finally.

"What? Because I'm such a planner?" That was a joke!

"No, normally you'd be able to tell us how many days you had until you got home," Stacy replied. "You really *are* feeling at home there, aren't you?"

"Isn't that what you guys said to do?" I felt a little stung at their response, for some reason. "I'm having a pretty good time. I do miss you guys, of course, more than you'd believe. And Ethan. I made such a good case, I'm staying over at his place the rest of the week—and my dad barely blinked."

Perry let out a low whistle. "You must've been pretty persuasive."

"Well, they figure we're probably going to get married at some point," I said.

"Yeah, how's that going?" Stacy leaned forward, all excited at catching some gossip. "And you know I'm planning on being matron of honor, right?"

"Of course," I said automatically. "I don't know. I'm sure there's a plan of some sort, and it'll all fall into place once I get home. I'm not worrying about it for the moment."

"Okay, now you're just acting weird," Stacy said, pushing back from the table. "You've wanted to marry Ethan for years, and now you're all casual about it?"

"I love Ethan, and I want to marry him," I snapped. "Jeez, why is everyone acting like I'm the one with the problem?"

Perry and Stacy stared at me, and suddenly I felt as if I'd thrown a temper tantrum—pulled an Ichiro, basically.

"Sorry," I said, rubbing at my eyes with the heels of my hands. "It's just . . . I am having a good time, and I'm just . . . chilling, I guess. I'm taking a vacation from my life. I'm sure I'll come back, and I want to get married, and I'll probably get my old job back if they'll even take me. But for right now, if I focus on that, I'll just make myself miserable while I'm gone. And I don't want to feel that way. You know?"

They nodded, but they still looked kind of wary. "We're not trying to push you," Perry said. "We just, well, we miss you."

"Should've thought of that before you convinced me to go," I pointed out, only half-joking.

"Believe me, if we'd realized what it would be like with you gone," he said, "we might've."

We all laughed at that one, although it occurred to me later that it really wasn't all that funny. Which explained why I felt so uncomfortable.

CHAPTER 11

June 13, Tuesday

ETHAN'S GRADUATION WAS BEAUTIFUL. I WAS IN THE CROWD, SIT-
ting on a hard plastic seat, wearing a pink sundress and trying hard
not to get sunburned. The ceremony itself was typical, with a few
speakers who were boring although trying very hard to be inspirational. With my last residual bits of jet lag, I was lucky not to simply
nod off with my usual travel-narcolepsy. But I'd made it this far, and
I saw him, fidgeting, looking great in his navy blue robe with various
tassels and stuff, that represented the honors he'd gotten.

"Ethan Lonnel!" the speaker finally said.

Ethan stepped forward, took his diploma, and shook hands. Then
he turned to the cameraman waiting and flashed a smile brighter than
any I'd ever seen on him. His family and I were cheering wildly, and his
mom was taking pictures while crying. I waved and he winked at me.

It was a great moment.

Afterward, Ethan's parents and his aunt and uncle took us out to dinner. Ethan looked drugged, he was so relieved. He kept laughing, no matter what was going on. I was glad to see him so relaxed and happy. I didn't realize just how tightly wound he'd been, the whole time I'd known him.

He leaned over and kissed me, in front of his parents and everything. "I'm so glad it's over," he said, for what had to be the thirtieth time.

"I'm glad, too," I said.

"So, what now, kiddo?" his father asked, swirling his whiskey sour around in his glass. "MBA, that's a big step."

"I've got some interviews lined up in the city," Ethan said, and I could see some tension creep back into his body as he spoke. I put a hand on his knee, nothing sexual, just comforting. He grinned back at me. "It shouldn't be that bad. Some places I talked to while I was still in school. I'm hoping, with offers and counteroffers, to have a new job by August or so."

"Wow! That's fantastic!" His mom beamed. She was short, with dyed honey-blond hair and a round, moonlike face. "I'm so proud of you, Ethan."

He looked bashful, which was cute as all hell. I was glad I was staying at his house tonight. My family was having a little get together for me on Friday night, and they'd made it a celebration for him, too, but for now it would be nice to just be the two of us for a few days. He'd even taken a few days off to be with me. I was looking forward to seeing what life was like with a laid-back Ethan, twenty-four seven.

"And what about you, missy?" his dad asked.

I realized he was referring to me—"kiddo" and "missy" were his favorite appellations for people younger than he was—so I spoke up. "I'm very proud of him, too."

He laughed, a booming laugh. "That's not what I meant. What are your plans?"

"I'm still finishing up my internship in Japan," I said, looking at Ethan. I thought he'd told them, but maybe he hadn't—he had been awfully busy. "I won this contest—"

"Oh, yes, dear, we know all about that," Ethan's mother said, waving her hand. "But now—"

"Mom, you're spoiling it," Ethan said warningly.

I had no idea what was going on, so I looked at Ethan, waiting for him to explain.

"Man, do you guys have to be so impatient?" Ethan asked around a sigh, and his tension level was suddenly back. "I was going to do this later, around dessert, but I guess now's as good a time as any."

I stared at him as he pulled a small felt box out of his pocket and got down on one knee. The noise level in the restaurant quieted to a low hush, I noticed.

"Lisa Falloya," he said, looking directly into my eyes, "will you marry me?"

I made a little gulp noise. I knew I'd marry Ethan. Sometimes it felt as if I always knew it. Hell, we'd talked about it like it was a foregone conclusion for as long as we were going out. But now, with him kneeling there, box in hand, with his family staring holes into me . . . it didn't feel real. I didn't know what to do.

I must've been frozen like that for a while because he laughed nervously. "Aren't you going to open the box?"

"I thought that was your job," I said inanely, because it hadn't even occurred to me to open it. He laughed again and opened it. The ring was gold, with a big honkin' diamond flashing obscenely.

"It was my mother's," his mom said proudly.

"Wow," I said.

"Is that wow, yes," Ethan pressed, "or wow, I can't believe you're doing this in front of a big crowd of people?"

I looked at him and noticed that he was starting to sweat ever so slightly.

"That's a wow, yes," I said quickly. "Sorry. You really should give a girl a few weeks off from jet lag before proposing to her!"

"It's all the window I had," he said, and then he kissed me, lingering and sweet. I was vaguely aware of his parents cheering again, like they had at the graduation, and people in the restaurant clapping. It was like a big performance. It felt very unreal.

For the rest of the dinner, I sat in a daze, the ring on my finger distracting me. It seemed to clink on the silverware; the diamond flashed at me like a blinker. I kept staring at it.

"I can't believe it, either," Ethan finally whispered to me, and I quickly and reflexively smiled.

"Well, you were planning on it," I replied. "It just . . . feels weird."

He frowned at that, but before he could pursue it, his aunt cleared her throat. "Have you kids set a date yet?"

I stared at her. He'd just asked me twenty minutes ago, for God's sake. How quickly did these people . . .

"I was thinking next spring," Ethan said. "Actually, maybe June at the latest."

I stared at him. "Really?"

He nodded, that easy grin still in place. "Sure. That gives us nine months to a year, and that seems like a good time frame to plan a wedding," he said. "Didn't Janie plan her wedding in ten months?"

"Yes, and it was beautiful," his aunt said. "Of course, June is a beautiful month for a wedding, and that gives you a whole year."

"What do you think, sweetie?" Ethan said. "Do you want to be a June bride?"

"Uh . . ." This was happening awfully fast, was all I could think. "I'm not sure, actually."

"Well, you'll have a little time to think about it," he said. "But not too long. There's a lot involved, I think."

"I'll have Janie get in touch with you," his aunt said. "Would phone be best?"

"E-mail would be better," I said automatically, although I wasn't sure I wanted to be talking to Janie at all, much less about weddings. "Japan has a long time difference, and it's hard to coordinate."

There was a little lull at the table. "Right, Japan," Ethan's mother said. "That could pose a challenge."

Ethan frowned. "What do you mean?"

"Well, you can't possibly expect the girl to plan a wedding from that far away," his mother said, and I could've stood up and hugged her. "When is your internship over, dear?"

"I'm scheduled to get back in December," I said.

"What?" Apparently, Ethan's father hadn't gotten the full briefing on my situation. "What are you doing over there, again?"

"I'm working with a comic book publisher," I said. "I'm editing and working on a series that they're trying to market to the United States."

"How long have you been in that line of work?"

"I haven't, really," I replied. "That's why I agreed to take the internship. I wanted to break in."

Of course, I hadn't realized just how much I meant that until I said it, just that moment.

"How likely do you think it is that you'll get a job in this profession?" his father badgered.

"Harold," Ethan's mom said, with just a note of disapproval.

Ethan's dad winced. If I didn't know better, I'd swear that she kicked him under the table. *Oh, I like you.*

"I'm sure you kids will iron it all out," his father finally conceded.

I looked at Ethan, eager to laugh about this later. But I noticed that Ethan's relaxation had ebbed away, and now he was wearing his "concentration" frown.

"You okay?" I whispered.

"Fine. Just thinking," he said, and I suddenly had a bad feeling about all this. He was counting backward from June.

He was *planning*.

So much for relaxation, I thought, and finished my dinner, my diamond mocking me the whole time.

June 16, Friday

The Falloya Family Get-Together had seemed like a great idea on paper. It was still nice to see the whole family. Unfortunately, I'd told my parents about Ethan's proposal and our impending marriage, and per the family grapevine (which makes the Internet look slow), everyone was congratulating me and family was popping out of the woodwork to see me. It was a little disorienting to see everybody at once. We were at Nana Falloya's house, since that's where most important gatherings happened. I was sitting at her round glass kitchen table, surrounded by aunts, uncles, and cousins. Ethan sat next to me, smiling, rubbing my back, taking the whole thing in stride. Since he'd graduated, he was like Gumby—very mellow, very pliable. It was nice to see, really.

It would've been nicer if I hadn't taken up the role of stress case. I had to pack. My flight left in two days, but I had stuff to mail, stuff to take care of, and all I could think of was, how am I possibly going to handle all of this?

"So you're finally getting married!" my aunt Delores crowed.

I sighed internally, smiled externally, and reached for another cookie.

"You'll spoil your dinner," my mom said automatically, as she breezed through the kitchen getting napkins and silverware. "Your nana made your favorite, stuffed shells."

I put the cookie down on the napkin in front of me.

"So have you set a date?"

"We're thinking spring, June at the latest," Ethan said.

We still hadn't discussed the timing or the planning, really. I had still felt pretty stunned, and we'd been so happy when we were together at his apartment that I hadn't wanted to ruin it with talking about the future.

I seemed to be doing that a lot lately.

"That's a lot of planning," Aunt Delores said, whistling appreciatively. "If you need any help, dear . . . *don't* call me! I barely survived your cousin Iris's wedding!"

My uncle Charlie nodded silently at that one and took another draw off his long-necked Bud Light. My cousin Iris's wedding was legendary. They'd rented out the Groverton Country Club, and the wedding had been outside, with about a million peach roses. The bride had been brought to the carpet in, I kid you not, a white carriage drawn by four white horses. She had a train, six bridesmaids, a ring boy and flower girl, and released butterflies. Uncle Charlie was going to be paying the thing off for years.

"I don't think we're going to want anything quite that elaborate," I said quickly.

My dad grinned, entering the kitchen with more food. "God, I hope not!" He laughed. "But I'm glad my little girl is happy."

I felt a pang of warmth and homesickness, and it only got worse as the rest of my family laughed and Ethan put his arm around my shoulders. This, *this* was what I'd missed when I was in Tokyo. As good a friend as Yukari was becoming, as much fun as I had with Chisato and Morimoto, they couldn't compare to real family. So what was I doing, over there knocking myself out?

My mom walked in. "The table's set, Nana," she said.

"Okay, kids, let's everybody sit down while the food's still hot." Nana was eighty years old but still moved pretty well . . . and still cooked up a storm.

The family erupted into chaos as they left the kitchen. Ethan excused himself to go clean up. I hung back, waiting for everybody else to be seated. My mom hung back, too, I noticed.

"I'd forgotten," I said to her, in Japanese. "I missed this."

She gave me a startled look, then laughed softly. "We never spoke Japanese here," she said. "It's odd to hear. But nice. Your accent is getting very good."

"Well, I use it a lot," I said.

"Are you okay?" she asked, still in Japanese. "You seem a little tense. I didn't want to bring it up in front of the others."

This was odd, this ability to speak frankly at a family gathering. My mom loved the Falloyas dearly, but I knew that she often felt like an outsider. Being the only Japanese person in a full-blooded Italian family would do that.

Funny, I knew exactly how she felt. It seemed as if I'd felt like an outsider most of my life. Now, in Japan, I was the ultimate outsider: the only difference was, I was reveling in it.

"I'm just a little stressed," I replied in Japanese. "I'm back in Tokyo in a few days, I need to pack, and work over there is pretty hectic. I mean, nothing like what Tony's dealing with . . ."

"Never mind Tony," she said. My brother, Tony, couldn't make it to my get-together because he was traveling, for his job. I think he was in Chicago. He said he'd catch me at Christmas. "You've never been the type to be overly stressed out by work. Is anything else the matter?" She paused. "With the wedding?"

"I just have no idea how I'm going to plan it," I said.

Ethan walked in on that and looked at us. "Wow. I've never heard you guys speak Japanese."

"Dinner!" Nana's imperious comment came from the dining room.

My mom and I exchanged a conspiratorial smile, then we all went in and sat down. Sixteen people for dinner—small, by our standards.

Nana said grace, and I dug in. At least I knew there wouldn't be oc-topus smuggled in my entrée, I thought.

"What are you smiling about?" my cousin Anna asked.

"I missed Italian food, real Italian food," I explained, then shared my birthday dinner story. Everyone laughed.

"God, octopus," Nana said. "You must be dying to get home. Oc-topus! In fettuccini alfredo!"

"You get used to it," I said. "Besides, I can get great sushi. I can't get that here."

"Sushi, ugh," Aunt Delores said.

"Still, you must be tired of being so far from home," Nana pressed.

I shrugged. "Actually, I'm getting used to that, too," I said.

The family looked momentarily stunned.

"That is so weird," Anna said. "You used to get homesick going to summer camp. And that was an hour away."

"The first month was tough," I said. "But now, I'm getting better at the language, and I really like my job, and I've got some friends. The really hard part is over."

"It's been a good experience," Nana summed up.

I nodded. "It's been a fantastic experience."

I noticed Ethan looked surprised at that statement.

"When are you supposed to come home?" Nana asked.

"December," I said. "At least, that's what my contract says."

"Contract?" Her fine white eyebrows jumped up. "You had to sign a contract?"

I ate some more shells, enjoying the red sauce and ricotta cheese, and sighed. I finally nodded. "It's hard to get the work visa without one," I said.

"So you're stuck there?"

"Well, I guess so." Although I wouldn't have put it that way.

"There are exit clauses," Ethan interjected. "If she's unhappy or they're unhappy, either one can terminate the contract." He smiled.

"I had just finished business law and looked over her employment contract."

I ate some more of my food. It had been nice of him to look over my contract. He hadn't mentioned the exit clauses before, though.

"So she could leave," Nana said, with a small smile. "If she wanted to."

Uh-oh.

Ethan nodded slowly, and I realized he'd known the same thing. Which was why he'd suggested I come home earlier. "She can leave at any time," he said.

Then he looked at me.

I felt irritation—no, temper—flaring. Suddenly, I was less enthused about my meal. "I made a promise," I said. "I gave my word."

"You just made a promise to get married," Nana pointed out. "That's all I'm saying."

I frowned. "I'm still getting married."

"But the planning!" Aunt Delores put that one in. "Trust me, honey, you're going to want to be here for that. It's harder than you think. Why, when I had to find those damned horses . . ."

Aunt Delores launched into another horror story about Iris and the wedding planning debacle. Ethan rubbed my knee under the table, and I tensed.

"You okay?" he whispered to me.

I didn't answer him for a second, until he squeezed. Then I looked at him.

"I'm still going to Tokyo," I said. "I'm going back."

The rest of the table went quiet at that remark.

"Well, nobody's telling you to drop everything," Nana said, even though, yes, she'd basically said just that. "We're just suggesting you prioritize, dear."

"Churches are hard to reserve," Aunt Delores added helpfully.

I sighed. God save me from helpful relatives.

"It is something to think about," Ethan whispered. "You've got a ton to plan, and it's not like it's a real job. I really think you should consider it. For us."

I grimaced, looking away. Add "helpful fiancés" to the God-save-me list.

June 19, Monday

It was almost a relief to be at the Sansoro office. I was still a tiny bit loopy from the trip back, but I'd discovered that Dramamine had a good effect on me—not that I got airsick or anything, but the stuff knocked me out like rhino tranquilizer. I had slept through the whole flight from San Francisco to Japan. It was nice to wake up well rested. I was still adjusting to time, but I got the feeling I just might be getting the hang of this whole travel thing. The trip from New York to San Fran hadn't been as pleasant, partially because of turbulence and partially because the tension between Ethan and me was still lingering. I kept replaying our conversations in my head, at weird times, when I used to replay stuff like kisses or little moments we'd have together. Now, instead of memories of things that were tender or precious, I was just recalling stress and discomfort.

I thought things were supposed to get more romantic when a guy proposed to you. Of course, I'd never had a guy propose to me before, so I really didn't have a basis for comparison.

I went into Sansoro determined to just buckle down to work and not give Ethan a second thought. I didn't know how well I'd be able to keep that promise to myself, but considering I never really had an ambitious career path or anything, it was amazing how well work could effectively block out any other pesky issues. Like a fiancé who wanted you to cut your trip short and come back and rush a wedding because he's got big business plans and he doesn't want to be put off.

I sighed, putting my lunch down on my desk. *Oh, yeah, Lisa. You're doing a fine job forgetting about Ethan and your little situation.*

The S-girls were already there, not a big surprise. They greeted me quietly, but they seemed strangely subdued. I mean, even for them.

"Is everything all right?" I asked Sakura. She was usually more forthcoming than Satomi.

Sakura looked at me. I know how they got the term "inscrutable Asian." She could clean up at poker with a face like that. She simply shrugged. "Akamatsu-sensei will probably meet with you today," she said, no inflection, no note of worry or concern.

Which meant something had gone down. Yoda didn't meet with people. He chewed people out, fired people. I was the only person who actively looked for the guy, it seemed.

I sighed and I looked over toward Satomi. She wouldn't even glance my way. Which suggested that I was in bigger shit than I realized.

Fabulous. What now?

I decided to go to my good buddy Morimoto, who, unlike Sakura, had no poker face whatsoever. If it was in his head, it showed through his expressions like sunlight through a pane of glass. The guy was as inscrutable as a puppy.

He was working at his desk, looking a bit more college-freshman than usual. The guys who were joking and ribbing one another around him took one look at me and fell quiet, going back to their respective little desk-sections and getting down to business.

Oh, crap, I thought. If the guys weren't going to look at me, this was trouble in an epic kind of way. I cleared my throat. "I'm back from vacation, Morimoto-san," I said, by way of preamble.

He looked up at me. His concentration had caused him to scrunch up his face, but I could see his tension from a mile away. He had dark circles under his eyes, and if possible, he looked thinner. Like a breeze from an oscillating fan would knock him out. What the hell had happened?

"I just wanted to check on the progress of the manga project," I said, and my voice was hesitant.

He winced. If we were in the States, I'd suggest we go down the street for some coffee, but they didn't really like off-site breaks here. And it wasn't like I could ask him to go to the ladies' room, although I get the feeling even the S-girls would probably look askance on an invitation of that sort if I asked them, and they were girls. It's all cultural.

I leaned toward his desk, even though it was somewhat bad form to be that close. "What happened?" I whispered to him.

He gave me a rolling-eye look, like cows that were terrified of a slaughterhouse or something. He shook his head. "Not now," he whispered back. "Later. After work."

After work? Epic, my ass. This was downright catastrophic.

I went back to my desk. There were some proofs that needed reviewing, more pencil work to erase—the usual lackey stuff. I did it as quickly and carefully as possible, trying not to make eye contact with anyone for any reason, even when I got up for bathroom breaks. First the Ethan stress, now this. Ugh. It was shaping up to be a hell of a month.

Finally, Yoda came in. I don't know where he'd been all morning, but with that tie of his, I suspected a meeting with the higher-ups on the higher floors. Mahogany Row, we used to call it at the plant. He had the same look that our boss used to have when he visited the muckety-mucks. The kind of look that said "I just got my ass handed to me, I'm looking to pay it forward." He scanned the crowd. I don't think I'd seen the editorial room that quiet in the entire time I'd been at Sansoro.

"Risa-san," he said, and I could almost feel the collective relief from the other people in the room whose names had not been spoken. "Please accompany me to my office."

This was shame-walking, a whole different sort. Everyone stared as I got up from my desk and followed Yoda back to his claustropho-bic lair. He closed the door behind me and sat behind his desk.

I waited for him to start. I didn't have to wait long.

"The project," he said, "is in shambles."

No, really? "What happened?" I said instead.

He grimaced at me. Perhaps I should've apologized first. It was my project and, presumably, it was my fault the project was a failure. Maybe he knew he shouldn't have let me go on vacation for Ethan's graduation. Of course, at this point, I had some similar sentiments about my trip home: it had definitely been a bad idea.

Don't think about that now, idiot.

"Nobuko-san has been having some . . . issues, with the material and the direction," he said, and I knew he was being diplomatic. Which meant that Nobuko was throwing every frickin' monkey wrench she could get her manicured hands on into the works. "She has submitted sketches, but she insists that Morimoto's direction is simply not adequate. She also does not like the characters. She thinks that it should be a Japanese city, not an American city . . ."

"It's not an American city, though," I said. "It's a fictional city."

He sighed. Apparently he'd already had this discussion. "Yes, but it feels like a fictional American city. She thinks a fictional Japanese city would be better."

"She's digging her feet in," I said, more to myself than to him. "She's trying to make it traditional."

"Yes, and Morimoto-san . . ." He sighed again, only there was a wealth of frustration in that one sound. "He cannot stand up to Nobuko-san. He is being wrung out. He has already offered me his resignation."

"He did *what*?" I didn't mean to yelp that. Yoda's grimace sank even deeper into his face, making him look like a beige raisin.

"He thinks the project is failing because of him," Yoda answered.

"He thinks that because he suggested the project, and it's failing, that he should leave the company."

"That's ridiculous," I said. "He's a great editor. Besides, he's working on twenty projects already. Who would take those over?"

Yoda finally nodded. "You understand why I could not let him go. Still, Nobuko-san must be appeased. When I told her of our misgivings, she said that since she had her doubts about the viability of such a project, she has no problems with postponing it—indefinitely."

Damn it! Damn it. She'd planned this. From the moment she knew we were working on it, she'd only stepped in and taken the job so she could sabotage it. I figured she was up to something, but I also thought she was just using it to grandstand, to show she was still young, still hip, still up to new challenges.

The thing was, she was the big fish in the pond. She didn't need any more challenges. And she didn't like that changes were being pushed on the company. She liked things the way they were, thanks very much.

"She also mentioned that she didn't think it was appropriate for an intern to try anything so substantial," Yoda added, his tone elaborately casual. "Especially one who has never done any editing before in her life."

I couldn't help it. My hackles raised at that one. I bit it back down. This wasn't the States, I kept reminding myself.

Still, as she'd so caustically pointed out, I wasn't Japanese, either.

"She's quite right," I said carefully, "I don't have experience. But I was hoping that you felt I learned quickly. I have already been of help to Satomi and Sakura on their projects. I know that you are understaffed. And I have learned a great deal in the six months that I have been here."

He made a dismissive gesture. I think my immodesty bothered him. I should be apologizing and backing down, so he could just chalk up the project as a bad experiment and go back to it. Or at least, that's what I thought he was hoping for. His next statement made me wonder. "This would have been a good project for Sansoro," he said in a low voice. "The executive board is looking for—how would you Americans put it?—fresh blood. Tanaka-san had high hopes for this project. Now, it looks very bad for us."

Not for us, I realized. For him. Yoda's butt was on the line, all because Morimoto and I had a brainstorm.

"If we'd started small, like we originally proposed," I asked, "and Nobuko-san was not involved, would we still have the same issues?"

He looked puzzled by the query. "Possibly not," he agreed.

"I don't think the project is a failure, and I don't think it's dead," I said. I could feel the stubborn gene, the Falloya trademark, digging in its heels. "I need to think about it."

One eyebrow went up as he surveyed me.

Oops. "May I— If I can come up with a workable solution, can I bring it to you?"

He glared. Anybody else in the editorial staff would've backed down by now, gone running for the break room. But I wasn't. Hell, the worst he could do was deport me, right? And Ethan kept telling me I didn't have a career here, that it wasn't a real job. I didn't have anything to lose, just as I'd originally thought.

"Talk to me first," he finally said, and I nodded. I left the room, going back to my desk, ignoring the curious stares.

So I needed to figure out a way to save the project and our collective asses. On the plus side, I hadn't thought about Ethan's ultimatum for a good five minutes. When life hands you lemons . . .

CHAPTER 12

June 19, Monday

TODAY HAD BEEN A TOTAL BUST. I'D WORKED HARD, TRYING TO ignore the S-girls' curiosity and Morimoto's near nervous breakdown. I'd missed a call from Chisato because I'd shut my K-tei off. I got the message from Yukari, of all people, when I got home.

"We have to go see Chisato," she said, already glammed up and ready to roll.

I kept my work clothes on. I didn't really have any intentions of a late night of bar hopping or karaoke, not with so much on my plate. "Why do we have to see Chisato? I mean, I want to see her, but what's up?"

"You mean you don't *know*?" She stared at me, the "what kind of friend are you" stare.

I sighed. Tonight was not getting much better, apparently.

We met Chisato at a dessert bar off the Omotesando, a new find of Yukari's that she was very proud of. It was very posh, with dark sage green walls and dark walnut tables and trim. The desserts were traditional Japanese. I found Chisato sitting at a table, with what looked like a bowl of ice cream in front of her. She was pushing it around listlessly with her black spoon.

"Get me whatever you're getting, please," I told Yukari, handing her enough money for both of us, and then I went to Chisato and sat next to her.

"What happened?" I asked.

Her hair was back in its customary mop in front of her face, but when she pushed her bangs away, I saw that her eyes were filled with tears. "She has asked me not to work for her anymore," she said, and let out a hiccupy little crying noise.

"Oh, God," I said, patting her shoulder. "I'm sorry." Working for Nobuko had to suck, but getting fired always sucked worse. "What reason did she give to let you go?"

"Reason?" Chisato blinked at me, not comprehending.

Apparently there weren't a lot of wrongful termination suits here in Japan, I thought, filling with righteous anger. Where was a lawyer when you needed one? And how often did *that* statement come up?

"I feel responsible," I said, as Yukari sat down in front of us, carrying a tray with two bowls that resembled Chisato's. I took mine without even studying it. "If I hadn't pushed you, you never would've gotten on her radar screen. She would've left you alone."

"I contacted you, Risa-san. The fault is completely with me," Chisato said loyally, and I blessed her for it. "She said she'd been unhappy with my work for some time."

"Does she have another *assisto* lined up?" I asked, taking a spoonful of my dessert. Then I paused with it in my mouth. The flavor was sort of familiar—green tea, red bean, and something else. Like Jell-O, but less benevolent. I quirked an eyebrow of inquiry at Yukari. *What am I eating, now?*

"Agar, red bean, and green tea ice cream," she explained. "You like?"

I swallowed. Agar was seaweed, which explained the Jell-O wannabe. "Interesting," I said, then turned back to Chisato.

"No," Chisato said. "As far as I know, she does not have another *assisto* lined up. But it's only a matter of time. She's famous, and too many people want to break in." She paused. "That's how I got the job."

My heart broke for the kid. She'd worked so damned hard! "Certainly, with your résumé and credentials, and *talent* . . . surely you can get another job. As an *assisto,* if nothing else!"

She shrugged but looked troubled.

"It's not easy to get a job if you've been fired," Yukari said to me. "It looks bad."

I made a noise. "Well, it's not like it looks good in the States, but people do manage to get hired," I said, and they both looked at me with the same damned look I was unfortunately getting used to: *well, maybe in the States but not here. Not in Japan. If you were Japanese, you'd know that.*

I sighed. "Well, there's got to be a way. Does Morimoto-san know about all this?"

Chisato's lip trembled. Ah, shit.

"He feels it's all his fault," I quickly answered my own question. "And he's beating himself up about it."

"He won't return my calls," Chisato said, and the tears trickled down her face. Yukari handed her a wad of napkins, and she hastily mopped at the overflow.

I took a deep breath. A week and a half. A frickin' *week and a half,* and now it was chaos.

"Listen, I'm going to come up with something," I promised rashly. "I will work on a solution. You'll get a job, one way or another."

"How?" Chisato asked, her voice tiny, like a mouse.

I had no idea. Still, sometimes it was better to sound confident to instill confidence. "Don't worry about it," I said. "I'm American and pushy, remember? I'll come up with something."

"There is that," she said, which was vaguely insulting. Still, she'd cheered up a bit, and that was the whole point. Of course, now not only was I committed to developing some kind of solution to the American manga project and saving Morimoto's sanity, I was also responsible for getting Chisato some kind of job.

I knew I was trying to avoid thinking about my wedding planning and my irritation with Ethan, but this was getting sort of ridiculous.

"I appreciate all of your help," Chisato said, after she'd finished her dessert. She stood up and bowed. I felt embarrassed. "I know if anybody could help me, it's you. I'll wait for you to contact me."

With that, she went home, and I finally understood what those old adventure movies meant when a guy took responsibility for another person's life because they owed them big-time. Not that I necessarily owed Chisato. I just couldn't see leaving her behind.

No good deed goes unpunished. I could hear Nana Falloya's voice in my head. She would've thought this was dumb, and she'd be right.

Of course, she would agree with anything if it'd get me home earlier. She didn't like me being this far away or putting my wedding second to a job.

Yukari was leisurely eating her dessert. "Up for a party tonight?" she asked, as if I hadn't just had that conversation with Chisato. As if everything were just hunky-dory. "Nori-chan is having a party at her apartment. It should be super-fun."

I sighed. "I'm a little too busy for super-fun tonight, Yuki-chan. But thanks for the invitation."

She grimaced. "I don't just party, you know."

I stared at her. "Okay, hello, left field."

Now she stared at me. "Left field?"

"Sorry, it's an Americanism." I should've known better. "It means I don't understand where that came from. I wasn't accusing you of being silly or childish or anything. I'm sorry if you thought I was."

She shrugged, but I could tell she was still sort of annoyed. I ate another few spoonfuls of my clear Jell-O agar. Whee. I'd stop by a convenience store and grab some true candy on the way home. Home, meaning the Kanai house.

"I'm sorry," Yukari came back, sighing heavily and leaning back. She looked like a bored supermodel, all done up as she was. But her eyes were more serious than I'd ever seen her. "You're my friend, right?"

I nodded. "I like to think so."

"I can't talk like this to my other friends," she said slowly. "They don't seem to understand. But lately, I've been feeling . . . adrift. " She frowned. "Unhappy. I think I may have felt unhappy for some time. I was usually not sober enough to notice."

That was an astute observation. I finished the dessert, just listening.

"Now I'm not sure what to do." She sighed. "My mother has suggested that I get a job. They have not complained up to this point. They have not commented at all on my life. I thought they understood my choices."

That fateful night when I'd eavesdropped on their financial woes came back to me in a flash. "They may have other reasons for asking you," I hedged.

She looked at me. "There are no good jobs out there," she said. "And if there were, what would I want to do, working myself to death for a corporation? One that won't even care about me? I've seen what they've done to my father."

I shrugged. She kinda had me there.

"And I don't want to be like my mother, no life but my children." She tossed her hair in a perfect wave. "That is what they would want for me!"

"I don't think that's it necessarily," I said slowly. "But I understand what it's like to have family pressures. It's hard to ignore."

Her eyes rounded. "What is your family unhappy about?" She sounded incredulous. "You're working at a manga publisher. You won a national contest! That's very big!"

I loved her for making the comment. "They don't really see it as a career, though," I said. "And my family would rather I came home to plan my wedding."

Yukari nodded, feeling my pain, obviously. "Weddings," she scoffed. "I was married once, you know?"

My eyes bulged. She was twenty-one! Finally, I shook my head. "Ah, no. You didn't mention."

"He was older," she said. "Very successful. We met through my family's friends. He made a lot of money. We had a large wedding, and then we went on a honeymoon. To Hawaii."

Sounded idyllic so far. "What happened?"

"I love traveling," she said. "He hated it. He hated what I was like when we left the country. We wound up having a conversation about what we wanted." She sounded incredibly bitter for someone so young. "He wanted a stay-at-home wife. I wanted some adventure before we had children. We got divorced as soon as we came home." She smirked, without humor. "Surely you've heard of the phenomenon. They call them 'Narita marriages' because they don't survive the trip back from the airport."

I was shocked. The girl had floored me.

"So I didn't get a job because I wasn't set up for one. And I didn't get married. I just became . . . this."

She sounded sad. Horrified, I felt bad for her. "You know," I said, tentatively, "you'd probably love the States."

She looked at me like I'd suggested commuting to the moon.

"Your English is good," I said. "And you love traveling. I don't know. I'm just throwing it out there. And you wouldn't have the same cultural issues."

She looked intrigued. "Hmm. America."

"My mom seems to like it," I said. "I can give you her e-mail, if you like."

"I need to think about it," she said, and I got the feeling she really would. "Sure you won't come to the party?"

"No, thanks," I said. I had too many problems to deal with, and I knew that drinking and karaoke weren't going to help.

June 20, Tuesday

By the next night, I felt like I was going to explode. Or implode. Perhaps both. I couldn't remember being under this much pressure before, where so many people I cared about were about to be affected by whatever solution I came up with. *If* I could come up with a solution, which, so far, I hadn't. I left for a week and a half, and all hell broke loose. Now, it was about ten o'clock and I was desperately trying to figure out how to patch up the situation, before Morimoto and Chisato both committed hara-kiri.

Admittedly, it wasn't like I'd held guns to their heads, but they'd both been so passive, just saying "go do this" in a forcefully persuasive voice had about the same effect. Thanks to my invasive efforts, Chisato needed a job and Morimoto was low man on the totem pole and probably would be for years.

My head was starting to pound, and my stomach clenched into a tight, painful ball.

Yukari was out for the night, and she'd already tried to cajole me into her version of a solution: drinking myself into insensibility. While part of that really did sound like a good idea—the situation well and truly sucked—I thanked her and sequestered myself in her room, instead. I wasn't going to find the answer to this in a sake bomb, that was for damned sure. I had to seriously brainstorm.

Unfortunately, the Kanai parents were also out, at some business function or something, leaving me with the homebound emperor Ichiro, who was taking advantage of the situation by blasting his music as high as the volume permitted. I didn't know how the neighbors stood it. I'd escaped it at a nearby Starbucks for a few hours, but I couldn't stay there all night, so now I was trying to ignore the screeching waves of "J-pop" and video game noise coming from the other room.

I pulled out a pad of paper, jotting down notes. I always thought better when I could sketch and write. *Problems: Chisato needs job, rescue reputation; Morimoto needs help, rescue from Nobuko; Akamatsu needs . . .*

I heard Ichiro laughing, derailing my train of thought. I gritted my teeth. The worst part was that I knew it was over nothing. He was just trying to make more noise; it was fake laughter, way too loud and abrasive. He wouldn't behave this way if his parents were home, I felt sure. He'd still be loud, but this was deliberate, a *fuck you* to the gaijin girl.

Focus, I counseled myself, flipping to a clean sheet of paper. *Possible solutions: get Chisato to another company? Get them both to another company? That would look bad for Akamatsu. How to handle Nobuko?*

"Ha ha ha!" Then a loud thump. He'd obviously thrown something at the bedroom door—something heavy. Then he started singing off-key to whatever poppy little song was playing.

I was gripping my pencil hard enough to break it. I forced myself to put it down. I could feel my pulse, pounding in my chest like a jackhammer. I could feel my blood rushing, specifically to my temples, which were beating in time to the music.

I didn't realize I'd stood up until I found myself on my feet, my fists clenching and unclenching.

I had a lot of shit going on, and I was close to the edge. The last thing I needed was an uppity preteen trying to goad me.

I stalked out into the living and screamed: *"TURN IT DOWN!"*

He stared at me, his fake laughter dying immediately. He probably thought I'd gone mad. He wasn't really wrong in that assessment.

I walked over to the television, found the volume button, and turned it down myself, then turned down the stereo. "I am trying to think," I said, slowly, in a low voice that would've done Dirty Harry proud. "And you're listening to things way too loud. You don't need everything that loud. So stop it."

He was still holding his controller, and he was slowly beginning to get his bearings back. He dropped the controller on the coffee table and grabbed the remote.

"Don't . . ." I warned, but he'd already turned the volume all the way back up.

I wasn't going to get involved in a button war with this guy, so I calmly walked around to the back of the television and yanked out the power cord. The TV shut off with a dull *boooooooop*.

"Hey!" He was on his feet, his face cherry red. He glared at me like I was the Antichrist. Or maybe like *he* was the Antichrist.

I stood in front of the outlet and crossed my arms.

"You put that back!" He was screeching by this point.

I shook my head.

He took a step toward me, then another, not stopping until he was a foot in front of me. He was hyperventilating, he was breathing so hard and so angry. I was calm, but my stomach was a solid ball of lead. I was ready for anything.

He made the mistake. He made a move to slap me, his thin arm making a long arc toward my face.

I was beyond pissed, and I'd had it. I grabbed his arm. He went at me with the other one, and I caught that, too, then shoved him back toward the couch. I remember fighting with my older brother this way when we were kids—and yeah, we'd probably been this mad. I knew it wasn't right, he was just a kid, but when a kid tries to get violent, tries to hit *me*, well. That shit is just not going to fly. I had had enough.

He started to come back at me, and I said, in a freezing cold voice, "Ichiro, you come at me again, and I promise you, I am going to beat you to a pulp."

Something in my voice must've finally registered that I wasn't kidding. And I wasn't. If he took another swing at me, I was making him sorry for it, one way or another.

He was so pissed, so frustrated, little tears leaked out from the corners of his eyes as he pounded the sides of the couch. "My parents will punish you! You can't touch me!" He made another step forward, as if trying to use that excuse to get his courage up to take me on.

I smiled, an evil smile. "Yeah, but your parents ain't here." I actually said that in English—I didn't know the Japanese equivalent.

Still, the English stopped him, as did the smile. "You can't do this to me," he finally said, his voice plaintive.

"You've just done whatever you wanted, whenever you wanted, and your parents have let you. Well, that's their problem. But you're starting to bug the hell out of me. And yeah, maybe they'll punish me. Maybe they'll kick me out. But it'll be worth it, because I have *had* it with your shit. So knock it off, or I'll make sure you do."

With that, I turned and walked back into Yukari's room. My pulse was going a mile a minute, and my temper felt like poison in my bloodstream. Part of me felt vindicated—*about time somebody told that little bastard off!*—and part of me just felt bad, like I'd smacked a toddler or something.

It remained blessedly silent for about five minutes, and I settled on the twin bed, trying to get in the right frame of mind to consider the Morimoto-Chisato problem. But then I heard the sounds, low at first, then growing in volume.

Ichiro was crying. No. Ichiro was *sobbing.*

I felt like complete, utter shit. Finally I got off the bed—there was no way I could work through this, especially since that guilty little part of me *knew* I was responsible—and I went out to the living room.

He had his head on one of the couch pillows. He was strewn across the couch itself like he'd thrown himself there. He was weeping like a little kid, snot running down his nose, the whole nine yards.

I sighed, sitting down next to him. "Come on," I said, trying to soothe. "I'm sorry. I shouldn't have yelled at you like that."

He made a small, pausing hiccup, looking at me cautiously.

"Why do you hate me so much, anyway?" I asked. I didn't want to play armchair psychologist, but damn it, he had to have *some* reason for doing what he was doing.

He shrugged. Of course, he was a teenage boy in the making. Not the most verbal creatures in the world.

I sighed again. At least the crying had died down a bit. I got up and grabbed him some tissues, waiting for him to blow his nose and clean himself up a bit. When he was done with that, I asked him again, "Why do you hate me?"

"I don't know," he said, in the most reasonable, nongrunting way I'd ever heard from him. "I don't really hate you. Not really."

"So, what's with all this?" I gestured to the TV and the video games.

"Why do you hate me?" he countered.

"I don't hate you," I said. Then silently amended *at least, when you're not trying to keep me awake or bug the crap out of me.*

"You think I'm a freak," he said. "I think— I heard you tell your American friends. You think there's something *wrong* with me. You think I'm a . . . a creep!"

I sighed. I probably had made some offhand comment to that effect to Stacy or Perry. I didn't realize he'd heard. "But you've acted like this since the day I got here," I said. It wasn't a great defense, but at least there was a reason. Man, rationalization was a bitch. "Why do you act like this? You don't go to school; you don't go to your room. You expect your mom to wait on you hand and foot, and you've deliberately tried to irritate me. What's the story?"

He stared at me. I guess nobody had really asked him the question before. It wasn't like child psychologists were jumping out of the woodwork—I imagine in this society, it would be something of a shameful admission, like you were truly insane or something, to go to a psychologist. They'd probably wait until Ichiro acted like the other problem children I'd read about, like that little guy who had beheaded his classmate. And that kid was only nine years old.

I shuddered.

"I'm not trying to be mad at you," I said, as gently as I could. "I just really want to know: What's wrong? What are you feeling?"

He didn't say anything. His lip just quivered. Then, before I knew it, he'd pitched himself forward, into my arms, and he was crying again.

He cried for a long time, soaking the front of my shirt. I just let him, stroking his back occasionally, making little comforting nonsense noises, the kind you might make to a baby. I had no idea what just happened. I just hoped it was a step in the right direction.

He cried like that for a while, then he pulled away, wiping at his eyes with the back of his hands. He got up. I waited for something, some kind of explanation.

"I'm sorry," he finally said. "Don't tell my parents."

With that, he retreated to his room. I didn't see him again for the rest of the night.

July 10, Monday

I felt wrung out, like someone had put me in the spin cycle. When going into the office felt like a reprieve, you *know* life was beginning to suck.

I stood in Akamatsu's doorway, without any sort of summons, early that morning. Yoda always came in early, so I was catching him at a relatively good time. The editorial staff was still straggling in, and they were getting settled—they didn't notice my intrusion.

"Akamatsu-sensei?" I said, knocking softly.

Yoda's bushy eyebrows jumped toward his hairline. I don't know how common it is for subordinates to do "pop-ins" with their bosses, even if it is common for Americans. He didn't look pleased at my presence. "Is something wrong, Risa-san?"

"I wanted to talk to you privately, if possible."

Now his eyes bugged out slightly, as if I'd come on to him. He made some strangled noises. "Again, is something wrong?"

I glanced around. I had no idea if Nobuko had any sort of confederates in the editorial pool—she was feared, but I didn't know if that extended to spying. "I wanted to talk to you about the American comic project. I think I've come up with a solution." After many hours of cudgeling my brain, I'd developed something. I just hoped it was workable.

He relaxed visibly. Maybe he really *did* think I was coming on to him. I'd find that amusing later, I was sure. "It's out of my hands, Risa-san," he said. "I don't think there is anything that can be done."

"I disagree," I said, and his relaxation disappeared in a wave of shock. Nobuko might be a terror, but Yoda was no slouch, either, and I got the feeling people didn't disagree with him a whole lot. Hence the *sensei* appellation. They didn't throw that term around lightly. He was our leader and our teacher. It would be like me telling a professor the theory he'd based his entire career on was wrong.

"Come in," he barked. "And shut the door."

I was already closing it when the order came. I sat down and belatedly realized he hadn't asked me to. If possible, his eyes widened at that one as well.

I wasn't getting off to a good start here.

"Morimoto-san has a good concept, with the adventure-romance thing," I said. "I think, if the drawing was good and the story line was spiced up a bit, it could really sell in the American market."

"We've been over this," he snapped impatiently. "And the project is dead."

It's dead because of Nobuko, and we both know it. Still, even I wasn't ballsy enough to bring that one up, point-blank. I think his head might have exploded if I did. "There were definitely some problems with the project," I said, starting to dance around the subject. "But I think that trying to court the American market with more than translations, by attempting a true cross-cultural hybrid, might really work."

He sighed. "Japan and America are too different, Risa-san," he said. "Besides, Americans like things that are Japanese. We are better off doing what we have always done."

He was digging in his heels, getting entrenched. He'd really gotten his butt in a sling when Nobuko burned us. "But there's room for growth," I said. "And the executive board wanted to explore a hybrid."

"We did explore it." He shrugged. "Apparently, we couldn't make it work."

I did what I could not to tear my hair out. I wanted to say that Americans never acted like that, but I'd worked with enough managers to know differently. However, I knew in my bones that Yoda didn't feel that way. He might not be a huge hell-raiser, waving the banner of change, but he wasn't as fiercely reactionary as Nobuko. She was the reason he'd changed his mind. Nobuko and the pressure she'd brought to bear from the higher-ups. I sighed heavily.

"Perhaps . . . perhaps the problem was that too much importance was given to the project," I ventured. "I think that a small test run might be a better way to go."

"We don't have the resources to do even a small test run," he said. "We'd need an editorial team, and an artist, and funding."

I knew Morimoto, and I knew Chisato. We had two out of three. "Perhaps someone on the editorial staff would be willing to volunteer extra time," I said. "And I believe we could get a relatively unknown artist to work on spec."

His eyes narrowed now, and he sighed. "Risa-san, I know what you're doing. And you have to stop."

That did it. All attempts at gently pussyfooting around the issue went out the window. "Why? Morimoto-san really believes in this project, and he thinks it'd be the best thing to get Sansoro competitive. I'd be willing to dedicate my time, since Nobuko-san doesn't want me working on anything substantial here anyway, and you've made it clear that I'm just an intern. Chisato-san is out of work, and she'd love the opportunity to work on a new project. Why wouldn't that work out?"

"You have no idea . . ." he started, shaking his head and making an empty gesture with his hands, as if he was at a loss for words on how to get the concept across to me.

"Yes, I do," I interrupted, and his lips pulled taut, almost disappearing into his craggy face. "I know it's political. Nobuko-san doesn't like me. She doesn't want new projects. She wants to stay the big fish in a relatively small pond."

He choked at that one. "Risa-san, that is disrespectful."

I knew it was, and I shut my mouth for a moment. It was true, yes, but it was disrespectful; she was a successful artist. And who was I? A hired flunky, some gaijin they'd picked up in a contest as a publicity stunt. One she was more than willing to deport, given any opportunity, so things could go back to the status quo.

But where did that leave Morimoto or Chisato? Hell, where did that leave me? Sharpening pencils and erasing for another five months? I didn't want to go back to that, not after I'd had a taste of how much more I could do. I didn't like doing just busywork. I could be home in Groverton if I wanted to do that.

Man, that came out bitter.

I shook off the observation and worked on rephrasing. "Sansoro went through all the trouble of giving a contest, looking for an American manga artist," I said slowly. "It was very good publicity. It could be even better if I got to work on a small project that could then be publicized. You would get even more contest entries, maybe something even workable. And you'd make more sales in the U.S."

It sounded logical to me, and Yoda calmed down enough to listen to me. He even nodded a little. "Still, I don't know how the executives would take this," he said. "And Nobuko-san will find out and be unhappy."

I nodded. I had a pretty good idea how unhappy Nobuko would be when she found out. "We'd keep the project relatively secret. The executives would never have told her, and she wouldn't dare defy them outright."

"No," Yoda admitted. "Apparently you're the only one with the audacity to do that around here."

I smiled. "It's the American thing," I joked.

He took it seriously, nodding in agreement. "You are lucky," he said. "If you were Japanese, there would be no way your behavior would be tolerated."

I stared at him for a second. By this point I knew better than to make the argument that I was half-Japanese. There was no such thing, by their definition—it was like being half-pregnant. Either you were Japanese or you weren't.

I used to be bothered by that. Now, finally, I was seeing the advantage.

"You could use that, you know," I pointed out.

"Use what?"

"The fact that I'm American," I said, thinking quickly. "The executives want to be able to leverage more publicity off of me. This project came up. I was pushy. You just have to put me in front of it.

Make it seem like I railroaded Morimoto-san and Chisato-san into helping me."

"You mean you aren't?" he asked mildly.

I didn't glare at him, though I wanted to. "I'm just trying to help," I said. "It's a great opportunity. They both have talent, and they both really want to try something new. I know how hard it is to get something new started around here. If you make it seem like a publicity stunt, and spin the pushy American angle internally . . . it could work."

He leaned over his desk, cocking his head to one side, like a curious and wary bird. "Is this how you do things where you work, in America?"

"I don't generally need to," I replied. "But in Japan, let's just say I'll do what I have to do."

He cogitated on this for a few minutes, absolutely silent, absolutely still except for the occasional knitting of his prodigious brows. Finally, he spoke.

"Let me put this before the executives," he said slowly. "They did like the idea of approaching the American market but were convinced that the scope of Morimoto-san's original project was too ambitious, perhaps because of Nobuko-san's input."

That's putting it politely, I thought, but kept my mouth shut.

"And I will tell them that it's a small project, and that you're spearheading it," he said.

I nodded, excited. He was going for it.

"And if the project winds up being a fiasco," he continued, "I'll tell them that we will release you from your contract, and advise them not to run the contest again."

I let out a little squeak of protest.

"I can't set a precedent here of letting interns run rampant," he said sharply. "You have good ideas, but you've never worked in publishing. You have a lot of energy, enthusiasm, and ambition . . . and you don't like Nobuko-san, but she does have a lot of experience. If you believe in this so much, then you must be willing to sacrifice something besides your precious free time. Is this so?"

Now he was Akamatsu-sensei, now he was formidable. And he wasn't kidding.

I nodded.

"All right," I said. "We'll pull the project together. And if the executive committee doesn't like it, I'll leave."

I couldn't believe I'd agreed to it. My family and Ethan would be thrilled—they wanted me to come home early anyway.

Still, wouldn't it be a kick if I didn't fail?

CATHY YARDLEY

July 30, Sunday

IN A STRANGE TURN OF EVENTS, I WAS HOSTING A PARTY . . . OF sorts. After clearing it with the Mr. and Mrs. Kanai, I had asked Chisato and Morimoto over for a brainstorming session on how we could improve, and develop, the still "on spec" (read: unpaid) and untitled "American manga project." We still had Chisato's original drawings, but Nobuko had screwed with the plot outline so many times that Morimoto and I were a bit lost as far as what story we wanted to tell. She'd made a couple of good points, surprisingly, and we wanted to be sure we incorporated them . . . without making them a simple knock-off of Nobuko's earlier work, which was obviously where she was going with it.

"You need more action." This from Ichiro, who was acting as our focus group. Ever since Ichiro and I had had our blowout, I had wound up having more conversations with him, usually after his parents were asleep. He wouldn't talk with his mom hovering around, for whatever reason. The conversations were short, at first, but they were getting more open. He'd asked what working for a manga publisher was like. He'd asked about America, more than once, and that's how I found out he'd read several American comics that he'd swapped with friends, notably the *Sandman* series from Neil Gaiman and a lot of *Batman* and *X-Men*. Older classics, but still great. He turned out to be perfect for what we were working on. It was also nice to see him interact with humans other than myself and his family. I got the feeling he was missing that, since he wasn't in school, and he was at the age where socialization was pretty important. I'd hate to see him wind up some kind of hermit.

Which suggested *I'd* come pretty far since I first got there, when I thought he was the Antichrist and wanted him dead.

"More action," Morimoto said reflectively, nibbling on one of the appetizers Mrs. Kanai had put out. She was both nervous and sort of happy, I think. The Kanai clan didn't really entertain a whole lot, I'd noticed, probably due to their financial situation. Also possibly because of the relative size of their apartment, although I couldn't imagine any of Mr. Kanai's coworkers having anything bigger. At any rate, I'd given Mrs. Kanai more than enough money and begged for her help in "entertaining" my two work colleagues. She was pleased and had provided quite the spread. I hoped she had change, and that she was keeping it.

"But you don't want to lose the love story," Yukari said, throwing in her two cents. She was our other focus-group person, being an avid manga reader. She was a *shojo* fan, someone who loved the romance stories. Of course, her stuff was pretty racy. I remember going to a club with her on a train and having nothing to read. She'd dug in her purse and gave me a slim volume. It seemed sweet, until I turned the page and found a guy going down on a woman who was obviously in the throes of ecstasy. I shut the book with a snap and blushed. The old guy to my right was startled. Yukari, on the other hand, had giggled like a fiend and embarrassed us both.

"Don't lose love story," Morimoto noted.

"The way you've drawn the love scenes are very romantic," Yukari added, to Chisato specifically. "She's so beautiful and so sad."

"And she kicks butt," Ichiro remarked.

I thought I heard a choking cough coming from the kitchen. I had the feeling Mrs. Kanai was listening to everything. Apparently she took a little umbrage at her son's remark.

I was just walking to the kitchen, to ask if Mrs. Kanai herself would like to become a member of our impromptu focus group/think tank, when the phone rang. As I got there, she turned to me, handing me the receiver. "It's your friends," she said.

I glanced at my watch. Nine o'clock at night, which was, what, eight o'clock in the morning in New York? I answered the phone. "*Mushi*, er, I mean, hello?"

"*Mushi-mushi,*" Perry answered. "That's so cute, by the way. Stacy and I are on conference again. We hadn't heard from you in so long, we thought maybe you'd died or something. What up, homegirl?"

I grinned. Perry trying to talk "street" was like Al Gore trying to rap . . . amusing, but it just didn't fly. "Just doing some work, actually," I said. "Hold on a sec."

Mrs. Kanai was hovering, fiddling with yet another wave of appetizers. "Would you care to join them?"

She blinked at me, then shook her head, reddening. "No, no, I wouldn't want to bother," she said, and her cheeks pinked a little. "That's for young people."

"Do you read manga?"

She looked surprised by the question, as if I'd asked, Do you watch TV? "Of course," she said offhandedly.

"We're still determining our market. I'm sure they'd love your help."

She paused, uncertain. "I don't want to disturb Ichiro and Yukari," she said.

I sighed. It was hard to get parents to hang with children successfully. "The offer's always open," I said.

She smiled, then retreated to her bedroom.

"Sorry about that," I said.

Now Stacy was on the line. "How's the planning going?"

I grinned. "We're just going over high-level stuff in the plot right now, and fine-tuning the characters, but I think the basic story line's tight. We'll get the whole thing written out by Wednesday and then Chisato can start drawing. It'll be great."

"Uh, what the heck are you talking about?" Stacy laughed. "I meant *wedding* planning."

"But what you're talking about sounds interesting," Perry interjected.

"Sorry. Sorry." I shook my head to try and clear it. "We've been working on this thing for hours. Honestly, it's consumed my life."

"So you haven't picked from any of the dresses I e-mailed you, huh," Stacy said. "For the bridesmaids, I mean."

I felt guilty. I hadn't even looked at them. "Um, I'm still thinking it over."

"You didn't even open the attachment."

I sighed. "Sorry," I said, feeling lame.

"If you guys are going to get married in June, honey, these things take *time*."

"I know," I said. "And I'll buckle down. We have to give our big presentation on September fifteenth. After that, I'm sure—"

"September?" Stacy laughed. "You're going to be having your wedding in Ethan's apartment if you wait until September to reserve a place."

I sighed. "Maybe we'll do that, then. I'm still thinking eloping."

"Cool," Perry said. "You could do Vegas. I'd fly out for that."

"Perry, don't be an ass." Stacy could be abrasive when she wanted to be. "Honey, I know this is stressful, especially with you being so far away. But I'll help you. At least it'll be something to get my mind off the pregnancy."

"How's that going?" I asked.

"Worse this time around. More morning sickness, more everything, and I'm the size of a tour bus . . ."

I chuckled, then stopped when Ichiro came in. "Hold on a second," I said. "Everything okay?"

"Does she have to kill the guy at the end?" Ichiro asked me. "We're starting to think that's not a good idea."

I liked the way he said "we," like he was on the team.

"Well, he's not really dead, but we want people to think he is," I explained. "I thought Morimoto-san knew that."

"He didn't say."

I sighed. It was nine. Morimoto would have to leave pretty soon, and we still had details to knock out. "Tell him I'll be out in a minute, please?"

Ichiro grinned and left.

"Sorry," I repeated to Stacy. "It's crazy around here."

"I don't mean to be interrupting," Stacy said, sounding hurt.

"And I'm sorry I don't have more time," I said. "Listen, can I call you back later? Maybe before I go to work . . . so tonight, for you?"

"I'm out tonight," Perry said. "But it sounds like I don't need to be a part of this conversation anyway, if you're just going to talk wedding stuff."

Now *he* sounded offended. I was spreading myself just a little too thin.

"I don't know. I don't have a lot of time with Roger as it is," Stacy said, and I knew she was just peeved and getting even with me.

"I really am sorry," I said.

"I'm just, God, this is going to sound bitchy, but I am kind of concerned about your priorities."

I blinked. That had stung like a slap. "I just— I really like this, Stacy. I'm really enjoying what I'm doing."

"Yeah, that's great. But after December, it'll be done, you know?"

"All the more reason to enjoy it now, right?"

She huffed. "Okay. Call me whenever."

"I'm sorry . . ."

She hung up.

"Perry?" I said.

He sighed. "She's just pissed lately. A lot of work trouble. She's been covering a lot of slack since you left, and now she feels like you're just dropping the wedding in her lap."

"I didn't ask her to plan the wedding!" I yelped.

"She's just that way. You know that," he said. "Listen, say hi to Yukari for me, and check your e-mail, okay? These conference calls aren't cheap."

"Okay. Sorry, Perry."

"Talk to you later." He hung up.

I went back out to the living room, my enjoyment somewhat soured.

"Everything all right?" Morimoto asked, with a note of worry.

I shrugged. "It is what it is," I said. My brother, Tony, said that all the time. I think for the first time I understood what he meant.

August 9, Wednesday

"Would you just relax?" Yukari said, sounding impatient. "It's no big deal."

I stood at the foot of a large wooden bath. I don't know why I listened to Chisato and Yukari when they said going to "the baths" would be just what I needed. I'd read about baths and stuff, and of course I'd seen plenty of Japanese movies where they went to bathe. It always seemed like a spa experience, and that should be no big deal. But I couldn't help it. The Falloyas might be loud and boisterous, but when it came to stuff like showers at gym class, we were regular Puritans. I hadn't had a roommate in years, but I couldn't remember ever parading around a roommate naked. And now, I was with not only my roommate but my coworker. I could guarantee I'd never seen a coworker naked before. With good reason.

We'd taken showers and gotten all cleaned up beforehand, and there were special robes, which I now hesitated to get rid of. Yukari was standing there naked, motioning me toward the tub. Chisato was already in it, and I have to say, she did look beatific. I sighed, took the robe off, and handed it to the silent bath attendant. The place smelled like a spa, only less chlorinated because there was no chlorine. I made an effort not to shield myself and followed Yukari, who popped into the tub with a huge sigh of satisfaction.

I followed suit—or at least, I tried. I put my foot in and promptly parboiled. *"What the hell?"* I yelped, yanking the foot out again.

All the women in the bath looked at me strangely. I was embarrassed but not enough to get over the fact that I'd scalded myself. That water was insanely hot. I looked at Yukari, who had just slipped into that sucker like a Cheerio into milk. "How can you just get in there when it's so hot?" I asked her.

She shook her head, smirking at me. "It's not that bad. You just have to get used to it."

I looked at Chisato. She had a light sheen of sweat, but she still sat there, smiling softly, like some kind of Buddhist figurine. "It's nice," she said.

Well, I knew that Chisato was even more stressed than I was. She had no income, she'd been fired, and now she was working on a renegade project with a junior editor who was having second thoughts about being her boyfriend, and a crazy American intern who had delusions of grandeur. If something as simple as hot water could make the girl feel better, I might as well try it.

I put my hands in first, gradually getting used to it by gritting my teeth. Then I wrapped my hands around my foot and lowered that in, repeating with the other foot. The butt and my breasts were the worst. Eventually, I finally lowered myself in up to my chin. The whole process took like twenty minutes. The girls watched me with amusement the entire time.

"You are so funny, Riri-chan," Yukari said around a giggle. Chisato giggled, too. It was probably the first time I'd ever heard so carefree a sound.

"You realize, of course, I may never have children, sitting around in water this hot," I pointed out.

"Hasn't seemed to stop us," Yukari countered. "You Americans. You're so 'hard core' and you can't even handle a bath!"

I leaned my head back against the corner of the tub. It was sort of nice, now that I'd acclimated. I could feel my muscle tension melt away—probably literally. What hope did knots have against boiling water?

I was enjoying myself, closing my eyes, and listening to Yukari and Chisato talk about clothes. I'd suggested to Yukari that Chisato could use a wardrobe upgrade, and in typical Yukari fashion, she'd doggedly pursued the issue. I knew Chisato didn't have a chance. As soon as she got some more money, she'd probably be one of the most fashionable *assistos* out there.

"Well, I did not expect to see you here, Chisato-san."

The voice was vaguely familiar. Yukari and Chisato fell silent. I cracked an eye open to see who was talking.

Nobuko was standing at the edge of the tub, her hands resting on her hips in a gunslinger's pose, surveying all of us as if we were peasants and she was an empress. She was wearing her usual makeup and her hair was up.

She was also buck naked.

Oh, Jesus, Mary, and Joseph, I thought, using my grandmother's favorite expression of dismay. *I could've lived my whole life without seeing this woman naked.*

For whatever age she was, she was remarkably well preserved, although I could see a few telltale scars—she'd had work done. Although I couldn't quite understand why someone who got a boob job would get what looked like A-and-a-half cups. I mean, if you're going under the knife, might as well make it count, right?

"Nobuko-san," Chisato finally stammered out, and I could see all the tension flood back into her body, hot water or not. "What are you doing here?"

"Isn't it obvious? Just taking a bath, like everyone else." Nobuko's laugh was like tinkling crystal. Anybody who didn't know what was going on wouldn't think twice; they'd probably assume the four of us were friends, or at least good acquaintances. "There's room here. May I join you?"

Yukari was looking at me, as if I had the authority to make the decision. I wanted to say no, but I couldn't think of how to do it politely . . . and I didn't want to piss her off any more than she possibly already was. None of us said anything, so she just went right ahead, sitting across from me and to Yukari's right.

Well, this isn't awkward, or anything.

She stared at me, sort of challenging. God as my witness, I had no idea what I ought to say to the woman. Then she glanced at Yukari and smiled.

"I'm sorry," I finally said. "This is my roommate, Kanai Yukari."

Yukari nodded her head, and Nobuko followed suit. "What do you do?" Nobuko asked.

Yukari shrugged. I could almost hear the response in her head.

You're *lookin' at it, lady.* But Yukari, while frivolous, would never dream of being so rude.

"I see. A 'Parasite Eve,' then." And she laughed at her little observation. "You don't have any aspirations to work in manga, do you? I need an assistant."

Chisato turned a deep, unpleasant red. How could this woman get away with being rude when we couldn't?

Because she made a lot of money, my subconscious reasoning supplied. Because she meant a lot to Sansoro, and so far, we were just peons, little cogs in a big machine. She was somebody. We weren't.

I stood up, the cold air a pleasant shock after the heat of the water. I was almost light-headed from the contrast. "I'm sorry, Nobuko-san," I said. "I'm not used to water this hot. I think I need to leave." I turned to Yukari and Chisato, who both stood as well. Chisato looked relieved.

"If you must," she said. "Oh, and I'm so sorry the project got postponed. It had potential."

I looked at her. Was she mocking us, taunting our efforts? Or did she really not know about the coup we were planning?

Yukari looked like she was about to say something, and I put a hand on her arm, stopping her by shaking my head slightly. "There will be other projects," I said to Nobuko.

"I suppose there will be," she said, lounging with her arms against the side of the tub. "But then, you're leaving in December, aren't you? They won't need their intern for show anymore. I don't even think they're having another contest. I don't think the publicity they have been getting did what they thought it would." She smiled, her teeth flashing abnormally bright and white. "I advised them against holding the contest in the first place, did you know?"

What? Nobuko advising against doing anything that might cause her competition? Now there was a shocker. I grimaced. "We'll see."

I could feel waves of outrage coming from Yukari, and I was get-

CATHY YARDLEY

ting pretty pissed myself, so I turned and the girls followed me, leaving Nobuko to laugh in the water to herself as we retreated.

"I don't like her," Yukari muttered, as we got dressed in our street clothes again.

"She's going to try something," Chisato said, her voice drenched in fear. "She must know what's going on. And she's going to want revenge."

I sighed. Any relaxing effects the hot bath was supposed to have evaporated with just one encounter. My shoulders felt like they were pinned together, and every vertebrae in my neck felt fused into a solid column. I was beat, and frustrated . . . and tired.

"I need a vacation," I joked.

Yukari brightened. "That's perfect! You really should get away, get out of the city." Her eyes sparkled. "A bunch of us are going to spend the weekend in Odaiba, on the eighteenth. You should come!"

I shook my head. Odaiba was a completely constructed place, on an old landfill I think. It had a beach and a huge theme park. Sort of like Disneyland but not, since Tokyo already had one of those. Odaiba also had casinos. Not that gambling was legal: you could go and learn how to gamble, instead. They were waiting out the legislation, so when gambling was legalized, they'd be ready. It was a weird place, not unlike Pleasure Island in *Pinocchio*. I knew that Yukari and crew were going to have a blast, but it wasn't my idea of relaxing. "I was thinking of something quieter."

Chisato bit her lip. "I'm going to be drawing all weekend," she said, meaning to finish the project. "But my family knows of a wonderful *ryokan* in Kyoto. It's far, and it's probably expensive, but you could take the Shinkansen to get there. And it is very peaceful."

I smiled at her. Taking the bullet train to Kyoto, on the other end of Japan? The place of a thousand temples? I'd read about how beautiful it was, and I'd sort of hoped I'd get there at some point.

"That sounds perfect," I said.

I'd never taken a vacation by myself, for good reason: I generally hated traveling, hated new things, hated feeling like a stranger. Hated feeling like I didn't know what to do or what was expected of me. Hated feeling *different*. I'd always liked comfortable surroundings. My job. My friends.

My life.

I was learning all kinds of new things in Japan. About it and about myself.

August 13, Sunday

"Lisa, honey, did you get my e-mail?"

I was sitting in a park, not far from the Kanai condo, looking at swans on the pond, talking to Ethan on my K-tei. It was a hot day, but there was a cool breeze and I was enjoying it. At least, I had been.

Ethan had been e-mailing me steadily for the past few weeks, since his graduation. "Which e-mail?" I asked, sighing.

He sighed back, a sound of singular impatience. "The one about the church. Which church did you want to get married in? I know how Catholic your family is, but my family's Protestant, not that they'd care."

I hadn't really thought about it that much, so I frowned now. He was in such a hurry—he was in "plan" mode, I could tell. He wanted to get ducks in rows, get plans in order, get on with the next phase. Operation Marriage.

I saw a swan glide gracefully through the air before touching down with a soft sound onto the glassy surface of the lake. Snowy white, with just that mark of black over the bill; it circumnavigated the water lilies with a delicate ease. I smiled.

"Are you even listening to me?"

I turned my attention back to my stressed-out husband-to-be. "Ethan, do I need to figure this out right now?"

He huffed. "It's August," he pointed out, as if I were crazy. "If we want to be married by April, then that's going to be tight enough as it is. Only eight months."

"April?" Did I agree to April? "I thought we were talking about June!"

"That was last month," he said. "I e-mailed you. April would be much better. I'm starting a new job and April will be just after my six-month review. I can take a little time off then. And June should be busy because we'll have summer launches, if I go with that sports-drink company I was telling you about. I don't want to take time off for a wedding when there's something that big." He paused. "Don't you want to take a nice honeymoon? This would work much better. I was thinking the Caribbean."

I sighed. His brain was revving so high, it was amazing he didn't have smoke coming out of his ears. "Oh, I forgot about that. It's just— There's so much planning."

"This would be easier if you were over here," he said, with just the slightest caustic edge.

I wasn't going to get sucked into this argument. "I made a commitment to stay here, you know that," I said as mildly as possible. *You wanted me to go.* "So we'll just work around it, I guess."

"Hmmph." His tone was vaguely conciliatory. "Well, at least there's a lot you can do through the Internet."

I felt a stab of irritation. It wasn't my fault that a summer wedding would interfere with his work schedule. So why, exactly, was I knocking myself out from ten thousand miles away, just so he could stay on target?

"Did you get that checklist I sent, by the way?"

I gritted my teeth. "I'm sure I did," I said, not caring either way.

He was silent for a second. "Are you mad at me?" He sounded astounded.

"Irritated," I said finally.

"*You're* irritated?"

He was walking a fine line. I stared at the swans like they were some kind of visual Prozac, as if they could help me calm down. "I'm doing the best I can," I finally said. "But this isn't ideal, and frankly, you're pushing me."

He paused at that one. "Don't you want to get married?"

"Why do you keep asking me that?" That was a little louder than I intended, and several people looked at me. The swans even ruffled their feathers and swam away. I took a deep, cleansing breath. "Yes, of course I want to marry you. I love you. I just think you're rushing things and pushing me to make sure everything works on your damned schedule, when you *know* I'm way over here and trying to get my own stuff in order."

"Come on, Lisa," he said. "I'm about to choose a job that ought to have us covered financially for the next three years, at least. I'm about to make some huge career moves. You're finishing up an internship. You can't honestly tell me that's comparable. I mean, do you even know what you're going to do next?"

"Please tell me you're not taking it there," I said in a frosty tone.

"Sweetie, I know this has been a dream of yours. But we've got to be realistic, too," he said, and his tone of voice wasn't deliberately condescending or anything. I knew he was really just trying to be as rational as possible, which made it worse. I was getting more angry because he was belittling what I was doing, but at the same time, he was just "looking out for me." He really was genuinely concerned.

"I took on this job, and I'm getting lots of new opportunities," I said. "Remember my e-mail? The one where I told you about the projects I'd been working on? The American connection? Ring any bells?"

"Sure," he said quickly.

"Oh, really?" I leaned against the back of the bench, crossing one leg over the other. "Why don't you tell me about it?"

"Come on, Lisa," he snapped. "Could you tell me about the Wilcox account I was working on last month?"

"Isn't that the one where the guy in charge was an asshole and lost three sets of presentation slides?"

He was quiet for a minute. Yes, I thought. I do pay attention when you send me stuff. Especially when it's not wedding-related.

"I can't remember," he finally admitted. "But it's been crazy around here."

"It's been crazy here, too, believe me," I said. Between the Ichiro weirdness and the office politics, how could he say it *wasn't* crazy?

"Yeah, but in December you'll come home and it'll all be over," Ethan countered. "This is the rest of my life, Lise. The rest of *our* lives. Can't you see that that's more important than what you've got going on?"

I swallowed hard. I should've seen— I mean, he was probably right. But it was *my* life he was trivializing. And I really, really liked it. For the first time in my life, I felt . . . *present.* I felt I was really living my life, instead of just passing time in it.

He sighed again, and this was one of submission rather than frustration. "I did not mean to get into all of this with you," he said, with a heavy voice. "I don't want to fight."

"I don't want to fight, either," I agreed.

"But . . . there's stuff that needs to get done, and I need your help." He was putting his best managerial voice on, and it grated on me. I bit my lip. "So, will you look into churches or halls?"

"Not a church," I said. "At least, not a Catholic one. They expect you to take classes for months beforehand . . . my cousin went through all that."

"Got it. So a hall or something. That can't be too bad. I'll e-mail you what I see as our budget. I know your parents are planning on giving a contribution, but since I'm doing well and I figured we'd want our freedom, I've put aside money, too."

"You know," I said, "we wouldn't have to plan at all if we just eloped when I got home."

There was silence on his side. "My parents would be really disappointed," he said.

"Mine, too. But it's our decision," I said. "And it would be easier. You wouldn't have to worry about any kind of timing or anything. Just a quick jaunt to Atlantic City, maybe, or something. Get the license. No muss, no fuss."

I thought it was a good concession. And at least I wouldn't have to think about things until I got home.

"Nope," he said, after a long moment. "I mean, we'd have to deliberately exclude people, and they'd know we were getting married because of the honeymoon."

"Maybe we could wing the honeymoon," I said, seeing my perfect solution start to evaporate.

"Honey, I won't be able to take a vacation easily once those launches happen," he said. "And I don't want to just jaunt off. At least if I say it's for my honeymoon, my boss will cut me some slack. And we'll be able to register—I've got plenty of family who would love to buy us stuff. That'll help when we set up the house, you know?"

He was still giving me all kinds of rational reasons for why we ought to stay on plan. I just felt . . . I can't even describe how I was feeling. Sick. Sad.

Emotions that really probably shouldn't have been related to a wedding, I realized. Especially not my own wedding.

"So, are you working this weekend?" he said.

"Yes," I said, automatically. "But I'm taking next weekend off."

"Great," he said, sounding relieved. "Then you can focus on the details."

"Actually," I said, "I'm taking a vacation. I'm going to Kyoto. I need some down time."

"Kyoto? Who are you going with?"

"I'm going by myself."

"You're going on a vacation by yourself?" He sounded baffled. "I don't think I've ever known you to take a vacation by yourself."

"Well, there's a first time for everything." That sounded snippy, and I didn't mean it to be. I just wanted to get back to some relaxation.

"There's no reason you can't be on vacation and still work on this stuff," he said. "I might even take a vacation myself, before the new job starts. Call me when you get back, and we'll get some more stuff nailed down. I have to run, love you, sweetie."

"I love you, too," I said, but it sounded and felt way too wooden. I hung up and stared at the swans.

Kyoto might be the most tranquil place on earth, according to some of the brochures I'd picked up. But they'd need to have Valium in the water for me to have tranquillity after all of this.

CHAPTER 14

August 25, Friday

I'D NEVER TAKEN THE SHINKANSEN, OR "BULLET TRAIN." IN Tokyo, I didn't have any need to. I found out that although Japan looks like a tiny island on every map and globe I'd ever seen, apparently it's the size of California. The whole state, that is. That was pretty nuts, and I wasn't sure I got it right. Still, with all that, I took the bullet train, and it took me maybe two hours to go what would've been an eight-hour drive or an hour-and-a-half flight. Since I'm still not a huge fan of flying, that was infinitely preferable.

While riding the train, I went over the manga pages that Chisato had completed. They were ready to be inked, and they were gorgeous. The whole shebang was due on the fifteenth of September, so she was even a little ahead of schedule. I leaned against the dark blue, plush cloth-covered seat, watching the "train stewardess" come by with a cart full of food and drinks, all available for purchase. The train was spotless and very luxurious. It was well worth it to travel this way.

I'd even used the time on the train to sketch out some wedding ideas, which I'd e-mail to Stacy. It was unnerving. I still couldn't quite understand why I couldn't get more enthused about the whole thing. I did love Ethan, and I did want to marry him. It was stupid, ridiculous, not to leap right into the thing. But for whatever reason, I was dragging my feet. I managed to come up with a couple of themes, and I knew that I wanted mini wedding cakes: little three-layer deals, decorated like the big cake. I'd seen it once in a magazine, and it had looked really cool. I also knew that I wanted chess pieces instead of traditional wedding figurines—largely because wedding figurines always looked so damned cheesy to me.

By the time I got to Kyoto, it was dark and I was tired. I just wanted to get to the *ryokan*, grab a bite to eat maybe, and get some sleep. I grabbed a cab. *Ryokans* are traditional Japanese places to stay, like bed and breakfast places back home. I got there, apologizing for being late. The owner and proprietor, Haruka Kiriyama, didn't seem to mind.

"Your room is already made up," she said, and took me there, her slippers making no noise on the woven tatami rugs. She pushed the door open. It looked like rice paper, but it was actually frosted glass made to look like rice paper—a bit more practical. It was hot, being August, but not unpleasant. The futon that would be my bed was rolled out on the floor and made up with pretty floral sheets and a comforter, not that I thought I'd be needing it.

"Thank you," I said sincerely. I decided food could wait, and I dove for bed. The futon was more comfortable than any futon I'd ever slept on, including the one in Yukari's room. I sank into a dreamless sleep in a matter of minutes.

The next morning, I slept in a little. It was amazing how much sleep you could get when your roommate wasn't coming in at four, and when you couldn't hear video games going till one in the morning, or the head of the family making his breakfast at six. I must have been more exhausted than I'd realized, to drop off like that. I got up, cleaning the place up as best I could. The proprietor offered me breakfast, and I ate it: fish and rice with some miso soup. It was a little more substantial than what I was expecting, but it did taste good and I was hungry. Then, they rolled up the bed, putting it out of sight, and gave me a map of the area.

In the daylight, Kyoto was just as beautiful as I'd always read. It also had a certain intangible sense of quietude that needed to be experienced to be truly understood. I wandered the streets, looking at other tourists taking pictures of the various temples, both Buddhist and Shinto. I watched Buddhist monks in their orange robes as they did their silent walking meditation. The gardens were beyond lovely. I finally went to a Shinto shrine, feeling less invasive there.

The shrine had a large red post gateway that led into the courtyard. I watched as worshippers walked up to the courtyard, where there were incense sticks and a large barrel that held water. To either side of the barrel were long-handled ladles. I watched as they washed their hands, pouring water with the ladles over first one hand then the other. They wafted scented smoke over themselves. Then the worshippers walked up to the shrine itself.

I have no idea what the statue signified, but it was large and gold. In front of the statue was a lattice. People would throw money at the lattice, letting their offering fall to the ground beneath. I guessed that the lattice kept people from just sticking their hand in and taking some out, which made me sad. After the money was thrown, the person would bow his or her head in prayer, and then, when they were finished, they'd clap, twice, loudly. That was "amen." There was a fortune-telling system involved, too, but I was too chicken to try it out. I know that it involved buying a number and then going to a row of drawers, like the old card catalogs libraries used to have. You went to your "number" on the shelf and pulled out your fortune.

I didn't feel like finding out what the future might hold for me—again, probably too chicken.

But praying . . .

I was a good Catholic girl. I'd gone to elementary school at Mount Carmel, gone through everything from first communion to confirmation. I had been taught by nuns who would probably be horrified that I was sitting in a Shinto shrine, contemplating what I was. But I desperately needed some peace. So, nervously, I washed my hands, then mimicked the actions of the old woman next to me, fanning my wet hands to direct the incense smoke over me. It was thick and pungent, reminding me of the incense Father Gregory used to use on Easter. It had been years since I'd thought of it. Years since I'd been to church, now that I thought of it.

I walked tentatively up to the shrine. Did I send the prayer to the gold thing in the middle? Did I pray to the Catholic God of my childhood? Or did I just throw some money, send the prayer out there, and see who answered?

I felt in my pocket for a few hundred yen pieces and tossed them in. Then I bowed my head.

I don't know who this is for, I thought. *But I am very stressed out. I didn't know I'd like the job this much. And it's not just the job. I like who I am now. I don't know how to go back to my old life. I miss my friends, but I don't want to be what they want me to be. I love Ethan, but I don't like getting married on his schedule. I like being the one people turn to. I like being the one who takes risks to get things done. I like helping.*

I don't want to be a supporting player anymore.

I let that spin around in my head for a minute. Then, as I realized people were moving around me, I clapped my hands twice.

Thank you, I concluded in my head. That's all an "amen" was, anyway, right?

I walked to the side, where there were some walkways and mini-shrines, nestled in thickets of bamboo. I went to a stone bench, hidden behind some foliage.

I don't know how long I'd been crying, but I sat there until the tears abated, wiping at them ineffectually with the backs of my hands. I had a forlorn tissue in my purse, and I used it to blow my nose, since by that point I was crying for real, the whole ugly nine yards. I didn't know I'd been so unhappy. Sure, I wasn't completely fulfilled, but hey, who was?

I didn't even want to come to Japan, but I got nudged into it, and now I couldn't imagine going back. My job felt more real to me than processing inventory. I wasn't drawing, but editing was cooler than I thought. I had a say in how the story went. I saw a finished project, not the never-ending battery of "this week our mission is" or other corporate nonsense. I didn't have to worry about sales numbers for little pieces of metal and plastic that meant nothing to me.

I didn't know if I could explain that to Ethan, but I got the feeling that I should. It bothered me that, now that he had time to focus on our relationship, he expected me to put aside everything and be full-steam-ahead with him. I was to blame for that, since that was how it had always worked for us: I never cared enough about what was going on in my life, and I felt that my "purpose" was being a good girlfriend.

Now I had something I felt passionate about, and I prayed he'd understand what was happening to me, even though I was just getting a grip on it myself.

I walked around the city for the rest of the day, eating noodles for lunch in a tiny hole-in-the-wall *udon* house and having delicious sushi for dinner. I watched the stream of people. I never turned my K-tei on once. I must have walked ten miles that day, but my legs weren't tired. When I got back to the *ryokan*, my bed was waiting for me. I was asleep by eight o'clock, feeling like a little kid who was all cried out.

Things were going to change, was my last thought. I was ready for them to change.

August 29, Tuesday

I was back at work, refreshed and raring to go. I'd been helping Satomi and Sakura with some of their projects, but that had all been easy stuff, secondary. The American manga was taking up all my time. Morimoto and Chisato had still not gotten back together, not as a couple, and Morimoto was working his butt off on his usual workload as well as Chisato's work. Chisato was burning the midnight oil. The drawings were gorgeous, and her ink work was brilliant. And, immodest though it might sound, the story was pretty damned good, too. We were supposed to meet tonight to go over how the climactic battle scene and the ending were working. Chisato thought they lacked structure and needed more oomph while Morimoto thought they were properly subtle and had "emotional depth." I was referee. I thought uncharitably that if they'd just sleep together, we wouldn't keep having these fights.

Maybe that was the American in me.

I was just packing up to head back to the Kanai house when my K-tei rang. I thought it was Chisato or Yukari, but I didn't recognize the number. "*Mushi-mushi?*" I said.

"Lisa."

It was Ethan. I smiled, although after my little Kyoto epiphany, I realized that I needed to talk to him more than he probably realized. *But not until after the project is finished.* If I became an emotional wreck before we got this thing done, there was no telling what shape I'd be in. I couldn't contribute. And it just seemed like such a waste, to puncture my own tire this close to the finish line.

"How are you doing?" I said into the phone instead, making sure my voice was bright and cheerful, and in English. "Started that new job yet?"

"Nope. I've got another week or so. I decided to take a break."

"That's good," I said, and meant it. He'd been relatively relaxed when he first graduated from business school back in June, even though that now felt like forever ago. I hoped he was getting a little down time in. Then I glanced at my watch. "Wait a second. What are you doing up? It must be the middle of the night for you!"

"It feels like it," he said ruefully. "Surprise, honey."

I did not make the connection. "Surprise, what?"

"Surprise, I'm in Tokyo."

I felt my stomach fall to my knees. "What? Why?"

There was an irritated chuckle. "Um, that wasn't the response I was looking for."

"You're here? In Tokyo?" I just couldn't wrap my head around it. "Why didn't you . . ." *Warn me?* I quickly changed the verbiage. ". . . tell me?" I finished.

"I wanted it to be a surprise." He made a low groan. "Jesus, how do you deal with this jet lag?"

I grinned. He'd often teased me about jet lag. It was nice that at least now he'd understand a bit better, even though I hated that he had to go through it. "Don't fight it. If you're sleepy, just sleep."

"That's not what the books say," he countered, and I could hear the frown in his voice. "I want to get on a regular schedule. Are you off work yet?"

"Well, yes . . ." I said, thinking of my Morimoto-Chisato meeting. "But—"

"I'm at the Westin Tokyo," he said. "I was hoping you could meet me here, have some dinner. Spend the night."

I smiled. It sounded romantic, and under any other circumstances, it would be wonderful. "I need to make some calls."

"Why?" Again, that slight edge of irritation.

I sighed. "I was supposed to have a story meeting tonight," I said, and I caught Satomi's surprised gaze as I said that. She then quickly nodded good night, which I returned, and I watched her get ready to head out the door "You know I've got that project on the fifteenth. We're in the final stretch."

"Oh." He made a disgruntled noise, as if he was annoyed and he was stretching to try and alleviate his discomfort. "So, are you saying you can't see me?"

I sighed. He'd come all these thousands of miles. I might love what I was doing, but I really did love the guy. Especially with a grand romantic gesture like this. "I just need to call to get out of it."

"That's my girl." I could hear the smile back.

"And I need to call my host family, so they won't worry when I don't show up," I said. "Oh, and I ought to grab my bag. You know, clothes for tomorrow. For work."

"That makes sense." He sounded magnanimous now. "What do you want for dinner?"

"Probably room service," I said, thinking of his jet lag.

I went back to the Kanai house, told them I would be out, and left messages for Morimoto and Chisato, telling them I'd have to bow out of the meeting tonight. Then I headed for the Westin, with an overnight bag and a sense of tension.

The Westin was part of a block of opulent, Western-style, luxury hotels in the heart of Tokyo. You could tell the minute you walked past the liveried doormen, in their immaculate uniforms, and into the sumptuous lobby that was filled with white people, that you were in tourist central. I hadn't heard this much English spoken in one place since I'd gone to a gaijin club in Roppongi with Yukari and crew, and that was months ago.

I went up to the room number that Ethan had told me, and he

opened the door. He looked tired. He was wearing a T-shirt and a pair of jeans, and his hair was rumpled. His eyes looked bleary.

I grinned. "You fell asleep," I said.

"It was like frickin' narcolepsy," he said. "I was sitting there, watching the TV . . . some movie in English with Japanese subtitles. Next thing I knew, an hour and a half had passed." He shook his head. "I drank coffee and everything. I thought I could beat it."

"Jet lag hits some people especially hard," I said. "And you haven't done a lot of international travel, huh?"

"Well, neither have you." He said it like I'd been trying to one-up him. "You sound awfully worldly."

"I've done the New York–Japan run three times now," I said. "I've got a few tricks for the ride back, if you want."

"I've got Ambien for the ride back," he said. "Should've used it this time, but I didn't want to miss anything."

Hmm. I didn't ask him where he'd gotten the Ambien, although I wondered if he had his own prescription. He didn't sleep much when he was stressed out. "So, you've got the new job and everything. You must be excited."

He stretched out on the bed, and I stretched out next to him, like we were back at home. He leaned up on one arm, studying my face. He looked weary, and I got the feeling it was more than just travel exhaustion.

"I've worked my whole life toward this. At least, that's what it feels like." He turned on his back, head cradled on the pillow, staring at the ceiling. "Now that it's done, I don't know. Sometimes I wonder if it was worth it. The job's gonna be a bitch, Lise."

I stroked his hair, making sympathetic noises. He'd spoken like this occasionally, just before a hard test or a performance review at work. But he'd never looked quite this beaten up before. "You'll get through it. You always have."

"I just— I feel like if I can just get stuff in control, it won't roll me, you know?" He looked at me, blue eyes pleading. "If I can just get everything to the point where I don't have to worry about it, then I can calm down. It's uncertainty that makes me nuts."

I knew that about him. He was almost obsessive when it came to his life. His organizer looked like a travel-worn Bible, the kind that preachers carried with them everywhere.

"So, you're worried about the new job," I said. "You've got the offer, but you haven't started. I know you. You'll get a system in place in a few weeks, maybe a month. It won't be that bad."

He stared at me a minute, then shook his head.

"I'm not worried about the job," he said, sounding surprised. "I'm worried about *us,* Lisa. Why else do you think I came all this way?"

I stared back at him. "Because . . . you missed me?" Maybe he was more insightful than I'd given him credit for. Maybe he knew I was having doubts, that my life was changing. Maybe . . .

He snorted. "Well, yeah, but you'd be home by December at the latest. That's not that far, I could've managed."

I sat up. "So, wait a minute, why *are* you here?"

He sighed and also sat up. "The *wedding,* Lisa. I know you sent some stuff to Stacy, and I've been talking to her. But damn it, I want to go over this with my *wife.* My future wife."

"You're here because you think the wedding's off track?" I said it out loud, but it still didn't make sense.

"Yes," he said, sounding relieved that I finally got it. "I brought a bunch of stuff for you to make decisions on. We don't have to go over it tonight, but I'm only in town for six days. We'll have a little time."

I was aghast. "I've got this huge project I'm supposed to be working on!"

He smiled sadly. "I know. I'll work around it if I have to. But this is the rest of our lives, Lisa. This is important."

I didn't want to have this conversation. I didn't want to do this at all.

"Listen, I'm going to take a shower. I'm feeling pretty grungy," he said. "Then maybe we can have dinner downstairs and go over a few brochures. Just look," he said, when I must've glared at him. "And then . . ."

His smile turned sexual, and he winked.

"I've missed you, Lisa."

I didn't say anything as he went into the bathroom to take a shower. I just stared at the door.

September 4, Monday

"Welcome to Narita International Airport," the voice over the loudspeaker said in accented English.

I'd accompanied Ethan here to send him off. He could've taken a shuttle just as easily from the hotel, but he wanted to take the subway. He was impressed that I knew how to negotiate the trains. "Why do they make everything so confusing?" he'd asked. I didn't have an answer to that. I'd felt the same way when I first got here, but now I was used to it, so used to it that it never even crossed my mind.

Yoda let me have the day off so I could see Ethan to the airport. I'd even brought Ethan to the office one day, just to show him around. Being tall, with light hair, he'd stood out like a beacon, and even the rowdy guy editors had fallen silent. Ethan got that a lot, when we were on a train or wandering around Shibuya or Shinjuku or the Ginza. He got attention, whether he wanted it or not. I think he was torn between being proud and being embarrassed by the stares.

Ethan and I sat next to a convenience kiosk and a few airport shops. "Well," he said, expectantly.

"Well," I replied.

"We got a lot done, I think."

I didn't want to respond to that. We'd decided on the number of guests (fifty), the kind of food (Italian), and the location (a restaurant). We decided on a budget, mostly Ethan's job since he wanted to pay for the bulk of the wedding. He'd nixed the chess pieces idea, thinking it was too weird. We agreed not to have any figurines at all. We'd decided that the colors would be light blue and light green. He said he'd okay the mini-cakes if I got pricing. We were all systems go for April.

"You're still pissed at me, aren't you?"

I sighed. He knew I was angry. I was tired and stressed—all the tranquillity from my Kyoto trip had been sapped from me, and now I was resentful and I knew I had no good damned right to be. I'd worked with Morimoto and Chisato as best I could, and they'd stepped up to the plate. Ethan had tried to amuse himself while I was working, but mostly he'd spent time in the hotel, playing video games or watching American movies, saying he was "catching up" on all the stuff he'd missed while he was in school. I just felt . . . spread too thin.

"You knew this had to get done," he said.

"No, actually, I don't know that," I snapped, and surprised the both of us.

"What's that supposed to mean?" he asked, when he recovered.

"Why April? Why do we have to move so fast on this?"

I should've said this earlier. I shouldn't have waited until I was about to put him on a plane for fourteen hours or so before having this conversation. Natch: *argument*. Because it definitely had all the earmarks of an argument.

"I've explained it till I'm blue in the face," he replied. "How many—"

"No, you've explained that *you* need to have the wedding in April because of *your* work schedule. You wanted me to go to Japan in the first place, even though I didn't want to, because *you* felt guilty at not being able to spend time with me and you thought I'd be occupied and amused and out of your way. Then *you* expected me to quit my internship and just fly the hell home to plan *your* wedding."

"*Our* wedding," he corrected.

Our voices were raising, and people were starting to look. I deliberately took some calming breaths and lowered my voice to a near-whisper. "Our wedding," I conceded. "On *your* schedule."

"Jesus, why didn't you say all this earlier?"

"I've been mentioning that it felt too rushed and too soon," I said. "I said it when I was home in New York. I've sent some e-mails. I just didn't get mad. And apparently you don't hear me unless I'm mad!"

"This is because of that little 'project' of yours, isn't it?" he asked.

I could've killed him. In that moment, I could've killed him.

"Why is it," I said instead, still in that low voice, "that when it's for business school, it's important, but when it's my job, it's just a 'little project'?"

"Don't pull that on me. You know it's different. And no, I'm not being some sexist fascist pig," he said sharply, "so don't even try it. It's *you*, Lisa. You might be totally competent at your job at the plant, but you've never cared about your 'career' in your life. I know you. When we talked about you staying at home with the kids, being a stay-at-home mom, you were fine with it, so I'm not being the macho asshole here."

I reddened. "I wouldn't have minded," I said, realizing that, on some level, I minded now. I mean, I loved kids and wanted some of my own.

But I wanted it to be a choice, not a tacitly accepted fallback or an escape from a crappy job.

"So now you're telling me you move to another country for a few months, as a frickin' *intern*, and now you're Ms. Ambition? Come on. You're just a glorified secretary! No matter what you're working on, do you really think they're going to offer you a job at the end of the day?"

His words stung, and I had to blink back tears for a minute. "I guess it is unreasonable," I said. "But even if they don't offer me a job, I'm working on an actual *book*, Ethan. I'm doing something I never dreamed I'd be able to do. My name's going to be on it as an assistant editor." I swallowed. "That may not sound like much to you. But it means a hell of a lot to me."

"Enough that you'd put off your own wedding for it?" He stroked my cheek. "That's all I'm asking. For you to put it in perspective, Lise. To figure out what's really important."

I pulled away from his touch. "I think what's bothering me the most is that you don't seem to get that I can have something important that doesn't have to do with us," I said quietly. "With *you*."

He shook his head. "That's not fair. That's not fair at all. You make me sound so damned selfish."

"I'm not trying to," I said. "But . . . it's been your way or no way. There hasn't been a lot of compromise, is all I'm saying."

"And there's compromise your way?" His voice raised, and I gestured to him to quiet down. "No, damn it, I won't lower my voice. If we put off the wedding, I have no idea when we'll be able to get married. I don't know when I'll have the time. Are you willing to do that?"

"I could move in with you," I said.

"Oh, your family would love that one," he said, rolling his eyes.

"Screw 'em," I said, and he was surprised enough to be quiet. "It wouldn't be much different. We'd be together. I just don't want to rush this. I want to have more in my life than just . . ."

I couldn't finish it, knowing it would sound too harsh.

"More than just our marriage, huh?" He finished it for me, and it sounded as brutal as a knife wound. "More than just *me*."

"You would want me to have my own life, too," I argued passionately. "You wouldn't want some clinging little wife. I might be on to something here. I just want to see where it goes. Then I'll marry you, whenever we can. But if I have to leave, or if you keep browbeating me because I'm not focusing enough on what you want, from thousands of miles away . . ."

"Stop making me sound like a monster!"

I sighed and let the tears fall. I looked down.

"I'm just asking for a little more time," I said.

"You know what? Take all the fucking time you need." He grabbed his bag and started heading for the security checkpoint.

"Ethan," I yelled, running after him and grabbing his arm. People were staring, but I didn't care. "Ethan, please, don't leave this way."

He jerked his arm away. "I'm trying to make everything right for us, and I'm tired of feeling like the villain just because I want to move ahead with our lives," he said. "When you get your priorities straight, then you can call me. But until you do, I don't ever want to have this goddamned conversation again. Do you hear me?"

Like he was reprimanding a child or a dog. His voice was razor-sharp and menacing.

I stood back. "You're absolutely right," I said, quietly. "I won't call."

"You do whatever you have to do," he said, determined to get the last word.

I let him. I walked away from him and the airport, heading for the trains. I didn't know who was right, but I did know that I was tired of feeling this way. I might be crazy or selfish, but I had to go with my gut. Or else I'd hate him and myself forever.

September 12, Tuesday

"EASY, RISA-SAN," YUKARI TOLD ME. "THAT'S YOUR FIFTH SHOT OF sake. You might want to slow down."

I nodded. We were at a noisy bar in Roppongi, one of the typical sleazy club joints. The music was blaring electronica and J-pop, and the crowd was young and mixed—Japanese and gaijin.

The project was almost finished. The presentation was scheduled. It was, as my brother, Tony, used to say, "all over but the shoutin'."

So, unfortunately, were Ethan and I. At least it felt that way.

I hadn't called him since our blow-up at Narita. I hadn't e-mailed him, and true to his word, he hadn't tried to contact me. He was like that: not exactly inflexible, but his word meant a lot to him. He'd rather eat fiberglass than go back and say he was wrong or break his promise. He said the ball was in my court. It would be until I did something. He'd die before he reached out to me.

I admired his sense of loyalty and his commitment. And hey, the jury was still out on whether or not I was a complete bitch. But I had my pride, too, and I still wasn't ready to call him.

"You should not let it all upset you very," Yukari said philosophically and in English.

"Shouldn't let all what upset me?"

"You know," she said, unwilling to mention it. For some weird reason, she'd been speaking English tonight, on and off, heavily accented and strangely cadenced. I wondered if it had to do with us being in Roppongi, which had a lot of English-speakers. "I think it great that you came to Tokyo!"

I smiled, answering in English as well. "Thanks, Yuki-chan. I'm glad I met you, too."

She smiled brightly. "You are brave to follow your dream."

"That's what I thought," I said, taking a sip of water. My head was starting to swim, ever so slightly—aftereffects of the sake.

"I want to be brave like you!"

"You are!" I said, as only a drunken friend can. "I'm sure you can do whatever you put your mind to. Don't let anything stop you!"

"Exactly!" With that, she did another shot of sake and then coughed a little because she'd downed it just a wee bit too fast. "Exactly," she repeated, sounding less triumphant and more like a croak.

"So, what do you want to do?" I said, trying to switch from my miserable life to Yukari's Grand Plan, which apparently required bravery.

"I," she said, and stood up with a little wobble, "am going to America!"

She said this loudly enough that several people nearby, mostly white guys, cheered for her. She smiled at them, then sat back down.

"Congratulations," I said, and motioned the waitress to bring us two more shots. "Any idea where?"

"New York City!" Like she was singing it. She rested her head on her hand, smiling at me goofily.

"Good choice," I said, as the waitress put our drinks down and I paid her. "If you can make it there, you can make it anywhere. Etcetera."

"I can make it there," she said. "I am making it there!"

"I'm glad for you," I said, and I meant it. She had a lot of energy and a lot of spirit. She was too young to let one bad marriage and a bad job market make her into a "Parasite Eve" as Nobuko had deemed her. She could still do plenty and enjoy her life. "So, any idea what you'd want to do in New York?"

"I will be work at a hotel," she said, and her voice was a little less goofy and a little more determined. "I will be an . . . associate."

"Sounds like you've got a good idea," I said. "You've done some research. That's good."

She took a second, as if she were processing what I'd said in English. Then she shook her head, and I wasn't sure if it was translation error or drunken misinterpretation. "I did more than research. I am going."

I blinked. Now I thought maybe I was having the drunken misinterpretation problems. "You're going? To New York?"

"*Hai.*" She picked up the shot and drank it without a bobble. Then she put the glass down and studied me, switching back to Japanese. "I just found out today. I've been accepted to the foreign associates program at the New York Hilton. They liked my English, they liked that I was a university graduate. They said that I had the right personality." She smiled again, her mega-watt best. I'll just bet they thought she had the right personality. She was a walking welcome advertisement. The fact that she was pretty probably helped.

"That's fantastic," I said in Japanese. I drank my shot of sake, feeling the burn down the back of my throat. It took me a second before

I could speak, although I'd developed something of a tolerance by now. "Congratulations, again! You've been keeping secrets!"

"I didn't want to tell you, not until I knew for sure," she said. "It's been fun to watch you and Chisato-chan working, and having Mori-kun come over. You seem to love what you do so much, and you've got . . . *purpose*. You want something. I forgot what it was like to want to do anything."

"Are you sure?" I knew that I'd mentioned America, and I thought she'd like the lack of strictures. Still, it had been my idea. I'd hate it if she wound up going and feeling awful.

"Well, I won't know until I get there," she said, shrugging, but her eyes twinkled with excitement that I hadn't seen before. "But, oh, I've read books! And it just seems so exciting. So *glamorous*. And it'll be different. I am sick of Tokyo. I'm sick of Japan. I need a change."

I smiled. "Well, you'll have that. What do your parents think?"

Now her face fell, and she stared at the surface of our little bar table.

"Uh-oh," I said. "You haven't told them yet?"

She shook her head.

"When were you planning on telling them?"

"Soon," she said, in a singsong tone, like a little kid would use. "Soon" meaning "not now, and probably not until I absolutely have to."

"When do you leave?" I figured she'd probably try to hold off on telling them until the last possible minute.

She sighed. "I should leave in November or December at the latest. They are still working out the details."

"Well, that gives you a little time," I said thoughtfully. She'd be leaving around the same time I did, come to think of it. "But you probably don't want to wait too long. You'll need to get ready, and I'm sure there's stuff you need to do. Medical stuff, paperwork." I thought of the hoops I had to jump through before I made it to Tokyo. "You can't just hide that from them. I'm sure they'll start to notice that you're leaving the house during the day, and they'll get curious."

"You're right," she admitted. "I am not looking forward to it, though. I don't know what they'll say, but I am certain my father won't be at all happy about it."

I nodded sympathetically. Fathers were like that. "They want you to be happy," I said.

"He'd rather I was safe."

I wondered about that, considering Yukari basically did whatever the hell she wanted in Tokyo. If she was my kid, I'd picture her dead in an alley in Shinjuku faster than I'd worry about her taking a job somewhere. Still, New York City didn't exactly have a reputation as the safest city in the world, so I could see how her choice would disturb him. It wasn't like she was taking a position in Boise, Idaho.

"I'm sure they'll be supportive," I said, trying to be encouraging and positive.

"Your boyfriend was not supportive of your move," she pointed out, and just like a set of stitches being pulled, that pain came rushing back. "How do you handle that?"

I sighed, taking a deep breath. I was already feeling fuzzy enough that it was hard to focus. I couldn't take another anesthetizing shot of sake, no matter how badly I wanted to descend into oblivion. "He wasn't always unsupportive," I defended. "Besides, he's just doing the best he can. I have to do the best I can, and whether or not he supports that, I have to do what I think is right."

She thought about that for a long minute, then she nodded, as if I were an oracle or something. "That is good," she said. "That is what I'll say to my parents."

"Good," I echoed. "Just . . . you might not want to tell them that I said it."

She grinned. "All right," she said. "You about ready to go home?"

I stood up, and the room made a slow, lazy spin. "Um, yeah," I said, grabbing the table until I felt steadier. "That might be a good idea."

September 15, Friday

This was it. The big presentation. Yoda would be there; his boss Mr. Tanaka would be there; and according to Yoda, two members of the executive board would be there, a Mr. Ogawa and a Mr. Hatagami. They would be our final pass-through. They would decide if the book went into production and, if so, how, and all the marketing decisions that would go with that.

Or, conversely, they would decide if Chisato had just wasted several months of her life, completely unpaid. And they would decide if Morimoto had just staked his career on a flop that would probably haunt him for the rest of his career at Sansoro, which pretty much meant the rest of his career. Meanwhile, the worst that could happen to me, in theory, would be getting fired and sent home unceremoniously, sort of like a dishonorable discharge. In this case, almost literally.

My stomach hurt. Chisato looked ill. Morimoto looked dead, he was so pale.

We were in the same well-appointed conference room on the twentieth floor in which I'd first met Mr. Tanaka. It seemed smaller, possibly because the aura of power and respectability that surrounded Mr. Ogawa and Mr. Hatagami was so impressive. Yoda bowed low, as did Mr. Tanaka, so the rest of us followed suit. And, once again, I was the only one who didn't have business cards. Not the best way to start the meeting.

"She's our American intern," Yoda said, by way of explanation. He did everything but clap me on the back, and for some strange reason, he was taking me at my word and really pushing me out in front of this. "This was Morimoto-san's idea, but she has really done an incredible amount of work. It was her idea to bring it to me, and when they say that Americans are tenacious, they are not joking. She has brought this to bear through sheer power of will!"

They all laughed at that, and I chuckled without really getting why it was funny.

"She will be doing the presentation today," he said.

I glanced at Morimoto and Chisato nervously. That wasn't what we had planned. I knew that I was the fall guy for the project, but I never dreamed that Yoda would take this big a risk. Putting an intern, a nobody contest winner, in front of something that would require money? That was nuts!

Morimoto, however, looked like he'd dodged a bullet. He really needed to work on his public speaking skills. And Chisato looked at me with eyes full of trust, as if she felt that if anybody could get her project sold, it would be me.

No pressure, Lisa.

I cleared my throat. "I apologize for any mistakes I might make," I started. "My Japanese has improved through working at Sansoro, but as Akamatsu-sensei has pointed out, I am American." God willing, that would get me a few get-out-of-jail-free points . . . the ignorant gaijin defense.

They nodded. Mr. Ogawa said, "By all means, go on. We are very interested in the project. We thought that Nobuko-san was no longer interested in it, so it would not come to fruition."

"Nobuko-san had some . . . philosophical differences," I said, as diplomatically as possible. "And she decided to postpone her participation and focus on some of her other deadlines. Instead, we have been working with a . . . colleague of hers. Chisato Kiriyama." I gestured to Chisato, who blushed and nodded her head. "Chisato-san was Nobuko-san's *assisto* for five years and learned a lot in that . . ." I searched for the word. "Apprenticeship," I finished.

I shot a quick glance at Yoda. He looked reluctantly impressed. Probably didn't think I could be that delicate or diplomatic. Hah.

"So, you went ahead with the project with a relative unknown," he said. "Not to offend Chisato-san's talent."

She shook her head. Of course she wouldn't be offended by the executive board members!

"We did decide to go ahead to meet the executive board's deadline," I said, feeling stupid. "I think that the story line and the art speak for themselves. Perhaps that would be the easiest way to proceed."

The triumvirate of Tanaka, Ogawa, and Hatagami nodded.

The next hour was pure torture. They went over the copies we'd made of the drawings, in minute detail. They debated story points. But worst of all, they'd be stone silent, watching me. I turned to Chisato and Morimoto on a couple of occasions. Morimoto had stuttered but stepped up to the plate. Chisato was much more charming and surprisingly eloquent about her own work. I couldn't get any reading from any of the men's expressions about how they felt about the whole thing, whether it was a waste of time or what.

Finally, the thing ended, after they'd asked questions in a flurry and fallen silent again. "Thank you for your time," I said inanely, then turned to Yoda for help.

He stood. "That concludes the presentation," he said very formally. "We look forward to hearing the executive board's decision on the matter."

The triumvirate stood, and everybody bowed to one another. Mr. Hatagami had to leave immediately to attend another meeting, as did Mr. Tanaka, but Mr. Ogawa lingered behind, so I couldn't be relieved that the thing was over. At least not yet.

"That was an interesting presentation," he said to us, leaning against the conference table, looking supremely comfortable.

"Interesting" wasn't exactly a ringing endorsement, but I still said, "Thank you, Ogawa-san."

"I have seen so many of the same sort of projects coming out of Sansoro," he mused. "So many manga that are . . . safe, shall we say. This is a breath of fresh air."

I felt weak and boneless for a second. That was an endorsement. "Thank you," I said again, and this time I meant it.

"Chisato-san, was it?"

Chisato nodded, blushing like a rose.

"Your penwork is remarkable. And your style . . . I can see Nobuko-san's influence, but there is something that is distinctly your own about it."

Now she was practically crying.

"The balance between the action scenes and emotional scenes was very deft," he said, and now it was Morimoto's turn to straighten with pride. "Excellent editing. Considering this was a side project with very few resources, I know I am very impressed with what's occurred here."

I felt like I'd swallowed the sun. He had liked it. He had really liked it!

"I will do everything I can to get the board to see the viability of this project," he said, "and the efforts that the three of you have made. And Akamatsu-san, I will recommend you for commendation as well. They have progressed very far under your leadership."

"Ogawa-san is too kind," Yoda said, bowing slightly. "They had their own initiative. I simply guided the process."

"We need more innovation. Now more than ever," Ogawa said, his tone very sober and low. "America is a market we need to exploit more than we have. I would not have expected we would get so much out of our little contest."

I smiled at him.

"Your internship is up in December, isn't it?" he asked.

I nodded.

His expression turned shrewd, and he crossed his arms. "You have a talent for manga," he said. "Have you considered continuing in it? As an editor?"

My smile broadened. "I've discovered," I said, "that it's something I love to do. If I can get the opportunity to continue, I certainly will."

"You know," he said, "you work very well with our staff. And as I've said, we need someone who understands Americans, as well as someone with your innovation and, pardon me, tenacity."

I stared at him. Was he . . . wait a minute. What *was* he saying?

"Have you been enjoying your stay in Tokyo?" he continued innocently.

I nodded. "Very much."

"Would you perhaps consider staying here," he said. "Maybe on a more permanent basis?"

I blinked. Son of a bitch.

He *was* offering me a job.

I jibbered, "I had not realized it might be an option," and then burbled into incoherence. I knew what Morimoto felt like.

He shrugged, as if he'd just exchanged pleasantries and not made an obscure offer to change my life. "Again, it's something I'll discuss with the board," he said. "But I think you should consider it, very seriously."

He made his good-byes and returned to his office. Yoda beamed at us. I think it was the first time I'd ever seen him truly, unqualifiedly happy.

"We did it!" Chisato said, then turned to Morimoto. Had it been anywhere but Japan, they probably would have hugged. But in Japan, even couples who had been together for years didn't hug in public—and these two were still under the impression that they weren't a couple. Nonetheless, they smiled foolishly at each other.

"So, Risa-san," Yoda said, stretching back with a smug grin, "what are you going to do now?"

Throw up, more than likely. I sent him a wan smile. "I guess I have a lot of thinking to do."

And God as my witness, I had no idea what conclusion I was going to come up with.

September 16, Saturday

It was afternoon. I was still riding the buzz from Friday's presentation. They were talking about offering me a job, getting me a work visa. Having me live in Tokyo. It was enough to make me start hyperventilating. Still, it brought up all kinds of questions. For one thing, it was just under two weeks since I'd last seen Ethan, and that had gone terribly. I still hadn't talked to him, although I'd sent him an e-mail. He hadn't answered. I didn't know how to patch it up, but I was fairly certain that telling him "oh, by the way, congrats on the great job but I'm moving to Tokyo" wasn't going to really mend matters.

Which brought up the question: Did I want to mend matters?

I sank back against the couch. Ichiro was in his room—he was there a lot more lately, I'd noticed. His parents seemed skittish about it. I was sure he'd be back out at some point, but for the moment, I had the living room to myself, and I was using it the way the monks did in the Kyoto temples. I had my legs crossed and I was trying my damnedest to be meditative.

I loved Ethan. It seemed like I kept trying to justify that to myself lately, but the fact was, I really did love him. When I'd first met him, he was a lot less stressed. He liked to talk to me about everything and anything. He was driven, granted, but I'd known a lot of driven people in my life: my parents, my brother. If anything, they always wondered why I wasn't more driven. In a family full of businesspeople, it was hard to feel like I fit in.

Ethan, on the other hand, really had his act together. I guess I found that appealing. And he knew immediately that he wanted me to be a part of that act. By our third date, he'd told me I was a keeper. By our one-month anniversary, he said he wanted to be sure I was in his life for a long time. By our one-year anniversary, he told me he'd marry me. It wasn't a proposal. It was a statement of fact. At the time, it had seemed wildly romantic and, to be honest, really comforting. I knew where he was going in life, and I was very happy to be a part of the team that got us there.

The problem was, I didn't really have any picture of where *I* wanted to be in life. I was happy to be part of the team. Now I was developing my own life, and he didn't seem to be at all interested in that. He wanted his team member back.

I closed my eyes. That sounded terribly unfair. In fact, it made him sound like an asshole. But he wasn't, not really. He just hadn't bargained for this. Hell, *I* hadn't bargained for this. Who knew that at twenty-nine, the opportunity you've only let yourself dream about could fall into your lap? I hadn't planned for any of this, it had just happened, and now I wasn't sure I wanted to walk away.

That made it sound like I was having an affair, I realized. *I didn't plan for this to happen, it just happened, but I can't walk away.*

I had always thought that marriage would mean more to me than that. It *ought* to mean more to me than that.

I needed to talk this over with somebody I could trust. I got out my K-tei and dialed blindly.

"Hello?" I heard Stacy's voice, and it felt like a lifeline.

"Stace," I said, and heard her boy, Thomas, warbling loudly in the background. "Is this a good time?" Just because I was having a breakdown didn't mean I had to interrupt her life.

"It's okay," she said, but her voice sounded guarded. "What's going on? Did you finally turn in that big project you were working on?"

"Yeah, it's finally finished," I said. "I'm sorry I couldn't talk with you and Perry before. It's been really crazy."

"I know how that is," she said, but her voice still sounded remote. "Between work and the baby coming . . ."

"How are you feeling?" I asked. Since she'd pointed out how busy I was the last time I called, I didn't want to just leap in with my problems. "How far along are you now?"

"About five-plus months, and I'm showing like you would not believe," she said, warming a little. "I look like a mini-van. I'm gaining more weight than I did with Thomas, that's for sure."

I made an encouraging noise. "That's gotta be rough."

"It's not easy," she said. "And they desperately need to hire someone. I've been screaming, and they've been blaming it on hormones, but if they don't hire somebody soon, I swear I'm going to kill someone." She grunted, and I imagined her shifting position on her chair, maybe even rubbing her belly. She did that a lot when she was pregnant with Thomas. "I think they were really spoiled by having you there, and they can't find anybody good enough to fill your spot. If you showed up tomorrow, I bet you could negotiate a twenty percent raise, easy."

"Really?" That was a surprise. They were nothing if not cheap. Hell, they were still making do without even replacing me.

"If only to shut me up," she added, then laughed. "I don't know that I can hold out till December, though. I was wondering, honey, I don't mean to push, but have you given any thought to coming home early?"

I swallowed hard. "Uh, no, not exactly."

She paused. "What's going on? You sound weird."

"A lot's happened in the past few weeks," I said. "Ethan came out to see me."

"He went all the way to Tokyo?" Stacy sounded floored. "Wow. That guy really loves you!"

"He wanted to use the gap between quitting his old job and starting his new one," I started, not eager to go into specifics. "He wanted to talk about wedding details."

"Oooh, fun!" She sounded chipper and perky, and it only made things harder. "I've said it before, I'll say it again: I'm matron of honor!"

"Wait for it," I said. "The thing is, he wants us to get married in April. That's coming up pretty quick. And he wants me to handle all the details—or at least, he did. Then he said he'd handle more of the details, but he was pretty pissed about it. He's totally fixated on the April Wedding Plan."

"And you?" Stacy prompted.

"I don't know why he's in such a big rush," I said, and the guilt that accompanied that statement was overwhelming. "I mean, I know why he is, intellectually. He's got a big product launch thingy in June, so that's out, and he needs to really make his mark in the next year, so no vacations, no time off for good behavior. He's got to buckle down. And nobody buckles down like Ethan," I said with feeling.

"Not if the way he attacked grad school is any indication," she agreed, and I immediately felt better.

"So I'm not crazy," I said. "God, that's a relief."

"If you didn't get married in April, when could you get married?"

"What, you mean per his schedule? I have no idea," I said, feeling glum again. "He doesn't even want to discuss the option. He doesn't seem to understand that planning a wedding from a foreign country is really a bear. He just keeps saying that I don't want to get married."

Stacy paused again. "I don't want to say anything that might piss you off, but you really don't sound excited about getting married."

"I just don't like how this is coming around," I said. "And Stace, there's a whole new element now. Remember that project I was working on?"

"The one that kept you so busy?"

Obviously she was still pretty pissed that I hadn't been able to talk to her, which seemed weird. "Yeah, that one. Well, it went over really, really well. The higher-ups were really impressed."

"That's great," she said, but it sounded, oh, I don't know. Maybe I was just being completely paranoid and insane by this point. Maybe I was expecting too much.

"The thing is, they talked about maybe offering me a job, including a work visa." I waited a second for her to make a comment, and when she didn't, I clarified, "Meaning they'd want me to move here."

Stacy went silent on the other end of the line.

"You still there?" I finally asked anxiously, after a long, painful minute.

"You mean, you'd move to Japan?"

"That's the idea," I said. "Believe me, no one was more shocked than me."

"What does Ethan think about this?"

"I haven't told him," I said. "We're sort of fighting right now. When he left, he said I was too uninterested, and that we'd talk later. We haven't talked since. It's pretty bad."

"Do you want to stay over there?"

Now it was my turn to pause. "I don't know," I said in a small voice. "I thought I'd hate it, but I'm really starting to like it over here. And I don't know what to do."

"You'd really just move away? For a job?"

I couldn't believe I was hearing this. "It's not just that," I said. "I love doing this. You and Perry both said you wished you had the opportunity!"

"Yeah, but that was just . . ." She sounded awful. "You really wouldn't come back? It's one thing to take a shot at a dream for a year. That's like, I don't know, a long vacation. But you'd leave your family and your fiancé and all your friends? You're not that materialistic. I know you're not like that."

"It's not about the job, exactly," I argued. "It's . . . the chance. It's . . ."

I didn't know how to explain it. If she didn't get it, I didn't know how to get her there.

"Listen," she said, and her voice sounded tight. "I'm sure you'll make the right decision. Thomas is fussing, and Roger's waiting for dinner, so I gotta go."

"Okay." I clutched my K-tei like a life preserver.

"You'll make the right decision. Just sleep on it," she said, and her voice sounded tentative, like she wasn't sure I'd make the right decision. It was unnerving.

We said good-bye and I hung up. Then I put my head against the couch, ready to weep.

"You okay?" A voice said to my left.

I looked. It was Ichiro, looking worried.

"Yeah, just got a lot of stuff going on."

He sat next to me. He was looking better lately—eating more, sleeping more. Those scary dark circles under his eyes had pretty much vanished, and he was more normal teen boy, less feral video game creature. "Like what?"

I thought about it. Well, my best friend didn't seem to have an answer, my future husband didn't have an answer . . . maybe my twelve-year-old ex-enemy might have an insight. "I love Ethan, but he wants to get married and he wants me to plan everything and do a lot of work from here, and go back home early if I can, and he doesn't understand that I love what I'm doing—I love being an editor for manga. He wants me to give it up. And now I might have a chance to be an editor for good and live here. But I don't want to abandon Ethan. And I don't want to resent him if I give this up. So I have no idea what to do."

He pulled his knees up to his chin, nodding sagely. He looked like a mini-Buddha, wearing a Niketown T-shirt and baggy sweats.

"So, what do you think I should do?"

"What do you want more?" he asked.

"It's not that simple," I said. "I mean, I don't even know if the manga thing would work out in the long run. And I don't want to be the sort of person who chooses a job over love."

"But you really like the manga," he said. "You're good at it. It makes you happy. That's kind of love, too."

Damn, the kid had me there.

"Your boyfriend should understand," Ichiro said.

"That's very progressive of you," I joked. "Man, you're wise."

"I try," he joked, and I reached over and ruffled his hair. He made a dissenting noise. "I made a decision today," he added.

"Oh, yeah?"

"I'm going back to school." He looked at me, part assertive, part scared.

I nodded. "I think that's a good idea."

"I figure, if you're brave enough to go for what you want, even if you might not get it," he said, "then I guess I could, too."

He let that simmer for a moment, then grinned. "I'm calling a friend to go hang out at an arcade."

He walked out, leaving that bomb in his wake. He thought I was brave for being there. For going after what I wanted, even if it meant failure.

He had a point.

September 19, Tuesday

IT WAS EARLY IN THE MORNING, AND I WAS ALREADY UP. I'D SLEPT
lousy the night before, thanks to a last-minute missive from Yoda.
Just before I'd left the office, he told me to be sure to be "prompt" because I was supposed to talk to Mr. Ogawa. I knew the basic hierar-
chy of the Sansoro power structure. Mr. Ogawa was just under God
when it came to manga projects. If he wanted to talk to me, it was
probably related to giving me a job and relocating me to Tokyo.

I was excited. And terrified. And terribly, terribly confused.

I got dressed quietly and headed for the kitchen. I figured I'd stop
off at a Starbucks for my usual coffee fix. To my surprise, Mr. Kanai
was up and at the kitchen table. I mean, I wasn't surprised that he
was up, although at six a.m. it seemed almost a little late for him,
since he was usually out the door and didn't linger over breakfast or

anything. What was worse, he looked like he was sitting at a board-room desk rather than a kitchen table. He stared at me expectantly.

I wasn't sure what was going on. "*Ohayo gozaimasu,*" I greeted him.

He didn't respond in kind. "I have been waiting for you. There are some things we need to discuss."

I swallowed, glancing at the clock on the wall. I had time. It'd just cut into my Starbucks experience. Still, this sounded ominous. I never talked to Mr. Kanai. I sat down. "Is something wrong?"

He sighed heavily. "Yes," he said. "As you know, there have been many changes. Some of these have been . . . unsettling."

Ah, the gift of understatement. "You mean, Yukari moving to New York for a year?"

He scowled at me. Apparently it was okay to refer to things obliquely. Coming right out with the unpleasantness, that was just not done. "That is part of the issue."

"I see." I wasn't quite sure where I fit into all of this.

"I was thinking that, perhaps, she would listen to you," he said. "She is still young and impressionable. It seems like a bad idea for her to move so far and to so large a city at this time."

I stared at him. Of course, the fact that she ran wild on the streets of Tokyo, and the fact that he was basically subsidizing her to do so, was perfectly all right. Again, I didn't get this family. Maybe he fig-ured that here at least he was able to keep an eye on her. Perhaps it was a wildness that was culturally acceptable?

I took a deep breath and then said, "I don't think that I would be very convincing, Kanai-san," I said, putting as much politeness and respect in my voice as possible. I certainly didn't want him thinking I was insulting him. "I moved here from New York, so I've moved an equal distance. And I went by myself." I waited a second and then said, "I'm not sure, but I think that might've been part of her inspi-ration."

His scowl deepened. "I had suspected, as well," he said. "But I felt sure you would not encourage her in such a pursuit. Besides, you are older, and you have a marriage proposal. You know what you are going to do with your life. She has none of these options."

My back straightened. This was weird on about eighteen levels, especially considering the meeting I was going to have today. I didn't necessarily want to mention that the marriage proposal aspect was on shaky ground, since he'd probably blame me for it. Maybe rightfully so.

Probably rightfully so.

"Kanai-san," I said slowly. "I respect and appreciate your desire to protect your daughter. However, Yukari-san has a strong personality. She is a determined person. She will do very well, I think. You don't need to worry about her."

Now he looked insulted. "I know my daughter."

I nodded. "Of course you do. But—"

"I do not need you to tell me what she is like. I know that she has wanted this for some time."

I nodded again.

"I also know," he said darkly, glaring at me, "that it was all just a fantasy until you moved into this house."

Aha, so he *was* blaming me.

"And now, Ichi-kun has decided to go back to school," he said. "While I am happy about this decision, since I think it will be good for him, his mother is somewhat upset."

I could imagine. I was proud of Ichiro, too, for going back to school. But that did leave Mrs. Kanai with a whole day filled with waiting for her son to come home. Well, she'd get a hobby. Lots of moms did.

"She's talking of possibly getting a job," Mr. Kanai said.

"Well, that would be good," I said. That beat a hobby, especially if they were having some financial difficulties. Although if they weren't supporting Yukari's partying habits and clothing budget, they were probably going to be coming out ahead anyway.

He leaned forward. "I don't think— You can't possibly under-stand," he said. "I have worked very hard for many years, to provide for and protect my family. There have been some challenges. It has not been easy."

I wasn't sure if he was referring to the problems with Ichiro, or Yukari's parasitism, or what. Maybe he meant the financial diffi-culties.

"But I have done what I had to, even when it was against my na-ture," he said. "I have recently gotten a new position, at a different firm. My new job starts in a month."

My eyes widened. "Congratulations," I said and meant it. I knew in Japanese culture, working for a corporation was like being married— you thought you'd stay there for life, and it was more like a marriage commitment than just something that gave you a paycheck, like in the States. If he got a new job, it had to be traumatic for him on some level.

"I can now afford to pay for this place and support my children, without making concessions. Even get tutors for Ichiro. Yukari does not need to leave." He paused for a second. "And we no longer need the small income from your stay here."

I stared at him. "Are you— Am I being kicked out?"

He winced. "It simply is not necessary for you to stay here," he said. "Yukari is your friend, and she will be leaving. There is no rea-son for you to stay."

He *was* kicking me out.

"My wife is still very upset at the prospect of her children leav-ing," he added. "She sees you as responsible. That could cause prob-lems."

Now he was pulling out the big guns. They wouldn't say "we ex-pect you out," but they would say "it would be better for everyone," counting on my sense of social decency to fall on my sword, as it were, and prevent the situation from getting any worse.

"I will need a little time to find a new place to stay," I finally said, feeling numb.

He smiled, a small quirk of a smile, more of satisfaction than of happiness. "Of course," he said. "We expected that. And I will ask around for a new place for you."

"I appreciate that," I said in formal tones. I glanced at the clock. Six twenty. Damn. "I am sorry, but I really must go to work now."

"Of course," he repeated and stood up, obviously glad that the whole ugly situation was over. Then he looked tentative and said offhandedly, "If you reconsider talking to Yukari about her decision . . ."

The guy had nerve, I'll give him that one. "I will think about it," I said. Japanese culture didn't like saying "no" outright, and, strangely enough, with all my changes, I did find myself being more Japanese. Still, he got the message and nodded glumly.

I got my jacket and portfolio and headed down the street toward the subway, merging with the people already heading down the stairs. It was commuter rush hour. I didn't feel the jostle of bodies. All I could think of was that Mr. Kanai thought I had my act together. He thought I was doing this all on some kind of grand plan. And now, here I was, with the opportunity to move here, the chance to take up one dream but abandon another.

And he thought I was just trying to screw up *his* life.

I WAS still reeling from my conversation with Mr. Kanai when I went into the office to meet with Yoda. I wasn't ready for this conversation, not really. It had been different, staying in Tokyo with at least a host family and not on my own. I mean, it had sucked initially, when Ichiro was still being a terror and before I understood and befriended Yukari, but it had become something of a haven. Now, if I took the job, it would mean starting fresh, and Yukari would be leaving, and I probably wouldn't see Ichiro anymore. Beyond that, there was the

Ethan issue. I didn't want to lose him, and I didn't want to leave him, did I? No, I didn't. I couldn't.

But haven't you sort of left him already?

I'd been sweating about it the entire train ride to the office. Now, taking the elevator to my floor, I still hadn't come to any conclusions.

I walked in, and there was a palpable electricity in the air. People knew that something was going on, they just didn't know *what*, and I could see speculation on their faces. Something big. Something involving their intern. In some of them, I could sense a little resentment. They'd been here for years, and now some little gaijin intern flunky gets a big chance?

I didn't blame them. Hell, if I were in their positions, I'd probably feel the same way. Again, not making my decision any easier. Of course, part of the reason they were offering me anything in the first place was because I went for it. I went against protocol, I ignored the chain of command. I even managed to circumvent one of their biggest artists. Japanese culture might tell people to wait until they're called on, but that wasn't what was going to make Sansoro successful, and the executive board seemed to realize that. If Sony could make a white English guy their president, then apparently a smaller publishing company like Sansoro could hire a Japanese-Italian-American editor.

I walked to my desk, putting my lunch down and hanging my coat on the back of my chair, my usual ritual. Satomi and Sakura were there already, and to my surprise, they actually put their pens down and started talking to me.

"What's going on?" Satomi said.

I blinked at her. "What do you mean?"

"Ogawa-san is coming down," she said. "From the twentieth floor. He *never* comes down to this floor."

I swallowed. "I think it may have to do with me," I hedged.

"Really?" Sakura's eyes were round as saucers . . . or at least as round as you can get with an epicanthic fold. "Are you in trouble?"

"No," I said. "It had to do with this project I was working on."

Satomi's eyes narrowed. "The American-manga hybrid?"

I stared at her. I knew I hadn't said anything directly to her, and I doubted Morimoto had spilled the beans—he had just as much riding on it as I did. And Yoda wouldn't say anything. At least, not to Satomi.

"Something like that," I finally said. Satomi had always seemed friendly, but now she seemed angry. I had no idea why, exactly, although I could hazard some guesses. "Is something the matter?"

She shook her head. "No, no. Of course not. What would be the matter?"

Okay, she was definitely put out. What'd I do? It wasn't like I was going to become her boss or anything. She had her own projects, and she was definitely senior in her own right. I think she was editor number fourteen, or something.

Yoda came out before we could continue the conversation. "Risa-san? Could you please come in here?"

I nodded and quickly went into the office, sparing only one backward glance for the S-girls. Sakura seemed to be still in shock. Satomi just went back to her work, scratching through drawings as if she wanted to stab something with her pen.

Mr. Ogawa was already in the office. He didn't look comfortable. Of course, he was behind Yoda's desk, which meant he was flanked by two of the most precarious towers of paper in the whole little room. I wouldn't be comfortable, either. He stood, bowed slightly. I bowed in return.

Yoda shut the door and sat next to me. I could feel my heart beating a mile a minute in my chest, and my mouth went dry.

"We need to discuss some things with you, Risa-san," Mr. Ogawa said, and his voice was low and rumbly and very, very serious. "The executive board has voted on the American manga project. I want you to know, it was a close decision."

I rubbed my palms on my thighs, as subtly as I could. I was so nervous, I could barely stand it.

"Although they had many reservations, we were finally in agreement. We want to take the chance," he said. "We are going to publish it and then see how it does in foreign markets. Specifically, the United States."

I smiled, feeling my chest expand as I finally took a deep breath. I knew it was iffy, but I also knew it was good. No matter what else happened or what I decided, I was glad that it was going to happen. I felt proud enough to pop.

"However," Mr. Ogawa continued, "there are some details of the work that have provoked some . . . controversy."

He said "controversy" the way some people say "bestiality." It was obviously a distasteful thing for him and for the executive board.

"As you know, Nobuko-san was under the impression that she would be the artist for this manga."

I swallowed hard. Of course, Nobuko. Should've figured she wouldn't just roll over and let it go.

"She heard about the presentation through one of your editors. Now that we've agreed to go through with it, it's hardly something we could hide from her, nor would we want to. She is a member of the Sansoro family and we value her input."

I nodded. They were still going through with it at least. But what was the cost going to be, to appease the vindictive woman?

"She felt that the editorial staff that would be needed to continue the series was inexperienced," he said.

She was targeting Morimoto, damn it.

"She also did not think the art was necessarily professional enough. And, of course, the story line will need revision, down the line."

I swallowed. No, she had stayed true to form and criticized all three of us. "I'm sure those things can be worked out as the project moves forward."

He sighed and looked at Yoda. Yoda's voice was soft and gentle, completely out of character in some ways, and in other ways more true than any of the rough posturing that he'd ever done, that James Jameson act he put on for the editorial floor.

"Risa-san," he said, "she is willing to accept Chisato-san as artist. And she is willing to accept Morimoto as a senior editor for the project. She is also willing to be completely removed from the project, letting it go forward without her name or influence."

I waited for the catch . . . and then realized that they'd made no mention of me.

"She wants me off the project," I said.

Yoda nodded, even though Mr. Ogawa frowned at his openness. "She thinks you are a bad influence. And you are only an intern. She feels it would set a bad precedent and would demoralize other members of the staff." He let out a deep breath. "She is not far wrong with that."

I nodded, looking at Mr. Ogawa.

"I would have liked working with you," Mr. Ogawa said, and I believed him. "You have very interesting ideas. A lot of spirit. We could use that."

I swallowed hard. "Thank you, Ogawa-san. You are very kind."

"Unfortunately," Yoda continued, "this means that your internship with us is over."

"Wait," I said, stunned. "What? I thought I would only be fired if the project was a failure!"

He sat there, silent, waiting for me to understand.

"That's part of the condition, too," I said, after rolling it around in my head for a while. "She doesn't just want me gone. She wants me gone *now*."

"My assistant has arranged for your travel, to go home," Mr. Ogawa put in. "And we will pay out the rest of your contract. I have also taken the liberty of upgrading your airplane ticket to business class. It seems the least we could do."

Yoda looked like a basset hound, mournful and solemn.

"So that's it," I said, feeling even more numb. It was all going so well, and now it was over. I don't even know if I would have taken the job, but to have it suggested and then ripped away . . . the whole thing was unreal.

"Yes," Yoda said.

"Is today my last day? I mean, do I leave right now?" I couldn't imagine going through the motions of work.

He nodded. "We will miss you."

I nodded back, then bowed to each of them. Then Yoda put his hand out, American style. I shook it.

Then I walked out of Sansoro. I didn't go back.

September 23, Saturday

I was sitting in, of all places, a Denny's in Hamamatsu, Tokyo. Yukari was throwing me a going-away party, and she'd pulled out all the stops. Her party crew was there, of course (whether they knew me or not, a party was a party), and to my surprise, her family was there, too. I figured that Mr. Kanai felt guilty, perhaps, or at least somehow indebted since I was a guest in his house. Mrs. Kanai looked different, because she was dressed up. I'd seen her in house clothes for so long, I had no idea how pretty and sophisticated she could look when she really tried. Apparently, Yukari was not a fluke. And Ichiro was there, as well, which I was glad for. We swapped e-mail addresses. He had just started school again, and while he proclaimed it was a drag, he had made a few friends and sounded happy to be out of the house. It was going well.

A contingent from Sansoro showed up, too, which I was thankful for. Morimoto and Chisato, naturally, as well as a couple of guys from the editorial floor. Sakura made it, as well. Satomi did not.

"Satomi-san is the one who told Nobuko-san about the project," Morimoto told me, pulling me aside. "She knew you were working on something with me. Nobuko-san had offered her an *assisto* job, with a fast-track to becoming a *manga-ka,* if she would be a spy."

I'd suspected, but I hadn't known. It hurt. "Satomi-san was doing what she felt was right, I'm sure," I said, trying to be Zen about the whole thing.

Morimoto shrugged. "Nobuko-san is furious, although she's glad . . ." He paused. "Well."

He meant, she was glad that she'd at least managed to get rid of me. "So, is Satomi jumping ship?"

"She starts at Nobuko-san's on Monday," Chisato said. "I can't think of a more fitting punishment."

Chisato had changed quite a bit, as well. She'd gotten her hair cut into a stylish shag that brushed past her shoulders. She'd also spent some of her advance money, apparently, and taken Yukari's advice. She was wearing a cute little dress and heels. Morimoto was having trouble not staring at her. She smiled at him, a little smile that I could instantly tell meant she was going to make sure they were a couple, officially, by the end of the night. Success had made her confident. Couldn't have happened to a nicer girl.

"Now that you're going home, what are you going to do?"

This from Red. It seemed that this was all the girl thought about when she was near me. "I have no idea," I said, wondering if the menu offered Moon Over My Hammy, like the Denny's back home did. Yukari picked this place because she thought it'd be fun and "American-like," while at the same time, Denny's was a relatively upscale dining establishment.

Transitioning back to the States was going to be tough, I could just tell.

"Are you going to keep going with manga?" Morimoto asked.

"It would be a shame if you didn't," Chisato added. "You are really a talented editor. You translate well . . . from words to pictures."

I sighed. "Unfortunately, there's not a huge market for manga editors in the States," I said.

"I wish they'd offered you the job," Chisato said. "I wish you could stay in Japan."

I smiled at her, patting her shoulder. "I don't know that I would've taken the job anyway," I said. "I have a fiancé back home, and family. It would have been very hard. But it would have been nice." I felt tears welling up and quickly cleared my throat and brushed my hand over the corners of my eyes before I really broke down. "Besides, you can always come visit me. Once the manga gets distributed in the States, maybe you could come and do a book signing in New York or something!"

Chisato's eyes sparkled. "I'd never even dreamed of that," she breathed.

Morimoto nudged her, smiling at her. "You would be fantastic."

They were so cute. For a second, I missed Ethan painfully, like a knife cut. I hissed from the sheer emotional pain of it.

I was going home now, early, just like he'd wanted. But he'd know it wasn't necessarily my idea. And even if it was my idea . . . we'd said an awful lot. I don't know if we could just pick up where we left off.

Yukari stood up. "A toast! To my American friend, who is going to New York before I do!"

I grinned. Weird toast, but everybody cheered and was happy. Yukari was Yukari. It would be fun to see what she did in a different country.

Mr. and Mrs. Kanai decided to leave and gave me a card, basically saying farewell. I was all packed. My plane was leaving tomorrow. I got the feeling they'd be giving me a wide berth until I did. Ichiro gave me a hug, which was surprising to everyone, possibly even Ichiro. They quickly shuttled him away.

The one person I had hoped to see, strangely enough, was Yoda. He'd been a pain in the ass, granted. But he'd been a sweet sort of pain in the ass, and he'd actually been a really cool boss. "Is Akamatsu-sensei coming?" I asked Morimoto.

Morimoto looked uncomfortable. "I didn't ask him," he said. "But Akamatsu-sensei does not come to these kinds of parties. It's not personal."

I still felt a little crestfallen. It was personal to me. I thought of him as a friend as much as an employer. Still, that probably wasn't how things were done here. I thought he was proud of me, though.

I wondered, but I really did think so.

Finally, we moved to a bar and did karaoke until one in the morning. I wound up singing "Proud Mary" with Sakura, Yukari, and Chisato as my backup singers. It was hilarious, and I was pleasantly buzzed by the time Yukari and I went back home. I was feeling the pain of missing all my new friends, but it was a dull pain—like Jerry Maguire said, where you don't feel it now, but you get an inkling of what you're in for in the near future.

"What are you going to do when you go home, Riri-chan?" Yukari asked me quietly, in the cab on the way home.

I looked out the window, and the tears I'd been fighting all night slowly leaked out. "I don't know, Yuki-chan," I replied. "I really don't know, and it's scaring the hell out of me."

I cried harder, to the cabdriver's consternation. Yukari made little soothing noises and patted the back of my head awkwardly, trying to console me. "It will be all right," she said. "I am sure everything will be all right. You've been so brave this far. It can't be that much harder to be brave there, yes?"

I hiccupped. "I have to figure out where to work, where to live, whether or not I'm getting married. I just have a lot of stuff to deal with."

"But you did all that here," she said. "And you didn't even know Tokyo. It will be much easier in your hometown."

"From your mouth to God's ear," I muttered in English.

"What?" she asked.

"Nothing. Never mind," I said. "You've been a very good friend, Yuki-chan."

She smiled. "So have you. Now come on, you've got a big flight ahead of you."

September 27, Wednesday

FOUR DAYS, SEVEN HOURS, AND A LIFETIME LATER, I TOUCHED
down at JFK, and my Tokyo adventure was officially over.

My cousin Anna picked me up at the airport and talked nonstop
all the way back to Groverton. I catnapped the whole time, not even
trying to make sense of all the family gossip and personal drama she
was relaying. I knew Anna—she didn't mind, she just liked talking,
and whether I was paying attention or even conscious didn't matter.
As we got closer to my parents' house, she finally asked about me.

"What's next for you?"

"Sleeping," I replied promptly. "For like forty-eight hours."

"Well, yeah, okay. But then what?" She took after Nana Falloya:
she could badger anyone, for any length of time. If she wasn't already
a damned good graphic designer, she'd probably have made a good

lawyer. Or police interrogator. "The job thing. You going back to the plant?"

"Anna, I just got off a fourteen-hour plane ride. I'm jet-lagged and totally wiped out," I said. "I don't know what I'm going to do. I'm sure I'll figure it out."

"Because if you go back to the plant," she said, as if I hadn't said anything, "you might be able to get Louise a job. She's my room-mate. Oh! And that reminds me . . . roommate. Are you going to get your own place again? Or are you moving in with Ethan? Hey, how *is* Ethan, anyway? I haven't heard about him in forever. You guys are still together, right? Nana will be pissed if you move in before you're married, though. First, because of the sin thing, of course, but she also always says that people who live together before they get married get divorced like eighty percent of the time . . ."

I let her words batter at me, trying to get back to a place of tranquillity. I mentally pictured walking around Kyoto. It helped. A little.

"Man, you *are* out of it," Anna finally pronounced. "Well, here we are! Your parents'. I'll help get your stuff."

The house looked just the same as when I'd left it, not surprisingly. Maroon-red siding with white shutters and a black roof. Snow hadn't fallen yet, but it was cold and the trees had turned. I wished I'd paid more attention to it before, when I was growing up here, when I was working here. Autumn leaves in upstate New York were as breathtaking as the cherry blossoms in Tokyo, even if we didn't have a big statewide party for it.

Maybe we should, I thought, bemused.

My parents came out, hugged me, and helped me into the house. My dad put my suitcase in my old room and assured me that I could stay "as long as I wanted."

"Are you hungry?" my mom asked quickly. "You must be exhausted, but you'll probably want to stay awake. You know, get on a normal schedule."

The comment reminded me of Ethan, when he'd gone to Japan. I felt tears choking at me, and I said, "I am thirsty."

"Okay," she said, obviously surprised at my emotional state. "What would you like? Soda? Juice? Or I could make some coffee . . ."

I swallowed. "Do you have any green tea?"

My dad walked in on that one. "Did you say green tea?"

I nodded. It just sounded comforting. I'd drunk like four cups a day when I was working with Morimoto and Chisato, and they'd always had a big pot of it going at work. I could still remember the smell.

"I do have some green tea," my mom said, leading me to the kitchen table. "Come on, sit down."

"You look terrible," my dad said, as my mom went to work getting the teapot ready.

I smiled at him wryly. "Thanks."

"You know what I mean," he said, and he frowned. I was always going to be Daddy's baby girl, and right now, that worked for me. "You never should've gone so far away. Look at you! Skin and bones . . ."

"Honey," my mom said, in a warning tone of voice.

He sniffed. "Oh, all right. Your mom made me promise not to bug you to death after you got home." He shrugged. "I know how you are, about traveling and all."

I smiled. Thank you, Mom.

"But you probably want to call Ethan," he added.

"I will," I said. And I knew I would. I just didn't know when.

I slept for the next day, on and off, my body trying desperately to adjust. I put off calling Ethan for a full day. I knew he wouldn't call me. I just wasn't sure what to say to him. I waited until Thursday night.

"Hello?" His voice was a little brusque.

"Ethan," I said, feeling terribly vulnerable.

There was a pause. "Lisa?"

"Yeah, it's me," I said, my voice shaky. "You told me to call you."

I took his responding silence as assent.

"Could I see you?" I said.

"What, you're home?"

"Yup. Got in yesterday. I've been trying to sleep it off."

"But . . . it's not December," he said. "What happened?"

"I'll tell you when I see you," I said. "Are you in New York or Groverton?"

"Groverton," he said. "I'm still getting an apartment in the city, but I'm having a hell of a time, well, never mind. Do you want me to come pick you up? Are you at your parents?"

"Yes, to both," I said.

We went to a diner. I ordered a real burger and peanut-oil fries, and my usual chocolate–peanut butter shake. He ordered the same but barely touched his food.

"So what happened?"

I relayed my story. "So they sent me back early," I finished. "But at least I got to fly business class."

He was silent and strangely calm during the retelling, but his face was somber, just this side of unhappy. "Would you have taken the job?"

I'd had some time to think about it, but I wanted to be honest. "I don't think so," I said. "I don't want to leave you, Ethan. I really do love you."

"I love you, too."

"I just— I thought we'd talk about it. I mean, that would've been a real opportunity, not just an internship. You would've understood that, right?"

He shrugged. "Yes, of course. But Tokyo . . ."

I sighed. "Well, it's a moot point now," I said.

"So now what are you going to do?"

"I'm getting that a lot," I said. "I'm still not sure. I need to lick my wounds a little bit, get my bearings. I really liked that job, Ethan."

"It was a good opportunity, and you had an adventure," he said, his voice sympathetic. "Most people never would've even gotten a shot. You should be proud of it."

"I think— I might like to keep pursuing it," I said, glad that he was being so understanding.

He went still. "What does that mean?"

"Not in Japan," I said. "Here, in the States. Of course, most of the publishers are on the West Coast, but there's got to be a publisher or distributor here in New York."

He sighed. "Well, okay. But how long were you going to pursue it?"

I frowned. "I don't know. I mean, I'm just coming up with the idea."

"I still love you," he said. "And I want you to be happy. But you don't have a lot of experience. Getting a job with your Japanese publisher would've been a long shot."

"I know . . ."

"I don't mind if you want to pursue it," he said, "but I do mind if you're going to keep pushing things aside just to go after this dream, you know?"

"The wedding," I said.

He leaned back, crossing his arms. "I've been patient, Lisa. But right now, I just wonder if maybe you're using this job thing as a dodge. If you really wanted to marry me, you wouldn't keep throwing up these roadblocks. I've had a lot of time to think about it, since I graduated."

I pushed the rest of my food away. I didn't want to keep having this fight—this same, repetitious, painful fight.

"I just think that if you really loved me, you'd put this first."

"Like you are?"

He nodded.

"So why April, Ethan?" I asked. I was tired of being the flake, the dreamer, the one who wasn't buckling down and dealing with what needed to be dealt with. "Why not September? Or even July?"

He shook his head. "You know why . . ."

"Because of your *job*. But because my job would pay less and I haven't been planning for it since birth, it's not as important."

"Do we have to go through this again?" he said sharply.

"The bottom line here is, you don't see that my life and my choices are as important as yours. You just see me as a piece of your life, and you're pissed that I'm not fitting in." I felt tears sting, and I let them go. We had to stop doing this in public places. Of course, the way this was going, we weren't going to do this again. This was the finale. This was it.

"I do think your life is important," he said. "But I'm the major breadwinner. I'm going to pay for most of the wedding, and I'll be supporting you when we have kids. If that isn't what you want, that's what you were supposed to decide. You tell me now: Is that or is that not what you want?"

I bit my lip. I wanted to be married to him. I wanted his kids. I had dreamed about it for so long.

But I didn't want to make all my decisions with him as final judge. I didn't want to be his support staff anymore. I wanted to be equal. And I didn't think that was a bad thing.

"I want to be your partner," I said. "I want to have my own life. I want to be responsible for my own choices. And I want you to respect and value what I bring to the table."

He growled in frustration. "Damn it, what do you think I do now?"

"I think," I said, "you're in charge. And I don't like it."

"Fine," he said, putting money on the table. "I'll take you home."

I went back with him, silent the whole way. He dropped me off in my parents' driveway. "I can't believe it's ending like this," he said, as the car idled.

"I can't either," I said.

He leaned over and kissed me, and I could taste the anger and frustration and sadness. I clung to him.

"You don't have to do this," he whispered against my cheek.

"Yeah, I do," I whispered back. "But if you change your mind, you know where to find me."

With that, I left the car blindly and went back into the house.

September 29, Friday

Perry and Stacy came over, the usual twosome, on a lunch break. Stacy looked very pregnant, while Perry still looked very thin. I'd been home for two days, and I hadn't seen them or called them, which I felt guilty about. I think I was just hibernating. Of course, I'd already seen Ethan, which could also account for why I wasn't seeing anybody else. I know talking with someone probably would've helped, but I just couldn't see calling them up and whining about what was going on. There wasn't anything they could do, and I just felt . . . wounded, I guess, and raw.

Stacy led the way, as usual. "I'm so sorry you got fired," she said. "What happened?"

I went over the details—the project, the success, Nobuko's betrayal. Ogawa's decision. They made noises of shock and anger in all the right places, which was gratifying and did make me feel a bit better, but at the same time, going over the details just seemed to re-open the wound.

"It wasn't fair," I concluded, taking a long swig of chocolate milk. At least chocolate still had its deliciously antidepressant effects. "If I'd just done a lousy job, that would be one thing. But I worked my ass off, and they knew it, and the project will be coming out and it'll probably do really well. And I didn't even get a thank-you. They didn't want to piss off their senior artist. I had to take the fall so they could keep the project. It was totally personal."

"That majorly sucks," Perry said, shaking his head and also swigging chocolate milk, probably to be companionable.

"Can you sue them?" Stacy's eyes snapped with anger. She looked like a fiery fertility goddess, all belly and baleful stare.

I shook my head. "I mean, I guess I could, but it's just not done. It's not the thing to do."

"Why not?" she asked, incensed. "They screwed you! They're going to make money on all the work you did, when they were just paying you a crappy stipend! You should take them to the cleaners!"

"I'm not going to sue Sansoro," I said. "I mean, I understand why they did what they did, even if I don't agree with it or like it. I know what kind of a bind they're in."

"Are you kidding me with this? Nobody held a gun to their heads!"

"Stace," I said, trying to calm her down, "it's a Japanese thing."

She made a harrumph noise but left it alone. "It's not like you're Japanese or anything," she said. "That shouldn't apply to you."

I remembered a song from forever ago, something about asking a guy if he was Christian, and his answer being, "Ma'am, I am tonight." That's sort of how I felt.

When I was in Japan, I wasn't Japanese—or at least, not enough to matter. But in this case, yes, ma'am, I certainly was.

"So now what are you going to do?" Perry was never pro-lawsuit, so he was eager to change the topic.

"I'm not sure." I sank back against my chair, feeling deflated and wishing I'd run out and bought some cookies or candy or some other sugary comfort food. "I'll need to get a job, that's for sure. I can't live here forever."

"Are your parents pressuring you?" Stacy asked, her mothering taking on a different bent now.

"Not really," I admitted. "Actually, they seem . . . weird. They're not quite sure what to do with me."

"What do you mean?" This from Perry, who had finished off his milk and was now rummaging through the pantry.

"They act like they don't know how to treat me. My mom is talking to me a bit more, but she keeps saying stuff like 'you don't have to hurry' and 'I don't want to upset you.' Like I'd tried to kill myself or something." I shuddered. "It's kind of creeping me out, actually."

Stacy and Perry exchanged a look, and I got the same disquieting feeling I'd been getting all week from my parents.

"Okay. What *is* that? Have I been that psychotic?"

"I wouldn't say psychotic," Perry demurred.

"You have been different, though," Stacy said.

"Different from *what*?"

"Different from how you used to be." Stacy rubbed her burgeoning stomach absentmindedly. "I don't know if I can explain how, exactly. You're just more, well, irritable. And depressed, I guess."

"Depressed?" I felt irritated more than sad at the moment, even though I knew they were trying to help. "Well, I had a shot at a dream job and I got fired instead, and my fiancé and I are probably broken up, and I'm living at home without a job. Okay. I can see the depression thing."

Perry sat down with some Fig Newtons he'd scrounged from the pantry. "What's up with Ethan? I thought he'd be thrilled that you're home."

"He sort of is," I said, feeling like an idiot all over again. "The thing is, ever since I went to Japan, I've been reevaluating things. And I just need a little more time to sort things out. I don't want to rush into something just because it's comfortable. I need him to understand that."

Stacy clicked her tongue. "Ethan's waited for you for a long time," she said.

I stared at her. "How do you figure?"

"He wanted you to come home after he graduated, but when you went back, he was okay with it," she said philosophically.

"First of all, he wasn't okay with it. Second, I'd made a year commitment. I wouldn't ask him to quit business school just because I wanted to get married sooner," I said.

"It's not quite the same thing," Stacy pointed out, "but never mind. The point is, you're back now, and you love the guy. Why make it harder? You can still figure out what you want to do *and* get married to him, right? I have to say, I love you, Lise, but it's sort of like you're just jerking him around now. I mean, you don't even have an excuse anymore."

I sat down, feeling tears stinging my eyes. Was that what I was doing? I didn't want to jerk Ethan around. But I just wanted things to slow down a little so I could sort them out. Things just didn't seem as cut and dried.

"I just wanted things to work to *our* plan," I said. "Not just *his* plan. I know plans mean a lot to him, but we've got to be an equal team on this."

"It doesn't seem equal to me," Stacy said. "Sounds like you want it all your way."

"I don't mean to sound uncharitable," I replied, "but you're supposed to be *my* friend. I don't think I'm being that unreasonable, here. I'm just asking for some more time."

She sighed. "Well, we'll just agree to disagree on that one."

I couldn't believe it. This, from my best friend?

"Anyway, at least I think I've got a solution for one of your problems," she said, and she was smiling broadly now. "They finally approved a new budget at work and can hire somebody, and when I told them you were back in town, they were ecstatic. You would not *believe* how hideously the temp they brought in screwed stuff up. They would hire you back in a minute, with a guaranteed seven percent raise. And they'd want you to start as soon as humanly possible. So now you don't have to worry about the job! And you'll get enough money to move out quickly, too," she added. She cleared her throat. "Unless you decide to move in with Ethan after all. I mean, I'm not pushing, but it could happen."

It did seem like a neat solution. In fact, it would be like slightly interrupted service—*we now bring you back to your regularly scheduled life, already in progress.*

I liked the people at the semiconductor plant. I had gotten some job satisfaction in getting stuff done. But I'd also been bored out of my mind. I hadn't had the same charge or challenge that I had at Sansoro. *That* was what I wanted, I realized. The ability to be creative. The ability to do something I loved, not just something I could tolerate that I happened to be good at.

I smiled back at Stacy, not so brightly. "Thanks, Stace," I said. "I really appreciate it."

"I'll tell them on Monday, then," she said. "I took today off for a doctor's appointment. Of course, I could call Todd this afternoon, I'm sure he could set up something on Monday, I don't know that you have to reinterview—"

"Actually," I interrupted, "how long do I have to think about this?"

Now Perry pushed back from the table, as if sensing explosions were about to happen. "You know, I'll bet I'm late for work," he said, glancing at his watch. "I've been taking too long a lunch break lately. Stacy, I gotta run."

"What do you have to think about?" Stacy asked me, ignoring Perry's plea. "You were complaining you didn't have a job, you need the money, you're miserable. We talked about this before you got back. It sounds sort of ungrateful, actually."

I knew she needed the help. I knew she trusted me. And yeah, we'd talked about it—although she'd done most of the talking. "I just really miss my job," I said. "I miss working with manga. I miss working in publishing. I was thinking I might try for a job like that over here."

"What?" Now she looked aghast. "But . . . you've got like no experience. You're never going to make enough to move out that way. And where would you go? Not back to Japan, would you?"

"No, not that far," I said. "But I'm sure there are places in the States. I just thought I'd give it a try, Stacy. It won't be forever. I'm not asking you to hold the job for me indefinitely. I just need to try this."

Stacy stood up with difficulty, considering the bump, but she glared at me the whole time. "Fine," she said. "Think about it. We have to go."

"See you at anime club?" Perry asked, eager to defuse the situation.

Stacy tugged on his hand. "She might be too busy," she said, and they walked out.

October 6, Friday

I WAS NERVOUS. I'D TAKEN THE TRAIN IN, UNGODLY EARLY, TO make sure I got to the interview on time. I'd killed the past hour and a half at a nearby ubiquitous Starbucks, and strangely enough, that reminded me of Japan, of all places. But now, I was here.

BubbleMech wasn't a leading importer of Japanese manga in the United States, but it was competitive—and, more important, it was in New York, unlike the other top publishers who were all on the West Coast. They had been interested when I sent them the manga that won the Sansoro contest and by the fact that I'd worked with the publisher on an upcoming manga project. When the human resources people called, I had enthusiastically accepted the interview. That was a week ago. Thanks to stress and uncertainty, I'd lost about three pounds in the interim.

"Ms. Falloya?"

I looked up. The receptionist was pretty and dressed reasonably sharply—I was in Manhattan, after all. "Yes?" I finally said.

"Mr. Zorin is ready to see you," she said. "Would you follow me?"

I did as instructed, clutching my little black portfolio in a death grip. I didn't need to be this nervous. The thing was, nobody knew that I was coming here. Stacy and Perry still hadn't spoken to me, Ethan was still angry . . . and I didn't know how to talk to them regardless. I'd mentioned it in passing to my parents because they were so worried at my "pajama zombie" act, as my father called my restless house haunting. They wanted me to get a job and to eventually move out and resume a life of my own. Not to put too fine a point on it, but they were also worried that I was so listless.

This was something that excited me. This felt *right*. More right than going back to the semiconductor plant. More right than getting married and pretending I didn't want a job at all. I still loved Ethan and my friends, but this felt like *me*.

I walked down a long hallway and passed what had to be the editorial offices. They didn't have the cluttered bullpen-styled situation that Sansoro did; instead, they had the usual maze of cubicles, just like my old job. But the drawings on the walls, and the toys, and the general atmosphere were common enough to warm my heart. The only thing missing was a big urn of green tea where the coffee machine currently sat.

The receptionist led me to a small office, and to Mr. Zorin, head of the editorial department. "Thank you," I said to her, bowing reflexively. She gave me a puzzled look and a smile, and then left.

"Mr. Zorin," I said, accepting the hand he put out to shake with, and then giving him a business card with both hands. It wasn't an affectation, the Japanese were on to something with the business card ritual. It was just formal enough to have a sense of importance, and it also got past the awkwardness of "when do I give him my business card?"

"How are you doing?" he asked.

"Fine," I said, sitting down when he gestured to the chair.

"I've really been looking forward to this. We don't get a lot of people with your background."

What, in electronics inventory management? I bit my tongue. That wasn't going to help matters any. "Thanks," I said instead. "I'm excited at the opportunity."

"So, you're Japanese?"

I sent him a small, Zen-like smile.

"I'm Japanese," I agreed, then shrugged. "Japanese enough, anyway."

"You speak Japanese, though, and read it," he continued, not getting the joke.

"Yes," I said. "As you know, I've spent the past nine months in Tokyo, at an internship with Sansoro Publishing. It was a great opportunity."

"I hear you got to work with Nobuko. She's a legendary *manga-ka*, I gather."

I nodded, a little wary.

"Tell me," he said, leaning forward, "is she as difficult to work with as I've heard?"

My eyes must've widened. Still, I was loyal to Sansoro, no matter what had happened.

"She's a brilliant artist," I evaded. "And I didn't work with her on a one-to-one basis."

He nodded with a knowing grin, as if acknowledging the political motivations behind my careful answer. "That's good," he said, and I didn't know if he was referring to Nobuko's brilliance or my refusal to badmouth the woman. "And you did editorial work?"

I outlined what I'd managed to work on.

"You actually got to manage projects?" He interrupted me. "As an intern? I figured that you'd just be doing dumb stuff—copying, running proofs back from the printer. I wasn't sure how you'd managed what you included on your résumé."

"I took on a few experimental projects," I explained. "They wanted to conduct some tests with the American market and try out a more American attitude and style. I was sort of a, well, a bridge between cultures, for lack of a better term."

A bridge.

Yeah. That resonated. The Japanese-American bridge.

"A bridge," he repeated, looking contemplative. "Huh. That's funny, actually, because that's what we're looking for."

I perked up immediately, my heart beating a little faster. "Well, I'd like to think I can help."

"Actually . . . can I be blunt with you, Lisa?"

I nodded. Why not?

"I thought your résumé was total bullshit when it first crossed my desk."

Now my eyes almost popped right out of my head. "Uh, okay," I floundered, completely at a loss.

I guess I was expecting Japanese blunt. *American* blunt was more like a shotgun blast.

"Seriously. It was an internship. Nobody does all this at an internship," he repeated, shaking his head. "You got to rub elbows with a top *manga-ka,* you got to present ideas to the top brass . . . you've got to see why I was skeptical. So I thought, I just *had* to meet the person who had the *cojones* to turn in this kind of résumé."

I could feel my cheeks heating with a blush, both anger and shame. This wasn't a real job interview. This was . . . I couldn't come up with a word for what it was. It was a reality check. He just wanted to see what sort of con I was pulling. He wanted to see what sort of liar I was.

They didn't want to hire me. They wanted to screen me. They wanted to laugh at me.

I came all this way for nothing.

"I didn't lie," I said coldly. "I worked my ass off at Sansoro. And I'd do the same for your company, given the opportunity." I felt a burst of fire surge through me, and I leaned back in the chair. Let them throw me out, but not before I had my say. "I'm fluent in Japanese, spoken *and* written, both kanji and *higana*. I can translate. I understand how manga works, I know how to work with artists, I know the process. I've studied the market, read about a zillion different comics, and that's just in the past year."

I stood up, my voice colder than an Antarctic iceberg. "I know how the Japanese work. I know how to be diplomatic and build consensus. And I'm American enough to know how to push things through when diplomacy and group-think cause bottlenecks. I know I'm inexperienced, but the only thing that'll fix that is working. And I really would've worked hard for you, Mr. Zorin."

I'd said my piece. I didn't have anything else to add, so I turned toward the door.

"Whoa," he said, getting to his feet, too. "I'm sorry. Damn it! I shouldn't have been *that* blunt," he added, and he really did sound remorseful. "I don't know why you . . . why the Japanese . . . oh, hell. There's no way I can say this without getting in even more trouble."

I stared at him, but I did sit down.

"I have trouble working with our Japanese publishers," he admitted. "I seem to put my foot in my mouth all the way to my damned knee every time we work together. I know we can make a killing, but I don't understand for the life of me how they work. So what I need is a 'bridge,' just like what you said. Someone who understands the Japanese but still understands American ways enough to kick some butt and get stuff done. I need that very badly."

I nodded, feeling the excitement build again. "I could do that," I said, in a quiet, confident tone of voice. And I meant every word.

"I know," he said. "I had a talk—well, a sort of stilted talk—with one of your supervisors."

"Really?" Now he'd caught me off guard. "Who?"

"A fella named . . ." Mr. Zorin riffled through some papers on his desk. "Akamatsu."

"You spoke with Akamatsu-sensei?" Now I was more than off guard. I was incredulous.

"He had nothing but good things to say about you. Raved."

"Now you're bullshitting *me*," I said, stunned into cursing, and it hit exactly the right note. Mr. Zorin relaxed back into his chair, chuckling.

"Tough sonofabitch, huh? I got that impression. Gruff. But he spoke very highly of you," Mr. Zorin said. "He said if anybody could work with both cultures and get her way, it'd be you. He said you weren't afraid of anything, even when you should be. That's when I knew you weren't making up the stuff on the résumé. And that's when I decided to call."

I sat there, dumbfounded. Akamatsu-sensei had stuck up for me. Wonders never ceased.

"I have a good feeling about you," Mr. Zorin said. "Here's what we'd expect you to do. And here's your starting salary . . ."

He named a number, and I nodded. It was not huge, but I wasn't expecting it to be. Still, it would be enough to compensate, for the time being.

"Think you could move to New York?" he said. "Groverton's a bit of a commute."

I couldn't afford Manhattan, not on this salary. But maybe Brooklyn.

There was always a way.

"When do I start?" I said instead.

He smiled. I had a job.

October 28, Saturday

It had been a long time since I'd been back to the anime club. I recognized most of the faces, although there was always a rotating group of college students, from Dutchess Community College or Vassar or Marist, coming by to watch new cartoons. They were going to be airing *Appleseed* tonight; I still hadn't seen it, after all this time, but I was looking forward to it.

More important, I had to find Perry and Stacy.

They were sitting near the back, talking. "Hi," I said.

Stacy sent me a frosty look but said "hi" back. Perry stood up and gave me a hug. Good old Perry.

"How are you feeling?" I asked her.

"Not bad," she said reluctantly, "for being this huge. And they did finally hire somebody at work, so I have help. Of course, I need to train him, but he seems pretty on the ball." She shrugged. "I held the job open as long as I could for you, Lise. Sorry."

She didn't sound sorry.

"No, I'm the one who's sorry," I said, and I meant it. "You really counted on me, and you wanted me there. I just . . . I didn't want to go back."

"Why are you even hanging out with us at all?" she snapped.

That hurt. "You're my best friends," I answered quietly.

"We're not too *boring*? Too *American*?"

"Okay, what the hell?" I snapped. "What, you think I turned racist when I moved to Japan?"

She blinked, then grimaced. "No, of course not. It's just . . . you went off to Tokyo, and then all of a sudden, everything in your old life just wasn't good enough. Your job. Even the guy you were going to marry."

I winced at that. Ethan was plenty good enough, but I couldn't get into it. Not then.

"So what chance do I have?" she finally said, with a sniffle. "I mean, here I am, just a community-college graduate with the same boring job and the same boring *life,* and you're moving on to all these—" She hiccuped, then tears started pouring out of the corners of her eyes. "Damn it. Frickin' hormones."

I went on instinct, hugging her tightly. "I love you, you idiot," I said. "I haven't moved on to anything. I need you, and I'm not leaving." Now my eyes were watering, too, and I brushed tears away with my wrist.

We just stayed like that, looking like two loons, holding each other.

"Jeez," Perry said. "I feel like I've fallen into a Lifetime movie."

"Oh shut up, Perry, you missed her, too," Stacy said, and we all sat down. She seemed a little better." So, I'm scared to ask, but have you figured out what you are going to do? If you're not going to go back to the plant?"

I leaned back, unable to contain the pride I was feeling. "I got a job," I said, with a broad smile but as much nonchalance as possible.

"Where?"

"In the city," I said.

They both stared at me, slack jawed. "Doing *what?*" Perry finally asked.

"I'm working for BubbleMech as a translator and editor," I said. "With time, I'll be able to take on new projects."

"Holy crap," Perry said reverently. "You made it. You're *in.*"

"Well, the pay's not all that great, and I'll probably have to move to the city," I said. "But I am getting tons of experience. And I gotta say, I love doing it. I love the job." Then I looked at Stacy carefully. "But I'll visit a ton. And I'll e-mail every day, I swear."

"Oh, Lise, you look so happy," Stacy responded with wonder, and I could tell we'd turned a corner. "I feel like such a bitch! Trying to make you feel bad, just because I'm not going to have someone to have lunch with all the time or have coffee breaks with. Why didn't you tell me you were going for a job in manga?" Then she grimaced. "I guess I wasn't that supportive, huh?"

"I didn't know I could do it, either," I reassured her. "I mean, if I saw anybody else going through what I was, I probably would've said go with the safe bet at the semiconductor plant, too."

"No, you wouldn't," Stacy countered. "Not anymore."

I thought about it. "You're right," I realized. "I wouldn't."

"Kinda makes me want to quit my job at Super Electronics," Perry mused.

"And do what? Be that porn star you've always wanted to be?" Stacy joked.

"You've gotta dream," he answered, then winked.

Dreams. Yeah. I liked the sound of that.

November 21, Tuesday

I'd been in Brooklyn for about a week now. My roommate, Felicia, was pretty cool. She was a reporter for AP who dreamed about writing a novel. The apartment was small, but after Tokyo, it was downright spacious, and at least I had my own room. Besides, Felicia had an active social life. I'd met her friends, who seemed cool as well: writers, artists, and various "bobos" as they were called—Bourgeois Bohemians. So far, I'd gone to drinks with the crew once. It wasn't karaoke, which was actually a good thing, and it was nice to do something out on the town. I promised to bring Perry up and introduce him around, and I filled Stacy in on the details, which she ate up. I still made it back to Groverton most weekends, though. My parents missed me, and it was a nice transition, still spending time at home, with my friends and family, on my old stomping grounds.

I didn't want to abandon my old life entirely. I was just adjusting it to accommodate my new one.

I liked my new job, too. It didn't have hellish hours, although I brought a lot of work home, and I sometimes worked long hours to accommodate talking to our Japanese partners. Mr. Zorin, or "Z" as we called him, turned out to be a fun if unconventional boss. I can see how he probably stepped on a lot of toes with Japanese companies. He had no internal censor and spoke his mind. Often. Bluntly.

I was training him not to do that—or at least, not to do that with anybody outside our office.

Tonight, I'd turned down Felicia's invitation. I was catching the train early tomorrow and heading for Groverton. Z had given me the day off, and I was going to help my mom prep for Thanksgiving. In the meantime, I was reading a manuscript and double-checking the translation, making sure that the concepts were adaptable to the American market. When my cell phone rang, I didn't recognize the number, but I answered it anyway. "Hello?"

There was a pause. "Risa-san?"

"Um, yes," I said, trying to place the voice. It was a woman's voice, soft and tentative, and obviously Japanese accented. I wondered if there was a work call I'd forgotten I scheduled.

"It's Yukari."

I sat bolt upright on my bed. "Yuki-chan! It's great to hear from you!" I said, shifting quickly back into Japanese. Then I realized: it was November. "Wait a second. Where are you calling from?"

"I'm in New York." She didn't sound terribly enthused.

"When did you get in?" I was thrilled for her, even if she wasn't.

"I arrived a few days ago."

"Do you have a cold?" I asked. "You sound . . . different."

I didn't know the right translation for *under the weather.*

Another pause. "Oh, Risa-san," she finally said, and it was punctuated by a sob. "I'm so homesick!"

I smiled. I wasn't happy that she was homesick, mind you. I just knew exactly where she was coming from. "Where are you, exactly?"

"I'm staying in the hotel," she said. "They've got these quarters for their international interns . . . it's a big room, and I have no roommate. I am all alone."

She sounded forlorn, downright desperate. "Give me the address," I told her.

An hour later, I'd made my way to Yukari's doorstep. When she opened the door, I almost didn't recognize her. Instead of the usual glam Parasite Eve getup I was used to, she was wearing what I had to assume was her work uniform: a pair of black slacks, a white shirt, and a black bowtie with a kelly green vest. "I think I've made a horrible mistake," Yukari said, without preamble. She wasn't even wearing sparkly makeup, and her hair was pulled back in a severe ponytail. She looked like a clone, or somebody who had had a close encounter with a body snatcher pod or something. She looked *awful.*

I did something I never did with her . . . I gave her a hug. She looked surprised, but she didn't seem entirely uncomfortable. She shut the door behind me.

I reached into my pocket and brought out my stash: a bag of Pocky, Kit Kats, and some other assorted candy, plus a big bag of green tea that I'd gotten from J-town, the Japanese section. She squealed happily and hit the Pocky like a freight train.

"Haven't you been eating?" I asked, taking off my coat and putting it over the small couch. It was a nice little apartment—a small suite, with a little living room and a small bedroom with a full-sized bed. Still, it looked like a hotel room, and considering she didn't have stuff strewn all over the place like her room at home, it didn't even look like someone was living there.

She shrugged, focusing on eating the Pocky before answering. "I found a noodle place around the corner, but it was terrible." She sighed heavily. "The food here is awful! And the Italian food is *weird*. How do you eat here?"

I laughed, which only deepened the severity of her pout.

"I don't know anybody here," she complained. "I miss all my friends. And the work is very hard. I'm on my feet all day! And the people—you have never heard such whining!" She looked beyond miserable. "I don't know why I came here. I hate it. I want to go home."

"Honey, you haven't even been here a full week," I said, and suddenly I realized why Stacy and Perry had been so tough with me, when I'd been bellyaching my first month in Tokyo. "You've got to give it a little time. It's not what you're used to, but you'll surprise yourself, if you just give it a chance."

She looked dubious as she tore into the Kit Kat.

"I hated Tokyo when I first got there," I admitted. "I didn't know anyone. I didn't know what I was doing. Work was not what I was used to—a lot of busy work, a lot of simple stuff that only made me feel stupid. And I really wanted to go home. But I didn't."

"Why not?" she asked, as if it wouldn't even occur to her to tough it out.

I grinned. "My friends wouldn't let me."

She frowned and sniffled a little. "My friends won't care if I come home," she said.

I crossed my arms. "I'm your friend," I said, in a serious tone of voice. "And I know how unhappy you were, even with all your partying. So I'm not letting you go home until you give this a good, solid chance."

She looked at me, and then, slowly, she smiled. "Well, it does help to have a friend in the city," she said in a quiet voice.

"Now, why don't I take you to a Japanese restaurant, and we'll get you acclimated," I said. "Change out of your work clothes, put on something warm, and we'll head out. My treat."

She smiled even more widely and retreated to the bedroom. I felt good. I felt like I was returning the favor, literally.

I took her out to a place not too far away. She disdained the subway, which was nowhere near as clean as the ones in Tokyo. She also looked in shock at the people yapping away on their cell phones or carrying on loud conversations, and shied away from people who would dare to make eye contact. It was going to take her a while to get used to things.

At dinner, I asked about her family, how they were doing.

She reddened a little. "I'm so sorry they wouldn't let you stay. They're still getting used to the idea of me being over here."

I shrugged. It stung at the time, but I could understand. They saw me as responsible for turning their world upside down. With a little distance, I realized I knew exactly how traumatic that could be. "It's fine," I said instead. "How's Ichiro doing?"

She grinned. "He wants to e-mail you. He's doing well in school, and he's thinking of designing video games. He says hi."

I was glad. He wasn't so bad a kid, when you got down to it. He just needed a little, I don't know. Tough love?

"And your mom . . . did she get a job?"

"She had one," Yukari said, surveying the sushi they put down in front of us with a little skepticism. "She didn't like it. She left after a week and refused to pick up her paycheck."

"What was it?" I asked.

"She was in an office. I don't know what she was doing, but apparently she felt very unfulfilled." She picked up a California roll, bit into it, and then made a face. Manfully, she swallowed but put the rest down on her plate. "She's thinking of maybe doing child care."

That would actually suit her perfectly—if she didn't get brats who burned the joint down.

Yukari and I hung out for a while, got a drink in the hotel bar, and then I walked her back to her apartment. It was nine. I had to get going, to get enough sleep to catch that early train. Besides, I could see she had the creeping edges of post-jet-lag and first-workweek jitters.

"Do you want to come to Thanksgiving dinner with me?" I asked, sad that she'd be without family.

"I don't even understand this Thanksgiving," she said, "but I can't anyway—the hotel needs us to work. But thank you."

"I'll get you to see Groverton at some point, don't worry," I told her. I wanted to see her face when she had her first chocolate–peanut butter milkshake. "In the meantime, if you feel down, call me."

"Risa-san," she said, "you didn't mention your fiancé. Are you still getting married?"

I thought about my last conversation with Ethan. It still hurt, like an abscessed tooth. I shook my head. "I don't think so."

She tilted her head, appraisingly. "Was it worth it?" she asked, in a small voice.

I thought about it. I thought about him.

"I love my job," I replied. "But honestly, I'm not sure. I wish it could have worked out."

"Oh, well," she said. "You were the one who kept saying that there's always a way."

We said good-bye. I mulled over her words the whole way back to my apartment. I didn't get to bed early as I had planned. I was still brooding at midnight. Finally, I opened my laptop, got on the Internet, and typed in Ethan's e-mail address.

"Hi Ethan," I wrote, and then froze. What was I supposed to say to him? *Sorry that whole marriage thing didn't work out. Otherwise, how are you doing?*

Or maybe I should just be honest. But what was that? *I miss the*

hell out of you. I'm glad I made the choice I did, but I still don't under-stand why you couldn't be a part of it.

I was confused and hurt and probably shouldn't be typing at all. But I still couldn't bring myself to shut it down. Finally, I just typed: "Hi. I'm going to be in Groverton tomorrow. I don't know if you're in California for the holiday or what, but I wanted to say . . . I think about you. Hope you're doing well."

I hit SEND, and then refused to think about it anymore. Whatever happened, happened. I'd done all I could.

Still, I had trouble sleeping.

CHAPTER 19

November 24, Friday

I WAS STILL STUFFED FROM THANKSGIVING, THE DAY BEFORE. Nana's spread had been incredible: turkey, mashed potatoes, sweet potatoes covered in marshmallows, green beans with almonds, stuffing, homemade cranberry relish. And three kinds of pies. I could barely fit into my clothes.

I decided to stay at my parents' house through Sunday. My crazy cousin Anna was having a party for the younger Falloyas, and that sounded kinda fun. I was also catching up with Stacy and Perry and a few of the anime group, who wanted BubbleMech to do some kind of promotional stuff with them. And I was reading through some Japanese stuff that needed translation.

I wanted to think I wasn't waiting to see if Ethan stopped by.

We'd had our first real snow, and I was shoveling the driveway, just like I used to do when I was a kid. My parents were out, visiting a friend of my mom's, and I had the place to myself until Anna's party.

Ethan's car pulled up, right into my newly cleaned driveway. I gripped the handle of my shovel tightly, ignoring the beating of my heart.

He got out. "Need help?"

"Just finished," I said, putting the shovel aside. "Did you want to come in? I was about to make some hot cocoa."

"Sounds good," he said and followed me.

We were quiet for a long minute . . . an awkward, expectant quiet.

"So, how've you been?" Ethan finally said.

"Good," I said. "Got a new job and a place to live."

"Really? Where?"

"Brooklyn. That is, I live in Brooklyn," I corrected. "I'm working in Manhattan."

He looked surprised. "I live in Manhattan now," he said. "Where are you working?"

I told him.

"My office isn't that far away," he said. "I probably walked by you on my way to lunch. That's bizarre."

"Well, we've been pretty busy," I said. "I don't go out for lunch a whole lot."

"Come to think of it, neither do I."

We both laughed, a little stiffly. He sat down at the kitchen table.

How do you get past this? I thought glumly. Could you ever get past it? It wasn't as if we hated each other. We just couldn't seem to see eye to eye.

"I've been doing a lot of thinking," he said, as I made cocoa on the stove. "About our fights. About what you said."

I bit my lip. I felt like apologizing, but there wasn't any point. I'd meant what I said, just like he had.

"You had a point," he said, then took the mug of cocoa out of my hands. "Thanks."

I warmed my hands on my own mug. "I never wanted to hurt you," I finally said.

"I know that," he said, blowing on his cocoa.

We both sipped at our drinks in silence.

Finally, he looked at me. "I had a lot of shit happen to me when I was younger. My parents divorcing, stuff like that."

I nodded. I knew about it, even though he didn't like to talk about it.

"I know that there's probably some kind of psychobabble excuse for it," he said, "and maybe I'm old-fashioned. I just thought I had everything in line, and when you changed, I thought that was it . . . that it was all over. Black and white. I even started dating other people."

I went cold at that one and clutched the cocoa mug like a life preserver. I got up, paced a little, leaned against the kitchen counter.

I had trouble looking at him.

"I didn't sleep with anybody," he assured me, and I believed him. "But I thought, well, it didn't work. Time to move on to another plan."

I swallowed. "That makes sense," I said, feeling numb. I'd moved on with my life, gone in a new direction. Why ask him to wait for me?

"But here's the thing," he said, and he got up and stood next to me, leaning against the counter. He took one of my hands. His hand felt warm, big, and comforting. "You were always more than just an element of a plan. You weren't just the wife piece of the puzzle, you know?"

I nodded, swallowing hard against the lump that was forming in my throat.

"I wanted a wife and kids and the whole nine yards," he said. "But if it's not you, then I can't just find someone else to make that work.

I love you and I want to be with you. I figure I can handle the rest as it comes along." He looked at me carefully. "If you can."

"Ethan," I said, getting up and hugging him. He held me tightly, more tightly than he'd ever hugged me.

"Why don't we start off slow? Start over," he said. "I made a lot of assumptions. We're both different. Maybe, I don't know, like a first date."

I smiled. "Okay," I said. I sat down at the kitchen table, pretending it was a bar or a restaurant. "Hi, what's your name?"

He grinned. "Smart-ass."

"Right, Mr. Ass." I held out my hand.

"Ethan Lonnel, miss," he said, playing along. He shook my hand, then sat down next to me. I could smell his cologne, feel the heat coming off him.

"Ethan. Nice name." My voice shook a little. I cleared my throat. "So, what do you do, Ethan?"

"I'm director of operations at a software firm," he said. "And you?"

"My name's Lisa Falloya," I said. "I work for a publisher of Japanese comics. I'm an editor, translator, and project manager."

"That sounds interesting," he said, and to his credit, it sounded like he meant it. I could feel his leg brush against mine, very softly. "Been doing it long?"

"No," I said, distracted. "Not very." Then I looked him in the eye. "But I love what I do."

"I can see that," he said, scooting his chair closer to mine. There was determination in his eyes—and softness. Forgiveness, both given and requested. "I like a woman who loves her job," he said in a low voice.

It was a bridge, crossing the distance between who we'd been and who we were becoming.

"You'd better," I said, and then I kissed him.